RUNNING SHOES

A Young Man's Journey in Pursuit of His Dream

CLIFFORD JAMES

Copyright © 2023 Clifford James

All rights reserved.

ISBN:

TABLE OF CONTENTS

CHAPTER 1 BROTHERS 1

CHAPTER 2 ZAK 7

CHAPTER 3 JEAN 14

CHAPTER 4 THE AFTERMATH 22

CHAPTER 5 RESPITE 26

CHAPTER 6 THE LAKEHOUSE 34

CHAPTER 7 BILLY 41

CHAPTER 8 WHAT REMAINS 49

CHAPTER 9 SAYING GOODBYE 58

CHAPTER 10 COPING 63

CHAPTER 11 TODD 73

CHAPTER 12 DANI 79

CHAPTER 13 GOOD TALK 89

CHAPTER 14 NATE 97

CHAPTER 15 AWAKENING 109

CHAPTER 16 GAIL 114

CHAPTER 17 DANI'S SECRET 121

CHAPTER 18 TIME TO GO 138

CHAPTER 19 GENEVA 146

CHAPTER 20 THINGS LEFT BEHIND 165

CHAPTER 21 MOVING FORWARD 180

CHAPTER 22 REVELATIONS 199

CHAPTER 23 THE GARDEN 209

CHAPTER 24 JUST ANOTHER MEMORY 219

CHAPTER 25 TRUST 230

CHAPTER 26 TRUTH BE TOLD	242
CHAPTER 27 SEASONS CHANGE	252
CHAPTER 28 LOST AND FOUND	267
CHAPTER 29 REUNITED	279
CHAPTER 30 LIFE CHANGES	289
CHAPTER 31 THE BACKUP PLAN	300
CHAPTER 32 LET ME TELL YOU ABOUT BILLY	314
ABOUT THE AUTHOR	323

CHAPTER 1
BROTHERS

It had been two years since he drove this lonely highway. In the darkness, he was lost, not sure of where he was or what he would find. He had made life-altering decisions over the past two years. The first to leave behind what could have been, in search of a lifelong dream. The second to regain what was left of his family, now torn apart by death and deceit. The Third, acquiescence, turning from a selfish dream to sacrifice. And finally, to seek out once again what he had given up two years before. The only difference now was he was sure of what he wanted, what he needed. But would it still be there? This could be his final doing...or undoing. He had miles to go and would drive through the night, with hours to think and reflect on what had brought him to this moment in time.

***

The dreams were more frequent now. The details of each moment of that fateful night became more clear with each fitful episode. And in this latest rendition, he could see clearly from the bedroom window the line of vehicles turning down the long drive of the neighbor's farm. The flashing lights shone brightly, surrounded by the darkness without and within. He had no option now. It was too dark to run from his fears, and there was little left to do but wait. "Dear God…" he whispered to himself but was unsure of what should come next. He didn't know what was happening, except that Billy had not come home.

RUNNING SHOES

He wished Todd were there. He always found consolation in Todd, no matter the situation. Todd would have the right words to calm his fears. But he wasn't there, and he would have to deal with his anxiety by himself. His mother had not been able for some time now, ever since the accident. His thoughts were interrupted now by the sounds below. He jumped from the bed and ran to the window once more, and observed from above. A single vehicle had come down the drive, and he watched as the sheriff walked quickly toward the porch and then out of site.

He heard the front door open and listened intently as muffled voices broke the unnerving silence, which ended as quickly as it had begun. The door closed, and he turned his eyes once again to the vehicle below, watching as his mother and the sheriff drove hastily down the drive under the strobe of flashing lights until it disappeared into the darkness.

He returned to his bed and lay down to wait for the inevitable, the final act of a once insouciant childhood. Thoughts ran rampant through his head, the kind that made him anxious and afraid. Since the accident, as things had become more unsettled, he had found running as a means to cope. As long as he had that and Todd, he would survive, but it was dark now, and he would have to wait.

He drifted into a restless sleep. It was a dream within a dream, having found consolation in the happier thoughts of days past and the sanguine life he lived and loved. Those were the moments spent with Todd and his best friend Zak while shrouded with the love of his mother. Those days had become a fleeting moment in time and lost forever.

***

"Where you off to, Nate?" Todd sat on the front stoop of the farmhouse, strumming his guitar as he watched Nate come out the front door.

"Going to Zak's, then to the barn. Billy's there, and we're gonna ride."

"How about going to the river this afternoon? We can fish, maybe pitch a tent. See if Zak wants to come."

Nate nodded, then began jogging across the open meadow toward his best friend's house. He looked up to his big brother Todd and liked to do things with him, like fishing, camping, swimming in the pond at the far edge of the property, and sports. They played all kinds of sports together, like baseball, football, soccer, and basketball. Todd was good at them, and Nate learned from him. And best of all, Todd seemed to enjoy doing things with him, not like his other brother Billy or sister Gail.

Baseball was his favorite sport, and he and Todd spent hours playing catch in the yard. At night, they watched the Red Sox on TV. Most folks in the upstate part of Connecticut rooted for the Red Sox. Farther south in the state, it was a tossup between the Sox, Mets, and Yankees. Someday I'm gonna play in Fenway Park, he thought to himself as he neared Zak's house. He had shared that thought before with Todd and Billy. Todd approved. Billy, on the other hand, had guffawed. "You're living in a fantasy world," he had mocked.

Zak was waiting for him on the back deck of the house. "How're the new sneaks?" Zak asked as he approached.

Nate knew it was said in jest. Just yesterday, he shared with Zak that he had gone shopping with his mother to buy new running shoes and had to enlighten her on the difference between plain sneakers and the running shoes he required. "Running shoes are meant for running. Sneakers are too heavy and just slow you down," he had said to her.

"You're the expert," she had conceded. "Just remember, they are much more expensive than sneakers, and you need to take good care of them."

"The new running shoes are great. Check them out." Nate sat down next to Zak and stuck one of his feet in his face. Zak grimaced and pushed it away.

"She lecture you again on taking care of them?" They both laughed. They had talked about this too. Nate was continually outgrowing his running shoes. Every six months, he had to get a new pair. Taking care of them was superfluous. He couldn't wear them long enough to worry about mistreating them.

"Todd wants to take us fishing and camping later down by the river. You want to come?"

"Yeah, that's cool."

"Come on, we gotta head to the barn. Billy's waiting for us."

Nate followed Zak to the garage, where he climbed on his bike. Nate had a bike too, but preferred running and seldom rode it. That was OK with Zak. Neither of them ever criticized the other for their differences. That's why they got along so well and were best friends. They had known each other since Zak and his parents moved in next door a few years back. Their dads were best friends, so it only seemed natural they should be too. Theirs was a friendship that would last forever. It was predestined. But it was also a friendship that would be tested over time and distance, which neither of them foresaw.

***

The Woods' property had once been a crop farm, back in the days when small farms thrived and provided fruits and vegetables to the surrounding community. It had been passed down several generations now, and Nate's dad, Mark, had inherited it, then moved in after a stint in the Marines. Today it was an open meadow-land except for the maples, oaks, poplars, and apple trees that overshadowed the large farmhouse and barn in the middle of the property. The open area that once served as farmland had reverted back to its natural state with open fields that provided the boys with ample room to run. A stream-fed pond sat at the edge of the property where Mark and his boys had built a dock into the ten feet of cool murky water. The pond and dock provided opportunities for swimming and diving during the warm summer months and ice hockey in winter.

The larger of the fields toward the front of the property had been transformed into a baseball diamond, complete with a backstop, dugouts, team benches, and bleachers for the fans. The neighboring families had participated in its conversion and helped to maintain it for use by the local little league teams.

Nate and Zak were fearless tree climbers, with Nate ascending to the highest limb of the tall pear tree, their favorite. Zak contented himself perched one limb below, where they both stopped to observe the world surrounding them. From this observation point, they planned their next adventure, whether it be chasing butterflies with their homemade nets, looking for crabs under the rocks in the creek, or kicking the soccer ball around the yard. Later, they would spend time on the tire swing that Nate's father had hung from one of the older maple trees, each daring the other to swing higher and higher.

When they eventually tired, they moved to the back porch and rested in the hammock, which had barely enough room to accommodate them both. Their rest was only momentary, however, as they proceeded to swing it back and forth with one purpose in mind; to each make the other fall out. Bumps and bruises were the price you paid for such gratifying play, and neither one ever walked away without a bruise or battle scar, evidence of a game well-played.

***

Next door was a twenty-acre horse farm owned and operated by the Elliotts. Sarah Elliott had trained, ridden, and competed in horse shows over the years, as evidenced by the numerous blue ribbons prominently displayed in the barn above the stall gates. Now retired from competition, she still trained young riders, and Nate's other brother Billy was one of her prime students.

Nate rode occasionally but was more interested in baseball. Billy was much more purposeful in his riding and, having mastered the quarter horses, looked forward to the day that he could learn to ride the saddle bred and someday compete. His interest stemmed from his mother, Jean's upbringing on a horse farm. Billy was noticeably impatient, not satisfied with the slow progress that Sarah Elliott encouraged. While she never rebuked him for it, she expressed her concern about overconfidence. "It's not just you knowing how to handle the horse," she reminded him. "Each horse has a personality of its own. They need to get to know you and trust you before you can trust them."

***

All the Woods boys were natural athletes. Todd, the oldest, excelled in both baseball and football. He was selected as captain of the football team, playing quarterback alongside Billy, just a year younger, who played wide receiver. Many of the team victories were attributed to the throwing and receiving talents of the Woods brothers.

Todd was, by nature, more reserved and cautious. He wasn't afraid of much, but he didn't take unnecessary risks either. In contrast, Billy was a risk taker and more daring. Being the oldest and more cautious, Todd took responsibility for his younger siblings whenever the situation required.

Todd frequented the barn too, but not to ride. He enjoyed working on the farm, everything from cutting and baling hay, transporting it to the barn and especially driving the John Deere tractor. Jim Elliott had engaged Todd's help from the age of twelve and rewarded him by teaching and allowing him to drive the tractor and operate the other farm equipment. As Todd grew older and stronger, he baled and then loaded the hay onto the wagon for the Elliotts. He enjoyed the outdoors and the physicality of it all.

During the warm evenings of summer, Todd would load the hay wagon several bales high, then proceed to drive around the neighbors' properties, picking up folks along the way for an evening hayride. The ride would end in the field at the front of the Woods' family property, where a bonfire awaited. Nate, Zak, and the other younger children would sit on logs next to the fire, roasting hot dogs on their makeshift skewers made from maple twigs, followed by marshmallows. Many of the kids in the neighborhood could be heard running here and there, playing games such as Kick the Can, Capture the Flag, or whatever other game suited them at the time. The older kids played volleyball and basketball while the adults would simply stand near or sit by the fire, chatting about this and that. It was the way of life in this close-knit community of Plainville, Connecticut.

CHAPTER 2
ZAK

Nate and Zak finished their rides and headed home to the farmhouse. Todd was waiting for them with camp and fishing equipment ready for their excursion to the river. "Grab your swim trunks, Nate. And get a pair for Zak. We're going to be jumping into the river from the railroad trestle." Nate and Zak's eyes lit up. They had gone to the river before with Todd and watched him jump from the bridge but never dared do it themselves. "Don't worry. I'll go first and wait for you down below."

"Cool," Nate decided after quick consideration.

"I'm game," Zak agreed, never to be outdone by his best friend.

They set up camp first at the edge of the river, then changed into their trunks and climbed to the top of the railroad trestle.

"How far is that?" Nate was looking down at the water below in nervous anticipation and then up at his big brother standing next to him.

"About thirty feet, I guess."

"Can you touch the bottom when you jump?" Zak asked with apprehension.

Todd shook his head. "Never have. I suggest you don't even think about it. Just jump in. I'll be waiting for you." He suddenly stepped off the bridge and fell quickly toward the water. Nate and Zak watched nervously from above as they waited for Todd to resurface.

Todd then waved to them from below. "You ready?" he shouted up to them.

"I think I might yell on the way down," Zak confessed.

"Me too," Nate agreed. "Let's do this together. That way, we can't ever say one of us did it before the other. Agreed?"

Zak nodded. "On three, then?"

"OK."

Zak started to count. "One...two..." Nate suddenly jumped before Zak finished the countdown, screaming and flailing his arms on the way down.

"No fair," Zak shouted and followed Nate down toward the water. Todd was waiting down below and watched carefully as they resurfaced.

"Awesome, guys. I was scared shitless the first time I jumped," Todd commended them.

"How old were you?" Nate asked as they swam to the shore.

"About your age, I think."

"I was just scared too," Nate admitted.

"So was I" Zak laughed. "But we did it. That was awesome!"

They fished for trout, and Todd showed them how to skin and filet them to cook over the camp fire. Later he played his guitar and sang a couple of country music songs as Nate and Zak just listened. Finally, Todd set his guitar back in its case. "I'm going to get some sleep. You guys don't stay up too late." Todd disappeared into the tent.

"Hey Todd," Nate called after him.

"Yeah, bud."

"You ever think about girls?"

Todd laughed. "Sure. Why do you ask?"

"You don't have a girlfriend. So I was just curious."

"Well, I have a couple of thoughts on that. First, I haven't found a girl that I really really like. I've dated a few girls, sure, but it's important to me to really like a girl before she gets to be my girlfriend."

"And what's second?" Zak asked.

"Thinking about girls comes without saying. I'm a guy; I think about girls." Todd thought for a minute before continuing. " If you guys don't yet, don't worry about it. You will soon. And if you don't...well, that's another story, and we can talk about it if you want. But what's important is that when you find the right girl, you won't just think about her. You'll feel it right here." He pointed to his heart. "Our thoughts are just a distraction from what's here, in our heart." Todd laughed as he observed the puzzled looks on their faces. "Someday, you'll get it," he said before disappearing into the tent.

Nate and Zak lay beside the campfire, looking up at the stars. "Your brother is pretty cool," Zak observed.

"Yeah," Nate agreed.

"I heard you can buy a star and have it named after you," Zak commented as they looked into the night sky.

"Well, I guess there are enough of them to go around," Nate responded.

"I wonder how they keep track of who gets which one?"

Nate thought for a moment. "I heard there is something called the star registry. There must be a map of the stars so they can keep track of who owns which ones."

Zak nodded. "That would be a good way to keep track. I think someday

I might get one. Then I can just look up in the sky, point at it and say, 'That one is mine.'"

"Maybe I'll get one too, right next to yours. We'll be neighbors, even up there."

"And when we get older, we can just look up at the sky, wherever we are, and remember this night," Zak added.

***

Their mother, Jean, had worked at the local branch of the bank after college, up until she married Mark, and they had their first child, Todd, followed by Billy, Gail, and Nate, each a year apart. She and Mark had met when she was working as a bank teller. He had just returned to Plainville after serving six years in the Marines, and he needed to open an account for his new insurance business. Jean was the teller who handled his account.

Even after four children, she still managed to stay active outside the home in several volunteer opportunities, mainly through their church. Her forte was in care ministry, which often provided home-bound parishioners with meals and offered assistance with food shopping, driving them to doctors' appointments, and even occasional assistance with house cleaning. She was wrestled from her pleasant thoughts as she heard Nate and Todd enter the kitchen.

"We caught some trout for dinner. Nate helped me fillet them, and they're ready to fry." Todd placed the cooler on the counter.

"Good catch," she acknowledged, opening the cooler. "Now go wash up for breakfast. It will be ready in fifteen minutes. And Nate, take off your dirty sneakers!" she shouted after him as Nate and Todd left the kitchen.

"They're running shoes," Nate said under his breath so as not to be heard contradicting his mother. Todd elbowed him gently in the ribs and laughed. He knew the distinction.

They passed through the dining room, where their sister Gail was meticulously setting the breakfast table. "I heard he's moving," Gail said out of the blue. Nate expected his sister to say and do things just to provoke him and get him to react. It was her nature to taunt and tease him, seizing upon every opportunity. For the most part, he just ignored her, but out of curiosity this time, with Todd at his side, he decided to engage her, if only briefly. "Who's moving?" Nate asked.

"Your friend Zak. Hasn't he told you?" She seemed to delight in the possibility that she knew something about his friend that he didn't.

Zak had not mentioned anything about moving, so he simply dismissed Gail's prodding. "I don't think so" he shrugged and followed Todd up the stairs toward their rooms.

"He is so!" they heard her shout gleefully as they hurried up the stairs.

"What's that all about?" Todd asked before entering his room.

"Who knows" Nate shrugged and continued down the hallway.

Sitting on his bed, he removed his running shoes, admiring them for a brief moment before setting them neatly in his closet. He was reminded of the conversation with his mother about running shoes, how they were so much better than sneakers, that they were more expensive, and that he better take good care of them because they would have to last. He laughed to himself again, thinking how silly for her to say that. These running shoes would soon have to be replaced, just like before, regardless of their condition.

***

Their father, Mark, had seated himself in his usual seat at the head of the table. Jean's chair at the other end remained empty while she carried dishes with pancakes, sausage, and fruit from the kitchen to the table, assisted by Gail. Nate took his customary seat to the right of his mother. Todd and Billy were already seated across from Nate and Gail.

Once Jean was seated, they passed the dishes around the table. Mark then announced they would be visiting Aunt Susan and her family in Florida over the Easter break and renting a place on the beach. Gail seized upon the opportunity to be heard. "I think we should move to Florida. It's too cold here. And it's like summer there all the time."

"That's not true," Billy countered. "It gets cold there sometimes in the winter. And you don't even like the heat. You hardly ever go outside in the summer because you think it's too hot."

"It will be nice to visit Aunt Susan and enjoy some warm weather after winter." Their mother was the peacemaker, and this was her way of quashing any disagreements between her children.

Mark agreed. "A vacation in Florida will be nice." He then continued: "But before that, we are going to build a baseball field in the front lot. I've talked with some of the other parents, and we have enough boys in our neighborhood to form our own little league team. Nate, you and Zak can play. We're meeting Saturday to get started on the field. You older boys can use the field too in preparation for high school ball."

"I don't know how much time I'll have for that," Billy countered. "I want to focus on riding. Mrs. Elliott says I'm almost ready to ride the Saddlebreds."

"Zak's moving," Gail blurted out. She looked at Nate, waiting for his reaction. No one responded, and Nate ignored her. He had been listening attentively to their father and was excited about playing little league for the first time. He and his brothers had played baseball many times in the yard with their makeshift bases and pitchers mound, but nothing like the real thing.

"Todd, maybe you can help coach the team," Mark continued.

"I'd like that," Todd responded, looking at Nate. Nate liked the idea of Todd being his coach. As for Billy and Gail, they were both too self-absorbed to be bothered with him.

Jean turned the conversation back to Billy. "So you're going to be riding the Saddlebreds? You know, I grew up with horses, and Saddlebreds can be skittish and unpredictable." Jean admired each of her children, in spite of and because of how different they were from each other. She viewed each of their differences as strengths that would lead to independence at an early age. Todd was the strong, reliable, and sensible one. Billy was confident and adventuresome. Gail was responsible and resourceful. And Nate, fearless but sensitive and still finding his way. But she had a special fondness and connection to Billy. Of their four children, he was the only one who showed any interest in some of the things she grew up with. He was an independent thinker and not easily influenced or swayed by others' opinions, much like herself. "Now, who is going to help me clean up?" she said as she stood and started collecting dishes.

Gail stood from the table, taking her dish with her. "Not them, that's for sure," she said, eyeing her brothers grudgingly as she left the dining room.

***

The boys were practicing on the new field when Zak arrived with his father, Ben. Zak had been noticeably missing while the field was being readied, and the boys gathered to play. Ben approached Mark as Zak took a seat on the bench to watch the other boys. "Field looks great, Mark. Sorry, I haven't been around to help."

"Yeah, everybody stepped up to help make this happen. It's what I love about this town."

"I know. And I hate to be leaving. But I think you probably heard I got that promotion at work, and I'm transferring to Texas. I couldn't pass it up."

"Congratulations. I hate to see you leave, but I get it."

Mark turned his attention to Nate and Zak, who were now sitting together on the bench. "They're going to miss each other. When will you be leaving?"

"In about two weeks. I've talked to Zak about it, but I don't think he really understands that he won't be seeing Nate every day."

"I still need to have that conversation with Nate. It will be hard for him too."

"Well, I wish we could stay and be a part of all this, but we have to get home to help with the packing." He then turned his attention to Zak. "Come on, Zak. We have to go."

CHAPTER 3
JEAN

To Nate, it began as a day like any other. He got dressed, ate a quick bowl of cheerios, put on his running shoes, and told his mother he was going out to play. He ran to Zak's house, fully expecting him to be waiting on the back deck. When he arrived, there were men loading a large moving truck in the drive. He watched curiously for a minute, then saw Zak's bike being loaded. He had an uneasy feeling now as it hit him. Gail was right. Zak was leaving.

He made his way around the truck to the back of the house, where he spotted Zak out by the garden. Nate noticed that the garden looked untended and badly in need of water, but Zak just stood quietly, staring off into the distance. Nate just looked at him, anxious at the prospect of his best friend leaving and his world suddenly changing. Neither of them spoke.

Zak's mother came out the door and spotted the boys near the garden. She only glanced at them momentarily before calling to Zak. "It's time to go, Zak. We have a long drive ahead of us." As the boys approached, she turned her attention to Nate. "I'm sure he'll write to you," was all she said before walking slowly away toward the car in the drive.

"Well, I guess I gotta go," Zak said solemnly. Nate was unable to speak as his emotions welled up inside him. Zak passed by and gave a quick glance back before walking to the awaiting car.

RUNNING SHOES

"Bye," Nate whispered, more to himself than Zak, who was now beyond hearing range. He stood alone for a moment, completely enveloped by that uneasy feeling. It was all real. His best friend was leaving. Nate walked to the drive and watched for a moment as the car began to speed away. He found himself running down the street, behind the car, in a vain attempt to keep up with it, hoping for that one last moment with his friend. Zak was watching him through the back window and offered one last wave as the car sped out of sight.

Ending his pursuit now, Nate turned and ran towards home. Once inside, he hurried up the stairs to his room, closed his door, and sat quietly on his bed as thoughts continued to rush through his head. His best friend was gone. Tears welled up in his eyes as he tore his running shoes off his feet and flung them as hard as he could against the bedroom door. He was too old to cry, he told himself. But then he lay down on the bed and sobbed into his pillow.

Outside his room, Jean heard the sound of shoes hitting the door and listened closely for sounds from within. She knocked on the door softly and spoke gently to him. "Nathan, are you OK?" Nate did not respond, so she slowly opened the door, but only half way as the thrown running shoes prevented it from opening further. She peaked around the door to see his body moving ever so slightly in rhythm with the soft sobs emanating from the pillow.

"Nathan, what's wrong, honey?" she asked as she sat slowly on the bed next to him. Nathan quieted himself now and moved closer to her, laying his head in her lap. She stroked his blonde curls and continued to speak softly to him. "Can you tell me what happened?"

"He's gone," was his short response as his whimpers began again. Jean knew this day would eventually come and how close Nate and Zak had grown.

"I'm sorry, Nathan. I know it hurts when people leave us, and you're going to miss Zak. You can write to him, and he can write to you, and you'll soon have lots of new things to tell him." He lay there in the comfort of her lap as she dried his tears. Neither of them knew what was to come, that moments like this and the closeness they shared would soon be lost to them forever.

***

Shortly after Zak left, Nate began seventh grade, Gail- eighth grade, and Billy and Todd in ninth and tenth grades.

Nate liked school, especially gym class and any physical activities that allowed him to run around the gym and outside on the track in his newly acquired running shoes. He showed them off proudly to the other boys in the class. The girls seemed to have no interest, but he didn't mind that. He thought about Zak and missed having him around. It wasn't easy making new friends, and he had no interest in trying.

He managed to keep busy through the fall and into the winter. He would go with Billy to the barn, and sometimes even Gail would tag along, usually whining and complaining about the wet, dreary Connecticut weather or muddy walk or smelly barn. Nate didn't understand why she complained since none of those things bothered him. Billy just ignored her complaining as he fed and watered the horses, then groomed and readied Molly, the quarter horse, to ride.

Billy rode her for several laps before bringing her to the rail. Gail was supposed to ride next but declined at the last minute, so Nate climbed into the saddle. He had learned enough already to ride on his own and began immediately trotting around the ring. After they rode and put the horses out to pasture, the three of them started walking toward home. Nathan was still animated by the ride and took off running as fast as he could. "Weird kid," Gail whispered just loud enough for Billy to hear.

"He likes to run. I like to ride. What do you like?"

"Neither of those things, that's for sure," she said stubbornly. "I don't think I'm going to ride anymore. It's boring."

"Suit yourself. Makes my life easier."

Todd and Nate were shooting a basketball into the hoop mounted at the peak of the garage, and Billy joined them. "How was your ride?" Todd asked.

"OK. Mrs. Elliott says I'll be able to ride a Saddle-bred soon."

"Good for you," Todd said approvingly. "Mr. Elliot said that maybe you could work at the barn too. He'll pay you to help care for the horses. So I'll be baling the hay, and you'll be feeding it to the horses. A brother team. I think mom and dad will be OK with that, don't you?"

"Yeah, I guess so," Billy said without much enthusiasm. He was more interested in riding the horses than anything else. Caring for the horses and baling hay would take away from his riding time. It had begun to rain, so the boys hurried into the house. They met their mother by the door, and she was carrying a covered casserole dish in her hands. She was clearly flustered and in a hurry, as she approached them.

"I'm late, and I need to run this over to the church. Your father should be home soon, and I shouldn't be more than 30 minutes," she said, handing the dish to Todd to free up her arms and put on her raincoat.

"OK," Todd responded, handing her back the dish. As she went out the door, the sky had turned dark, and rain began falling heavily. He watched as she hurried to her car and drove away.

***

Several hours passed, and there was no sign of their mother returning. Their father should have been home from work hours ago, but he, too, had not shown himself. Todd debated calling either of them on their phones, which he wouldn't do unless there was an emergency. Was this an emergency? He decided no and tried to shrug off his concern, concluding their mother must have been delayed at the church and father at work. His thoughts were suddenly interrupted by a phone call. He listened carefully to his father and sensed both anxiety and fear in his father's voice. "Todd," he began. "I'm at the hospital with your mother. There's been an accident."

"Is she OK? Is she hurt?" Todd replied with trepidation. Billy and Nate were standing nearby, overhearing the alarm in Todd's voice but not able to hear their father's response.

"Your mom is a little shaken up, but we should be able to leave the hospital in a couple of hours. She made dinner earlier, and it's in the refrigerator. Can you make sure everyone eats?"

"OK, but what should I tell them?" Todd waited anxiously for his father's response.

"Just tell them your mother is OK, and we'll explain when we get home."

"OK, Dad...but is she really OK?" There was a momentary silence on the other end before Todd heard voices in the background that he couldn't immediately identify. But he distinctly heard his mother's crying voice before his father hung up the phone.

Todd gathered his siblings around the table and passed the casserole. "Dad called and said he and mom would be home in a couple of hours."

"Where are they?" Gail demanded. "They should have been here hours ago." Nate sat quietly, eating his dinner and listening. Todd would tell them if there was any information to share.

"That's all I know," Todd said and continued eating in silence before changing the subject. "What say we go fishing tomorrow? We haven't all been in a while, and the trout are biting."

"I wanna go," Nate spoke up excitedly, and Billy nodded. "I have to feed and water the horses in the morning, and we can go right after."

"How about you, Gail?" Todd turned his eyes to her.

"You know I don't like to fish," was all she said.

***

It was past nine o'clock when they finished dinner and heard a car come down the drive. Their mother had left nearly five hours earlier, and their dad had not been seen since morning when he went off to work. All were curious about what had transpired over the past few hours that kept them away from home, and they waited anxiously at the dining room table for their parents to enter.

They listened as the front door opened and then heard one set of footsteps go immediately up the front stairwell. Momentarily, their father entered the dining room and stood before them. He looked pale and tired. The expression on his face was one that Nate had never seen before and would see only twice in his life, an expression of remorse and sorrow. They all listened attentively as their father began to speak.

Nate had never heard his father speak without exuding confidence and strength. His voice was shaky, and he was clearly fatigued. "There was an accident," he began. "Your mom was on her way to church and..." he hesitated. The next words came hard to him. "...Bobby Winston was riding his bike. It had started raining, and Bobby rode his bike into the street...she didn't see him until it was too late."

There was silence around the table as they tried to grasp the situation and continued to watch their father struggle with this news. "Is he going to be OK?" Billy finally asked.

Mark closed his eyes momentarily and shook his downcast head. "Your mom is taking this really hard and blames herself. She'll need some time."

Nate continued listening, not sure what it all meant or if he should ask questions now. He was about to when Todd looked squarely at him and shook his head no. Then Todd spoke.

"Billy and I are taking Gail and Nate fishing tomorrow, so we'll be keeping busy."

"I think that's a good idea." Mark excused himself from the room, and they listened quietly as he ascended the back stairs.

They proceeded to clean up in silence and then headed up to their own rooms without further conversation, each lost in their own thoughts about this terrible tragedy. Nate was awakened in the middle of the night by the sound of his mother's crying in the bedroom next to his. He lay there and listened to the muffled voices and her occasional sobs, knowing that something terrible had happened, but he would not begin to comprehend the impact on him or his family for years to come.

When morning came, Nate found his brothers and Gail already eating breakfast in the kitchen. Todd had put out the cereal, bowls, and milk. Their father and mother were nowhere to be seen. "We'll all head to the barn, get our chores done, then head to the river," Todd announced.

"I'll go fishing, but I don't want to go to the barn," Gail insisted.

"You can't stay here by yourself," said Todd.

"Where's mom and dad? Aren't they here?"

"You heard what dad said last night. Mom needs some time to deal with this," Todd said with frustration. "So you're going to have to go with us." Gail reluctantly conceded as they finished breakfast and headed for the barn.

After their chores were done and they had settled by the riverbank to fish, Nate decided it was time to ask questions. "Is Bobby Winston dead?"

"Dad didn't say, but it sounds like it," Todd said as he began to bait Nate's hook for him.

"I can do that." Nate took the bait from him. "You taught me, remember?"

"Mom could go to jail," Gail said definitively. Nate felt a brief moment of panic.

"Bullshit," Billy scoffed. "It was a stupid accident. They don't put people in jail for accidents."

"They can if it's your fault," Gail retorted with certainty.

"It was nobody's fault. That's why they call it an accident, dummy," Billy chided.

"We'll see," was all she said, and silence prevailed as they continued to fish.

RUNNING SHOES

Nate turned to Todd. "Do you think mom will go to jail?"

"No, bud," Todd reassured him.

CHAPTER 4
THE AFTERMATH

The next few days went by quickly as they all returned to school. Things were definitely different as there was no breakfast prepared for them by their mother before school; in fact, they did not see her at all on those mornings. For the first week, they didn't see her in the evening either, as she never left the bedroom. Dinners now consisted of takeout and packaged foods such as mac and cheese, pizzas, and whatever else they could muster on their own.

As they approached the second week following the accident, Nate again overheard sounds in the night, louder this time, coming from the bedroom next door. He could hear his mother's anguished cries and then shouting, presumably at his father. It seemed to go on for hours as Nate pulled the covers over his head to drown out the woeful sounds of his mother. He couldn't sleep and sat up for a few minutes before picking up his pillow and making his way down the hall to Todd's bedroom. He knocked on his door softly, and a sleepy Todd opened the door. "What's up, bud?" he asked, rubbing his eyes.

"I can't sleep," Nate answered with a sullen look on his face. Todd knew why. He was not oblivious to what was happening in the bedroom next to Nate's.

"I see you brought your pillow. Come on in." Todd ushered him into his room and closed the door behind them.

RUNNING SHOES

***

After school, when the kids all arrived home, their father unceremoniously herded them into the dining room to speak with them. "You all know your mom as been struggling since the accident. It's been over a week now, and she is still not feeling well, so today, we decided it would be best for her to go into the hospital until she feels better."

Nate had a bad feeling about this. He hadn't felt like this since the day that Zak left. Now it was like his mother had left without even saying goodbye. "Is she ever coming back?"

Mark moved behind Nate's chair and put his hands on his shoulders reassuringly. "She hasn't been herself. This has been traumatic for her. So she's in the hospital where they can help her recover from this. Hopefully, she will be back to her usual self and be able to come home soon. We all miss her."

"When can we visit her?" Billy then asked.

"I don't know," Mark responded, knowing that a visit to the hospital was not likely. "Let's just hope that she won't be there for long."

Billy looked at Todd, then back to his father. "What's wrong with her? Is she sick?"

"Billy, it's not that kind of hospital."

Todd didn't speak, but his father's uncertainty about how long their mother would be away concerned him.

***

Several days passed without a further discussion about their mother. It was after school one day that they came home and found an unfamiliar face working in their kitchen. She looked up from her work on the counter at Todd and Nate as they entered.

"Hi, boys. Which one of you is Todd, and which one is Nathan?" she asked as she continued preparing a salad for dinner. Nate observed that she was probably older than their mother based on her salt-and-pepper hair. She was a little weighty but not unpleasantly so and had rosy cheeks and a pleasant smile.

"I'm Todd, and this is Nate," Todd responded respectfully.

"It's nice to meet you, Todd and Nate. You can call me Bella. Dinner will be ready by six. If you have any special requests for dinners in the future, just let me know. I can be very flexible and accommodating."

"OK," was Todd's quick response. "I'll let everyone know," and he led Nate from the kitchen.

"She wants to know what we like to eat. Sounds like she will be here awhile.' Nate was concerned and looked to Todd for an answer. Todd thought for a moment but deferred. "Let's go out to the field and have a catch," he said as they headed up the stairs to their rooms. Nate agreed and went to his room to get his glove.

On the field, as they tossed the ball back and forth, Todd was unusually quiet. Nate was aware that Todd seemed lost in thought and tried to strike up a conversation. "Do you think mom's ever coming home?"

"Of course, she will. This is just temporary."

"But she's been gone a week already."

"Yeah." was Todd's response, again lost in thought.

Shortly before six, Billy arrived at the field on the way back from the barn. Nate was the first to speak. "There's a strange lady in our kitchen," he announced to Billy.

"I know," Billy began. "I met her earlier before I went to the barn. Dad hired her to cook and clean while Mom is away. She looks familiar. I think I've seen her at church."

They returned to the house and washed up for dinner. They found Gail assisting Bella, bringing several dishes of food to the table. As they all sat, Nate was keenly aware of the empty chairs of their parents. It was unsettling to him.

Nate heard his dad arrive around 7:30 and listened to muffled sounds coming from the kitchen. He thought again of this new person who had replaced his mother, which meant she probably would not be coming home soon. He retreated to his room, put on his running shoes, and went outside. It was nearly dark but not dark enough to stop him from running, so he ran as quickly as he could out the drive and toward the barn. It was his safe place, and this is where he ran in times of confusion and uncertainty. And his mother was no longer able to reassure him.

CHAPTER 5
RESPITE

Their new routines soon became the norm. For months there was little talk of their mother or when she might come home. Todd and Billy played basketball at the high school, and Gale kept busy with Bella in the kitchen. Nate continued to run daily, often thinking of his mother, but never sharing his thoughts, even with Todd. It seemed to him that everyone avoided any discussion about her.

Mark continued to come home late from work two or three times a week, presumably due to regular hospital visits. He attended the older boys' basketball games in the evenings when he was available and tried to maintain what normalcy he could under the circumstances.

***

In early April, the baseball season started, and Todd and Billy spent most afternoons after school and, again, Saturday mornings playing. Todd was one of the starting pitchers. Billy was left-handed, tried out for first base, and was selected as a starter too. When there wasn't a formal practice or game at the school, they practiced pitching, throwing, and hitting on their own baseball field. Nate was happy to be fielding the balls during their batting practice. Occasionally, other members of the school team, as well as little leaguers from the neighborhood, joined them, and they would divide up into teams and play an actual game.

In mid-April, Mark gathered all the kids into the dining room one evening to make an announcement. "I have some good news. Your mom is coming home tomorrow." It had been over six months since she left, and Nate, having convinced himself that he might forget what she even looked like, had found a picture of him and his mother and put it on his night stand. He had looked at it every night and promised her that he would not forget her.

"You have all been very patient and done a good job keeping things as routine as possible. Now I need you to help make her transition home as easy as possible. That means keep doing what you're doing, and we will all be fine."

There was silence while they all thought this over; then Gail spoke. "Is she better?"

Their father thought deliberately before replying. "She is the same mom she has always been. She hasn't seen you all for months now, so it will take some adjustment for her and all of us." Nate wondered what he meant by adjustment. He just wanted things back the way they were before the accident.

Mark continued. 'I have asked Bella to stay on for awhile." He wasn't specific, believing it best not to share any more information with the kids than absolutely necessary. So much of what was to come was uncertain. Gail smiled; she liked Bella and had gotten very close to her, working by her side in the kitchen. "Any questions, anyone?"

There was a momentary silence, and Todd once again assumed the role he had inherited as of late. "No sir, I think we are all good here."

"Can I go play now?" Nate was anxious and distracted by the thought of his mother coming home.

"Sure, Nate. And the rest of you as well. Todd, I would like you to stay a minute."

As the others filed out of the room, he proffered a chair for Todd and seated himself. Mark began. "I appreciate how you have stepped up and helped keep things going here. I know I put a lot on you, but I also knew you could handle it. I'm sorry that you had to bear so much of that responsibility. I think you're old enough to understand what happened to your mother."

Todd had suspicions as to their mother's condition but was never one to question his father's decision not to discuss it with the children.

"Right after the accident, your mom suffered a nervous breakdown. She feels guilty, believing she was responsible for ending that boy's life. Hopefully, she can now cope with this tragedy and stop blaming herself."

***

The next day was Saturday, and the first little league game of the season was scheduled for that afternoon. During the pregame practice, Nate warmed up in his usual short stop position, fielding balls and throwing them to first base. Then they had batting practice, and Nate managed to hit every pitch thrown to him.

The game started with the visiting team at bat. The pitcher was successful in striking out the first two batters, while the third one grounded to shortstop, and Nate threw to first base for the third out. When at bat, Nate grounded past the short stop and into left field for a double, but the inning ended before he could score.

The game continued without any runs until the fifth inning. Nate was at a shortstop, and there were already two outs when he was distracted by his father and mother approaching the field. He watched as they seated themselves in the home team bleachers. The distraction caught him off guard as the first pitch went across the plate, and a hard-hit ground ball went whizzing past him. Todd called time out and approached the short stop position to talk to him. "You OK, bud?"

"I'm OK," Nate quickly responded, pounding his fist into his glove.

Todd nodded and walked back to his coaching position. The next batter struck out to end the inning. Nate and the next two batters all got hits, resulting in two runs for the home team. The score remained two to one at the end of the final inning, and they had won the first game of the season.

Once the game ended and most of the players had left, Nate made his way up to the stands where his mother was seated. His father had left the bleachers and was talking to the two assistant coaches and Todd near the players' bench.

"Hello, Nathan," he heard her say as he approached. He expected her to reach out to him and hug him like she used to whenever they were apart for any extended period. But she turned her eyes away, seemingly unable to look him in the eyes. He expected her to say more, like how much she had missed him or at least how good it was to see him, but it was not forthcoming. He stood uncomfortably in front of her, waiting for some further acknowledgment, but to no avail. She slowly stood and made her way down from the stands, leaving him standing there by himself. He watched her walk away, paralyzed by the realization that this was the new her. She was different, and he didn't like it.

He watched as she joined his father. She put her hand on his arm, and they walked toward the house together. Nate gathered his bat and glove and made sure the rest of the equipment was all properly stowed, then sought out Todd and Billy, who were busy talking to some of the other players. He listened briefly before Todd broke away from the group to walk with him back to the house. "Did she talk to you?" Todd asked as they walked.

Nate shook his head no. Todd put his arm around Nate's shoulder as they continued on. "Don't worry, she will." Todd sensed that Nate was distraught when he thought he saw a slight quiver in his lips. "Don't worry, buddy, we just have to give her some time," he reassured him.

Billy caught up with them, and the subject was quickly changed. He directed his criticism toward Nate. "You really screwed up out there. You could have cost us the game out-right. You're lucky they didn't have many good hitters."

"That's enough," Todd said. "It's almost dinner time, so we better get changed." Billy increased his stride, leaving Todd and Nate to follow him into the house.

Nate changed out of his uniform, washed up, and joined the family in the dining room by six, as was customary. Gail had set the table and was busy putting some condiments out. They could hear voices coming from the kitchen and listened quietly. Bella was doing most of the talking, and there was an occasional acknowledgment by their mother. From what they could discern, it appeared to be a pleasant, though rather one-sided, conversation.

Mark entered the dining room from the hallway and sat himself down in his usual position at the head of the table. "Good game today, Nate" he complemented.

"Thanks," Nate responded. "My fielding could have been better."

Billy scoffed. "Almost lost it."

"Gail, thanks for bringing the lemonade," their father continued. "And good coaching job Todd" he added, looking at Todd.

Jean then entered, followed by Bella, each carrying dishes of food to the table. Jean sat, and Bella returned to the kitchen. Idle chatter continued around the table during dinner, and Jean's contribution was a simple acknowledgment of whatever the topic of conversation happened to be. Their mother was usually an active participant in all their discussions, no matter how random they were, but this first dinner since her return was noticeably different, and each of the children was keenly aware of how things had changed. At the conclusion of dinner, Jean stood from her chair and announced that she was tired and going to lie down. This, too, was unusual, as she typically would supervise the clean-up after dinner. She left the dining room, and they listened as she went down the hallway and up the stairs.

Todd took charge in the silence that had followed. "Everybody grab their plates," he ordered as he stood with his and walked to the kitchen, and the others followed.

***

They arrived at their beachfront hotel outside of Sarasota around noon time the next day and checked in. Mark's sister Susan and her family, including her husband and two kids, Bobby and Melissa, and Melissa's best friend, Allie, all lived nearby and joined them for the day. Mark and the boys began the day surf fishing. After lunch, the younger boys spent the afternoon jumping and diving into the waves along with Gail, Melissa, and Allie. Jean spent most of the day alone, reading, besides the pool while Susan kept watch over the kids from the shoreline.

In the evening, after dinner, the older kids hung out by the pool. Todd brandished the acoustic guitar that his dad had bought him for his previous birthday, and he idly strummed it as they sat around the pool. Todd took an immediate like to Allie and serenaded them all, paying particular attention to her. He had a deep mellow voice that complemented Allie's soprano delivery as they sang renditions of their country favorites, some separately, some together.

Nate managed to hang by the pool for a while, too, observing his older brother's behavior around this new girl Allie. Todd glanced toward Nate with a wink and a smile as he continued playing, and Allie sang. Shortly after, Nate was summoned from the hotel balcony above by Mark to come up for bed, leaving the older teens behind.

Each day of the vacation became a routine, including breakfast together, then time for swimming and fishing. By afternoon they were joined by their cousins and friends to surf, swim, and lounge by the pool. Nate noticed that his mother seemed to talk a little more each day, whether it be about how much she loved the warm weather and the beach or some other non-specific that had nothing to do with children, including her own, or anything that might be a reminder of what had transpired previously or could happen down the road.

This was a change from her pleasure in things past and her optimism toward things to come. Previously, she wouldn't hesitate to share how proud she was of each of her children for their accomplishments. She believed these were meant to be shared, not out of arrogance, but as a means of support for her children while encouraging the children of others. But things had changed; at the risk of celebrating her own children in deference to the loss of others, especially as a result of her own doings, would be inexcusable. As a result, she was at a loss as to what would be right to say or do, so she said very little if anything. And nothing about children.

Nate was not good at engaging people in conversations, especially adults. It shouldn't be that hard, he thought, especially with your own mother. But it had become difficult, as it seemed to cause her anxiety when he approached her with even the simplest attempt to engage her. He began to think that her lack of response to him was callous. She had not even touched him since returning home. Even an undeserved admonishment from her would be welcome attention.

All of these feelings would continue to well up inside him unless something changed…unless she changed. But he had no control over that. So over the course of the next few days of their vacation, Nathan regularly donned his running shoes and ran up and down the beach until he couldn't run anymore, all in an effort to overcome the anxiety he felt for something he couldn't fix.

***

After they returned home from Easter vacation, things settled down into a normal daily routine of school, baseball, and dinner together with family. Jean was making slow progress and engaging more and more with all of her children in limited conversations and attending school functions and sporting activities. She even made efforts to visit the barn on occasion to watch Billy ride one of the quarter horses.

Nate was aware, though, that she seldom laughed, if ever, and while she used to show much affection toward her children, that part of their relationship had changed since the accident. At first, he believed that her inability to show the affection he craved was somehow his fault. He was, however, reassured but not comforted by the fact that her lack of compassion was not just for him but for all her children equally. Even Billy, whom she always seemed to have a special affinity for, received no amount of affection from her.

When summer arrived, the boys began their usual fishing expeditions to the river and, on occasion, brought a tent and sleeping bags to spend the night. They routinely jumped off the thirty-foot bridge to swim in the river below. They also swam in the pond, diving from the dock into the cool water. Usually, it was just Todd and Nate, and on occasion, joined by Billy.

Little league baseball continued through the summer months, coached by Todd and several other players from his high school team. They practiced on the cool summer evenings and played their games on Saturday mornings. Nate's skill at the short-stop position improved every day, and he was well-suited for the position. He was not afraid to get in front of the ball, excelled at fielding and throwing, and he was quick. He loved the game, knew he was good at it, and planned on playing on the school team like his brothers when he was old enough. Occasionally he would dream of baseball and even one day playing in the big leagues.

The Saturday morning games were always well-attended, including Jean and Mark watching from the stands. Gail continued to make and sell her lemonade, now supplemented by homemade chocolate chip cookies that Bella provided.

The summer league baseball season ended in mid-August, two weeks before the start of school. On Saturday, Mark gathered the family in the dining room that evening for an announcement. "Tomorrow, we are taking a drive up to Candlewood Lake," he started. Candlewood Lake was the largest lake in Connecticut and one of the most popular recreational spots in the state.

" Why?" Billy pondered.

"Your mom and I have talked and decided to buy a vacation home on the lake."

Gail didn't show any enthusiasm or interest at all. "I have a slumber party to go to tomorrow. I don't want to go see some stupid house on the lake."

"You won't have to go if Bella can stay with you until the slumber party," Mark replied. In normal circumstances, he would have insisted the family go together, but considering Jean's fragile state, it was best to avoid arguments with the children.

CHAPTER 6
THE LAKEHOUSE

It was only an hour's drive from Plainville to the lake, and Jean was noticeably quiet throughout the trip. They parked on the black asphalt drive and observed a brick ranch house before them. It sat about half way down the sloping acre lot to the lake below. They could see the lake in the distance, which immediately got Billy and Nate's attention.

"Let us out," Billy said impatiently as he pushed his way to the door and opened it. Nate immediately followed and raced Billy down to the lake.

"Let's take a look," Mark said, opening his door, then turning to help Jean climb out. Todd was already two steps ahead of them, walking toward the lake.

"Todd, you gotta see this!" Billy yelled excitedly to him as he approached. Todd saw what the excitement was about; an outboard motor boat sat in the boathouse beside the dock. Nate was already climbing aboard the boat to check it out. It had a 150 horsepower Evinrude motor which appeared to be almost new. The boat itself had been well cared for and in good condition.

Mark inspected the boat and was obviously pleased with what he saw. "Let's take a look inside the house." He withheld any further comment about the boat, for now. Several boats went by as they looked out onto the lake. "Come along, Nate" Mark called to him as he took Jean's hand and walked back toward the house.

Nate got out of the boat and raced toward the house, beating them all there. Mark began informing them about the house as they entered through the front door. "The house is about twenty-five years old. They put on a new roof just five years ago. It has three bedrooms and three baths. It's an open living space with an updated kitchen. And there is a finished basement that opens up to the back yard."

Mark led them through the kitchen and open living space, then through the three bedrooms. He then led them to a door which revealed a stairway to the lower level. The basement was recently finished and included one large room with a wet bar and fire place, a big walk-in storage area, and a full bath. A large sliding patio door overlooked the back yard leading down to the lake.

"Does it come with the boat?" Nathan asked impatiently.

Mark smiled. "Yes, we bought the house and the boat...

"There are only three bedrooms," Jean observed.

They were still downstairs when Todd spoke up. "Billy and I could sleep in bunk beds down here."

"That would solve the bedroom situation," Mark said more to Jean than the kids.

"I want my own room," Billy objected.

There was silence for a minute as they thought about this obstacle. Then Todd spoke up. "Nate and I can room down here," he suggested, looking in Nate's direction.

Nate was startled by the proposal but immediately excited by the prospect of rooming with his big brother. He didn't care about having his own bedroom anyway, and a broad smile crossed his face. "That would be ok." He tried to hold back his excitement.

"Fist bump," Todd countered as they tapped clenched fists...

"That sounds like a good solution. Let's take another look at the rest of the house then," said Mark, leading toward the stairs.

***

Once in the car, talk about the house resumed. "I like it!" Billy announced as if they would all be surprised.

Todd laughed. "What's not to like? It's on a lake, you'll have your own room, and we have a boat. What do you think, mom?" he asked, trying to engage her in the conversation.

She sighed dismissively. "If it's what you all want..." Mark remained silent, knowing it would be best to address any of Jean's concerns privately before furthering the boys' excitement about the house and boat.

***

Gail and Bella were busy in the kitchen making cookies for the slumber party. Gail had remained unusually quiet until Bella queried. "What's going on in that head of yours? You're awfully quiet today."

"Do you think my mom will ever love me again?" Gail replied suddenly.

Bella stopped mixing the cookie dough for a moment and looked questioningly toward Gail. "What makes you think she doesn't love you?"

"Look who's helping me bake cookies," she shrugged.

Bella thought for a minute before speaking. "Well, buying a house on the lake is a big deal, and your mother should be there." Then Bella decided it best to change the subject. "You and I do so well in the kitchen together. I think you could be a great chef someday." She handed the bowl of cookie dough to Gail to spread on the baking sheet.

"She hardly even talks to me anymore. It's like I don't exist." This was clearly upsetting to Gail as Bella saw tears in Gail's eyes. Bella moved toward her and hugged her.

RUNNING SHOES

"I know this is hard for you to understand, dear, but your mom does love you, trust me. She has suffered terrible trauma. She feels responsible for that boy's death, even though we all know it was an accident." Bella was still holding her tightly.

Gail broke away and carried the baking pan to the oven. She then turned back to Bella. "She sure doesn't act like she loves me."

" I'm sure she does. This isn't about you, Gail. It's about her."

"What do you mean?"

Bella decided she would tell Gail a story that might help her understand. "I had a brother named Leo, two years older than me. When we were in high school, Leo got involved with a rough crowd, and he was constantly getting himself into trouble. One day, it all caught up with him. He was arrested and put in jail. He was incarcerated for almost eight years. In spite of what he had done, we all looked forward to the day he would come home. Unfortunately, when he was released, he didn't come home. In fact, we spent a considerable amount of time trying to find him."

"What happened to him?"

Bella continued. "We eventually found him in New Haven. He was homeless, living under a bridge."

"Why? Didn't he know that you all still loved him and wanted him to come home?"

Bella nodded. "Yes, he knew."

"Then why didn't he come home?"

"He didn't think he deserved it. He had let us all down, and he didn't think he deserved our love or the home and family he had given up."

Gail thought for a moment. "So our mom loves us but doesn't think she deserves our love? I understand what your saying, but I don't understand why she should feel that way."

"Well, just as my brother believed his behavior didn't warrant our love, your mother may feel the same way."

"But your brother made a choice; the accident was not her decision. She didn't choose to hit that boy."

"That's true. She didn't. But she still feels responsible for his death. She made the decision to go to the church, and it was during a storm. In hindsight, she could have waited or even decided not to go to the church that night. Then the accident could have been prevented. The bottom line is she blames herself for the pain and suffering she has caused that family. Consequently, she doesn't believe she deserves your love or even to be happy."

"It wasn't her fault he rode out in front of her. That isn't fair. She is not responsible for what happened!" Gail countered.

"Unfortunately, when we are involved in something bad that happens, even if it's not our fault, we may still feel responsible. And taking on that responsibility can do terrible things to us and everyone we love. I think if you can continue to show her how much you love her, by doing things for her, trying to get her to do things with you, telling her you need her... maybe, eventually, she will be able to accept your love and reciprocate."

Gail determined that she understood and that her mother really needed her now, so she would help care for her. In this way, she could show her mother how much she loved her and convince her that none of this was her fault. It all seemed so simple now in her mind. "I'm going to go pack for the slumber party while the cookies bake." Gail then left Bella alone in the kitchen.

***

The Woods family entered the crowded church, welcomed by friends and acknowledged by acquaintances, with Jean noticeably absent. Nate usually sat next to his mother during the service and felt a little uneasy, convinced that people were acutely aware of his mother's absence and whispering about her.

Todd sensed that Nate was anxious and elbowed him gently in the ribs to get his attention, then whispered to him. "At least we'll give them something to talk about," he chuckled.

Pastor Dan went out of his way following the service to greet Mark and the family. "It's good to see you all here," he addressed the entire family. He left it at that, purposely not mentioning Jean or acknowledging her absence.

***

Football season came and went with Todd and Billy both playing on the varsity squad; Todd as a quarterback and Billy as a wide receiver... Thanksgiving came, and the family spent more time together than they had in months. Jean took charge of the Thanksgiving festivities and assigned each of the children jobs to do in preparation for dinner. She had always been the one to take-charge during holiday meals, and this one was no exception, in spite of her otherwise reserved behavior since the accident. She enlisted Gail and Nathan's help in setting up the kitchen and dining table as she prepared the turkey for the oven. The older boys, including Mark, were in charge of all the side dishes. They could pick and choose who did what as long as everything on the menu was included.

College football games ran throughout the day, and they took time out from their various tasks to watch some of the games, including Cornell, which had become their favorite college team. By the age of twelve, Nate had already decided that Cornell was his college of choice and declared that someday, he would play baseball there.

Immediately following dinner, Gail and the three boys went out to the back yard and tossed the football around while Mark and Jean relaxed in the large living room that overlooked the lake below. Todd and Billy had retrieved some firewood and started a fire in the fireplace. Jean's smiles had been far and few between the past months. Today, she smiled and spoke softly to her husband. "This is nice," she said, sipping an after-dinner drink with him.

He reached for her hand and smiled, looking at her and then around the room. "The kids all seem to be getting along well," he observed.

They were silent for a moment, listening to their children talking in the background. She finally spoke, squeezing his hand. "Thank you. I needed this."

"We all did," he concluded as they listened in silence while the four children continued their banter outside.

CHAPTER 7
BILLY

Christmas was spent at the lake house, which had become their home away from home. Jean seemed comfortable in the new settings but often remained distant and detached, spending time alone in the bedroom.

Both Billy and Gail had set up their own rooms just as they wanted. Billy completed his setup with black lights and a blue tooth stereo connected to his new cell phone, both gifts at Christmas. Gail decorated by covering her wall with a tie-died sheet and various posters of the latest hot young actors and singers. She, too, had a new cell phone and was in constant contact with her girlfriends from home.

Todd and Nate had their bunks set up downstairs, out of the way, near the back wall of the large room. Todd gave Nate the top bunk, which he knew Nate would prefer. Their decorations were not as elaborate as Billy's or Gail's by choice. Neither of them saw much value in it, so they just hung up a few posters reflecting their music and sports interests. Their focus and time together were spent playing on their new Play Station 2 and strumming on their guitars. Todd got another new one for Christmas and was happy to hand down his old one to Nate, who was quickly learning the chords and playing along with Todd.

They would retire late in the evening and talk late into the night from their bunks. Their discussions were random, ranging from the events of the day to plans for tomorrow. Nate asked Todd if he thought he would be leaving after high school. This had been in the back of Nate's mind for some time now, and it would be hard to not have Todd around. Todd understood the reason for the question and wasn't sure how to answer it. First of all, he wasn't sure yet what he was going to do, and secondly, he didn't want Nate to worry about it. Todd finally responded. "That's a long way off, bud. We got a lot of fun to have before that happens. OK?"

"OK," Nate said.

"Good talk." This was how Todd ended their frequent talks now, and Nate knew it was time to turn off the light and get some sleep. It was comforting to have Todd close by, and Nate felt less anxious now about the distance that continued to exist between him and his mother.

"Yeah, good talk," Nate said, smiling to himself. He couldn't ask for a better friend than his brother Todd. He was surely going to miss him someday, but not tomorrow or the next. And when Todd did leave, he decided that he would message him every day so they could continue their talks.

When Easter break came, the family went on their second annual trip to Florida for a week on the beach. During their time there, Todd got reacquainted with Allie and spent all of his time with her. Billy and Nate spent most of their time either fishing or swimming in the surf. Gail, heeding advice given to her by Bella, shadowed her mother to the store, in the kitchen, and even out onto the beach, in an effort to engage her in conversation and elicit some kind of response that might reaffirm her affection for her. Mark spent his time surf-fishing with Nate and Billy.

"Why isn't Todd fishing with us?" Nate asked Mark as he cast his line into the surf.

"Well, he has other interests now," Mark responded, looking down the beach where Todd and Allie were sunning themselves. Nate followed his gaze.

"I'm glad Billy still finds fishing interesting," Nate observed, glancing Billy's way. Billy caught the look but couldn't hear them talking.

"His time will come. Then it will be just you and me, Nate," Mark added, laughing.

***

Todd had turned seventeen that spring and was saving money earned at the horse farm for a year now, hoping to buy a car after his birthday. Mark agreed to pay for half, provided Todd came up with the other half, so he began searching immediately for his first choice, a Jeep Wrangler. On his birthday, he and Mark test-drove a used Wrangler, and both being satisfied with its safety and handling, took the jeep home.

They were greeted in the drive by Billy and Nate, both excited by the prospect of having their older brother driving a jeep wrangler and the expectation that Todd would now be chauffeuring them around. It had a removable top, which Todd, in spite of the cool spring weather, promptly removed, oblivious to the cold wind.

"I'm saving up, too," Billy announced as they sat around the dinner table. Billy was now sixteen and had just gotten his license. His birthday was just a week later than Todd's, and although he would have to wait another year, he was already excited about getting his own car. "Same deal, right, Dad?"

Mark smiled. "Of course, Billy."

Baseball season had started, and both Todd and Billy played on the high school baseball teams again. Todd was a starting varsity pitcher, and Billy was at the first base position. Practice lasted about two hours every day after school, and games were on Wednesdays. Mark was usually working, and Jean had not resumed driving, so neither attended the games. Nate's little league season would start a little later and run through most of the summer.

Work for Todd and Billy continued at the barn, and now that Nate was fourteen, he helped them out. Nate had grown over six inches in the past two years and could now reach the clutch and brake pedals on the tractor, so Todd taught him how to drive. After all, Todd was going to be graduating soon. He hadn't decided yet what he would be doing after school but believed that whatever he decided, his time at the barn would end.

In the meantime, Todd baled the hay, and Nate drove the tractor and wagon while Todd tossed the bales onto it. When it was loaded, they drove the tractor back to the barn, and both carried the bales up the stairs into the loft.

Billy continued caring for the horses, becoming more impatient every day as he waited for permission from Sarah Elliot to ride one of the show horses. He was frustrated that she still felt he wasn't ready, and it annoyed him that she doubted his ability to handle the more fidgety purebreds safely. In spite of his frustration, when he was done feeding and watering, he helped unload the wagon.

This would be their routine until summer: baseball after school, working at the barn, home for dinner, then time spent on school work.

As the weather warmed, Todd and several baseball friends decided on Friday evening to drive out to the lake house. This would be the first time that any of the kids had gone to the lake house without the entire family there. Mark had approved it, after taking Todd aside with a promise not to drink and drive or engage in any risky behavior. Mark was realistic and forgo-ed any mention of "illegal" behavior, knowing full well that the boys would likely take some alcohol along. But as long as Todd and his friends weren't driving, he wouldn't concern himself with them drinking at the house.

Todd promised and, taking the cue from his father, responded in kind. No drinking and driving and no risky behavior. That was understood, and Todd added that he appreciated his father's trust.

Todd asked Billy to go, but he declined. He had an obligation to take care of the horses, so he decided it best to stay behind. Billy continued working in the barn until after dark, mucking the stalls and feeding the horses their last flakes of hay for the night. It had begun to rain, and he heard thunder rumbling in the distance as Mark and Nate arrived in the SUV.

Nate got out of the car to talk to Billy while Mark stayed inside, watching from the driver's seat as the rain intensified and the storm moved closer. "Hey. Dad and I are going to pick up some pizza for dinner. He said if you still want to go up to the lake house, he can take you tomorrow morning."

Billy thought for a minute, then declined. "That's OK. There will be plenty of opportunities for me to go to the lake house, and I really should be here to take care of the horses. The Elliotts depend on me. Besides, those guys with Todd aren't really my friends. They're his."

"You coming home for pizza?" Nate asked.

"As soon as I finish here. Should be in about a half hour," he said, returning to his work. Billy watched as they drove away and was suddenly startled by a loud clap of thunder directly overhead. He heard several of the horses stir nervously, one of them thrashing about his stall. Billy moved to the stall gate and reached in to calm the Saddle-bred gelding, but it backed away out of his reach and continued thrashing about the stall nervously. He knew this was one of Sarah's prize show horses that could easily hurt itself by kicking the wooden planks that lined the stall, so he decided he should try to calm the horse by whatever means necessary. He had watched Sarah Elliott many times and was confident he could handle the horse. And if he was successful, it would show her just how much he had learned, and he could be trusted to work with the show horses.

Without another thought, he opened the stall door and entered, speaking calmly to the horse and slowly reaching out to him, stroking his neck gently. The horse snorted and seemed to calm himself. Billy breathed a sigh of relief, and convinced that the crisis had passed, he turned to exit the stall. As he did, there was another sudden crack of thunder overhead, and the gelding was suddenly up on its hind legs. It then came down on Billy, who's body fell limp to the floor of the stall.

***

Mark and Nate arrived back at the house with the pizzas. Gail heard them arrive and busied herself pouring sodas in the kitchen when Mark and Nate entered. "Is Billy back yet?" Mark inquired.

"Haven't seen him," she responded shortly. There was another more distant clap of thunder as the storm began to subside.

"Nate, please go let your mom know that we're here with the pizza, then check Billy's room to see if he is there."

Nate went up the stairs and found his mother in her room, letting her know she should come downstairs to eat. He then passed by Billy's room; the door was open, and Billy was nowhere to be seen. He returned to the kitchen to let his father know.

"He's probably just waiting for the storm to let up. I'll drive over and pick him up," said Mark as he picked up his keys from the counter and headed out the door, leaving Nate, Gail, and Jean in the kitchen.

***

The rain had stopped when Mark parked the car in front of the barn. The lights were on, and he could see clearly the center hallway with the stalls on either side. Billy was nowhere in sight, so he climbed out of the SUV and entered the hallway. It was quiet until he called out Billy's name, and getting no response, he began walking down the long hallway, glancing briefly into each stall as he went. He had passed by several stalls when he stopped in his tracks and was filled with panic. Billy lay motionless on the stall floor, his head and upper torso covered with blood.

***

Nate, Gail, and their mother Jean sat silently at the table, waiting for Mark and Billy to return before eating. "It's going to get cold. Can't we just eat?" Gail asked impatiently.

Jean consented, and Nate ate two slices of pizza before retreating to his room. Several minutes later, he heard sirens in the distance but didn't pay much attention as he sat on his bed and strummed his guitar, practicing the chords he had learned from Todd over the past year. A few more minutes passed, then he hurried to the bedroom window as several rescue vehicles passed by with lights flashing and sirens blaring.

A single vehicle had come down the drive, and he watched as the sheriff walked quickly toward the porch and then out of site. He heard the front door open and listened intently as muffled voices broke the unnerving silence, which ended as quickly as it had begun. The door closed, and he turned his eyes once again to the vehicle below, watching as his mother and the sheriff drove hastily down the drive under the strobe of flashing lights

RUNNING SHOES

until it disappeared into the darkness.

The house was eerily quiet now, and Nathan made his way down the hallway, past the empty bedrooms. He stopped briefly by Billy's room, opened the door, and surveyed the walls within. He found himself surrounded by an eclectic collage of wall posters, including some girl clad in a skimpy bikini named Kate Upton, Yankee first baseman Mark Teixeira, Chance the Rapper, and a race horse named Secretariat, among many others.

His bat and glove lay atop his baseball uniform, unceremoniously lying in a heap in the corner. His bed, however, was made and conveyed more of an orderly appearance to the room in stark contrast to the helter-skelter atmosphere surrounding it, conveying that this was something he would need sooner rather than later and it would be ready and waiting for him. On the dresser between two baseball trophies, the first designating him as MVP and the other a team trophy, both earned during the previous JV baseball season, sat a picture of Todd, Billy, and Nate, taken at the river during one of their camping and fishing expeditions. It appeared to be fairly recent, but his mind was so clouded with current developments that he couldn't recall when it might have been taken. He finally turned from the room and left, closing the door quietly behind him, not wanting to end the peaceful quiet that had calmed his anxious fears.

Nate continued down the stairs and found Gail sitting alone in the living room. She sat motionless for a time, not acknowledging his presence as he sat in the lounge chair across from her. They both continued to stare blankly ahead but avoided any direct eye contact. The silence was abruptly ended when the doorbell rang. They remained still until it rang a second time, and Gail slowly arose from her chair to answer the door.

Bella had received a call from Mark only minutes before, explaining to her as exigent as possible that Billy had been injured, he and Jean were at the hospital, and could she possibly check on Gail and Nate at home? She now stood outside the door of their house, anxiously awaiting for Gail or Nate to answer.

Gail opened the door and led her to the living room without speaking so that Nate would know firsthand any news that Bella might share. "Your father called and asked me to come by," she began.

Gail didn't want to waste time with any perfunctory conversation. "Is Billy going to be OK?" Nate watched Bella closely for any hint of evasion.

"I'm sorry, I don't know anything except that he was injured by one of the horses. They are with him at the hospital and waiting to talk to the doctors. I'm going to wait with you both here if that's OK". Gail nodded in acceptance of the offer. Nate remained silent, his hope of Billy's well-being renewed by the uncertainty of his condition. If his parents were waiting to speak with the doctor, he must still be alive. He silently asked God for it.

CHAPTER 8
WHAT REMAINS

Midnight came and went, and there was no word from Mark or the hospital, so Bella finally convinced Gail and Nate to try to get some rest. They retired to their rooms, and Bella sat alone in the living room, praying for Billy, for the family, and for God's mercy on them. She then lay down herself, hoping to get at least some rest while they awaited news. Around seven the next morning, Bella was awakened by one of the young deputies at the door. As he entered, she read the name on his badge, Deputy Sanders. He was familiar to her, as most people in Plainville knew each other, especially the village law enforcement and emergency personnel.

He tipped his hat to her as he began to speak. "Good morning Ma'am. Mr. Woods asked me to stop by and check on things here." Bella nodded acknowledgment but wanted to know more about Billy. He continued. "I am driving up to the lake house to pick up Todd and bring him home."

This could not be good, she thought before asking the question. "What is his condition?" She knew the response would be vague as he had likely been instructed to say as little as possible.

He did not speak but merely shook his head with a blank expression. Deputy Sanders was new on the force, and this was his first experience in dealing with a family crisis such as this. He struggled to maintain his composure and finally spoke before turning to leave. "I'll be back with Todd in a couple of hours, and then we'll have to see where things stand. I'm sorry I don't have more to tell you right now." He tipped his hat again as he exited.

***

Deputy Sanders arrived at the lake house by 9:30 and rang the bell. No one answered, so he tried the door, which was unlocked, and entered the foyer of the house. "Hello, this is Deputy Sanders. Is anyone here?"

A young man dressed in gym shorts and a tee shirt appeared from the hallway. Deputy Sanders recognized him as one of Todd's baseball teammates. "Yes, sir," the young man spoke. "Can I help you?"

"Is Todd here?"

"He's probably still asleep…"

"I'm here," Todd interrupted as he emerged from down the hallway. He had heard the voice of the deputy identifying himself and quickly jumped out of bed, apprehensive as to the purpose of this visit that was out of the Plainville police district. "How can I help you, Deputy?"

"I'm afraid there's been an accident. Your father asked me to come pick you up."

Todd stared at him for a minute, a million thoughts running through his mind, before speaking. "Who?" was all he asked.

The deputy thought it unfair to withhold this small bit of information.

"Billy."

Todd looked toward his friend Johnny, then back at the deputy. He was afraid to ask the question but even more afraid to know the answer. "How bad?"

The deputy turned to Johnny without further discussion of Billy's condition. "I understand you rode up here with Todd. I need to take Todd home now; could you bring his car home for him later?"

Johnny looked toward Todd, who remained motionless. "Sure, I can do that."

"Keys are hanging in the kitchen," Todd finally said. "I'll get my things," he directed to the deputy and left the room.

***

Deputy Sanders remained silent during the drive back to Plainville, and he turned off his police radio to maintain the silence. Many scenarios ran through Todd's head; he knew how reckless Billy could be. Had he done something stupid, or was this really an accident? Knowing Billy, it was probably some combination of the two: risky behavior resulting in unforeseen consequences. And he had just promised his father he would watch out for Billy, keep him out of trouble. He knew any revelation about Billy's condition was not forthcoming from the officer, so he would have to wait.

As they neared town, Todd spoke up. "Can you take me to the hospital?"

"Your father asked that I take you home."

"Please, sir, just take me to the hospital." Todd was now insistent.

The Deputy thought for a moment before responding. "Alright, Todd."

Inside the hospital, Todd was directed to the ICU nurses' station. He approached a nurse seated at a computer. "I'm here to see Billy Woods."

"Your name?" she asked politely.

"Todd Woods."

"OK, Mr. Woods. If you would like to take a seat in the waiting room, I'll see if I can get someone to help you." She pointed down the hallway.

Todd made his way down the hall to the waiting room and sat, his mind racing in anticipation of news about Billy's condition. This time he prayed for

Billy, his family, and then his mother. If this was as bad as he imagined, he feared the worst for his mother. Her previous recovery had been long and hard, and it was far from complete.

His thoughts were interrupted by his father as he entered the room. His physical appearance shocked Todd; he was pale, disheveled, and weary. Todd stood to face him and waited for the news.

"Todd, uh...I didn't expect to see you here."

"I asked the deputy to bring me straight here. What's happened to Billy, Dad?"

"Let's sit," he ushered Todd to a chair across from him. He searched for the right words before continuing. "Apparently, Billy went into one of the stalls to calm one of the horses during the storm. The horse must have startled and...and it reared up and...and it came down on him." His voice began to fail him as he choked up. "That's where I..." he looked up at Todd, and tears filled his eyes. "I found him there." They sat quietly now, just looking at each other. Todd's eyes had filled with tears now too. Mark was finally able to continue. "He is on life-support. There's no hope..."

Todd sat for a few minutes, processing what he had just heard from his father. "This is my fault. I should have made him go with us to the lake house. I'm sorry, Dad." Todd was suddenly sobbing, and his father went to him, holding him tightly until he was able to calm himself.

"Todd, this is not your fault. It was an accident."

"I want to see him," Todd insisted.

"Todd, I don't think that's a good idea. You don't want your last memory of Billy to be this."

"Dad, please. I will always have fond memories of Billy. Saying goodbye to him won't change that. I want to see him."

"Alright, Todd. Your mother's with him right now. The doctor will be turning off life-support as soon as we allow. Give me a couple of minutes to let your mother know you are here."

**

Todd entered the ICU minutes later, where Billy lay. He was hooked up to several monitors and a breathing tube. His head was wrapped entirely in a bandage, with only two blackened eyes and several large abrasions across his nose and cheekbones visible. Todd stood next to his father, watching Billy's chest rise and fall in rhythm to the breathing apparatus that kept his body alive. Only a body; nothing else, Todd was thinking to himself. Why Billy? Why did you do this?

Their mother sat quietly at Billy's side, still clasping his left hand tightly between her two. She was no longer crying, having been drained of her tears and the energy it took to generate more. She did not acknowledge Todd's presence nor that of Pastor Dan as he arrived.

Pastor Dan exchanged brief words with Mark, then stepped forward with a bible opened and began to read several passages. "So will it be with the resurrection of the dead. The body that is sown is perishable. It is raised imperishable; it is sown in dishonor; it is raised in glory; it is sown in weakness; it is raised in power; and it is sown a natural body. It is raised as a spiritual body. If there is a natural body, there is also a spiritual body." (1 Corinthians 15:42-44)

"For our light and momentary troubles are achieving for us an eternal glory that far outweighs them all. So we fix our eyes not on what is seen, but on what is unseen since what is seen is temporary, but what is unseen is eternal." (2 Corinthians 4:17-18)

He then moved to Billy and anointed what was visible of his head with oil as he prayed, but the words Pastor Dan spoke were obscured to Todd. "I'm sorry, Billy," he said softly to himself.

When Pastor Dan finished, he stepped back behind Mark and Todd as the doctor and a nurse proceeded to turn off the breathing apparatus, the only remaining sign of life that once was a son and brother.

Pastor Dan then took Todd's arm and led him from the room, leaving

Mark and Jean alone with Billy. "Let's give your mom and dad a few minutes alone. We can go to the house ahead of them and talk to Gail and Nathan." Todd was numb, didn't speak, but just followed Pastor Dan's lead.

When they arrived at the house, Bella was waiting at the door. Gail and Nate stood apprehensively behind her. She scanned their faces but stopped at Todd's. His eyes were red, and his face remained downcast, avoiding contact with them. It took his best effort to remain emotionless for his sister and brother. Without speaking, Bella led them through the hallway to the living room, where all but Bella sat. She dismissed herself from the room, out of sight but within earshot of the conversation.

"Gail and Nathan, I'm sorry to have to tell you this. Billy sustained some serious injuries. There was nothing the doctors could do."

Gail immediately let out a wail and burst into tears, her sobs drowning out the deafening silence that preceded the announcement. Bella reentered the room, doing her best to remain composed, and sat next to Gail to console her. Nate was stunned and stared at Todd, looking for some kind of reassurance that everything was going to be OK. Todd brushed away several tears before looking up and speaking softly to Pastor Dan, seated next to him. "Thank you, Pastor, for being there for my mom and dad...and Billy. And for coming here to speak with us." He then quietly stood, glanced briefly at Nate, and headed upstairs to his room.

"Why did God let this happen?" Nate suddenly directed toward Pastor Dan.

"Nate, we don't know the mind of God and why things like this happen. All we do know is that Billy is safe with Him now, and God will care for him." Nate left the room without saying more. He hadn't cried; he didn't know why. Maybe he would do that later. Right now, he was angry and bitter. At God. At Billy. At everyone who could have prevented this terrible accident. He walked down the upstairs hallway toward his room, stopping briefly at Todd's closed door. He wondered what Todd was doing right then and if he could talk with him, but he decided that maybe Todd needed to be alone, so he continued onto his room.

Inside, he put on his running shoes. He would run now and try to make sense of it all. That's all that he could do at this very moment. It was nearly ten-thirty, and the fog was slowly lifting, letting the sun peak through. He began jogging at first, in the direction of the barn, his place of refuge. Once there, he stopped at the double doors leading in. They were closed, so he slid one side open to peer inside.

The aisle was clear, and there was silence inside except for the horses stirring about their stalls, so he entered, walking slowly down the hallway. He could see a yellow taped-off stall about halfway down the alley, reminiscent of a crime scene on an episode of Law and Order. He decided to break the rules and duck under the tape to look inside the stall. The stall was empty except for remnants of dried blood on the floor shavings. Nothing but the body had been removed from the previous night's crime scene.

He entered the stall and stared at the spot where Billy last lived. He sat down on the pine shavings and ran his hand through them, now stained with dried blood, all that was left of his dead brother. This was his refuge and his time to let his emotions take hold of him. He was alone now, just as Billy had been during his last moments. The sense of loss and sorrow overtook him, and he cried until he was emptied and no tears were left to shed.

***

News of the death of Billy Woods rocked the small town. Nate had completed his run around the neighborhood, draining him of what little energy he had left after his emotional outburst. There were at least a dozen cars in the driveway now and people standing around on the front porch when he arrived. Some familiar faces, some not, all with expressions of sadness and disbelief. He passed by them quickly, hoping no one would speak to him. That would require a response, and he wouldn't know what to say. He entered the house, and there were more people milling about, talking in hushed tones to whatever sympathetic ears were nearby. He passed by them quickly, too, and hurried up the stairs, hoping to find some solace in the quiet of his own room.

He came upon Todd's closed door once more, but this time stopped and knocked softly. He didn't know what he was going to say or what he expected from Todd at this moment, but he needed to know that they were going to be OK. There was no response from inside, so Nate slowly turned the knob and opened the door. The curtains were drawn, and the room was dark, but he could see a shadowy figure sitting motionless on the bed. Nate decided it was worth the risk. If Todd didn't want him there, he would let him know. He entered and stood silently just inside the door, closing it behind him.

"Hey, Nate." His voice was calm and reassuring. "Come in and sit for awhile. It's safe in here."

Nate took a seat in Todd's desk chair, wheeling it closer to where Todd was seated on the bed.

"I went for a run" Nate finally found his voice. He hadn't tried to talk to anyone since Pastor Dan earlier.

"Of course you did," Todd retorted in spite of the doom and gloom that had enveloped them.

"I ran to the barn," Nate continued.

Todd expressed his concern. "You probably shouldn't have gone there."

"I saw his blood on the floor. In the stall," Nate continued. He then stood, walked to the bed, and sat down next to Todd. "Why'd this happen? I don't understand. Why?" His run had only provided a momentary solace, and he felt himself losing control once again. But he was with Todd now, and he would understand, so he allowed himself to cry as Todd wrapped his arm around his shoulder, holding back his own tears.

"I don't know why, bud. It just did." They sat there for a long time in silence. Nate's crying finally turned to sniffles before either of them spoke again. "Do you run every day now?" Todd attempted to distract them both from their remorse.

"Usually. Why?"

"I was thinking maybe we could run together sometimes. Would that be alright with you?"

"Sure," Nate responded solemnly.

"I don't know if you'll be able to keep up with me, though..." Todd replied in an attempt to overcome the sadness that consumed them.

Nate temporarily overcame their moment of despair. This is why he loved Todd. 'It's you that will have to keep up."

CHAPTER 9
SAYING GOODBYE

The funeral for Billy followed two days later. Nate had never been to a funeral before, and while to his family, it was a monumentally sad affair, he was distracted by the seemingly hypocritical celebration surrounding them.

"I don't get it," he nudged Todd sitting next to him in the pew. Todd's attention had been drawn to the back rows of the sanctuary. Nate followed his gaze and spotted what Todd was distracted by. Aunt Susan and her family had arrived late and were seated in the back row, accompanied by Allie, whom Todd had spent much of his time with when they had vacationed in Florida.

"Don't get what?" Todd now turned back to Nate.

"Why does everyone seem OK with this? Are we the only sad ones here?"

"It all depends on what you believe, I guess. Some people overcome their grief by claiming this as a celebration of life." Nate just looked at Todd, more confused now than before, and Todd sensed it. "Look, bud, the whole purpose of church is to teach us that when you die, you go to heaven. You pass from this life to eternal life with God. There's a lot more to it, but that's the bottom line. And that's what the people celebrate."

"Do you think Billy's in heaven?"

RUNNING SHOES

"I like to think so..." Their conversation ended as the service began. Several scripture readings and hymns followed, then people were invited forward to share their thoughts and memories of Billy.

Todd stepped forward and began: "Enough has been said about Billy, so I'd just like to share with you this poem that I found, written by Edgar Guest.

"I'll lend you for a while, a child of mine," He said.

"For you to love the while he lives and mourn for when he's dead.

It may be six or seven years, or twenty-two or three,

But will you, till I call him back, take care of him for me?

He'll bring his charms to gladden you, and should his stay be brief,

You'll have his lovely memories as solace for your grief."

"I cannot promise he will stay; since all from earth return,

But there are lessons taught down there I want this child to learn.

I've looked the wide world over in My search for teachers' true

And from the throngs that crowd life's lanes, I have chosen you.

Now will you give him all your love, not think the labor vain,

Nor hate Me when I come to call, to take him back again?

Todd hesitated for a moment as he searched the eyes of his family. Nate was watching and listening intently as Todd continued.

I fancied that I heard them say, "Dear Lord, Thy will be done!

For all the joy Thy child shall bring, the risk of grief we run.

We'll shelter him with tenderness, we'll love him while we may,

And for the happiness we've known, forever grateful stay;

But should the angels call for him much sooner than we've planned,

We'll brave the bitter grief that comes and try to understand!"

He walked quietly back to his seat amid the silence, except for the faint sound of his mother's weeping.

***

They welcomed their extended family and friends to the house immediately following the service. Nate observed his parents, especially his mother, who had regained her composure now, but remained aloof as visitors wandered about the house, offering their heartfelt sympathy. While his mother sat quietly, his father stood rigidly behind her, acknowledging all who extended their condolences.

Todd had excused himself and made his way out to the back porch, where he and Allie sat together on the porch swing. She greeted Nate as he passed by them on his way into the back yard. There Nate found his best friend Zak, who had arrived during the night all the way from Texas.

"I'm sorry to hear about your brother…"

"Thanks. How do you like Texas?" Nate and Zak had kept in touch at first, but over time, their correspondence became less and less. Nate was glad to see him and that their friendship had not waned.

"It's OK, I guess. It's just me and dad now. My mom wasn't happy there and left." Zak changed the subject. "I miss the winters here. Doesn't snow very often in Texas."

"Sorry to hear about your mom. You playing any ball there?"

"Yeah, I joined a league. I'm playing catcher now. They needed someone who could actually catch the ball." They both laughed.

"Come on, follow me," Nate instructed, and Zak followed him to the pear tree in the sideyard. Nate climbed to the top, and Zak was close behind. They were quiet for a time before Nate spoke again. "Got any new friends there?"

Nate asked as they observed the people huddled throughout the yard.

"There are a couple of guys I hang with. How about you?"

"Not really."

"I'm irreplaceable, right?"

Nate smiled. "I guess so."

Zak continued. "Remember how we used to watch Cornell baseball?" Nate nodded. "I've already given my dad fair warning. When I get out of high school, I'm going to Cornell."

"Wow, you're sure planning way ahead."

"Well, it will happen before you know it. I know it's always been your plan to go there. It's mine too. If we both go, we could be roommates."

"I'd like that. Be kinda like old times camping together."

"Except there will probably be girls involved..."

"Yeah, I suppose you're right." They both laughed at the prospect.

***

"How long will you be here for?" Todd asked Allie as they glided gently forward and backward on the swing.

"A few days, I think."

"I know the timing may not seem right. Maybe it's totally inappropriate. But we could go up to the lake house for a few days."

"I'd like to, but your cousin Melissa would have to come since I am traveling with her."

"She could come too. Maybe it would be good for Aunt Susan and Uncle Matt to just stay here with my parents while we get away to the lake. When I say that, it sounds a little selfish on my part."

She touched his arm. "Don't be so hard on yourself, Todd. I don't think you're being selfish at all. Your brother and sister should come too."

"OK, I'll run it by my dad. Make sure he is OK with it."

CHAPTER 10
COPING

They arrived by ten the next morning and brought their things inside. Todd showed them all around the house and assigned rooms: Nate and Zak took the downstairs bunks; Melissa and Ali would stay in the parent's bedroom with the king bed. Gail had refused to come and took refuge with Bella. As they all took their things to their rooms, Todd walked alone, carrying his things to Billy's room, where he stood outside the closed door. He opened it slowly, stepped inside, and surveyed the melange of wall hangings and decorations that Billy had concocted.

They were so different, he and Billy, yet they had been so close growing up. It wasn't until their teen years that Billy stopped following his lead and struck out on his own. While they both learned to play guitars, Billy preferred heavy metal and jammed regularly with his friends. Todd preferred his acoustic guitar, soft rock, folk, and country classics. And then there were the horses; Billy loved being around them, and now, he was gone because of them.

There was a soft knock on the door, and Allie entered. She walked up to his side and slid her arm through his. She surveyed the room before speaking. "You OK?" she whispered.

Todd reached for the small framed photo on the dresser of Billy, Nate, and him. "This was taken last summer at our favorite fishing spot. It's funny; I think he has this same picture in his room at home." He handed the picture to Allie. She looked at it for a minute, then placed it gently back into its place on the dresser.

"You two were close."

"We used to be. Then we got older and had different interests." Todd chuckled. "Nate and I are a lot closer than Billy and I ever were, in spite of our age difference."

"From what I have witnessed, you and Nate are a lot alike. And I think he looks up to you."

"I haven't told anyone yet, but I've decided I'm going to enlist. I think maybe I will defer for a year, though. There won't be much left here after I leave. Nate and Gail don't really get along. Our mother is in a world of her own. Our father has escaped to his office and spends all his time there. I had hoped Nate and Billy could get closer; be there for each other. But with Billy gone, Nate won't have anyone." He stopped for a moment and dried his moist eyes. They stood in silence for a while; Todd inhaled deeply, then spoke again. "I can't sleep in here tonight. Come on. I think I'll use Gail's room." They left the room and closed the door behind them, leaving the room intact.

***

It was a warm summer day spent out on the lake. While the boys took turns diving into the lake from the boat, the girls chose to sun themselves and work on their early summer tans. The younger boys tied rafts to the back of the boat, and Todd towed them around the lake, occasionally making some sharp turns, creating a wake for them to bounce over.

For dinner, Todd started a fire in the fire pit and cooked burgers, and as dusk set in, they set camp chairs near the fire to ward off the chilly air of the evening. Todd and Nate played some familiar tunes on their guitars, and the group sang along. When they had finished, Todd stood and announced that it was getting late and everyone should get some rest, so the group followed him back into the house.

Melissa bid Todd and Allie goodnight and retired to the parent's bedroom. Todd and Allie sat together on the couch. He was captivated by this girl he barely knew. But even from a distance, he had developed strong feelings for her like he had never felt before. It was all instinctive and natural when he leaned in and kissed her. They lingered there for a moment before Allie let go of his hand. She smiled and spoke softly to him. "We both should get some sleep...and Melissa will be wondering where I am."

"Goodnight," Todd said as she rose from the couch and turned toward the bedroom. As he watched her walk away, he whispered softly, "I love you."

***

He was awakened in the night as a shadowy figure came through the bedroom door, closing it silently behind her. He watched as she moved closer to the bed, stood next to it for a moment, then dropped her robe to the floor. She then climbed into the bed and lay next to him with her arm across his broad chest and head resting on his shoulder. They lay there quietly for a time before he turned slightly toward her. He could smell her lightly scented perfume. It smelled of tangerine and honey. No words passed between them. She was there for him, and she was what he needed. He moved his right hand gently, first across her lips, then her ear lobes and neck. He wanted to feel her every part and continued a slow progression down to her soft breasts, teasing them ever so gently and listening intently as her breathing intensified in expectation of his every move.

His hand continued it's slow progression downward as he positioned himself to meet her lips with his own. This level of passion was all new for both of them as they continued their mutual exploration. "Are you OK?" and "I am now" were the only words spoken between them, and they continued on this new journey, with this moment that they would both remember forever in the life they would share.

After, he fell into a deep sleep and awoke several hours later to find she had retreated from their time together and gone back to the bedroom that she and Melissa shared so as not to be suspected by anyone in the morning.

When Nate and Zak arose, they found Melissa and Allie in the kitchen making breakfast of sausage, eggs, and pancakes. Todd appeared moments later and greeted Allie with a kiss on the cheek, then proceeded to pour himself a cup of coffee. Nate watched his brother closely; he was not usually this chipper so early in the morning.

"How did everyone sleep?" Todd asked, searching the faces of everyone and stopping for a moment when he saw Nate eyeing him.

"OK, fine, great," were the responses. "How about you?" Nate asked without assertion.

"Gail's bed isn't the most comfortable of beds; it's a little short for me, and my feet hung off the end. But other than that, I slept well." He turned his eyes away from Nate and spoke again. "Anyone up for a hike this morning?"

"Zak and I want to go out on the lake again."

"We'll do that this afternoon after our hike."

***

The landscape surrounding the lake consisted of some flat lands leading up to the foothills of the Berkshires that extended up into Massachusetts. Todd and Billy had found several hiking trails on one of their previous visits, suitable for all of them to climb. They carried backpacks with drinks and a picnic lunch which was shared at the top of the hill. Melissa, Nate, and Zak explored the surrounding woods while Todd and Allie settled on a large glacier rock overlooking the valley and lake below. She snuggled up close to him, and he put his arm around her shoulder.

"Billy and I found this place. I guess it will always remind me of him now." The melancholy was obvious in his voice.

"It's beautiful up here. This should be a good memory for you."

They were silent for a few minutes, listening to the sounds of the birds in the woods and the wind rustling through the trees.

"Last night tops my list of things to remember," Todd commented. Allie nudged him gently in the ribs. He smiled and turned his face to hers and saw that she was smiling too. Then he drew her in close and kissed her.

Allie finally shared her thoughts about the night. "I was hesitant, you know. I didn't know if...well...considering everything that has happened the past week."

"I'm glad you overcame your hesitation. I wasn't sleeping well, and I needed...wanted you...I wanted so badly to be with you. I have since the first time we met, you know."

She took his hand in hers. "We'll be leaving for Florida tomorrow." Now there was resignation in her voice.

"I'm going to find a job in the fall, but will take some time off between Christmas and New Year for a visit."

"What about your family?"

"I'll stay through Christmas day, then fly down the day after. It will get me there sooner if I fly, and we'll have more time together."

"You would do that for me?"

Todd laughed and spoke in his most sexy voice. "Baby, after last night, I'd do anything for you!" They laughed together until they were rejoined by the others.

***

Nate found Todd sitting alone on the pier, dangling his feet into the lake. He sat down next to his big brother, wondering what he was thinking; now that the funeral was over, Billy was gone, and he had to say goodbye to Allie. Before he could ask Todd his thoughts, Todd spoke to him.

"So you and Zak at Cornell, huh? I wish I could be there to see that. You two will make your mark there before long, I'm sure."

"Yeah, he's a good friend. I'm glad he came to visit, in spite of why he came."

"Ironic that you don't get to see the ones you're closest too until someone dies."

Nate wasn't sure exactly what Todd meant but would leave that for another time. "So, you and Allie are pretty serious."

"Was that a rhetorical question?"

"What's ironic mean? And rhetorical? "

Todd smiled. "I'm sorry, bud. Sometimes I forget you're only thirteen when we have such grown-up conversations. Yes, we are pretty serious."

"Almost fourteen. I'm almost fourteen, and I understand more than you think," he corrected, then suddenly added, "I saw her last night."

"Who?"

"Allie."

"What do you mean? When?"

"Coming out of Gail's room. I couldn't sleep. I was thinking about Billy. So I came upstairs and just sat in the dark on the couch for awhile. I saw her come out of Gail's room. I don't think she saw me, though."

Todd thought for a minute before responding. "Well, bud, I guess maybe it's time for another one of our adult talks."

"Not necessary. Like I said, I know more than you think. But I do have a question for you."

"OK, as long as it's not too personal."

"Sometimes I get on the internet and read stuff. Maybe it was meant to be funny. I read that sometimes men let their dicks do the thinking, and it gets them in trouble."

Now Todd laughed. "You can't believe everything you read on the internet. Seriously though, as you get older, you're going to have these urges."

"If you're talking about sex, I'm taking sex ed in school this fall."

"All they're going to teach you in sex ed is basic anatomy and how things go together. And the consequences if you're not careful. What I'm talking about is guys chasing after girls and wanting to have sex with them. It's a natural urge we have. But it's important to resist those urges until you meet the right person. Someone special. For me, that's Allie. I'm sure someday you'll meet that special someone too. I just hope you can wait until you do."

"Did you wait?"

Todd deflected." I've had lots of girls flocking around me during high school. Plenty of opportunities. But when I met Allie, I had someone special to look forward to, to share something special with, and it became a lot easier to avoid temptation." They sat in silence for a few minutes before Todd spoke again. "You know, Nate, I'd like you to remember something for me. And this doesn't just apply to sex; it's about everything. I believe that the thoughts in our head can be a distraction from what is in our hearts."

Nate thought about that for a minute and contemplated Todd's proclamation. "I remember you said that to me once before...when Zak, you and I were at the river."

"So you understand what I'm saying?"

"I don't know. I'm going to have to think about it. I'll let you know later if I believe it."

Todd nodded. "Good talk," he said and jumped into the lake.

"Yeah, good talk," Nate said and followed him in.

***

"Do you think it will be OK for me to work at the Elliott's now? I mean, since the accident, I don't know if they even want me there." Nate was asking

Todd's opinion as he drove them home from the lake house.

"Well, I don't know Nate. But are you sure you want to? It's going to be a constant reminder for you about Billy and the accident."

"I know. But the Elliotts need help now more than ever. And I'm OK with being reminded of Billy. It makes me sad, but the accident was no fault of theirs. Besides, Billy is in a better place now. That's what Pastor said."

"Well, if you're sure about that, we can stop by the Elliott's on the way home and see what they think."

"I didn't see them at the funeral," Nate commented.

"I'm not sure why they weren't there, but I'm guessing that they may not have felt welcomed."

***

They drove up the Elliott's long drive and parked near the entrance to the barn. As they exited the jeep, there was shouting in the direction of the house. The voice was familiar to them, but it was considerably louder and hysterical in nature. Todd immediately recognized it as their mother's voice.

He and Nate ran quickly to the house and found their mother on the sidewalk near the steps of the front porch. Sarah Elliott stood in the doorway, looking out. Her expression was grim.

Jean did not see her boys approach from behind and continued to rant at Sarah. "How could you be so reckless?" she demanded. "You allowed this to happen!"

Sarah was clearly distraught but did not speak. Todd came up beside his mother and took her arm. It was clear that this confrontation by their mother had been going on since before their arrival. "Mom, please, let's go home," he pleaded. She shook off his arm and began crying hysterically.

"You've destroyed our family. I can never forgive you for what you've done!"

Todd grasped his mother's arm again and forced her to move away. "Mom, stop." Todd was now demanding this of her.

Nate was getting anxious and upset by the confrontation. Was this how it was going to be from now on? he asked himself.

Nate followed them down the walk toward the jeep, then glanced back at Mrs. Elliott, who was wiping tears from her face. He continued to watch her as she turned away and closed the front door behind her. Their mother had become quiet now and did not speak to either of them as they returned home. She left them alone by Todd's jeep and entered the house in silence.

Todd put his arm around Nate's shoulders. It was an odd time for him to notice how tall Nate had gotten; he was just a head shorter now. It reminded him that their time together was running out, and soon he would not be there for Nate. There was no talk between them of what had just transpired. Todd believed there was nothing he could say to Nate that would help. It would be best to engage him in another fashion. "A good time for a run?" Todd asked solemnly. Nate nodded. This was just another thing he needed to run from.

***

Nate later overheard his father and Todd talking downstairs in the living room. "She's taking her grief out on others. Today it was Mrs. Elliott. She is blaming others for Billy's death."

"We need to give her time to grieve Todd. She...We...have just lost a son."

"And I lost a brother! I loved him too. But I don't blame others for this. In fact, if it was anyone's fault, it was mine. I promised to protect him...to protect all of them. And I failed." Tears had filled his eyes now, and he looked to his father for some consolation. But it was not forthcoming.

Instead, his father turned his back to him as he spoke. "We all lost him. And each of us has to deal with that loss in our own way. It's not something we can choose how to deal with. Your mother is handling this the only way she knows how. And so am I."

"I mean no disrespect, but isn't this a time our family should be pulling together? We are all going in opposite directions here. Our mother has been a recluse since she killed that boy. She barely talks to or even acknowledges her children. I don't know where Gail is or what she is feeling. Nate seems confused by it all. And you, Dad, where are you? We need you to hold us together. I just don't get it."

"Nothing compares to losing a child Todd. I don't expect you to understand that now, and I hope you never have to. But maybe someday you will be forced to, and if that day comes, then you'll understand that I only have so much to give. It's taking all my resolve to get your mother and me through this. I can't do this for everyone."

Nate could overhear the discussion and felt helpless. He retreated up the stairs, walking directly to his mother's room. He opened the door without knocking. She was lying on the bed with her back toward him. He walked to the bed and climbed in behind her, draping his arm over her shoulder and around her neck. He cried as he lay there, hoping that she could find it in herself to turn to him and comfort him. But there was no response as she lay there silently next to him. He could not see her face or the tear-stained pillow on which her head rested.

CHAPTER 11
TODD

Nate and Todd visited the lake house frequently during the summer, sometimes with friends and other times just the two of them. There were no family trips there together; it was as if the entire reason for the lake house had been forgotten. Now it existed only for them and them alone, and Nate had resigned himself to that. He often found Todd just sitting alone on the dock, seemingly in deep thought, maybe about Billy or his future plans. At those times, he wasn't sure. But he knew when Todd was lost in thought about Allie because his mood was not so somber.

It was the last weekend before school and their last chance to spend the entire weekend there. Nate awoke and found Todd's bunk below already empty but spotted him through the sliding doors, sitting alone on the dock. He had been working on the boat, checking the engine oil, and getting it ready for a day on the lake. Today, they would spend time fishing for lake bass.

"Do you really blame yourself?" Nate asked, sitting down beside him. Todd looked up briefly, then continued to look through the tackle box. "I overheard you and dad talking that night. You said it was your fault that Billy died. Why do you think that?"

"I'm the oldest. Billy was reckless. I promised dad I would watch out for him. I guess I didn't do a very good job of it." Todd climbed into the boat, and Nate followed. "I got us some sausage biscuits and juice for breakfast while you were sleeping. You snore, by the way."

"Thanks..." Nate sat in the boat and opened the tackle box to make sure they had everything they needed. "... for breakfast." He then continued, wanting to know more about Todd's feeling of responsibility. "You couldn't be expected to be there all the time, you know. We have to be responsible for our own actions and suffer the consequences."

"Listen to you," Todd commented as he removed his shirt and sprayed himself with sunscreen, then handed the can to Nate. "Here, put some of this on." It was the same ritual every time they went out on the lake; get the boat ready, bring the fishing gear, and put on sun screen. And Todd would either fix something for breakfast or run to the local Mickie D's while Nate still slept.

"No one blames you," Nate continued. "We all knew Billy was fearless. It was stupid what he did, taking a chance like that. If anything, dad shouldn't have let him stay behind when we went to pick up pizza that night. Dad trusted Billy to be sensible. To be smart. Why should you be responsible for something our own dad allowed him to do?"

"You know you sound a lot smarter than your age," Todd concluded. He started the engine and steered the boat out into the middle of the lake, then anchored it.

Nate was the first to speak again. "You going to miss playing QB this year?"

Todd nodded. "Why do you ask?"

"The last time you talked about football, you were looking forward to you as QB and Billy as your wide receiver."

"At least we got to play together last year. I thought a lot about it, and I don't want to play. Not without him."

"I wish I could be the one downfield to catch your passes."

Todd cast his line into the water and sat back down. "Yeah, I would have liked that too."

"I wish I was older."

"Don't wish your life away. These years will come and go before you know it. Then you'll look back and wonder where the years went."

"I don't think I'll be forgetting last year very soon, if ever. Do you wish you were young again?" Nate knew the implication of this question, and Todd laughed.

"You're funny. You know age is all relative."

"How so?"

"Think of it like this. I'm eighteen right now, and to me, thirty is old. When I'm thirty, it won't seem old to me anymore; fifty will. And so it's all relative, based on how old you are and what you perceive as being old."

Nate thought about this awhile as he cast his line into the water. "So, do you miss her?"

"If you're talking about Allie, yes, definitely."

"Do you love her?"

"Well, bud, I think I do. I know I miss her, and I can't stop thinking about her. I want to be with her all the time."

"You want to know my opinion?" Nate quipped.

"I don't know, do I?" Todd laughed.

"Well, speaking from my limited experience and from what I have read on the internet..."

"Do you have experience other than what you have read and seen on the internet?"

"What I was going to say before you interrupted me was that I think that if you just like someone, you're thinking with your head. But I think love is in here." Nate pointed to his heart. "And I heard it said that our thoughts can be a distraction from what is in our hearts. So, if you're still just thinking you like her a lot, then maybe the love is not in your heart yet."

Todd smiled as he pondered the wisdom of his younger brother. "So, do you have any advice then for me on sex?"

Nate flashed a smile. "Give me another year. Besides, I think you'll figure it out. If you don't, ask me again in a few years. Maybe by then, I'll have a good idea of what it's all about."

Todd nodded. "I'll do that. Good talk."

"Yeah, good talk."

***

The year passed quickly as Todd kept busy with school and working full-time at the factory loading dock. The family dynamics stayed the same through the holidays and into the spring. Todd utilized the time between Christmas and New Year's to travel to Florida. It was a grim reminder for Nate about how it was going to be when Todd left for good. The realization that Todd would be leaving seemed to be on his mind constantly. Combined with his mother's reclusive behavior and absence in his life and the deterioration of a once cohesive family unit, his anxiety reached new levels. His only escape was to run daily, sometimes twice, in an effort to get away and leave it all behind.

When Todd was around, they would run together. Once Todd left, he would have reminders of the past and worries about the future to contend with on his own. When he was with Todd, everything seemed right, and he looked forward to their time together. Nate kept busy playing baseball in his usual shortstop position and doing occasional chores at the barn with his father's blessing. He didn't know if his mother was even aware of the time he was spending at the barn.

In late May, just two weeks before school ended, Todd asked the family to meet him in the dining room as he had an announcement to make. He had not shared with Nate or anyone in advance, what that announcement would be, but Nate speculated he was soon to learn what Todd's future plans were.

The family gathered around the table in anticipation, Jean sitting silently in her usual chair, although it had been empty for some time now. It was not her choice to be there, but Mark insisted she should do it for Todd. She looked pale and disheveled. It had become the norm on the rare occasion that she participated in family discussions or activities. Her bedroom was her domicile. Her entire reality existed only within that fortress.

Nate turned his attention toward Todd as he began to speak. "Thanks, everyone, for being here. I don't want to make this a big deal. It's just easier to tell you all at one time and not individually. I have made the decision to join the Marines."

There was silence around the table. Todd had applied to and been accepted by several schools right after graduation, including Cornell, but deferred entrance. In Nate's mind, this announcement was even worse than he had imagined. If Todd had gone to Cornell, Nate had hoped to be there too, that their time there would overlap for at least a year. But Todd's enlistment in the Marines changed everything.

Jean's reaction was indignant, and she mustered what strength she had to object to his plans. "That's not what we planned for you, and we won't allow it! You need to go to college!" Mark remained silent, allowing Todd to speak for himself in response to his mother.

He stared directly at her as he spoke. Nate had never seen Todd speak to their mother with such firm conviction and in direct opposition to her. "I'm doing exactly what my father did. He joined the marines, then after he got out, he put himself through school. I'm sorry if you don't like my decision, but it's my decision to make. I've already enlisted, and I will be reporting for basic training at the end of June."

Jean slowly stood from her chair, refusing now to look at Todd. "This is not what we planned on all these years. Going off to some middle eastern country and getting yourself killed. Haven't we lost enough already? " She then stopped and looked at Mark. "Are you going to allow this to happen?"

Mark wasn't surprised by Jean's reaction and chose not to respond. Todd was old enough now to make his own decisions, and there was nothing left for him to say. There was silence as Jean slowly walked from the room and ascended the stairs without speaking again.

Todd continued. "I plan on spending a few years in the marines, then using the GI bill to further my education."

"Why do you want to join the Marines? Mom's right. You should be going to college," Gail admonished. "It's stupid."

"You understand, don't you, Dad? You're a Marine."

Mark nodded. "I do. I didn't know what I wanted to do when I got out of high school, so I enlisted. It will give you time to plan out the rest of your life."

"As short as that might be..." Gale interjected.

Nate observed that his father, who used to make excuses for their mother's behavior, no longer made attempts to rationalize for her. Everyone had spoken except Nate. Todd knew this would be hardest for him and turned his attention to him. "You got an opinion, bud? Everyone else has expressed theirs."

Nate nodded. "If I had a choice, you wouldn't be leaving at all. But like you said, 'our thoughts are just a distraction from what is in our hearts.' It's not what I think that matters. If it's in your heart, it's what you need to do. Just make me two promises. You will stay in touch with me, and you'll get home safe." Nate kept his emotions in check and stood to leave the room. This was the reality he feared most, and it would soon come to pass.

Todd nodded in agreement. His little brother was growing up. Hopefully, their time together had been enough for both of them.

CHAPTER 12
DANI

Nate excelled in football and baseball into his junior year of high school. Baseball was really his forte, and he still dreamed of someday playing in the majors. In the meantime, he accepted the notoriety of his athletic ability with pride but not arrogance and found he was constantly surrounded by new friends and often the center of attention. It gave him a new found confidence that he had lacked in his earlier years, especially with girls who now seemed to flock around him as they passed through the hallways and fought to sit near him in classes. He wondered if this was how it was for Todd in high school and laughed to himself.

In between classes, he stopped at his locker and noticed an unfamiliar girl several lockers down, unfamiliar in that she was not one of his "groupies" and wouldn't even acknowledge his presence. She is very pretty, he thought to himself. She had shoulder-length auburn colored hair tied loosely back into a pony tail and green eyes. He was still introverted in spite of his popularity around the school, and he was not accustomed to just walking up to strangers and starting a conversation. But he was determined to make use of his reputation, as it was, and put this newfound self-confidence to the test.

"Hi, I'm Nathan," he said as he approached.

She glanced at him for a second, then turned back to her open locker. "I know who you are."

"I guess then you have an unfair advantage over me" he smiled his best-dimpled smile. "And you are?"

"Not interested" was her immediate glib response. She closed her locker and started to walk away.

"Oof. That was harsh," he countered as he followed her down the hall". I haven't seen you around and thought you might be new and need a friend."

"If I were new here, I wouldn't already know who you are. All the girls gush about you, and the guys all envy you because of it. Does that about sum it up?"

"You're very pretty," he commented, still smiling and ignoring her tirade. This was unexpected and seemed to catch her off guard.

"Dani," she finally said, turning back to face him. "My name is Dani."

This is promising, he thought to himself, but he didn't want to overdo it. "It's nice to make your acquaintance Dani" he extended his hand out to her, but she did not reciprocate. He waited for a verbal response, and it became an awkward silence.

"OK," she acquiesced. "I give. What's your game?"

"My game? Well, I play sports, primarily baseball, as you may know. And I love sports analogies."

"So now that our introductions are out of the way, what do you want?"

His mind was racing; she didn't hold back. "Well, I was hoping you would go out with me sometime."

"And why would I do that?"

Nate shrugged. "Who knows? It could be a match made in heaven. We'll never know for sure if we don't give it a shot."

Dani thought for a moment, and her response surprised him. "OK." She then took out an index card and wrote on it. "See you tomorrow night at eight." She handed him the card and walked away.

He looked at the card, and she had written an address on it. Nate smiled, but only to himself, as she was now gone. Wow, that wasn't too hard. I'm pretty good at this. He couldn't wait for the next evening to come.

***

With Todd now gone, Nate had gotten his license and convinced his father that he needed a car to get around. Mark was agreeable as long as it was a reliable and practical vehicle that Nate could use through his college years. They settled on a used late-model Civic.

In preparation for his date with Dani, he put on a pair of khaki carpenter pants, freshly steam ironed and pressed by Bella, and a tightly knit collarless pullover that emphasized his physique. He examined himself closely in the mirror before deciding that it was not too pretentious for this first date with her. He just wanted to make a good first impression. His hair had always been blond and curly, and he kept it short but long enough to keep it styled. He added just a dash of cologne, one given to him by Todd the Christmas before he left, and who assured him it was the right one to attract girls.

Nate started his car, put the address from the index card into his phone, and proceeded to drive, a bit apprehensive but reassured that he was a natural and this was going to be a cakewalk. He arrived at the address and found himself parked in front of the church that he had frequently attended up until Billy's death. He rechecked the address, and he had keyed it in correctly. "Interesting place to meet for a date," he chuckled as he got out of the car and walked up the front steps and into the church.

The sanctuary was lit but empty. "Hello, is anyone here?" he called out.

"Can I help you?" A young man, a few years older than Todd, he guessed, called from behind him. His arms were filled with what appeared to be songbooks.

"Well, I'm not sure," Nate began. "I was supposed to meet someone here."

"Who might that be?"

"Dani?" He didn't know her last name; in fact, was Dani even her real name? "Had she really played him?" he said to himself.

"Dani is downstairs with the youth group. Come on, I was just gathering these songbooks. Maybe you can help me." He handed a stack of books to Nate. "I'm Rick, by the way," he introduced himself. "I'm the youth pastor here at St. Mark's. I'd shake your hand if I had one available," he laughed.

"I'm Nate."

"So, how do you know Dani?"

"We go to school together."

"So she invited you?"

"Sort of. This was the address where we were supposed to meet."

Rick laughed. "So you had no idea this was a youth meeting? She can be cunning, in a sweet sort of way."

"So I've noticed," Nate agreed.

They entered a large meeting room furnished with a half dozen couches, some padded folding chairs, and tables along the walls. The tables were neatly arranged with snacks, desserts, and bottles of soda. A large pull-down movie screen was at the front of the room. Nate estimated there were at least twenty-five teenagers milling about the room, engaged in idle chatter. He looked around the room, seeing some vaguely familiar faces from school but no one that he knew personally.

Rick spoke as soon as they entered the room. "Guys, we have a guest with us tonight. I'd like you to say hello to Nate."

They responded in unison. "Hi, Nate." It reminded him of television scenes from AA meetings. Nate searched the room and spotted Dani in the corner with several other group members. She was looking at him with a cunning smile.

So *this is how she plays*, Nate thought to himself. I like her already. She broke away from the small group and approached him. "Did you have any problem finding the place?"

"No problem. Your directions were impeccable. I am impressed. Your home is a cathedral." Nate was casual in his response and couldn't wait to engage her in further wit and cunning. "Nicely played, I might add."

"Were you expecting something else?" she mocked.

"You led me to believe I was picking you up and that we might be able to get to know each other. Not a church youth group meeting. What's next, confession?"

"We don't do that here, and I didn't mislead you. You just assumed. And you know what assume is. Besides, like I said, I already know all I need to know about you."

Rick started handing out the books and spoke again. "Before we watch the movie you all requested, we are going to sing a couple of songs together. Who wants to pick the first song?"

Nate whispered to Dani. "What's the movie we're watching?"

"'The Shack'. Have you seen it?"

Nate shook his head no. "I've heard of it. It's about the death of an innocent child."

"The group picked it because it's all about having faith and trust," she explained.

"You should probably pay close attention then. You may learn something." Nate was half serious, and she chortled at the inference.

They settled themselves next to each other on a couch near the back of the room. He could smell her perfume now, and it smelled of the lilacs that grew in their yard. Songbooks were passed around, and they shared one as Rick began to play the guitar.

"He's a great guitarist," Dani commented.

"Hmm," Nate shrugged. In his mind, it was all fairly simple chords being played. Nothing challenging and certainly nothing that he couldn't play.

"I suppose you could do better?" she quipped.

"You know all about me. *You* tell *me*."

"No, what I said was, 'I know all I *need* to know about you'."

"OK."

"OK? That's it? "

He nodded. "Like you said, you already know all you need to know."

When the singing ended, the lights were dimmed, and the movie started. Nate had heard bits and pieces about the story of The Shack but never paid much attention to it. The story before him was all new, and the first thirty minutes disturbed him. He became restless and shifted about in his seat. Since his mother's first accident and then Billy's death, his emotions sometimes got the better of him when, even in just a book or a movie, when a child was taken away or killed. Nate's restlessness soon overcame him.

"I need some fresh air," Nate said in a whisper to Dani, suddenly standing and leaving the room. Dani was taken by surprise and watched him exit before standing too and following him out. She called to him from behind as he walked down the hall to the stairs leading up to the sanctuary.

"Where are you going? Are you OK?" She called after him.

Nate turned and looked at her. "I think maybe this was a mistake. I'll see you around."

"Wait, Nate," she responded as she caught up to him. "If it was a mistake, it was my mistake. I'm sorry."

"That's OK. I guess you don't know everything you need to know about me after all." He turned to go.

"If you are trying to make me feel guilty, you've succeeded."

He turned once more to her, unsure of what his next move should be. "If there is one thing I have learned during my lifetime, I can't make anyone feel guilt or shame or joy or anything."

She approached Nate and took his arm, holding onto it with both hands. "Wow. There is a lot going on in that head of yours that I think maybe I should get to know more."

He looked down at her and forced a smile, thinking back to Todd. "You know, a very wise man once said to me, 'Our thoughts are sometimes just a distraction from what is in our hearts.' I do have a lot of thoughts going on up here.." he pointed briefly to his head…" but ultimately, that's not what matters."

"That sounds like a smart man."

"That man is my hero. Someday, maybe you'll get to hear more about him. But for now, I'd like to just blow this joint and get some real food. None of that snack stuff."

"OK, I have been guilt-ed enough into inviting myself along. Is that OK?"

"If you insist, but you're going to have to allow me to ask some questions and get to know you. I have serious trust issues with you as a result of your earlier deception."

They walked a short distance from the church to a small diner at the center of town and found a corner booth away from the other patrons. Dani sat first, sliding into the booth and across the seat next to the window. Nate observed that she purposely left room for him next to her rather than across from her, and he happily obliged.

"So, Nathan...or do you prefer Nate?"

"Nate is fine." It was rare that anyone called him Nathan other than his mother, and this was not the time or place to even mention her. It was possible he would never talk about her to anyone ever again.

"So then, Nate, what would you like to know about me?" She sipped a coke and awaited his response. "By the way..." she continued before he could speak. "You really smell nice. What is that cologne you're wearing?"

Todd was right. It was definitely the right cologne to attract a pretty girl. "Thanks, it was a gift," Nate responded, smiling. Nothing more had to be said about it. "You smell really nice as well. Lilacs, I think."

"You have a good sense of smell. Odd that we should be talking about smells, don't you think?"

"Only if they were bad odors. Good smells are...well, good, for lack of a better word, don't you think? No need to answer that one, but tell me, what made you change your mind?"

"About what?"

"When I first introduced myself, I said,' And you are?' and your immediate response was..."

"Not interested," she completed for him.

"So, what changed your mind? Why are we here tonight, together, just you and me?"

"You didn't flinch. When I gave you that smart answer, you didn't even flinch. You just continued on like it never happened. That was totally unexpected. It says something about you."

"That I'm not only handsome but witty? Shy but determined?"

"Not shallow like most jocks who only want one thing from a girl. Most guys look for easy targets. I'm not one of them, and I don't play those games."

"Well, you *do* play games," Nate observed, looking for her retort.

"I play smart games. They're fun. Stupid games are for stupid people. I am not a stupid person." Her smile captured his imagination. He wanted to reach over and kiss her but he knew this was way too soon.

"And I am not some stupid jock looking for a hookup...looking to get laid. I'd at least like to get to know you first."

She frowned a bit before speaking. "You could have worded that a little better. Just knowing me first doesn't qualify you for the bed Olympics."

"Bed Olympics? I hadn't heard that one before. Anyway, you're right. It definitely takes more than knowing someone well in order to qualify, as you put it. But seriously, it's the precursor to liking first and falling in love second. And besides, how can you qualify for the bed Olympics if you haven't at least practiced beforehand?"

"I just made that term up. Bed Olympics. Did you like it?" she nudged him and chuckled.

"Like I said, I love sports analogies. And the bed Olympics is a great one. I feel like I know all I need to know about you for now. I have enjoyed our first date."

"This was not a date. It was a youth group activity," she countered slyly.

"I asked you to go out with me. For me, it's a date. And where's the youth group? It's just you and me here, together, alone. And to make it officially a date, I plan on kissing you goodnight, at the right time and place, of course."

She sighed a deep sigh and rested her head on her hands. "OK, I give. I might allow you a quick kiss on my cheek if you get me home safe and sound."

They left the diner arm in arm, walking to Nate's car in front of the church. When they arrived at her house, they casually walked up the walk to the front steps. As Dani turned to say goodnight, Nate tilted his head down to kiss her on the cheek as she had indicated, but she quickly drew his face into hers,

RUNNING SHOES

and their lips met for the first time that evening.

CHAPTER 13
GOOD TALK

Todd had left nearly four months ago, and to the best of Nate's knowledge, his brother was stationed somewhere in the south, being readied for deployment to some far-off place like Iraq or Afghanistan. He missed their talks, but they texted as often as Todd's schedule would allow. Todd warned that, at some point, their contact would become less frequent once he was deployed. But for now, he insisted that Nate keep him updated on what was happening on the home front, especially news about Nate himself. They kept their texts short and to the point, injecting humor when possible and appropriate.

"Met a girl," Nate typed. He knew the best time to engage Todd in conversation was usually late at night, just before going to sleep. It reminded Nate of the many late-night talks they had and acted as a sedative leading to a restful night.

"Tell me," Todd immediately responded.

"Dani. Cute, auburn hair, green eyes, sweet smile, and she's hot!" (smiley face emoji).

"Ask her out yet?"

"She tricked me. I thought it was a date. More of a youth gathering."

"LOL."

"Still got to kiss her, though."

"And?"

"She tastes like strawberry."

"Yum."

"And she liked my cologne...the one you gave me at Xmas."

"What'd I tell ya? Never failed me! Going on a real date with her?"

"Haven't asked, but I will tomorrow."

"Remember our talk. KMI."

"How's marines?"

"Piece of cake. Hard for guys not in shape. Easy for me."

"Glad to hear. Any word on deployment?"

"No. Should hear soon tho. Miss you, buddy."

"Ditto that."

"Good talk."

"Yeah, good talk."

***

Nate caught up with Dani in between classes at her locker. Today her hair was not pulled back but hung down loosely to her shoulders. And she wore makeup, not like when he first approached her. She was radiant. While to him, she was a natural beauty with no blemishes to hide, he believed she was making a special effort to lure him in, and it was working.

"Hey," Nate greeted.

"Hey, back," she smiled.

"I was thinking maybe we could see a movie Saturday."

"What's in it for me?" She toyed with him.

Nate had prepared himself for her coy responses. "You're looking at it."

"Oh, so you're saying you're the reward...hmm...I was hoping for something a little more motivating."

"I'll buy you ice cream after."

She laughed. "OK, now you're talking. I think my calendar's open."

"I have another question for you," he added.

She opened her locker and exchanged books, then looked at him inquisitively.

"We have a game Friday night. Come watch."

Dani shook her head no. "I don't think so. I'm not into football. And that wasn't a question."

"That's disappointing. I was hoping you would at least be into watching me play."

She thought for a minute. "OK, here's the deal. I will come to watch you play if you do something for me."

Nate was cautious before committing. "OK, I'll bite. What exactly must I do for you to come see me play?"

"Sunday evening. Youth meeting."

"Not another movie about kidnapping and murder, is it?" He was half serious in his pensive response.

"No, I promise," she tugged his arm. "Come on, walk me to class." They walked down the hall together, hand in hand. People recognized him for who he was; they took notice of her for who she wasn't. Popular. Nate took pleasure in the winsome reactions of the many girls they passed. Dani took notice and seemed to enjoy the notoriety of this new coupling. They finally arrived at her classroom, and she made one last request. "Oh, and make sure to bring your guitar." She quickly entered the room before he could respond.

***

He spotted her in the stands as he took his position on the field. She was seated with a group of friends, primarily from the youth group, whose names he did not recall; in fact, he had not even made an effort to. It wasn't important to him at the time. But now that they were spending more and more time together, he understood the necessity to learn their names because they were part of who she was. And if she was the one who would be a part of his life, at least for the interim, it would be wise to make that effort for her.

Last year as a sophomore, he made the varsity team as a starter in the wide receiver position. It was the position Billy had played, and now he coveted, having experienced early on in life the personal satisfaction he received in catching the ball and then carrying it down the field doing what he did best, running. He was always in position downfield to receive the pass and, if the QB was on target, carry the ball in for a touchdown. He dispelled any notion in his own mind that he was arrogant or cocky. He was not vain or attempting to receive recognition from others for his accomplishments. He craved recognition from within that he had the ability to overcome any flaws in his being that were a result of his inadequacies.

His imperfection was not discernible from without; he was viewed by all as potent and likable. He exuded confidence and maturity. In his own mind, he knew it was just a front but acceptable as a goal to achieve. So what if these goals were already how others around him perceived him? This was all a part of his maturation and would inevitably result in him being exactly who he wanted to be. And these were not just idle thoughts in passing. He felt in his heart that he was going in the right direction, but he was not there yet. After all, he was still only sixteen, and life at this stage was all new to him.

Especially Dani.

She was waiting for him after the game. "You smell," she commented, but allowing him to hug her anyway.

"That's all you have to say? Not good game, or nice catch, or congratulations on your TD?"

"I told you I don't know anything about football, but I guess if you catch the ball and run all the way down the field with it, and the crowd goes wild cheering for you, and all the guys' high-five or chest bump you or pat you on the ass…well, I guess you played well?"

He found her sequitur amusing but amazingly succinct. "Well, if you put it that way, I was absolutely amazing out there." He kissed her gently on the forehead. "Some of the guys are headed over to the park. There's going to be a celebratory bonfire there. Are you up for it?"

"These guys are really not my kind of people," she resisted.

"Come on, just for a little while. Let me revel in my awesomeness. Besides, I am making and will continue to make an effort to get to know your youth group friends. It's only fair you try to get to know mine."

"Alright," she shrugged.

Later as they snuggled together on a blanket next to the bonfire, they listened to the wide displays of boisterous laughter and congratulations between the guys and their guests of a game well played. Several teammates approached Nate, congratulating him and acknowledging Dani as his new companion. Most of the varsity squads were juniors and seniors. Some were friendly to Nate, and others were jealous but tolerated him because of his demonstrated ability and contribution to a winning team.

Jake, the QB, regarded Nate as a valuable addition to the squad. When Nate was downfield and open, Jake regularly threw to him, knowing he was the most dependable receiver he had. As a result, he treated Nate with the utmost respect and paid more attention to him than the other guys. In Nate's mind, Jake was just a downright decent guy, and he was going to hate to see him graduate.

Jake approached them with a girl on his arm. Nate recognized her as Jake's long-time girlfriend. "Hey, Nate. Awesome game tonight."

"Thanks, man, you too. Your passes were right on target."

"This is Jeannie," he introduced the girl on his arm.

"And this is Dani," Nate introduced her.

"Mind if we sit for a few?" he asked Nate.

"Of course not," Dani immediately responded, happy to make a friendly acquaintance. She nudged closer to Nate and made room for Jake and Jeannie to share the blanket with them.

Dani and Jeannie engaged in idle conversation as Jake engaged Nate. "There's been some talk in the locker room about next season," Jake began.

"What's the latest?"

"Well, I'm graduating, you know. They're worried that next year, they won't have a QB to replace me. I'm not saying I am irreplaceable. I'm saying that there is no one in the ranks remotely qualified for the position."

Nate thought for a minute. "What about the JV quarterback? Why don't they just move him up a year early, like they did me?"

Jake shook his head no. "Have you seen him play? He shouldn't even be in that position."

"So, what are the options?"

"Well, I think you're an option," Jake responded.

"Me? Wow. How do they know I can even throw?"

Jake laughed. "Seriously, dude? Look, my name's going up on the board you know as MVP this year, just two spots below your brother Todd's name.

He was an outstanding QB, and if you're anything like your brother...well, you have a reputation to uphold...and wouldn't you like to see your name up there, sharing the honor with Todd?"

"Yeah, that would be kinda cool. Todd taught me almost everything I know about football, other than what I've learned from the coaches. They taught me the rules of the game; Todd taught me how to play the game."

"How is your throwing arm?"

"Decent. But I don't know that I'm the leader that Todd was."

"I think you underestimate your leadership skills. Tell you what, after practices this week, let's go out and throw some. See what you got. Just give it a try; you might surprise yourself." Jake then stood. "Come on, babe" he took Jeannie's hand, helping her to her feet.

Before they left, Nate responded to Jake. "Hey, thanks, Jake, for your confidence in me. It means a lot, and I appreciate it."

"Well deserved," he nodded before walking away.

Dani looked at Nate questioningly. "What was that all about?"

"Just football talk." It was a lot for Nate to think about but now was not the time. He would run it by Todd later in their texting. "You know next week is homecoming," Nate started. She waited. " Would you be my date for the homecoming dance?"

"You dance?" she asked, feigning surprise.

"I am a man of many talents, so I'm told." His mind was once again thinking about the discussion with Jake.

"Sure, why not? I've let down most of my defenses already; why not just throw myself into the game?" she quipped.

"God, I love those sports analogies." She managed to regain his attention and keep it for the rest of the evening.

RUNNING SHOES

***

"We won tonight. Scored twice on long bombs from Jake."

"Congratulations! How's the record?" Todd texted back.

"We're five and two."

"Not bad. What else?"

"Jake graduates this year. Gonna need a new QB."

"Who's next in line?"

"That's the problem. No one."

"So, what are you thinking?"

"Jake thinks I should step up."

"What's stopping u?"

Nate didn't respond immediately, thinking of all the good reasons not to step into the role. Todd continued. "You were fifteen when I left, and you could throw the ball almost as far as me already."

"I know. But it takes more than that to be a good QB."

"You are physically capable. The rest is psychological. You could out star me if you set your mind to it. But, if you try it and find your heart is not really in it….well, nothing ventured, nothing gained. I'm proud of you either way."

"Thanks, Todd."

"Good talk?"

"Yeah, good talk."

CHAPTER 14
NATE

Saturday night was supposed to be their first official date. Nate arrived at Dani's house at seven and was immediately ushered in by Dani's mother, who, by all accounts, was anxious to meet Nate and was more excited about him than Dani had, up to this time, portended to be. She introduced herself as Mrs. Lucas as she led him into the living room. She was about his mother's age, he guessed, and also had auburn hair like Dani's, with some graying at the temples. He imagined that she, too, must have been beautiful in her younger years, but unlike his own mother, Mrs. Lucas had aged well.

They were soon joined by Mr. Lucas, who took a firm grip on Nate's hand, and it nearly became a competition as to who had the strongest grip. Nate relented, allowing him the win but reassuring himself that if necessary, he could definitely "out grip" this man. He was shorter than Nathan by several inches, was balding with salt and pepper hair, and had a slight paunch. He was pleasant enough, and Nate, who, as an introvert, could find himself intimidated by the middle-aged parents of his friends, found both of Dani's parents to be down-to-earth and engaging conversationalists.

As they continued to talk and Nate feigned interest, he wondered when Dani would finally make an appearance. Knowing her, this was probably just part of the plan, something that had to be done with no forewarning, which might have unnerved him anyway. So ultimately, it was a smart and considerate move on her part. He talked primarily to Mr. Lucas, who expressed an interest in Nate's sports activities, including baseball and football. Having learned of Nate's starting position as a wide receiver, Mr. Lucas had to share that he, too, had played football and had the great hands of a pass receiver.

This prompted Nate to outdo what seemed to him to be a declaration by Mr. Lucas of their equality on the playing field by declaring that he would most likely be playing Quarterback next year.

"That seems like a rather implausible move, from wide receiver to quarterback," Mr. Lucas responded, expressing doubt and questioning the rationale behind Nate's change in position.

"I thought so too in the beginning, but I've been told that I have the physical skills already. I just need to work on the psychological side of the game. You know, confidence in leading the team, calling the right plays, those kinds of things." Mr. Lucas nodded, not that he agreed, but that he understood what Nate was saying. And for this, Nate determined that while he had conceded the battle of the grips, he had won the verbal dual.

Mrs. Lucas now took a turn chatting him up. "Dani tells me you have joined their youth group."

"Well, I'm not really sure what's required to join, but I have attended a couple of youth functions with her."

"And does your family belong to a local church?"

Nate was careful to respond. "St. Mark's is also our church." They hadn't attended on a regular basis in years now, and he didn't know if they were even members still, but there was no need to share that. Nate was relieved when Dani finally entered the room, ending the discussion with her parents.

"Hey," she greeted him and took his hand, leading him out of the living room and up the stairs. She then led him into her bedroom unexpectedly and closed the door behind them. There was soft music playing from several blue tooth speakers scattered about the room. Nate couldn't identify the artist.

"Parents are nice," Nate started.

She looked at him with an amused look on her face. "Uh-huh," she nodded, taking a seat on the edge of the bed. She patted the bed, beckoning him to sit down next to her, and he obliged. "I don't feel like going out tonight. Can we just stay in and watch a movie?"

"I guess. Still counts as a date, though."

"Really? Keeping count, are we? I only know one reason why a guy would count the number of dates he goes out with his girlfriend."

Nate took notice that she referred to herself as his girlfriend. This was significant, even though there was no one else there to overhear it.

"I told Todd I had met this really hot girl. He asked if we had gone out yet. If you hadn't tricked me, this would be our second date. It's hard to explain to my brother over a text message. Now we're still not going out, so I guess we're back to zero."

"So I'm a hot girl? Hm...OK, to be fair, yes, I did trick you. But we did go out after we left the church. That counts as date one. And you can still take me out for ice cream later. Date two. How many dates before something of significance happens? I mean, what are we aiming for here?" She was teasing and not serious, he knew, but he would play along.

"Well, by date three, which by my count now will be the homecoming dance, definite progress should be made toward my ultimate goal."

She raised her eyebrows at this revelation. "Which is?"

"You will have to wait and see. Anticipate something amazing."

"I'm not doing that. I'd just be setting myself up for disappointment."

He suddenly leaned in and kissed her. He loved the taste of her lips, the scent emanating from her neck, and the silkiness of her hair on his cheek. "You will not be disappointed, I assure you," he whispered in her ear and then kissed her again.

They remained motionless for a time, listening to the soft music, both content just to be near each other. "I think maybe we should go get that ice cream you promised me first, then come back and watch the movie. I would hate to fall asleep during the movie and miss out on that ice cream."

"I take it the movie is not action-packed. I was hoping for something like Xmen."

"Sorry, but no. We can figure it out when we get back."

They returned to Dani's house around eleven, and the house was quiet. Her parents had retired for the evening, so they relaxed on the couch. Dani lay with her head in his lap. No discussion was had on the choice of movies to watch. It wasn't important to Nate. She simply put some random movie on Netflix, and they watched in silence.

After a short time, she fell asleep. Nate remained motionless, with thoughts about how lucky he was to have met Dani and what the future had in store for them. Then he thought of growing up with Todd, the good times they had together, and how he was doing now. He would seek advice from Todd the next time they texted. This was all new to him. He had not known her long, yet already had strong feelings for her. How long should he wait before...well, he wasn't sure how to approach the topic with Todd. He wasn't sure why since Todd had talked openly about sex with him before. Why should it be so difficult now? His thoughts were interrupted as she stirred. It was now 12:30, and he should be going home. As delicately as he could, he untangled himself from her, then covered her with a nearby blanket. Before leaving, he gave her a goodnight kiss on her forehead. He determined it was too late to text Todd but assured himself sleep tonight would not be an issue. He had a lot to dream about.

***

Dani texted him the next afternoon, and they agreed to meet at the church for youth at seven. She reminded him to bring his guitar. When Nate arrived, the same group was gathered in the meeting room and extended a friendly greeting to Nate. They made him feel welcome, and he found he was comfortable in this setting. He observed Dani off to the side, talking in a hushed tone to the Youth Pastor, Rick. She finally walked over to Nate and gave him a hug. She was sanguine, joking now about the movie that neither of them watched, but that the promise and fulfillment of ice cream were all she needed.

Rick then spoke, offering a brief prayer for the gathering and an introduction to the night's proceedings. "I see several of you have brought your guitars. Now I hope you have brought your singing voices. For those who choose, the piano is an option for your selection of music. Volunteers, to go first?"

A small framed oriental girl in the back stood and was the first to sing. She sat down at the piano and began to sing along as she played: I Dreamed A Dream. Her voice was loud and strong, totally unexpected from her physical size. Several others picked various selections, some with religious overtones, some not.

"Have you decided what you will sing?"

"Well, you told me to bring my guitar. Didn't know I was expected to sing by myself. Another unexpected surprise, thank you."

"I'm sorry." Dani sounded truly regretful for putting him on the spot.

"No problem" Nate stood and moved to the front of the room with his guitar in hand. He had thought there was more to this than she had shared, so he was prepared but wanted her to at least feel a little guilt about not giving him an advanced warning.

"This song is for Billy," he announced. It was the song that Todd had sung at the lake house the day after Billy died. But he did not explain that to the group; the song would speak for itself. He began strumming the guitar and singing in his smooth baritone voice:

RUNNING SHOES

I can see it in your eyes that you are restless

The time has come for you to leave,

it's so hard to let you go, but in this life, I know

You have to be Who you were made to be.

As you step out on the road, I'll say a prayer

So that in my heart you always will be there.

This is not goodbye

I know we'll meet again

So let your life begin

Cause this is not goodbye

It's just "I love you" to take with you

    Until you're home again……

He continued singing and playing through all the verses. Dani had clearly been moved and wiped tears from her eyes. Nate stood and took an obligatory bow before returning to his seat.

As he sat, she intertwined her arm with his. "Who is Billy?"

"It's too soon. Someday."

"Well, that was amazing, Nate. You are a man of many talents, aren't you? And I'm glad you let down your defenses, if only for a moment. It's good to know that there is a soft side of you and that you're not all macho about every little thing."

"Wow. I never thought of myself as macho. Is that how I come across?" This was new to him and unexpected.

"Guys associate sensitivity with weakness. Everyone has some kind of weakness, but not many guys are willing to show their sensitive side. It's that whole macho thing that goes on. Some women do appreciate seeing vulnerability on occasion."

"So, what is your weakness? If everyone has one, what is yours?"

She suddenly dismissed the topic of their conversation. "I'm sure you will find out someday. But like you said, 'too soon.'"

***

Nate ended football practice over the course of the next few days by spending time with Jake, who enlisted two other senior players, both receivers, to run downfield as he and Nate took turns passing to them. Nate had not practiced the long throws since Todd had left but found himself quickly reclaiming what he had learned from his older brother, once the star QB.

By day three of their after-practice sessions, Jake was convinced of Nate's talent and informed the coach that if he was interested, he might want to observe from a distance. He was there, but Nate was unaware that the coach was watching and impressed by what he saw, and if Nate was willing, the coach would set him up at football camp with the express purpose of developing QB skills. This was something to be addressed after the final game of the season.

Saturday was homecoming, and games usually played on Friday night would be played Saturday afternoon instead. During the halftime celebration, the homecoming queen would be elected and then officially crowned at the homecoming dance in the evening. The game was won easily, and Jake's girlfriend Jeannie, who was also cheer captain, was elected queen. This was not unexpected as the couple had been very popular among the students and favored to win.

Nate arrived at Dani's house at 7:30 to pick her up. He wore a dark suit, one he had found in Todd's closet, with an athletic cut tailored white shirt, dark tie, and cuff links, also Todd's. He was awed by Dani as she descended the stairs in a light green ¾ length gown that sat low off her shoulders. Her auburn hair was in a French braid, exposing her neck, shoulders, and low cut back. Nate thought to himself that he had never seen anything so beautiful.

They spent the evening on the dance floor, Nate impressing her with yet another one of his many talents. He had considered continuing their evening by driving out to the lake house but thought better of it, not wanting to rush things with her.

Nate and Dani were seated with Jake and Jeannie when not dancing, and Nate was taken by surprise when his sister Gail approached the table. He was not aware that she was even there at the dance. She was escorted by one of the other senior football players. Nate didn't recall his name but identified him as part of the small group who clearly had disdain for him, having been a sophomore when elevated to a starter on the varsity team.

"Hello, little brother," Gail said in a vain attempt to be sweet. Nate sensed that she had been drinking and was feeling the effects.

"Hey, sis." Nate was cordial but cautious.

"And you are..." Gail said, looking now at Dani. All eyes turned on Dani. Nate secretly hoped for a witty response similar to what she had given him the first time they spoke. Something like "unimpressed," but Nate had never talked to Dani about Gail or their contentious relationship.

Dani politely waved her hand from where she sat. "Hi, Gail. I'm Dani. It's nice to finally meet you. Your brother has told me so much about you." Nate flashed a glance at Dani, then back to Gail.

"I'll bet he has," she laughed.

"And who is this handsome gentleman with you?" Dani asked sweetly. The handsome gentleman had remained quiet while staring Nate down.

"This is Dale. Isn't he cute, though?" She tweaked his chin with her fingers, and he flinched.

"Come on, babe. Let's go," he urged impatiently.

"Oh, alright," Gail sighed. She gave one last look at Nate. "Don't do anything I wouldn't do." They then sauntered off in the direction of the dance floor.

"There's nothing she wouldn't do," Nate said under his breath. Dani overheard his comment and elbowed him gently in the side in disapproval.

Jeannie had remained silent also, but Jake spoke. "That guy is bad news."

"Just her type," Nate added. Dani squeezed his hand resting in his lap and indicated she understood their contentious relationship and was glad he at least kept it civil.

"We can't control others' bad decisions," Jeannie volunteered. She, too, was well aware of bad boy Dale and had heard things about Gail that, if true, would tarnish any girl's reputation forever.

Later as they drove home to Dani's house, Nate decided to lighten the mood. "So, how would you rate our third date on a scale of 1 to 10?"

"Oh, is our date over?" She made fun.

"Well, it doesn't have to be. Is there someplace you would like to go?"

Taking a more serious tone now, she rested her head on his shoulder. "No, not really. Anywhere is nice with you."

"It's not too chilly tonight. Let's take a walk through the park. Check out the moon and the stars. Enjoy the sounds and smells of nature."

"How romantic of you. I like it."

Nate parked the car, and they strolled through the park. There was a slight chill in the air, so Nate removed his jacket and put it around her shoulders.

She looked at him with a broad dimpled smile. "Thank you, kind sir. How gallant of you."

"You are welcome, my lady. Wait. Listen." They both stopped and listened intently. "Do you hear that?"

"I don't hear anything."

"Exactly. That is the sound of silence."

They sat at the bandstand and were silent for a while before Dani spoke. "Tell me about Billy." It was not a demand but more of an attempt to learn more about Nate, not Billy.

"Let the dead rest in peace" was all he said.

She resigned herself to his vague answer. "How about Todd then?" A smile crossed Nate's face. "I bet you're a lot like him."

"I'd like to think so. He was there for me when my parents weren't." He was thoughtful for a minute before continuing. "When I was just thirteen, he told me I was his best friend. Can you imagine being thirteen years old and having your big brother tell you that you're his best friend?"

"I can't imagine."

"I am lucky to have him," he concluded.

"And he is lucky to have you," she added. They leaned back on the park bench, looking up at the stars.

"Growing up, my friend Zak and I used to camp out. We'd lay back like this, just staring up at the stars. We decided that one day, we would each pick a star and register it. They'd be right next to each other."

"What happened to Zak? I don't know anyone named Zak at our school."

"He moved away. We still email each other occasionally." Nate thought for a minute before continuing. "The last time I saw him was at Billy's funeral. He and his dad flew up from Texas. After the funeral, we got to spend a couple of days at the lake house before he flew home."

"He sounds like a good friend. So you have a lake house?"

Nate nodded. "It's on Candlewood Lake. Todd and I used to spend every weekend there in the summer. I haven't been there in a couple of years, not since Todd left. I'm not sure why my father has even kept the place. He hasn't set foot in it since before Billy died. But now that I have a license and my own car, I've been thinking about going there. Maybe invite some friends. Would you like to see it? Maybe help me get it ready for friends."

"I don't know if that's a good idea," she responded doubtfully.

"Football season is over. We could go out next Friday or Saturday." Dani didn't immediately respond, so Nate ventured further. "I promise you, I will be the perfect gentleman," he added.

Dani smiled. "I'm sure you will. Let me think about it."

***

"You there?" Nate texted Todd. It was already one AM, but it was Saturday night, going into Sunday morning, so he thought maybe Todd was still awake.

"Late night?" Todd asked.

"Homecoming game, then dance. I took Dani. Our third date."

"Sounds like things are going well."

"I told her about you."

"Good things, I hope."

"Told her you were not only my big brother but my best friend."

"No lie there. What did she say to that?"

"How lucky you are to have me as your best friend!"

"LOL. She's right about that."

"I asked her to go with me to Candlewood next weekend. She's considering it. I don't think anyone has been there in a couple of years. Now I can drive myself there. Clean the place up. Maybe invite some friends."

"Run it by Dad first," Todd cautioned.

"?" Nate wasn't sure why Todd was concerned.

"Dad has a 'friend,' and the house may be occupied. Just give him a heads-up that you're going. Could be awkward if you don't."

"Thanks for that." Nate thought for a minute before continuing. "Any advice for me? About Dani?"

"Go slow. Do what comes naturally. If she says no, she means no. And I don't need to remind you about our talk…"

"No, bro. You don't. Oh, forgot to mention. Football. Coach is grooming me for the QB position next year."

"You'll be awesome."

"Thanks for the vote of confidence."

"Glad you texted. Good talk."

"Yeah, good talk."

CHAPTER 15
AWAKENING

Nate rarely sought permission from his father anymore and simply left him a note saying he was headed to the lake for the weekend. His father was seldom home evenings, and when he was home, he was usually preoccupied, spending most of his time in his home office. Nate accepted his father's affair for now. He was not going to judge him for his indiscretion, condoning his behavior as therapeutic. He had witnessed his father struggle for several years, trying to remedy the maladies of his mother and supporting her through numerous unsuccessful treatments, including therapy and medications, all to no avail. Her condition had worsened over time and evolved into a mental illness that could not be cured and barely managed. Short of institutionalizing her, there were no other options than to accept what had once been a loving wife and mother for what she was now. As distant as his father had become, out of respect, he would simply let him know where he was. Nothing more, nothing less. "You never talk about your dad…or your mom…" Dani commented as they drove to the lake house.

"It's complicated. I like to keep things simple."

"OK." She resigned herself to letting him disclose only what he was comfortable and ready to do.

At the lake house, Nate proceeded to show Dani around. Everything appeared to be just as they had left it two years ago. He turned up the heat to take the chill off the cool November air and turned on the hot water in the lower level.

"This is where Todd and I stayed" he pointed out the bunk beds against the back wall. "

"So this is where all those late-night talks took place between you two."

"The first time we looked at this house before we bought it, there was some discussion over who would get what bedrooms. There are only three. One, of course, for my parents, one for Gail, and the original thought was that I would get the third bedroom. Todd and Billy would bunk down here. Billy didn't like that idea and wanted the third bedroom. That's when Todd spoke up and said that he and I would be bunkmates. I've thought about that day a lot over the past few years and came to realize that it was one of the best days of my life. Todd didn't hesitate to share this space down here with me. He just asked me if I was OK with that, and it was a done deal."

"Your brother sounds amazing."

"Yeah, you're probably getting tired of hearing that, though."

"It's obvious from what you've told me that he is the one constant in your family. That certainly makes him easier to talk about. And I don't tire of hearing it at all."

"Let me show you the rest of the place." Nate led her up the stairs into a huge open area consisting of living, dining, and kitchen areas, all opening out to the upstairs deck overlooking the lake.

"This is beautiful," Dani commented. Nate had never taken time to simply enjoy the view or aesthetics of the interior. To him, it was all about the lake and the boat. He took notice this time of the open beams that ran across the ceiling, the large stone fireplace, and the light gray tone hardwoods that ran throughout.

He set those thoughts aside and continued the tour. "The master bedroom is down that way" he simply pointed in its direction, "and this way leads to the other two bedrooms." He led the way down another hallway and opened the door into what was Billy's room as Dani followed him in. The room was unchanged, still displaying Billy's wall décor, nick-knacks, and furnishings. Dani walked over to the dresser and picked up the framed photo of Nate, Billy, and Todd.

"Oh my gosh," Dani exclaimed. "Look at you."

"That was taken the spring before Billy died. I was almost fourteen then. He had just turned 16."

"You sure were a handsome bunch," she smiled, setting the picture back down. Nate might have blushed if the circumstances were different, but he felt her compliment was meant more as consolation.

"Nothing has changed in this room. It's like they're expecting him to just show up someday. I don't suppose anything will ever change here until my mother is ready, which I doubt will ever happen now. "

This was all new to Dani; she knew nothing about the family dynamic. Only what little Nate had alluded to. And she was not in a position to advise or offer an opinion. Simply listen and respond if needed. Nate picked up the baseball mitt that was lying on the floor in the corner. He put the glove on his right hand, made a fist, and pounded it into the pocket of the glove. "This is a first baseman's mitt. The webbing is different than the fielders' mitts. And Billy was left-handed. Not much use for this anymore." He tossed it back onto the floor in the corner. A pile of old Sports Illustrated magazines lay on the nightstand. Nate picked them up and blew the dust off the top one. Beneath it was an equestrian magazine.

"He was into horses?" she asked, standing at his side, glimpsing the magazine.

Nate nodded. "It's what got him killed," he said without further explanation. He tossed the magazines on the bed. "Let's start a fire and get something to eat."

After dinner, Dani busied herself in the kitchen cleaning up. Nate ventured into the master bedroom. The king-sized bed was stripped of linens, so he found clean ones in the linen closet and proceeded to make the bed. This was where they would sleep. He had no particular plan in mind. He would heed Todd's advice. Just take it slow, and everything will come naturally. He did want her in a way that he had never felt for anyone before. But he didn't know if she wanted him in the same way. Her body language said yes, but he wasn't sure of her personal convictions and if she would allow it to happen.

He was distracted from his thoughts by her soft voice directly behind him. "I'll never understand why loving couples buy such big beds. They may as well sleep in different rooms." She was now next to him, her arm draped through his, just looking at the bed. "When I get married, I'm not sleeping in a bed like this," she declared, jumping onto the bed. She then reached out her hand to his and pulled him down beside her. "But for now, this will have to do," she sighed, laying her head now on his shoulder.

They lay there motionless for what seemed like an hour to Nate. He was nervous in anticipation of being with her...with anyone...for the first time. She sensed his hesitation and spoke softly. "I've never..." she started, looking into his eyes.

"Me neither," he admitted, letting down his defenses once again.

"I'm glad. This will be the first time then for us both."

This was his cue. They would learn together, discovering a world that neither of them had ever explored until that night.

***

"Todd?" Nate texted. He lay in his bed, having dropped Dani off earlier in the evening the following day.

"Nate. You good?"

"I'm great."

"Sounds like things went well at the lake."

"It was amazing."

"It was my first time there, too, you know."

"LOL. Yes, remember I saw her coming from your bedroom."

"You were only thirteen, almost fourteen."

"But I knew. I was happy for you."

"As I am for you. Anything else?"

"Not tonight. I have to get some sleep. Get my strength back (smiley emoji)."

"Good talk."

"Yeah. Good talk."

CHAPTER 16
GAIL

Nate and Dani continued spending what free time they had together, traveling to the lake house whenever they could. Nate had to divide his time between school, studying, working at the barn, and then baseball in the spring. Dani attended his games. She didn't need prodding, and Nate didn't have to bargain with her. She chose to be there to see him play, and Nate excelled in his shortstop position and in batting throughout the season.

The only days that allowed him extra time were on rainy afternoons when baseball practice was canceled and he headed home early. On this particular day, he entered the drive and parked next to an unfamiliar Toyota pickup. He gathered his backpack and proceeded into the house, thinking to himself that Gail must have a friend over.

Nate climbed the stairs two at a time on the way to his room. Passing by Gail's room, the door suddenly opened, and a familiar face stepped out of the room, adjusting the belt loop on his jeans. It was a senior member of the baseball team, one that Nate frequently heard making derogatory comments about his sister. He passed by Nate, grinning and forcefully bumping his shoulder into Nate as he passed him in the hallway.

The thought of this guy being with Gail and now purposely knocking into him infuriated Nate. He dropped his backpack and tackled the intruder from behind, knocking him to the floor. As Nate held him down, he continued hitting him in the jaw with his fist as the intruder struggled to free himself.

"What the fuck…" a shout came from behind Nate as another player came from the bedroom and pulled Nate off the first intruder. As the second player held Nate, the first one began pummeling him, first in the stomach, then a fist to the jaw, splitting open his lip.

Gail heard the commotion outside her room and came out dressed only in panties and a bra, yelling at the players to stop. They stopped, but only after Nate lay defeated, balled up on the floor. "Get out of here," Gail yelled at the two players as they quickly recovered and ran down the stairs.

Gail then sat down beside Nate and put his head in her lap. His head was spinning, his stomach was churning from the pummeling he had received, and the smell of sex emanating from his scantily clad sister caused him to vomit repeatedly as he lay there. Gail's sympathetic overture turned quickly to disgust and revulsion as she raised his head from her lap and retreated quickly to the bathroom to clean herself off.

Nate lay there until his head stopped spinning, and the pain in his abdomen subsided enough that he could get to his feet and down the hall to his room. He then lay on his bed and passed out, sleeping restlessly through the night.

When he awoke, it was nearly noon. He made his way down the hallway to the bathroom, passing by where he had been beaten just twelve hours before. The carpet was freshly cleaned, and there was no evidence of an assault. He looked in the bathroom mirror, examining his face and mouth. His lip was split, and his cheek bruised and swollen, confirming that this had not just been a bad dream. He ran hot water into the bathtub and climbed in, hoping to relieve the dull pain that continued within his stomach and now groin area. He lay there for nearly an hour. Half the day was already passed, so school was not an option. Maybe not tomorrow, either. He would not allow himself to be seen like this by anyone, including Dani.

Nate, dressed in sweatpants and a shirt, then made his way down to the kitchen for juice and some aspirin. Bella was busy working in the kitchen.

"Good morning Nate." She first just glanced at him, then took a second, longer look. "Oh my!" she declared, moving toward him as he opened the refrigerator and took out a bottle of orange juice. "You need to put some ice on that lip." Nate appreciated that she would not ask questions but knew she would be open to hearing anything he had to say.

Bella took a sandwich bag, filled it with ice, and handed it to Nate. "Here, it should help with the swelling."

"Do we have any aspirin?" Nate asked, holding the ice to his lip. Bella went to a nearby cupboard and handed Nate the bottle. He opened it and took two, along with a swig of orange juice to wash it down. "I'm going to skip school today and just take it easy. I'll see about tomorrow."

"OK. I can make some lunch for you if you're hungry."

"Thanks. Maybe later." Nate dismissed himself and returned upstairs to his room. Lying in bed, he decided to text Todd and take a chance that he might be available.

"Hey," Nate began. He was surprised when Todd immediately responded.

"Hey, Nate. No school today?"

"Not feeling so good. I need some advice."

"I'll do my best."

"I got in a scuffle with a couple of guys. Seniors on the team."

"You OK?"

"Split lip. Ribs hurt." Nate wasn't sure if it was anything more than bruised ribs and didn't want to worry Todd.

"What's their problem?"

Nate hesitated. How much should he tell Todd about Gail, the two guys coming out of her bedroom, the locker room talk?

"They still pissed that you were only a sophomore and made the baseball team?" Todd asked since Nate had not responded.

"I think that's part of it. The same thing happened with football."

"What else?"

"You have some time? I can give you all the details."

"I'll make time. Shoot."

Nate proceeded to fill Todd in on everything that had happened the previous day as well as the locker room talk that had taken place over time.

"My biggest concern is how you feel. You sure it's just your ribs?"

"No. My stomach and groin both ache. My stomach is purple from bruising."

"Ask Bella to take you to see the family doc. May not be serious, but you shouldn't take any chances."

"OK."

"Once the doc clears you, go back to school. Don't hide at home."

"I'm not hiding from anyone," Nate protested.

"I know you can handle yourself. But the perception by these thugs will be you're hiding. Don't give them the satisfaction."

"And the split lip? How do I explain that?"

"Be creative."

"OK. What about Gail?"

"It's unfortunate. She's searching for love. She has been since our mother abandoned us. There's nothing we can do about it. The good thing is she'll soon be graduating, and you won't have to deal with it anymore."

"She's not going anywhere. She didn't even apply to any schools. Says she can't go. Has to stay home to take care of our parents."

"She doesn't have to. It's her choice. It's not a reason for you to change your plans."

"Your advice is appreciated. Always on target. The only one I can depend on."

"I'm always here for you. Speaking of which, I'm shipping out in a few days. I'm not sure what communications will be like. I may not be able to respond to your messages right away."

"OK. How long are you going for?"

"Unknown right now."

"Be safe, Todd."

"I will. Good talk?"

"Yeah, good talk."

Nate returned to school the next day after Bella took him to see the family physician, who confirmed it was only bruising and the pain would subside gradually. He gave Nate some pain pills and a note for the coach with instructions that Nate not participate in the next game or practices leading up to it.

The coach questioned Nate on the cause of his "injuries," and he evaded the question. "Nate, is there anything I need to know?" he asked.

"No, sir."

"Anything I can do?" The coach was obviously suspicious, having heard rumors within the locker room.

"No, I'm handling it."

"I can't afford to have you on the injured list. So after this week, if I need to act to prevent this from happening again, you have to tell me."

"I can take care of myself.."

"I have no doubt. Who is your closest ally on the team?"

Nate thought for a minute. "I guess Jake. He's always been friendly. Seems like a solid guy. Never gave me a hard time about being a sophomore on the varsity squad."

"Jake's a good man. Level headed. Tough. Good guy to have on your side. How do you feel about confiding in him?"

"With all due respect, coach, I'm not going to rat on these guys or go whining or complaining to Jake."

"OK, Nate. You do what you think is best, but if things become unmanageable, I will take action against whoever I hear is causing the problem. In the meantime, come to practice, but sit it out."

"Thanks, coach." Nate left his office.

***

"Nate, what happened to you?" Dani caught up with him in the hallway. She saw his face and touched his lip.

"OK, you caught me. I've been seeing this other girl. We were making out, and then she bit me," he joked.

"Not funny!" She poked him in the ribs, and Nate flinched in obvious pain. She lifted his shirt and saw the bruising. "My God, Nate, what happened?" She was serious now and upset.

"You should see the other guy..really." He kissed her forehead. "Seriously, I'm OK. I went to the doctor, and he checked me out. There is nothing to worry about."

"So you're not going to tell me what happened?" Nate didn't respond. "I know you, Nate. Whoever did this ganged up on you. I have no doubt you can defend yourself against just one aggressor. And I'm sure you put up a good fight. Does that about sum it up?" Nate noted she still wasn't smiling. Nate shrugged without speaking. "So what are you going to do?"

"Nothing," he responded. She shook her head at him and walked away.

"I'll see you later," he called after her. She turned briefly, smiled, and waved him off.

CHAPTER 17
DANI'S SECRET

Nate missed the following week of practices and games but returned to active status the following week to finish the season. He heard there were college recruiters scouting the team, but he was only a junior, so he was not likely to pay much attention to him. Following his talk with the coach, Jake had purposely hung back whenever Nate was readying himself for play, not allowing him to be left on his own in the locker room. Nate concluded that the coach must have said something to Jake about the confrontation with several of the senior players, but he was OK with that. He liked Jake, and they developed a natural friendship. Jake shared with Nate that he had received two scholarship offers thus far, one to Cornell, knowing that Nate hoped to attend there.

Nate continued to text Todd with updates about school and the family, but Todd was not responding since being deployed. Nate wasn't concerned but missed their talks. Todd had warned him that he may not be able to respond.

When the school year ended, Gail graduated without much pomp and circumstance. Nate and Dani began spending every weekend at the lake house. He led her to the top of the mountain, and they sat on the big glacier rock, looking down at the lake below. They lay there quietly until Nate spied the tree nearby and the initials carved into it. TW+AM. "That's Todd and

Allie. He told me he was in love with her."

"Are they still together?"

"I don't know. He never mentions her in his texts. I guess maybe they went separate ways when he joined the Marines." Nate took a jackknife from his pocket and began carving his initials, then Dani's, into the tree. "What do you think?"

She wrapped her arms around his neck and kissed him. "Let's get back to the house. I need to shower. And so do you."

"Shall we save water?" he asked, grinning.

"Absolutely!" she laughed as they hurried down the mountain.

***

They spent as much time together as they could at the lake house up until Nate left for football camp for two weeks. His training for the quarterback position accelerated as he readied himself to be the starting high school QB the next month.

When school finally started, they returned to their usual routines; school, practice and games, the lake house on Friday nights, and youth on Sundays. Nate excelled at starting QB and quickly gained the respect of his teammates. He desired to do well and gave it his all but had no intention of changing his priority from baseball to football when it came to college. His desire had always been and remained baseball.

"When I first met you, Nate, I didn't want to get involved with a star athlete and one of the most popular guys in school. But from the start, you didn't come across as egotistical or arrogant. I didn't believe it possible until you proved to me that you could be all those things and not be an ass."

He laughed. "I will take that as a compliment."

***

This was the first time since before the accident that he could remember being truly content with his life. He had finally risen above adversity; the death of his brother, the downward spiral and mental illness of his mother, the indiscretions and distancing of his father, the sordid reputation of his sister, and Todd's departure. He continued to run every day, but it was becoming more out of desire than need. He was euphoric in this new life that he had found. He took notice now and reveled in the scenery of the hills and trees as he breathed in the fresh country air.

Nate and Dani celebrated the holidays together and joined with friends at the Lake House on New Year's Eve. Nate had received his acceptance and a full scholarship offer to play baseball at Cornell the next year, just days before, but had not shared it with her. He wasn't sure what it meant for them. But she knew it was coming, and he expected it was what she wanted for him. She had not indicated to him what her own plans were; his plans always seemed to take precedence, maybe because there was more at stake for him. He had worked hard both scholastically and athletically toward his goal and succeeded.

Dani was smart and had done well in school but didn't make a big deal out of going to college or getting a scholarship. They had talked briefly about her options, and her first choice was Quinnipiac University in Hamden, an hour south of Plainville, where she hoped to study English Literature and someday teach.

As the partiers reveled in preparation for the midnight hour, Nate took Dani outside into the chilly winter night and sat by a campfire to talk. "I got my acceptance and scholarship offer from Cornell," Nate began.

"That's great, Nate. I know you have been waiting for this. I'm really happy for you."

"Thanks. Have you received anything yet from Quinnipiac?"

"I have. I've been accepted." Nate noticed little enthusiasm in her response.

"You don't seem very excited." He thought maybe it was because they would soon be apart from each other after being together for three years.

"I think I may defer enrollment for a year," she confessed.

"Why?"

She looked at him for a moment before speaking. "Let's just celebrate your victory tonight. We can talk about me some other time." She stood to leave. "I'm cold. I need to go inside."

Nate sat alone for a while, pondering her response and her reluctance to speak further about it. It wasn't like her to be so dismissive. Their relationship proceeded to the point of honesty and trust, whereby they didn't hesitate to share their thoughts and feelings. It felt like something had changed or was about to, and it made him uneasy. These were the precursors to the anxiety of the past, and it made him uneasy. He just wanted to be with her now, and nothing else mattered, so he sought her out and stayed by her side. She remained somber all through the evening and past midnight. When they retired to the master bedroom around 2 AM, she rejected his advances, claiming fatigue, and turned away from him on the bed.

During the night, Nate was awoken by sounds coming from the bathroom. The sounds were muffled, but he recognized them as someone being sick and suffering the consequences of too much booze. He reached behind him and found Dani missing from the bed. She had not drunk anything that he was aware of. Maybe she just wasn't feeling well, which could explain her distant behavior. He waited quietly for her to come back to the bed.

"Are you OK?" he asked her as she slid quietly back into bed beside him. She didn't respond verbally but simply lay her head on his chest. She was shivering, and she began to weep gently.

"Just hold me," she whispered. Eventually, they drifted off to sleep.

The following morning when he awoke, she was already dressed and in the kitchen with several of their friends making breakfast. He saddled up close to her as he poured himself some coffee and kissed her forehead. She looked pale but acted more upbeat than the night before. "Feeling any better?" Nate whispered.

She smiled. "Must have been something I ate."

Nate wasn't aware of anyone else getting ill from the food but decided maybe something just didn't agree with her, so he didn't question it further. She would talk about last night when she was ready and not before.

***

During the next several months, their relationship seemed to be back to normal, and Nate was relieved. They drove to the lake house on the weekends with just the two of them. There were several occasions that Dani texted him to say she wasn't feeling well and wouldn't be in school that day. It seemed unusual to Nate. Since they began dating, Dani rarely missed school, and now when she did, it was usually for two or three days, not one, and it seemed to be more frequent.

It was late March, and they planned to meet at the youth gathering. When Nate arrived, he immediately observed Dani off in the corner with Youth Pastor Rick, engaged in a hushed conversation. Nate was reminded that when he had first met Dani, she and Pastor Rick were acting similarly, talking in secret. It was not a common occurrence since he and Dani had been together, and it disturbed him that it was happening again.

Was he just jealous? They seemed a little too friendly to him. And something about his own relationship with Dani kept him on edge. He sat down, watched, and waited for her to sit beside him, observing closely as Pastor Rick hugged her tightly before she finally extricated herself from him. As she approached him, he noticed her eyes were red, like she had been crying. She feigned a smile and kissed him on the cheek, but her smile was obviously forced and contrived. He had a puzzled look on his face which she recognized as she squeezed his arm and spoke. "Don't worry. I'm fine."

April and spring break came. Nate and Dani spent the entire week together at the lake house. Nate woke up at the crack of dawn every morning to run several miles, keeping in shape for baseball, which would start right after spring break. Dani was usually still asleep as he rolled out of bed, got dressed, and kissed her on the forehead. This particular morning, he noticed her forehead was warm, possibly too warm, but he allowed her to sleep and would check on her when he got back from his run.

When he returned, the bed was empty. He called out for her, but she didn't respond. The bathroom door was closed, and once again, he heard several episodes of vomiting coming from the room. He slowly opened the door and saw her kneeling by the bowl. He knelt beside her with a damp towel. She looked feverish, and perspiration covered her forehead. She gave him a glance, then proceeded to vomit more into the toilet. When she finished, she just laid her head down at the edge of the bowl and looked up at Nate. Several tears ran down her face, and he wiped them away with his finger.

"Here, let me help you back to bed." He helped her stand and then picked her up, carrying her back to where she had previously lain. "Feels like you have a fever. Let me get you some water and aspirin."

"No aspirin, just water." Her voice was hoarse, and her skin pallid.

"OK. Here, put this wet towel on your forehead. You definitely have a fever." He went to the kitchen for water. He thought to himself; it must be the flu. If it was, he would come down with it in a day or so but hopefully be over it when practice started next week.

Dani spent the day in bed, and her fever subsided during the night. She awoke when Nate returned from his morning run and said she was feeling better. It was their last day there, and they packed their bags and headed home. While she said she felt better, it was obvious to Nate that her energy level was lower than usual, and her spirits were dampened. Again, he thought it must be from a virus, and she would be back to her vibrant self in a few days.

Baseball started, and Nate was engaged every afternoon in practice with games on Tuesdays and Thursdays. Dani continued to miss school and all of his games.

He didn't ask her why. He believed she would tell him, whatever it was when she was ready. She would not like to be questioned. She had already told him she was fine, and it was nothing to worry about. He was becoming more worried every day, and his anxiety level was on the rise.

On Sunday, they were to meet at youth as usual. When Nate arrived, Dani was not among the group. He thought she must be late and sat down in his usual spot to wait. Several minutes later, Dani walked in with Pastor Rick. He tried to quell any suspicion of Dani and Pastor Rick in any kind of inappropriate relationship, but it bothered him. She looked OK, but he did notice that she was wearing more mascara than usual, but just enough to naturalize her color.

"Hey." She greeted him with a brief kiss and sat down next to him. After youth, Nate walked her to her car. "I'm going to miss school most of next week…" she began.

Nate looked at her, waiting for the answer to his fears. His mind was racing. Was there something going on between her and Pastor Rick? She continued. "Can we go to the diner and talk?"

"Sure. I'll drive. Ride with me." She agreed and got into his car. At the diner, they sat and ordered a couple of sodas.

"Do you want anything to eat?" Nate asked.

"No thanks. But you go ahead."

Nate wasn't interested in food right now. He only wanted to know about her. What was happening to them? To her? Was she about to tell him it was over between them?

"What'd you want to talk about?" he finally asked.

"I owe you an explanation…why I've missed so much school…why I missed your games."

"You don't owe me anything, Dani. But I am worried about you. About us."

"Us? What do you mean?" she asked.

"I've seen you with him…with Pastor Rick."

"Oh, Nate, it's nothing like that. He's just been helping me deal with some things." She reached across the table and took his hand. Her eyes welled up with tears again, but she took a deep breath and remained composed. Then she began to reveal the secret she had held onto since before meeting Nate.

"When I was fourteen, I was diagnosed with leukemia," she began. She waited for his reaction, and he just stared at her. "I went through chemo, got sick a lot, lost all my hair but eventually went into remission. About a year later, I met you. I wasn't looking to meet anyone. At least not until I knew I would be OK. I needed to be OK first and not let myself get involved with someone who would feel sorry for me or ultimately get hurt if things went bad again." She stopped and looked into Nate's eyes. He simply nodded.

"I can understand that" he smiled and continued holding her hand from across the table. As serious as their discussion might be, he wanted to avoid any connotation of this being hopeless or the end of their happiness together.

"Last November, it came back. I started chemo again just before Christmas."

"So that's why you have been sick," he acknowledged. "I wish you had told me sooner. How much longer for the treatments?"

"I have to continue them through June."

"And then what?"

"Then they'll tell me if they worked."

"I'm sure they will." While he tried to reassure her, he was not sure of anything. "So what can I do to help?" He watched her closely. She was beautiful to him, so loving and caring. And she had been trying to protect him through all of this. "I'll be with you through the rest of these treatments if you'll let me." He was searching for anything to reassure her of his commitment to her.

"I appreciate that, Nate. But you can't put your life on hold because of this. You have to finish the school year, and you have baseball. I just wish I could be there to see you play."

He had noticed that he didn't enjoy the sport as much when she wasn't there watching, but he wouldn't say anything to make her feel more regret than she already felt.

"OK, look," he resolved. "I'll be thinking of you while I'm out there in the field, and you be thinking of me during those treatments. We can be with each other in spirit, at least."

This brought a smile to her face, at last, Nate thought. "Deal," she said.

"And when you're not feeling well after your treatments, I'll try to be there to take care of you."

"OK, but be forewarned. You won't be seeing me at my best."

"I've seen you at your worst, and you were still beautiful to me."

***

Nate upheld his promise to be with her whenever he could. She was now having weekly chemo treatments, and he would take those afternoons off to sit with her at the hospital. He would then take her home and return to the school for practice, then back to her house again in the evening. Dani had become weaker as a result, but Nate took her out for walks around the neighborhood in the fresh spring air in an effort to help her regain some of her strength. Her mood remained positive, or so he thought. But deep down, he had doubts and believed that it was just an act done mostly for his benefit.

Nate brought her school assignments home daily so that she could graduate on schedule, and they often studied together. When she tired, he lay down beside her on the bed and held her until she fell asleep. Then he would leave her for the night, returning to his own home.

By early May, she had lost her hair once again, and her mother fashioned a scarf that fit nicely around her head to conceal her baldness. Dani had regained some of her strength and had a renewed energy as she began to tolerate the chemo better.

The Senior Prom was just two weeks away, and Nate urged Dani to go with him and at least make an appearance where all their friends would be. She agreed, as long as she was feeling better and on the road to recovery.

***

Nate dressed in a black tuxedo, white shirt, and black shoes, all rented. Prior to picking up his tux, he went to the local haircutters. He knew Dani was self-conscious about her appearance, having lost all of her hair, so he decided to alter his appearance to match hers. It would lighten the mood and possibly take attention away from the side effects of her treatment, so he had all of his curly blonde hair removed, and his head shaved. Looking in the mirror as he sat in the barber chair, he rubbed his hands across the smooth scalp. He determined it wasn't such a bad look, and maybe he would do this for a while, at least until Dani was no longer suffering the ill effects of the treatment.

He debated about renting a limo for the occasion but decided it would be best to just drive them there himself, just in case they could not stay at the prom the entire evening. He traded the Civic to his father for the occasion in exchange for the use of his Lexus.

Nate arrived at her house at eight, greeted at the door by Mr. And Mrs. Lucas. They expressed surprise but approved of his appearance as they waited at the bottom of the stairs for Dani to appear. Nate beamed as she descended the stairs in her ¾ length gown and matching headdress. When she reached the bottom of the stairs, she looked up at him with a big smile, then touched his shaved head.

"You won't be needing this. May I?" He asked, touching her headdress.

Dani smiled and nodded her consent, then helped him to remove it from her hairless head.

***

They arrived at the prom shortly after and found seating at a table with Nate's teammates and their dates. They listened to the music for a while before heading to the dance floor. Regardless of the music tempo, they danced together, slowly and at a constant pace, oblivious to those around them. When Dani tired, they returned to their seats and enjoyed the company of friends, who complimented them on their matching hairstyles.

They returned to the dance floor once again when Dani suddenly clung to him. "I need to sit," she said softly. He sensed she was out of breath, and they made their way toward their seats. "Can you get me some water, Nate?"

"Sure, I'll be right back." When he returned, a crowd had gathered around the table. Dani was no longer in her chair. She now lay unconscious on the floor.

When she came to just moments later, she lay with her head in Nate's lap. "Hey. It's not nice scaring me like that," he smiled.

"Take me home," she whispered as she struggled to sit up. Nate lifted her gently into a sitting position.

"Your parents are meeting us at the hospital. Just to have you checked out. Make sure you didn't hit your head or anything."

"It's nothing. You shouldn't have called them." She then tried to stand but didn't have the strength. Nate helped her to her feet, then picked her up. He had carried her like this before, and while she never seemed heavy to him, she felt even lighter now. The illness and chemo were taking its toll.

They were met by her parents at the emergency entrance to the hospital, where Dani was immediately wheeled in, and they began iv fluids. She was briefly examined, and her history was reviewed by the resident. "We need to admit her at least overnight for observation. It could be just dehydration, but we want to be sure. We'll contact her oncologist in the morning."

"I'd like to stay with her," Nate volunteered.

"Are you family?" he asked.

Dani's mother spoke up, touching Nate's arm. "Yes, he is."

The doctor looked at them doubtfully. "She's already sleeping. I suggest you go home, get some rest, then come back in the morning."

When Nate returned the next morning, Dani was already up, dressed, and sitting next to the hospital bed. "Hey, how are you feeling?" He bent down and kissed her forehead.

"Better," she smiled weakly.

"Good. I'll take you home then."

A nurse then walked in and looked at them questioningly. "You shouldn't be out of bed, young lady," the nurse said firmly. "The doctor has scheduled some tests for you and will go over them with you and your parents later." She then turned and left the room.

"Help me up," Dani said as she rose unsteadily from the chair. Nate held onto her arm, expecting to walk her back to the bed, but Dani resisted. "No, not there," she insisted. "Please get me out of here."

"But Dani…"

"Please, Nate," she said more firmly. "I can't do this anymore."

"OK," Nate nodded. He peaked out the door to make sure the hallway was clear. "Can you walk?"

"I'll have to. It would look a little suspicious, you carrying me, don't you think?" She took his arm, and they walked out of the room and made their way down the hallway and out of the hospital to his Civic. "Let's make a quick stop at my house. I need to pick up some things." Nate looked at her, puzzled. She sensed his confusion and expressed her immediate wish. "Take me to the lake house. I can get all the rest I need there…with you."

Nate thought for a moment. Was this really a good idea? What about her parents? Shouldn't they talk to them first?

He hadn't spoken those words, but she sensed his reluctance and touched his arm. "My parents will understand. If this last round of treatments doesn't work, there is nothing left to do but live for the moment. That moment is now, Nate."

"The treatments will work," he assured her. He started the jeep, and they drove toward her house.

"That's one of your best qualities," she commented. "Always so positive." Nate doubted that was true, but accepted the complement graciously.

They arrived at the lake house by lunch, and Nate prepared some soup and sandwiches. He carried them down to the dock where Dani was sitting, soaking up the bright warm sunshine. "I'm going to take a nap after lunch; then I want to go up the mountain...to the rock...and the tree."

"Sure, we can do that." They ate in silence, then Nate spoke again. "I'm sorry I pushed you to go last night. It was obviously too much for you."

They sat in silence for a few minutes before she spoke. "Nate, we need to talk," she started. "Better yet, I'll talk, and you listen. When I'm done, it will be your turn. But I already know what you're going to say."

"You think you know me that well? You remember when we first met, how you said you already knew everything you needed to know about me? Then you found out there was a little more to me than you expected."

"I've gotten to know you and how you think."

"Our thoughts are simply a distraction from..." he started.

"....what's in our hearts" she interrupted him. "And you have an amazing heart, Nate. I've never seen you intentionally hurt or even be mean to anyone. But at some point, you are going to have to do what is best for you and not everyone else, including me."

"I will never do anything to hurt you," he pledged.

"Nate, what will hurt me is if you don't listen and try to understand what I'm saying. No matter what happens to me, what would hurt me most is if you don't follow your dreams. Go to Cornell. Play baseball. Try to get drafted. It's all there waiting for you, and I can't be the reason you don't go for it."

Nate thought for a moment. "What about us, Dani? You know I love you."

"Love can wait. We're both too young to make that commitment. I'm planning on getting over this, then taking a year off, and then going to school. You need to focus on keeping your scholarship. For now, baseball has to be your first love."

"Is that what you really want? For us to take a break?"

"It's not a question of what I want, Nate."

Deep down, he knew she was right. But was it possible that she didn't feel for him the same way he felt for her? After all, he had just told her he loved her, and she didn't reciprocate the sentiment. "When I'm at Cornell, I want to stay in touch with you, know how you're doing, and maybe someday…" He wasn't sure how to continue.

Dani stood now and stopped briefly before walking toward the house. "I'm going to go rest for a bit. Wake me in an hour?"

Nate nodded. As he watched her walk away, he pondered their future. Was there a future for them, or would the time they had shared the past three years just become a memory? A part of life that passes them by. He knew she was right, though. If he was going to pursue his dreams, she would have to take a back seat. He couldn't put all his time and effort into baseball and expect her to be waiting in the stands. It wouldn't be fair to her. For now, though, she was the most important thing to him, and that wasn't going to change until it had to.

***

"Hey Todd," Nate texted. "You there?" Nate waited for a response, but there wasn't one. "It's been a while since we talked. I hope you are OK over there, wherever you are. The season's over, and I'm headed to Cornell next month. Dani and I are at the lake right now, talking things through. Looks like we will be taking a break so I can focus on baseball at Cornell. Text when you can. Lots more to tell. Miss our talks. Take care."

***

He awoke Dani from a deep sleep. "I don't think I can make it up the mountain," she concluded as she lay there.

"Climb aboard," Nate offered her his back. "We're going to the top of the mountain. There is a beautiful world out there, and we're going to take it all in." So she climbed onto his back.

They reached the top and sat upon the big rock where Nate, his brothers, and his sister had all sat before, looking down upon the valley and the lake below. Nate's melancholy mood overshadowed the ecstatic moment he usually felt when he was atop the mountain. There were so many memories here…of Billy. Of Todd. And soon, it would just be a memory of him and Dani, here together, alone.

"You have your jackknife?" Dani asked him. He took it from his pocket and watched as she carved the date beneath their initials which he had carved on their previous visit. She then returned to his side on the rock. "Have you heard from your brother?" she asked, breaking the silence between them.

Nate shook his head. "I texted him a while ago. He hasn't responded to my messages for quite some time now. He's somewhere in the middle east, I think."

She stood slowly, waiting for him to follow. "It's getting late. We should be heading back."

Nate remained motionless, deep in thought about their discussion. "I need to ask you something."

"Sure, Nate. What is it?"

"You and Pastor Rick. You are close with him?"

"Yes." He waited for her to elaborate, but she remained silent for the moment.

"How close?" He raised his eyes to her, fearing that his suspicions could be true.

"He's always been there for me."

Nate saw her response as evasive, at best. "That doesn't answer my question," he concluded.

"When I was first diagnosed, he was the only one I told. I didn't want it to spread around or for people to feel sorry for me. He kept my confidence. Whenever I was feeling down, he brought me back up."

"Hm," Nate responded. Her response didn't and wouldn't either confirm or deny his suspicions, and he was not happy with it.

"Since I told you about my illness, you've been supportive, too, and I appreciate that."

"So you appreciate that I've been supportive?" Nate said sarcastically, under his breath but loud enough for her to hear.

"Nate, what's going on? Why this sudden attitude?"

He looked at her for a moment, then hung his head. "I feel like I'm losing you."

Her eyes had now filled with tears, and her voice quivered. "How do you think I feel? I might be losing myself to this…disease…and if I lose to it, I lose everything. And if I have to continue to fight this, you won't be here to help me. Rick…" she stopped herself. "Pastor Rick will be."

"But I can be here…"

"No!" She cut him off in mid-sentence. "You can't be here. You can only help me by doing what is best for you and getting on with your life. And with you gone, I can focus on me…on me getting better and getting on with my life. Don't you get it?" She wiped the tears from her face with a sleeve.

Nate stood now. "I understand, but I don't like our options."

"There are no options, Nate." She walked ahead of him now toward the trail going down the mountain.

"Can I help you?" he asked as he followed her.

"It's all downhill from here," she sighed and continued down the path in front of him.

"Well said," Nate thought to himself and followed her.

***

Dani was exhausted physically and emotionally from their hike up the mountain and retired early to get some sleep. Nate walked down to the pier and sat on the edge of the dock. He checked his messages, no response from Todd. There was a message from Zak, though, saying he would be coming into town a few days before they had to report to Cornell and asking if he could stay at the Woods' for a few nights.

Nate responded. "Good to hear from you, Zak. We'll stay at the lake house and then travel to Cornell. Just let me know when to expect you."

Nate and Dani returned to Plainville the following day. He walked her to the door of the house. She had regained some of her energy and was feeling stronger today. She turned to him at the door before going inside. "Call me in a few days?" she asked.

Nate was used to seeing her often, and they talked daily; now, it had changed to a "few days." Their relationship was changing and would never be the same. He nodded, kissed her forehead, and watched as she entered the house alone.

When he reached his own house, he went to his room, put on his running shoes, and headed back out the door. It was time to run.

CHAPTER 18
TIME TO GO

He saw little of Dani over the next few weeks. He heard she had reentered the hospital for a few days, then was sent home. He saw her next at their graduation. He watched as she steadily made her way up to the stage to accept her diploma. She still wore the turban on her head, and the crowd applauded, recognizing her for her achievements, graduating while still fighting for her life. Nate rubbed his head, feeling the stubble that had grown back since the day of the prom, and stood with his classmates, acknowledging too her courage and stamina.

He searched the bleachers of the athletic field for his father. He was there, seated with Bella. It was foolish to think that his mother might actually attend his graduation. She had skipped Gail's the year before. It was rare now if she came out of her room, let alone out of the house. He tried to recall the last time they had even spoken to each other but to no avail. As he went forward to accept his diploma, he saw his father stand up and nod approvingly. This would be the extent of his graduation celebration. It was even more subdued than Gail's the year before. He had still not heard from Todd and was sure that, if Todd were able, he would have sent him a message on this occasion. He questioned his father several times, and he claimed to have not heard anything from Todd for several months.

Following graduation, Nate became fully engaged in work at the barn, cutting and baling hay. Tossing hay bails onto the wagon, carrying them up into the barn loft, and then his daily run provided a good workout for him each day. At the end of the week, he would reward himself and invite friends up to the lake house with him. There they would spend their days swimming, boating, and fishing on the lake. By dusk, they would begin the party ritual, friends bringing plenty of beer and some hard liquor. Nate found himself drinking more than usual in a vain attempt to forget about Dani, especially with all the guys and their girlfriends partying around him. Many evenings he would drink until he passed out and would wake up in different places, such as on the boat or the dock, not remembering how he got there.

Zak arrived the second week in August, just a week before they had to travel to Cornell. He was just as Nate remembered him from when he last saw him at Billy's funeral, but he had grown to nearly Nate's 5'10" height and solid 175 lbs. He sported longer hair than Nate's and obviously hadn't bothered to shave for several days. Their reunion was a happy one, and Nate was distracted from the melancholy of his separation from Dani. Nate invited a few friends for their last weekend of the summer at the lake house, including Jake, who was going back to Cornell as a junior.

Nate had paid little attention to their housing plan and learned from Jake and Zak that they had reserved a four-bedroom suite at the school. Tom Whitney, a left fielder and friend of Jake's, would be their fourth roommate.

Nate and Zak arrived at the lake house early Saturday morning to prepare for the arrival of the others later in the day. "So tell me about Dani," Zak entreated as they uncovered the boat.

"Not much to tell," Nate shrugged. "We had a good run. Now we're headed in different directions."

"Is she why you're drinking so early?" Zak had observed that Nate was already on his second beer, and it wasn't noon yet.

"This is only my second," Nate said dismissively.

"It's barely noon, Nate," Zak observed cautiously. "Look, Nate; I don't want to pry…"

"Then don't." Nate cut him off sharply.

"You know you can tell me anything. When you're ready," he added quickly. Nate was unresponsive. "So what's next? Anything you need me to do before the guys arrive?"

"Beer run." Nate reached into his pocket and pulled out a wad of bills.

"Go to the QuikMart. Ask for Zeke. He won't proof you." He handed the money to Zak.

"What, no hard stuff?" Zak said almost mockingly.

"No need. There's already a good supply here, compliments of my dad."

"Alright then" Zak shook his head, surprised at Nate's attitude and what he was hearing. "I guess I'll be back in a bit."

Nate watched him walk up the hill and out of sight, then sat down on the dock, hanging his feet in the water. It was a warm summer day, and the lake had warmed significantly over the summer months. He stood, removed all of his clothes, and dove naked into the lake. He swam out to the middle of the lake, then stopped to float while he rested. A boat with several teenagers sped by, then suddenly turned and stopped close to him. A girl passenger dressed in a thong bikini called out to him. "Hey, are you OK?"

"Yeah, I'm fine," he called back.

"You're quite a ways from shore. Want a ride?"

She was cute, and he was tempted, so he swam closer to the boat. He was about to climb up the ladder but stopped as he remembered he had no clothes on. "Stupid of me," he thought. He noticed that there were five people on board, three of them scantily clad females and two guys, all about his age, he guessed. "I appreciate your offer, but I live just over there, and it's not that far a swim."

"I can give you a towel" she smiled, and Nate now realized she could see he was naked through the clear water.

"Oh, what the hell" Nate mumbled and proceeded to climb up the ladder. After all, he had nothing to be ashamed of or embarrassed about. As he neared the top of the ladder, she handed him a towel, still smiling.

"I'm Sienna, and these are my friends….blah….blah…blah…" Nate wasn't really interested in the others, just the one who was paying him immediate attention.

"I'm Nate." He strategically placed the towel in front of him.

"Hasn't anyone ever told you it's not safe to swim alone? Especially halfway across the lake!"

"I'm not alone. My friend is over there," he lied, pointing toward the lake house. "You have anything to drink?" he asked, quickly changing the subject.

"Soda," she offered. She saw the disappointed look. "Alcohol is illegal on the lake," she added.

Nate smirked. "Right. So where are we going?" he turned his attention to one of the guys at the helm.

"Take us for a ride around the lake, Josh," Sienna instructed. He nodded and opened the throttle. Nate dropped the towel for a moment, watching Sienna out of the corner of his eye as he wrapped the towel around his lower half. She was definitely watching his every move.

"I'm having some friends come over this evening, and you're welcome to come," he offered her.

"Maybe. I'll have to see what my friends say."

***

It was two hours before they ended their trip around the lake by dropping Nate off at his dock. Zak was watching from the upper deck at the back of the house. He watched Nate as he hopped out of the boat, tossed the towel back to its passengers, and walked naked up the dock, picking his clothes up along the way.

Zak called to him from the deck. "Apparently, I am overdressed."

Nate looked up and smiled. "Sorry to abandon you like that. It wasn't planned."

"Spontaneous is good. I'm glad to see you smile finally. You'd better get dressed, though. There's a text message from Jake, and they will be here soon."

***

Their friends began arriving around four. Most of Nate's teammates were there, some with girlfriends in tow. Jake brought Jeannie, both of whom Nate had not seen since the Christmas holidays. They talked about baseball at Cornell the past year, and then Dani's name came up.

Jeannie was speaking as Nate opened his fourth beer of the night. He felt good for the moment with a slight buzz on and listened to the conversation taking place around him. "I heard you took Dani to the Prom." Nate glanced at her and caught her gaze but looked away quickly. He had avoided any conversations about Dani, especially explanations as to what had happened between them.

Zak was observing from a distance. Nate had shared earlier with him some of what had transpired with Dani and decided to run interference for him. He approached Nate from behind and tapped his shoulder. "Your friends from this morning are here." He pointed in the direction of the dock where Sienna and her friends were climbing out of their boat. Nate arose from his chair by the fire, and they all watched as he walked toward the dock.

"Hey," Sienna greeted him. "We're ready for those drinks now."

"Follow me," Nate said and led them toward a keg that had been tapped up on the deck. Zak watched as Nate led her into the house. It was several hours later before Zak would see him again. He found Nate sitting alone on the steps leading up to the deck. His eyes were glazed over, and he seemed oblivious to the people and sounds around him.

"Where's your friend?" Zak asked as he sat down next to him.

Nate shrugged. "Sitting right next to me, I reckon." He picked up a half-empty bottle of bourbon and took a long swallow. "Here, have some." He handed it to Zak, who took the bottle and set it down beside him without taking a drink.

"I'm good, thanks."

Nate was slurring his words as he spoke. "She probably thinks I'm an ass....and she's right. I am an ass."

"So what happened?" Zak took a sip from his beer.

"I assumed she wanted me. Hell, I let her see me naked. What's not to want, right?" he scoffed, reaching around Zak for the bourbon.

Zak was putting two and two together. "I guess she didn't take you up on your offer."

"Oh, she did alright. But I couldn't do it. I mean, I couldn't get it up. She must think I'm a freak."

"Who cares what she thinks? You've got a lot going on, dude. And you're drunk on your ass too!" Zak laughed.

Nate laughed too. "You're right, Zak. You know, you're a good friend." He clinked the bourbon bottle against Zak's beer. Nate began to reminisce, slurring his voice as he talked. "You were my best friend...hell, my only friend for a long time. Then you left, and I was all alone."

"You've always been my best friend, Nate. Even after I moved away, no one could take your place."

"Todd and I were close for a while. He even told me once that I was his best friend. You were hard to replace, but Todd managed to fill the void."

"And I thought I was irreplaceable." Zak chuckled.

"Well, you're back, and Todd's gone. So the honor is all yours. Here's to best friends." He clinked the bottle once more against Zak's beer, then gulped the last of the bottle before tossing it into the yard. Nate then struggled to stand and steadied himself with the stair handrail.

Zak stood, too, and had to move quickly to keep Nate from stumbling. He secured his arm around Nate's back and under his arm. "Steady there, bud," Zak implored.

"No one has ever called me that except Todd," he noted. "I need another beer. Want one?"

Zak suddenly felt all of Nate's weight on his shoulder as his legs went out from under him. Fortunately, Jake had spotted them, analyzed the situation, and come to Zak's aid.

"Help me get him upstairs," Zak said to Jake, and together they helped Nate upstairs and into the master bedroom. They laid him on the bed; Zak removed Nate's shoes and threw a blanket over him. Nate had passed out.

***

Nate sat strumming his guitar on the front stoop of the farmhouse. Memories of Todd sitting in this exact spot, playing his guitar, flashed through his mind. He missed him.

The car was loaded, and he would be leaving shortly for Cornell. The realization hit him during the night that he would soon be leaving what had been his home for eighteen years now. So many changes had taken place over the years, changes that had caused him so much pain and anxiety. A house once so full of love was now empty. It made it easier to leave, he supposed. But this could be a defining moment for him. It was going to be the rest of his life, but before he took that step, there was one thing left for him to do.

He picked up his guitar, went up the stairs, and stood outside his mother's bedroom door. He knocked softly, but there was no response, which wasn't surprising. He entered the room quietly and saw his mother laying still on the bed, her back to him.

Well mom, I'm headed out now and just wanted to let you know."

She had not stirred. He walked to the side of the bed that she lay facing, bent down, and kissed her forehead. Her eyes were opened, but she did not lift them to meet his or acknowledge him in any way except for the single tear that lay on her cheek.

CHAPTER 19
GENEVA

In their first year at Cornell, Zak and Nate took advantage of all the social events that the school had to offer, including fraternity and sorority parties, intramural sports, and their first year as players on the school baseball team. There was time for little else, and it passed quickly. Dani became more of an afterthought for Nate, and after several early attempts to reconnect with her, he accepted that their relationship was just a memory.

The summer passed quickly, and Nate did not return to Plainville but stayed at the lake house with frequent visits from friends. He then returned to Cornell for his Sophomore year.

"You need a backup plan." Jake, Tom, Zak, and Nate were all sitting in their suite, beers in hand, as Jake offered his advice. "There are no guarantees. As good as we are, baseball may not be an option as a career choice. So what are your backup plans?"

"If they won't let me play, I'll be a trainer. So I guess PE and PT will be my focus," Zak stated confidently.

"That's good, Zak. How about you, Nate?"

Nate was silent. He hadn't really considered what he would do if baseball was not an option. After all, he had never failed at it. "I don't know," he finally said.

"What would you want to do if baseball were not an option?" Nate wasn't sure if the question came from Jake or Zak. He was deep in thought, but his thinking was chaotic. It perplexed him. He had always known what he wanted before this. It just seemed that things were laid out for him, that they came naturally and easily. He hadn't given it much thought until now.

The silence was finally broken by Jake. "You don't need to decide right now, but it's something to think about when you register for classes. For now, though, we have to get to the team meeting."

Upon the advice of his adviser, Nate signed up for the basic freshman courses in his first year, with an emphasis on PE and Health. His adviser suggested that based on Nate's own propensity toward leadership roles in sports, he might be able to utilize them later in some kind of teaching or administrative capacity. Nate was amenable but wasn't passionate about anything now except baseball, and he was determined to someday make it his livelihood.

***

"Hi, Todd. I don't expect you to be there right now to talk. Just wanted to catch up on some things. Any chance you'll be home for Christmas this year? I don't expect there is. What's it been now, five years since I've seen you? Doesn't seem possible. And so much has happened. Anyway, I'm here at Cornell now, and things are going OK. I hope they are with you too. Text me when you can."

***

The fall and winter terms passed quickly, and both he and Zak made plans for the holidays. Zak would be flying home to Texas in a few days and had some time to kill. This was another decision that Nate had to make. Part of it came easily for him. He was not going home to Connecticut. There was nothing for him to go home to. And last summer, he had stayed at the lake house all summer, never visiting the house where he grew up. He had made that break when he said goodbye to his mother. "Come to Texas with me," Zak offered.

"Maybe. But we've got a couple of days to kill. I miss the lake, and the Finger Lakes are just an hour north of here. We can hole up there for a few days, and it's not that far to the Syracuse airport."

"Road trip. Cool. Let's do it."

They loaded up Nate's civic and headed north toward the town of Geneva on the north side of Seneca Lake. It was lunch time when they arrived in Geneva, and Nate parked the loaded car on the main street. "Let's get some lunch, and then we'll find a place to stay. Should be lots of places on the lake."

"Over there," Zak pointed toward a cafe intermingled among the various storefronts and small shops lining the street. The downtown area reminded Nate of his hometown of Plainville.

"Nettles," Nate read the large, faded, hand-painted sign across the front. "Looks interesting," he laughed. "Adventure number one." They crossed the street and entered the door to the cafe. Nate read the menu board. Primarily soups, sandwiches, and salads during the lunch hours. He observed the rustic furnishings of old maple-stained chairs and tables covered with red and white checkered table cloths. An artificial Christmas tree stood in the corner near the front window with abundant colored flashing lights and ball-shaped ornaments. It was atypical of the white artificial trees with white lights and gold ornaments seen in much newer and flashier commercial establishments.

A long walnut-stained bar with matching bar stools, but mismatched in color from the tables, was to the right, and there were several unoccupied stools. A young lady carrying a tray of drinks spoke to them briefly as she quickly passed by. "Sit anywhere," she instructed.

"This place is hopping," Zak commented, watching the server move away from them.

"A good sign. Let's sit over there." He led Zak to one of the few remaining booths. They sat and observed the crowd and wait staff as they waited. Nate picked up the poinsettia strategically placed in the center of the table. "Hm…" He examined it closely before setting it down. "Fake. Nice try, though."

"Everything is fake these days," Zak concluded.

"Enjoying the décor in our fine dining establishment, gentlemen?" The server now stood at the end of their booth, handing them two menus. Nate looked up and was immediately drawn to her beautiful face and smile.

"Yes indeed, Leah," he said, reading the faded name tag on her pale blue dress uniform. "I hope the food is equally rewarding."

She simply smiled and waited. "What would you like to drink?"

Zak had been observing their interaction, then spoke. "A coke for me, please."

"How's the water?" Nate asked seriously.

"Bottled fresh, right from the lake."

Witty, Nate thought to himself. "Sounds ebullient," he responded.

Her smile faded and turned to a frown. "Cornell, huh?"

"I guess the jackets gave us away," Zak said directly to Nate.

"Do you need more time with the menu? I can come back."

"Nope. Not a slow reader. Soup and sandwich," Nate responded. "Whatever the special is for today will be fine." He noticed she didn't write down his order. "You going to write that down?"

"No need. I have a good memory," she countered, turning her attention to Zak.

"I'll have a burger and fries," Zak added.

" I'll be back with your drinks in a minute." Leah turned and walked toward the kitchen.

"I think I'm in love," Zak whispered as they both watched her walk away. "And dude, what does ebullient even mean?"

"Not sure, but I wanted her to see me as more than just another pretty face. You know, intelligent AND good-looking."

They observed as several other young servers moved quickly about the establishment, taking and serving orders, but none as attractive as Leah, they agreed. When their food and drinks arrived several minutes later, Nate decided to engage her in more conversation.

"We just got into town and are looking for a place to stay for a couple of nights. Any suggestions?"

"This is a busy time of the year. I doubt there is much available on short notice. Most people reserve way in advance."

Zak responded first. "He doesn't plan ahead. You know, kind of spur-of-the-moment thing. We are on our way to Texas. That part was planned. This little excursion wasn't."

Leah smiled politely. "Does Cornell offer a class in geography? Texas is in the other direction." She then began writing on the back of the check. "Try this place. It's two blocks from here, right on the lake. Tell them Leah sent you. Oh...and ask for the penthouse suite." She laid the bill on the table and walked away, smiling to herself.

As they returned to Nate's car, Zak entered the address into his phone. "Turn right two blocks up, and the place should be on the left," he read. They pulled in front of a large country-style inn and parked in the street. The faded sign over the steps leading up to the wrap-around porch read "Nettles B n B."

Walking up the steps to the door, Zak commented. "I wonder how many establishments this Nettles person owns in this town." The sign on the door simply said "walk-in," which they did. They stood in the foyer. A large crystal chandelier sparkled overhead. To the right was a large dining room with gold-flecked leaves on the wallpaper. To the left, through double French doors, was the living room with dark wood-paneled walls.

"Wow. Retro," Zak observed. A grand piano sat by the front wall, and a large stone fireplace was visible on the side wall. The house was old-fashioned and ornate, clearly lacking in updates and a throwback to the last century.

"Hello," Nate called out as they stood in the foyer.

"Just a minute," a kindly voice called from beyond their view. A young couple entered the front door from the porch behind them, then walked past and up the long curved stairwell to the second floor, smiling pleasantly as they passed by. A slightly overweight lady, about five foot tall with curly gray hair, then greeted them as she dried her hands with a dish towel. She smiled pleasantly as she examined them. "How can I help you, gentlemen?"

"We're looking for a place to stay, just a couple of nights."

"Well, I'm afraid we're booked. Lots of folks like to come in for the holidays, and we fill up fast."

"I'm sorry to hear that," Nate responded. "This place looks perfect, right on the lake, close to downtown. Can you recommend any other places that might have a room available?"

"Leah sent us," Zak said before she could respond. "She said the penthouse suite might still be available."

"Oh, the penthouse suite," she said, nodding, containing herself.

She extended her hand to Zak and then to Nate. Her hand seemed to linger longer in his hand as she looked up at him. "I'm Lois Nettles, the owner of this fine establishment, but you can call me Grammy. Everyone does."

"I'm Zak, and this is Nate," Zak introduced. Nate smiled as she released his hand. He took notice of the calming effect she had on him.

"I do have one room available. It's on the third floor. You will have to share it, but there are two beds, a queen and a twin, unless, of course, you are otherwise inclined," she winked. "And the elevator hasn't worked in years, so you'll have to walk up a couple of flights."

"Sounds perfect. We really appreciate it," Nate said agreeably.

"At least you'll have your own private bath up there. You'll have to excuse me for not showing you the room, though. I'm getting on in years, you know, and I don't go all the way up there unless I absolutely have to."

"We totally understand and appreciate renting the room on such short notice," said Zak.

"Can I have the butler help you with your things?" she suddenly asked.

"You have a butler?" Zak said incredulously.

She laughed. "Follow me to my office so I can take your money."

"You want to start bringing in our gear?" Nate asked Zak. "I'll take care of the money since I brought you on this little excursion."

***

The room was on the third floor of the old country home. It was no penthouse suite; in fact, it looked to be an attic space converted long ago into a large bedroom that was seldom occupied. But it was clean and comfortably furnished, and they laughed at its misrepresentation by both Leah and Grammy Nettles.

The queen bed was a four-post bed with a canopy over the top. A second twin bed with a white cane head and foot board was brandished against the opposite wall. The bathroom displayed a new and updated sink and toilet but maintained the original flavor with a large claw-footed tub. A shower curtain wrapped around the tub. Zak found it amusing, while Nate reveled in its simplicity.

"I'm going for a run. How about you?" Nate asked as he put on his running shoes.

Zak lay back on the twin bed, reading messages on his phone. "I think I'll just hang here."

"I'll look for places to eat dinner while I'm on my run, then come back and shower before we go out." Nate walked down the flight of stairs to the second floor. He passed by four doors, two were closed with voices coming from inside, and two were open. He glanced inside and saw one was nicely made up and ready for expected guests. The other looked, by all appearances, to belong to a young girl, reminiscent of Gail's room when they were growing up in Connecticut.

He descended the final steps to the front door but stopped and listened to the sounds of the piano being played in the living room. He peeked inside and spotted a young girl seated on the piano bench with her back to him, reading from a music book and cautiously playing and counting each note. He recognized the song book as one he had as a child. There were

songs about Santa Claus and reindeer and Frosty, which he had learned to play on the piano before taking up the guitar.

He was going to walk away quietly, but she spied him in the mirror over the piano and beckoned to him. "Hi. I'm Molly."

He wasn't one to dismiss such a friendly overture, especially from an impressionable child, so he turned and entered the living room. "Hi, Molly. I'm Nate."

She extended her hand to him, but not as if to shake his. His reflex reaction was to take her hand and kiss the top of it as if in the first meeting between a princess and a suitor. She giggled, delighted at his gallantry, and withdrew her hand.

"I'm delighted to make your acquaintance."

"Do you play?" she asked, turning back to the piano.

"I can play. I'm much better at guitar, though."

"I've always wanted to learn to play guitar. Maybe you could teach me?"

Not to disappoint her after so soon meeting her, Nate relented. "Maybe."

"Will you come down later? I can play the piano, you can play your guitar, and everyone else can sing. We're doing some Christmas songs."

Nate thought for a minute. By others, she probably meant the other guests. He and Zak had no plans for after dinner. Maybe play it by ear and go to a local bar, but they could do that after the sing-along.

"I will try to come down later," he promised. "If you'll excuse me now, though, I have to run."

"Why do you have to run?"

Nate's response was immediate and didn't need any forethought. "I like to. It makes me feel good."

"My mom used to run. She said it calmed her fears. Are you afraid of something?"

"No, I'm not afraid. But I suppose for some people, that's true. Your mom sounds very wise."

"She died when I was six. But I remember she said it."

"I'm sorry about your mom."

"It's OK. She and daddy are with Jesus now."

Nate smiled and nodded. Her father too? He was at a loss as to what to say in response. "Well then, I guess I'll see you later."

"And we can talk more later about what you're afraid of," she concluded.

Nate smiled, turned, and left through the front door. He stood on the front porch for a moment, then went down the sidewalk toward the street before stopping at a huge oak tree at the front of the house. It looked to be a bit of a challenge, but the perfect climbing tree. And there was no better time to climb than now, so he made his way up the tree as far as he could, then settled down on a limb to gather his thoughts.

***

After returning from dinner, they made their way down to the living room, where a small group had gathered. Nate didn't want to disappoint his new friend Molly and brought his guitar. He noticed first the young couple from earlier seated on the couch. An older couple had joined them, too, and occupied two armchairs. Grammy Nettles was busy handing printed music to the participants, including Molly, seated at the piano. The last person to catch Nate's eye was seated next to Molly at the piano, still with her back to the group. When she finally turned, Nate's eyes stayed fixed on her until she returned his gaze and smiled. It was Leah from the cafe earlier that day.

Lois then took charge and spoke as she handed out the music. "Before we sing together, we should get to know a little about each other. So I will start, and then we'll go around the room. I'm Lois Nettles. People around here call me Grammy. I was born and raised here in Geneva on the lake and have been running what used to be this boarding house for almost fifty years now. Now it's a BnB. And I encourage you to add your names to the guest book. We've had guests from around the world stay here, including famous authors, actors, and sports figures. So welcome to all of you."

The older couple next introduced themselves, and Nate only half listened as the introductions continued around the room until it became his turn. "I'm Nathan Woods. Originally from Connecticut, now a student at Cornell. I'm not famous for anything…at least not yet. But I could be someday…I play baseball. So I will sign your guest book and someday may become one of those famous sports people you mentioned. That's it."

He turned his attention away from himself and now to Leah as she spoke. "I'm Leah Matthews, born and raised right here in Geneva by Grammy, who has taught me most of what I know."

"Like what?" Nate blurted his thoughts. All eyes turned on him. "What would you say has been the most important thing you have learned from Grammy?" he clarified.

All eyes now turned back to Leah, who thought for a moment. "She taught me the difference between pride and arrogance."

"What is the difference?" Nate continued their back and forth.

"The difference is humility. It's OK to be proud of one's accomplishments. It's not OK to be arrogant." An uncomfortable silence followed as they all seemed to wait for Nate to respond. Leah finally broke the tension as she continued with her eyes on Nate. He noticed she was smiling still, and he felt it was for his benefit. "I'm studying music at William Smith College here in Geneva, which, as you have probably noticed, is one of the most beautiful areas of the country."

"Hi. I'm Molly, and I'm nine years old, and I live here with Grammy and Aunt Leah. I'm learning to play piano, and Nate has promised to teach me how to play guitar." She was looking directly at Nate, who was only half listening while still looking at Leah. She caught his stare, and he quickly looked away, embarrassed.

"I am proud of my accomplishments, and I don't see myself as arrogant. I didn't mean to come across that way."

Zak elbowed him in the ribs. "Don't dig your hole any deeper, dude."

Grammy now took control of the conversation. "I think we have all learned a bit about each other, and I thank you all for sharing. Now let's celebrate the season with some songs." Leah and Molly turned back to the piano and began playing. The mood lifted considerably as they all began to sing. At one point, they all listened as Leah played and sang a solo rendition of O Holy Night. Nate closed his eyes and listened to the beautiful resonance of her voice. It reminded him of years ago when as a young boy, his mother would insist that the family gather together to celebrate in the days leading up to Christmas. At the time, the children resisted, bemoaning the tradition as banal. But it was a painful memory now, not because of its banality, but because it was a sad reminder of his troubled family and lost childhood.

He recalled hearing once, "What the child needs and doesn't get, he searches for his whole life." He couldn't remember who said it, but he believed it was true. His was a fractured life, broken into little pieces by the tragic events of his stolen youth. A mother's love should flow naturally from her to her children. It's the foundation that provides the strength for a family to endure hardship and loss. When this is missing or lost, we flounder as we search for a means to cope with that loss. We may thirst for a lifetime and never be quenched.

"Nathan...Nathan..." He was awakened from his daydream by Leah's voice from across the room. When she had gotten his attention, she continued. "Do you have a song you'd like to play and sing for us?"

Nate strummed his guitar for a minute as he thought. " I do have a favorite, but it requires participation. You all have to be the drum." Nate began to play the Little Drummer Boy and sang: "Come, they told him..." and the group sang "par-rum-pum-pum-pum" after each line.

When they had finished, Molly applauded, rose from her piano, and approached Nate. She wrapped her arms around his neck and exclaimed, "That's my favorite too!"

Nate was surprised by the sudden show of affection. He caught Leah's gaze and an approving smile from her. This vitiated the melancholy mood that had taken hold of him earlier in the evening.

The celebration concluded with refreshments of cookies and punch, then began to wind down as the group thanked Grammy and excused themselves to their rooms. Soon, all that remained were Zak, Nate, and Leah. Nate remained on the couch, and Zak vacated his seat, having conceded all hope of pursuing any semblance of a relationship with Leah to his best friend. "I'm going to walk into town and top off this celebration with a nightcap...a few nightcaps. If your up for it brother, feel free to join me later."

"Possibly. But don't forget tomorrow we're heading for the slopes and have to get up early," Nate reminded him.

"Aye, aye, mien cap-e-tan," Zak saluted and turned his attention to Leah. "Good night, fair lady," he added before leaving them alone in the room. Leah walked now from the piano to the couch where Zak had been sitting.

"You and Zak are close?"

"Yeah. Friends since we were kids. Now roommates at Cornell. Look, I'm sorry about earlier. It was rude of me."

She smiled. "Don't be silly. The exchange was enlightening. And I think Molly already has a crush on you. You were all that she could talk about at dinner tonight."

Nate nodded. "I do seem to have that effect on people. And that's not arrogance, mind you. It's pride."

"And your humility is beyond reproach, I'm sure."

"Yes, definitely…beyond reproach. Now let's talk about you."

"No, too soon," she scolded. "Besides, I'm transparent. I am what you see, and you have already seen me in my natural surroundings. But tell me, why are you here? What brought you here, and more importantly, why now? It's Christmas. It's time to be with family."

"Wow, that's a lot of questions. It's complicated."

"The questions or the answers? I could ask them more slowly if it helps." It took him a moment before he realized she was not making fun but humoring him.

"I've no family to speak of," he began. It wasn't a lie, really, he thought as he spoke. It was more of a half-truth about a broken family that he'd rather not talk about. "Zak is the closest family I have. We're leaving for Texas in a few days to spend Christmas with his father."

"So tell me more about you, Nathan." This caught his ear. No one called him Nathan but his mother, and it had been years since she even said his name.

"Please, call me Nate." He wanted to avoid formality in favor of a more friendly relationship. His thoughts about what that relationship might entail were precluded by her beautiful smile and her sparkling blue eyes. Physically, she was very similar to Dani in stature. But she had blonde, shoulder-length hair, similar in color and texture to his own, but without the curls. She was not only attractive but better defined as exquisite in appearance and demeanor. If perfection were attainable in the form of a woman, he was in her presence at that moment.

"I prefer to call you Nathan. It's much more nuanced, don't you think?"

Nathan chuckled. "Too big a word?" she teased. "You look more like a Nathan than a Nate. Besides, Nate is much too familiar. I barely know you."

"So our relationship must be a formal one?" he sighed in resignation.

She laughed. "I've known you for less than two hours, and we're already defining our relationship?"

"A man can dream, can't he?" It was his turn to make light of the situation.

She quickly dismissed his assertion. "So, why are you here? I know it's just a stop along the way for you. What drew you to this area?"

"Proximity mostly. Cornell is just a couple of hours from here and on the way to the airport at Syracuse. And the area itself. It reminds me of home. The lake, and the town, are alike in a lot of ways to where I grew up in Connecticut."

"And Cornell? What took you from Connecticut to an ivy league school in such a remote location? There are plenty of ivy league schools in New England to choose from."

"A scholarship. They were the only ones to offer me a full ride."

"Wow. Did you get an all-expense paid trip to Cornell? That is impressive. Maybe you do have cause to be arrogant."

"Proud, not arrogant. I don't flaunt the fact. But I am proud of it."

"You have every right to be. So what are you studying?"

Nate shrugged. "Just the basics. Until I know what direction to take."

"So they offered you a full-ride scholarship without any inkling of your scholastic goals?"

" The word scholarship is a misnomer. Not all scholarships are based on scholastic achievement. In fact, I'm a B student at best."

"Well, I was impressed," she laughed. "Now I'm not so sure."

"Don't underestimate me. I'm very good at what I do."

"I should have known when I first saw you. Collegiate jacket and all. And the way you dress."

"Should I be offended?"

"Well, you certainly don't try to hide anything, now, do you?" It was true. Intended or not, the clothes he wore always complimented his physique, which he took pride in.

"Neither do you," he observed.

"They're comfortable clothes," she defended.

"Uh-huh," he nodded. Tight jeans and sweater, he thought, but enough of that. He wasn't complaining.

"So baseball is your ticket?"

Nate nodded as he sipped from his cup of punch. "I'm good at it. But don't take my word for it. You should come see for yourself."

"I doubt time will allow for it. I've got school, work, all that good stuff that keeps me too busy to drive a few hours to see some baseball game."

"Oof...I'm wounded," he said, holding his hand over his heart. "But I understand. Between school and serving tables at the cafe, I can see how your time is limited."

She laughed. "You have no idea."

"So tell me then. I'm all ears."

"I waitress at the cafe and I manage it."

"I'm impressed. You already manage a business at such a young age. How did that happen?"

She looked away from him for a moment, thinking how much she should disclose and what were the consequences of telling too much. None that she could think of, so she continued. "Full disclosure. On the condition, this discussion goes no further, including your friend Zak."

"My lips are sealed."

"I own the cafe. It was owned by Grammy years ago, and she handed it down to my mother, then to my sister and me. We were supposed to be partners. But my sister passed, and now it's mine, for what it's worth. It's more headache than I need, but I keep it for Grammy's sake. She started it, and I can't finish it until after she is gone."

"That's a noble sacrifice," he said for lack of better words.

"And besides that, you see this place. Grammy still runs it like she did fifty years ago. Not much has changed or been updated. It's falling apart in places we can't even see. But it's hers, and she can't let it go. So I help her wherever and whenever I can."

"I'm sorry, that is a lot on your shoulders."

"Maybe, but there are rewards, you know. Grammy and Molly are all that's left. They are my family, and I'm blessed to have them. But enough about me. What do you plan to do after baseball at Cornell? Is there a career in it?"

"Right now, I'm just focused on playing baseball at Cornell. What I do down the road is totally contingent upon being drafted by the minor leagues and given the opportunity to work my way up to the majors."

"And if it doesn't happen?"

"Failure is not an option. What about you? Once you've completed your studies in music, what will you do after the cafe and this house are not holding you back? And I don't mean to be insensitive about all that."

"It's a fair question. I love music, and I love children. I'll get a teaching degree in music. It's all I'll need. I expect Molly will always be a part of my life. Another thing I've inherited."

"She seems sweet. And very smart."

"She is. To be honest, if it weren't for her, maybe I could have walked away from this all. It would have been hard, but Grammy would have understood. Now with Molly in the picture, it's not an option. Don't get me wrong. I don't blame Molly. In fact, I give her credit for keeping us all together as a family. And family is important." As she stopped speaking, she ascertained a pensive expression on his face. "I guess family is an issue for both of us." They sat in silence for a moment. "It's getting late, and I have to open the cafe in the morning. You should go hang with Zak."

She stood from the couch and looked down at him. Nate returned her look and smiled. "He's a big boy. He can find his way back. I think I'll just head up to bed. We have a big day planned for tomorrow. I enjoyed our talk. Maybe we can do it again before I leave."

"Maybe," she said before disappearing down the darkened hallway.

***

Nate and Zak spent the next day skiing, then prepared to leave for Texas. Nate had looked for Leah while back at the house, just to say goodbye, if nothing else, but their paths never crossed. Before leaving for the airport, they visited the cafe once more for breakfast. They spotted Leah busy behind the counter pouring coffee for the customers seated there.

"She's working the counter," Zak observed. "Want to sit there?" Nate agreed, and they found two empty stools.

"Good morning, guys. Coffee?"

"Sure, two cups. We have a long day of travel ahead of us," Zak responded.

She poured them each a cup. Nate had remained silent, deep in thought about what he should do. "So you're leaving today?" she asked.

"That's the plan." He was expressionless. He wasn't excited about going to Texas. And Connecticut was out of the question. He wished there was some incentive, maybe even encouragement, for him to just stay in Geneva through the holidays. But it was too much to expect too soon, and it was foolhardy for him to even think it.

"Molly will be disappointed." She handed them breakfast menus. "She was hoping you would stay awhile. Seems you promised her some guitar lessons?"

"I think she manipulated me into saying yes. She can be very persuasive." Nate sipped his coffee.

Leah laughed. "And she was hoping you would come to see her sing at the holiday concert. There is this song she really loves. I think it's called 'Walking in the Air.' Story about a snowman, I think."

"I would like to have seen that. Will you tell her I'm sorry I couldn't stay?"

"Sure. Merry Christmas and safe travels."

***

They left the cafe and climbed into their loaded car, heading for the airport. When they arrived, they checked in and made their way to the gate. Nate was quiet as they walked through the terminal. "You're pretty quiet dude. What's going on in that head of yours?"

"Too much. I'm too conflicted to even express how I'm feeling right now."

"The way I see it, you have a choice to make. You can continue to run away from things, or you can choose not to. You can leave this all behind, or you can choose to take a chance on life and stay. The uncertainty shouldn't stop you. I know Todd wasn't always the first to take chances, but he didn't run away from things, either. He ran towards them. You hesitate to take a chance. Maybe you've been running away from things too long and should start running toward them, as your brother did."

The announcement for boarding began, and Nate hesitated as Zak stood to leave. "You're a good man Nate. Do whatever is in your heart."

Zak helped to make Nate's decision now. He just needed a little nudge and encouragement from his friend that what he was thinking wasn't crazy. "Thanks, Zak. You're a good friend." Nate stood and embraced him. "I'll see you back at school then?"

"You bet. I hope your time here is well spent. And you have a great Christmas. Text me!" Nate watched as his friend disappeared down the walkway toward the plane.

CHAPTER 20
THINGS LEFT BEHIND

Nate drove back to the Nettles' B&B and parked on the street in front. It was still early afternoon, so Leah would still be at work. Grammy Nettles would likely be there, working in the kitchen. He crossed the street and walked up the sidewalk toward the house, stopping at the oak tree for a moment before beginning the climb to the top. He was having doubts, and this was a time for him to get his thoughts straight. Was he crazy to cave to these impulses? Was it foolish to think there was more to hold onto here than there really was? But then again, where else was there to go? Maybe Zak was right. It was time to stop running away and start running toward those opportunities.

He heard voices from below on the sidewalk as Grammy Nettles and Molly walked past. Molly suddenly looked up, spotting him in the tree. She laughed and tugged on Grammy's arm. "Look, Grammy," she pointed to Nate, seated on a limb near the top.

"Nathan, is that you? Good heavens, come down from there before you fall and break something," she scolded. Nate climbed down and stood, smiling, before them. She tried to be stern with him, but she couldn't conceal her smile. "How was Texas?" she suddenly asked.

She was sharp and witty. He loved it. "Let me help you carry those" Nate took two bags of groceries from her arms. "I was wondering if the penthouse suite is still available. I'd like to stay a little while longer."

"Payment is required in advance," she quipped, leading them back into the house.

"I knew you'd come back," Molly interjected. She was gleeful as she reached for his hand but was only able to grab two fingers because of the grocery bags.

"How could I resist your charm?" he teased her.

"So, how long will you stay this time, young man?" Grammy asked as she took the bags from him and set them on the kitchen counter.

"A few weeks if you'll allow it. I have to go back to Cornell right after New Year's."

"Then you'll be here for the holidays. Good. Get settled, and I'll collect payment later. Molly, you can help me put away these groceries." Nate nodded and excused himself from the kitchen, passing through the hallway and into the living room. He did a quick survey, estimating the height of the ceiling at about twelve feet. Plenty of space for what he had in mind. First, he would unpack his things, then take Molly on an adventure.

After unpacking, he found Molly in the kitchen making Christmas cookies. "I was wondering if I could borrow Molly for about an hour. I need her assistance."

"Molly, you can go help Nate as soon as we get these cookies into the oven."

They were soon in Nate's car and drove several miles out of town before Nate spotted a sign for a Christmas tree farm. He pointed to the sign as they turned. "I need your help picking out a really nice tree for the living room."

"Grammy has a fake tree," Molly said.

"No way. This year we'll have a real one. It will be a surprise."

"Grammy might not like that."

"Really? How could anyone not like a real tree? I bet she'll love it."

"OK, but I won't take responsibility for it if she doesn't."

"You won't have to, I promise."

"We have lots of decorations in the basement."

"How about a tree stand? You think she has one?"

Molly shrugged. "I don't know everything," she conceded.

"I guess we're a lot alike, you and me. I don't know everything either. Come on, let's find the best tree here." They soon found a Douglas fir that suited them both, full and about eight feet tall. A young man followed them around with a band saw and began cutting the tree. "This one will be nice and fresh and last us a few weeks."

After the tree was cut and the bottom branches trimmed, the assistant wrapped it in netting and helped Nate mount it on the roof of the car. They were soon back at the house, and Nate carried the tree inside without much effort. His days of hauling hay bales had paid off. "Let's sneak down to the basement and see if we can find a tree stand."

Molly was excited first by secretly getting a real tree, then sneaking into the basement with Nate to find the decorations, lights, tree skirt, and finally, a tree stand big enough to handle the trunk of the eight-foot tree. "Where does Grammy usually put the tree?"

"Here," Molly pointed out, and they moved the furniture just enough to make room. As Nate set the tree up, Molly advised him when it was finally straight, and he anchored it securely. Molly then began handing him the strings of lights, which Nate carefully wrapped around the tree from bottom to top. She then handed him an angel to be placed on the top and plugged in the lights of various colors, all twinkling individually. This was how Nate remembered it, not like the lights used today, all white and so commercial in appearance.

"OK, we are ready for the ornaments."

"We have to wait. That's something we all do together." Molly was firm in her conviction. They soon heard Grammy summoning Molly from the kitchen, where a scent of roast beef made its way into the outer rooms. "I'll see you at dinner."

Molly left him there alone until he heard the front door open and observed Leah as she entered. She had a stunned look on her face, staring at the tree, and then as she entered the living room for a closer look, she spotted Nate on the couch. She put her hand to her mouth in surprise.

Finally regaining her composure and seeing the broad smile on Nate's face, she searched for the right words. "My, aren't we full of surprises?"

"Pleasant ones, I hope."

"Well, you know Grammy loves her artificial tree."

"Do you think she'll be OK with an exception this year?"

"I think she will be quite pleased. I take it she knows you're back?"

Nate stood to face her. "Yes. I had to make sure the penthouse suite was still available. I think she's charging me more this time, though." They both laughed. "Listen, I need to go shower and make myself presentable for dinner. Can we sit and talk later?"

"I look forward to it. Especially an explanation as to why you are still here." Nate detected a wink from her before she turned and walked down the hallway. He hadn't really thought about where she disappeared to as she went down that hallway, until now. He had only explored this level of the house as far back as the kitchen. He determined that there must be several bedrooms behind it where Leah and Grammy slept. Someday maybe he would be invited back there to see. But that was a thought for another day. Today he would revel in his immediate situation and surroundings. After all, he had reserved a passage in his mind, taken from his study of Classic Literature and the Italian poet Cesar Pavlise "We don't remember days, only moments." And this was a moment he would never forget.

They sat down to dinner, and the conversation remained light-hearted. Molly was overjoyed that her new friend had decided to stay. Grammy expressed concern that Nate was not going home to be with family but assured him he was welcome to stay, no matter the reason. Secretly, she was more than glad to have him there, particularly for Leah and Molly's sake.

Leah was curious as to why he had decided last minute to stay but would save that discussion for later.

"I believe you have something to show me" Grammy said to him as she stood to unset the table.

"Molly and I can clean up," said Leah. "Why don't you show Grammy what you accomplished today?" she directed to Nate.

"Sure." He stood, and Grammy reached for his arm to lead her into the living room. She stood in stunned silence for a moment, staring at the beautifully lit yet undecorated tree.

She then inhaled deeply and sighed. "I love the smell of a fresh-cut tree. We haven't had one in years. Since Papa passed. The ceilings in here demand a big tree, bigger than I could handle. This one is perfect."

"Molly helped pick it out. I'm glad you like it."

"I do. But I have one request. Better yet, you need to make me a promise. When you leave, the tree has to go too."

"I promise. And I will even clean up any mess it leaves behind."

"You bet you will" She padded his arm, then moved closer to the tree to inhale its scent. She then picked up a box of handmade ornaments. Nate followed her instinctively, expecting a discourse on the source and history of the more elaborate decorations. "Most of these were made by my mother, my sisters, and me. Some of the newer ones were made by Leah, her sister, and her mother. And now, of course, Molly adds a few each year."

"They are beautiful. My mother was artistic and very talented in that way. She made many of the ornaments too. She didn't like store-bought or commercial-looking decorations. She didn't like garland either and made all of us string popcorn for garland. And when it was time to take the tree down, we left the popcorn on for the birds." He didn't often talk about his mother anymore, and this time he found himself speaking of her in the past tense. Yes, she used to do those things, but anyone listening to him now would think that she had died. For all intents and purposes, she was dead and had been for years now. But it was a slow death and not yet final.

"Cookies and punch," Leah announced as she and Molly entered from the foyer, setting the glasses and tray on the coffee table.

"Nate," Grammy started, then stopped. "I'm sorry," and she touched Nate's arm again. "Can I call you Nathan? I so like that name."

Nate looked briefly at Leah, who was anxious to hear his response, knowing that only Nate's mother and now her, Leah, had called him Nathan. "Of course," Nate replied.

They sat, and Grammy began speaking again. "Nathan has agreed to stay with us through the holidays so he can take care of the tree." Leah eyed Nate, suspicious of his true motives. First, the last-minute decision to not leave for Texas as planned. Then, his collusion with Grammy to stay and care for the sizable tree that none of them could handle or remove from the house when the time came. But based on what she had seen and heard so far, she liked him, even felt some attraction to him. However disconcerting it was for him to have inserted himself into their lives so quickly, she felt strangely comforted by his presence.

Other guests had now entered the living room, complimenting them on the tree as well as the hospitality that Grammy had shown them. All the guests were departing the next day, and no new ones were expected until just before New Year's Day.

As Nate listened to the conversation taking place around him, his phone rang, and he excused himself from the room. He stepped out onto the porch and answered. It was Dani. He hadn't spoken to or even received a message from her for over a year. He had mixed feelings about it. While he had thought less and less about her over time, he still wondered how she was. But not hearing from her made it easier to forget and think of her as nothing more than a memory.

"Hello, Nate?" Her voice echoed through his head. Familiar and sweet. He missed it.

"Hi, Dani," he answered.

"How are you?"

"Good. I'm good. How about you? You doing OK?"

"I am. Things are going well."

"And the Cancer? Any signs?"

"No. None."

"That's great." Under different circumstances, in a previous time, he would have exulted in the news. Now it was more of a feeling of relief for him, knowing that she would be OK.

"You must be surprised to hear from me."

He waited. "I didn't expect to hear from you unless you had some news to share, good or bad."

"I was wondering when you would be coming home for the holidays. I want to talk to you."

"So talk. I'm listening."

"I want to talk to you face to face. It's not something I can do over the phone. So are you coming home for Christmas?"

"You know the situation at my home better than anyone."

"You're not going to be alone at Christmas, are you?" She was now expressing concern. Nate didn't respond. "I'm sorry. This must be so hard for you, not coming home for Christmas."

"I've gotten used to the idea. It hasn't been a real home for years. You know that. And I still have my running shoes."

"So you're still running?" To Nate, it sounded more like an accusation than a remedy.

"Yes, I run almost every day."

"Good. I know how much you enjoy it. So it sounds like you don't have any plans to come home soon. When you do come home, I'd like to see you."

"We'll see. Merry Christmas, Dani. I better go now." He could have said much more about where he was and what his plans were, but that wasn't something to share with her now. And it struck him as she said goodbye and wished him a merry Christmas that this could be their last conversation and her voice just a memory.

He returned to the living room, and the guests had retired. Only Molly, Grammy, and Leah remained, and they were busy now hanging the last of the ornaments on the tree.

"Nate, will you come watch me sing tomorrow night?" Molly asked as she scooted next to him on the couch. He looked questioningly at Leah, who explained.

"The Christmas pageant is tomorrow evening at our church. You are welcome to join us. And it's Christmas Eve. Traditionally, we go to church, come back and eat dinner, then watch a Christmas movie. Either the Grinch or Polar Express or The Christmas Story. Molly gets to choose."

Nate had been somber since ending the phone call but managed to smile at Molly. "I'd like that, Molly."

"And since you are our guest, you get to pick the movie," Molly interjected.

Nate nodded, still distracted from the phone conversation. "Those are some hard choices. Let me sleep on that." He then stood from the couch. "If you will all excuse me." He left the room without further explanation, and they listened in silence as he went up the stairs to his room. There he changed into his jogging clothes and put on his running sneakers, then a knit cap. Winter weather had finally arrived, and it was chilly outside, but he warmed up quickly as he ran.

He passed by the living room, and only Leah remained, standing by the tree. She watched him pass by without speaking, and he soon disappeared out the door and into the night. She found herself worrying more than she should about a situation she knew nothing about. She had expressed interest in talking to him more, and the indication had been they would do that tonight. Clearly, since the phone call, he had become preoccupied with other thoughts, and their conversation would have to wait.

***

Nate drove them to and from the pageant on Christmas Eve. The decorations in the church, the Crismon tree, and the music were nostalgic for Nate, even after the years missed due to his mother's illness.

They returned home for dinner, ate dessert by the tree, and settled down for a movie. Nate's selection was not expected but wholly acceptable to Grammy and Leah. And it was one of Molly's favorites.

"It's a classic," he assured Molly. "It's one I grew up with and also one of my favorites." She shrugged and found her position on the couch, reserving Nate's seat next to her as "The Polar Express" began to play.

A few minutes into the movie, Molly was asleep with her head in his lap. "Maybe this was a bad choice?" Nate wondered openly.

"Oh, it was fine," Grammy assured him. "She always falls asleep about now, regardless of what movie we watch. I don't think we've ever made it through an entire movie." She stood and requested Nate's assistance. "And it's nice for a change that we don't have to wake her to get her into bed."

Nate took his cue and lifted Molly, easily carrying her up to her bedroom. Leah followed but stood back at the doorway leading in, observing from a distance. Nate laid her on the bed and pulled the covers securely around her. He was not aware of Leah's presence, just the girl sleeping peacefully now in her bed. He bent down and kissed her forehead. It was something his mother used to do, and it just seemed natural and right. She was so accepting of him and made him feel welcome in her home.

***

Nate was awakened at seven by the slight knocking on his bedroom door. Molly's voice called from outside, beckoning him to hurry downstairs.

"OK, I'll be there as soon as I get dressed," he responded sleepily as he sat at the edge of the bed.

"No time for that. Just come in your pajamas," she yelled before the sound of her footsteps faded down the stairs to the attic.

Nate thought to himself. Pajamas…I don't own a pair of pajamas. Oh well, this will have to do. He quickly picked a clean T-shirt and a pair of sweatpants from his dresser and put them on. He picked up his phone from the nightstand and saw there was a message from Todd, which he quickly read.

"Merry Christmas, little brother. I'm sorry I've been unable to message you until now. I am only in the States for a few days, then re-deploying. Things are really f'd up over there, so I don't know how long I'll be gone this time. I just wanted to tell you before I left again that I got married. It was a quick decision in between deployments, and we didn't want to wait any longer. I would have liked you here, but I know you're busy with school now. Take care of yourself, and good luck with baseball and school. I'll be in touch when I can. I miss our talks."

Nate set the phone down. At least I know he is OK, he thought to himself. But married. To who? That would have to wait until later. For now, they were waiting for him downstairs. He picked up several gift bags from beside his bed, one for Molly, one for Grammy, and one for Leah. His decision to stay was last minute, so he had to improvise the gifts and be creative as best he could.

Molly was seated on the floor, ready to hand out the gifts. Leah and Grammy were seated next to each other on the couch, so Nate took a seat in a nearby armchair. Christmas music played softly in the background as Molly handed the first of the gifts to Leah and Grammy. She then selected one for herself and then handed a gift about the size of a shoe box to Nate.

"Oldest to youngest," Molly announced, and Grammy opened her first gift. Nate was second, just a few months older than Leah, he discovered. Their birthdays had not been a topic of discussion previously. "That one is from me," Molly said as Nate began unwrapping the box. It was a shoe box with the label Nike across the side. "That's not what's in the box," she advised. Nate carefully opened the box to reveal a brightly colored hand-knitted scarf inside. He held it up to examine and for all to see. "I made it" Molly proudly announced. "I hope you like it."

"I can't believe you made this for me. It's beautiful. I think it's one of the best presents I've ever gotten. Thank you, Molly." He smiled broadly as he draped it over his shoulders, letting it hang over the front of his tee shirt.

Nate then handed each of them a gift bag. "I apologize in advance. I didn't have a lot of time to think about what to get everyone."

Grammy opened her bag first, pulling out a beautiful silk scarf. "Thank you, Nathan. It's gorgeous." She then dug deeper and pulled out an envelope with a card and note inside. She read the card and then the note. "My gift to you is to make repairs around your home wherever is needed, for as long as I am here," she read. She laughed. "That is quite a gift, Nathan. Are you sure you're up for the challenge?"

"You'll find I'm rather handy. My father and brother taught me well."

"Well, I will certainly accept your gift, provided you still take time for yourself while you're here. I can put a short list together for you."

Nate nodded, and then it was Leah's turn to open her bag. She, too, first revealed a beautiful silk scarf, which she immediately tied loosely around her neck. "Thank you, Nathan. It's beautiful." She then pulled out an envelope with a card and note inside. She read the card and put it aside. "I'll save the card for later," she said, looking at Nate. Next, she opened the note and read it aloud. "The guarantor of this note promises to provide repair and maintenance services at Nettles Cafe and the silver Volvo" referring to Leah's car. "Thank you, Nathan. That's nice of you. But how are you going to manage to do all of this before you go back to Cornell?"

"Well, that's the thing," he started and wrung his hands together with nervous anticipation of their response. "I was thinking that when school lets out in early June, I would come back here and work for the summer. In exchange, though, you will have to provide me with a room and occasional meal." He then looked up to see their reactions. Leah was smiling, but it was hard to read how receptive she was to the idea.

Grammy seemed more open to it. "I think the penthouse suite is available if you reserve it now. No deposit necessary."

Molly then opened her bag and pulled a book out, reading the title. "Robinson Caruso."

"It was one of my favorite books growing up. I hope you like it."

"Thanks. I'm sure I will." Then she, too, pulled an envelope from the bag and opened it. Inside were two ski lift tickets dated Dec. 30.

"Have you ever skied?" he asked. She shook her head no. "Would you like to learn?"

"Sure," she smiled.

"Good, because we will need to use those next week. Just me and you...if that's OK with Grammy, of course."

"Can we?" Molly asked excitedly, and Grammy responded approvingly.

"There's another gift inside," Nate added. Molly removed a handwritten note promising guitar lessons.

She quickly ran to Nate and hugged him tightly. "Best Christmas ever," she proclaimed.

Nate agreed silently to himself.

**

Nate made good on his promise to do some minor repairs around the house over the next few days, followed by a day of skiing with Molly. Leah surprised Nate with an invitation to go with her to a local pub on New Year's Eve but promised Molly they would first sit on the deck overlooking the lake to watch the fireworks.

As they watched the display over the lake, Nate spoke quietly to Leah. "I don't think I told you. I finally heard from my brother Todd on Christmas."

"How is he?"

"Hard to say. He was home for just a few days, then was being redeployed. Mentioned that he got married."

"I'm not sure what to say about that. You haven't shared much about your brother."

"It was sudden, between deployments, so not planned in advance. I would have liked to have seen him though."

"I can understand that. When do you think you will see him again?"

Nate shook his head. "No idea. He didn't say how long he would be gone."

After the fireworks display, Leah and Nate walked downtown in the cold winter air. It was snowing lightly, adding a clean, fresh cover to the previous snowfall. The sidewalk was slick, and Leah instinctively reached for his arm to balance herself as they walked.

Once inside, they found a table near a small stage where a microphone and stool were set up for open mic night. A server came to their table to take their order. "Just sparkling water for me," Leah responded.

"Stella, please," Nate added. "So, tell me more about you. You're going to school, you own and manage a cafe, you're helping Grammy with the BnB, and then there is Molly. That's a lot."

She nodded. "Is there a question in there?"

"Sure. How do you do it?"

"It hasn't been easy, but I know it won't be forever. Molly is nine and getting more independent every day. Someday I will sell the cafe. As far as the BnB, I may have to sell it, too, eventually. Once I finish school, I want to teach music. I won't be able to manage the BnB and teach too."

"If there is anything more I can do before I head back to school, please let me know."

"You've already done more than we could hope for, and we appreciate it." They listened now as a progression of singers took the stage, singing a variety of familiar country, folk, and pop tunes. "You should have brought your guitar," Leah commented.

"Not this trip. Maybe next time. What about you? Have you ever taken the stage here?"

She shook her head no. "I'm not much of a public performer. You know what they say, 'those who can do, and those who can't, teach'".

"I've heard you sing. You have a beautiful voice."

"Thanks. Maybe next time."

"We've only known each other now for a couple of weeks. Seems longer, doesn't it?" Nate asked.

Leah thought for a minute. "On the surface, yes, but all I really know about you is you go to Cornell, you love baseball, and you have a brother Todd that you don't hear much from anymore. You haven't shared much about your family, growing up in Connecticut, high school girlfriends..."

"I guess both of us will have a lot to talk about when I come back in June," Nate concluded. Although he liked Leah and knew she would be attentive, he wasn't ready to bare his soul in what little time he had left in Geneva. The countdown to midnight began as the noise level in the pub rose. At the stroke of midnight, cheers rang out, and toasts were made. Nate observed other couples around the room, kissing in the new year, but he held back the urge to lean over and kiss her. He was attracted to her, sure, but he still had an empty place for Dani in his heart that hadn't healed. Nate simply raised his glass to her in a toast. "Happy New Year, Leah."

"Happy New Year, Nathan."

CHAPTER 21
MOVING FORWARD

Nate returned to Cornell after completing two more days of repairs at the BnB, reassuring them all that he would be returning in June. Molly was hardest to leave, not wanting to let go of the goodbye embrace until she ran tearfully back into the house. Leah had wished him luck with his upcoming baseball season, and Grammy had handed him a batch of homemade peanut butter cookies, his favorite.

Zak had contacted Nate to pick him up at the airport, which gave them an opportunity to catch up on the drive back to school. Zak's first question was expected. He wanted to know how things went with Leah.

"Good," Nate smiled.

"That's it? That's all you're going to tell me?"

"I like her. She's sweet, she's nice."

"Nice? She's f'ing gorgeous, dude."

"Yeah, she is, isn't she?" They laughed.

"So, are you going to see her again?"

Nate nodded. "I'm going back in June. I promised to do some repairs around the BnB and the Cafe."

"Sly, dude. Do you think she suspects the real reason you're coming back?"

"I sure hope so."

***

Baseball became Nate's focus after returning to school. He had very little free time between baseball and academics to think about the past or maintain connections to it. Late in the evenings, before sleep set in, he lay in his bed and on occasion, would message Leah. Their correspondence remained cordial and friendly, lacking the affinity of any hoped-for relationship between them. Nate had to remind himself that their connection was still new and anything beyond that was a fantasy. He would have to remain patient until the summer when he could switch his priorities and focus more on her.

From the beginning through the end of the season, Nate found himself in his element, accomplishing all that he had hoped for that might lead him to a career playing the sport he loved. Scouts from the major leagues were frequent guests at their games as they searched for candidates to fill their minor league field teams, where their young recruits would have to prove themselves in order to fulfill their dreams of playing in the majors. Some of the scouts had become so familiar to Nate, even as a freshman, that he knew their names and which teams they recruited for. And rumors were that he was on their "watch list" with star potential. He determined that he would be patient and not seize the first opportunity that came along. He would consider any and all opportunities to pursue his dream.

The team performed well, placing third in the league that year. Jake, who was part of the pitching rotation, was approached by several scouts with opportunities to leave school early to enter the minors, but Jake declined. He reminded Nate and Zak that he needed one more year to graduate and be true to himself, affording him with a backup plan should his career as a pitcher in the majors not pan out. While Nate was happy for him and understood Jake's decision, he felt more confident in his own ability to achieve his goal and not worry about the risks.

While Nate, Jake, and Tom were assured of their starting positions the following year, Zak was not. He was unusually quiet as they each prepared to leave for the summer while discussing their status with the team and their future in the sport. As a sophomore, he still spent most of the season on the bench, pinch-hitting on occasion, but still hopeful that he would have a much bigger role to play during their junior year. His catcher position was currently held by a graduating senior, which would open up the spot. He had to be patient for now, but he was at a clear disadvantage, being out of view of the scouts who frequented the games.

"Next season should be a good one with all of us in starting positions," Nate reassured him as he drove Zak to the airport for his flight home.

"I'm not guaranteed a place on the team," Zak countered.

"What will you be doing this summer? You could come with me to Geneva," Nate offered. He hated to see Zak in his melancholy frame of mind.

Zak shook his head no. He would see himself as a third wheel and out of place there. "I'll work at my dad's company and focus on weight training in my free time. I need to build bulk if I'm going to make it to the minors. I don't have the advantage of size that you and the other guys have."

Nate nodded. "I get it." He was actually relieved that Zak would not be accompanying him to Geneva. He preferred to be away from not just Zak, but all the guys, for the summer. And he could spend whatever free time he had with Leah.

Nate's first stop in Geneva was the cafe. He entered unobserved and took a table by himself in a booth toward the back. He watched as the servers scurried about the cafe, taking and delivering orders to the lunch crowd. He spotted Leah as she carried several dishes from the kitchen to a nearby table.

An unfamiliar server approached Nate's table to take his order. "What would you like to drink?" she asked politely.

"Just ice water, please. And could you tell Leah that Nathan is here?"

"Sure," she smiled as she moved on to the next table.

***

"Hi, Nathan," Leah greeted as she set his water on the table. "How have you been?"

She looks more beautiful than ever, he thought to himself. "I'm great. How about you?"

"Busy as always, but doing fine. Have you checked in at the BnB yet? Molly has been excited for weeks already. And Grammy will be happy to see you too."

And you? He thought to himself. What about you, Leah?

"And I've got a wish list of things I'd like done here. My Christmas present from you, if you recall," she added with a smile.

"Of course," Nate responded, wishing she had given him at least a hint of showing interest in him in more than a business relationship. "I'll get to work on your list tomorrow."

While Grammy and Molly were openly affectionate toward Nate over the next few weeks, Leah continued to keep their relationship cordial and friendly. He saw her daily at the cafe, completing most of the repairs she had on her wish list. By evenings, they were both tired and did little else other than sit in the gazebo on the lake engaged in idle chit-chat. On occasion, Nate would walk to the end of the pier and dive into the cool waters of Seneca Lake.

One evening, as he climbed up the ladder onto the pier, Leah was sitting there waiting for him. She threw him his towel and began to speak. "If you're not busy Saturday, I'd like to show you something."

"I'm intrigued," he smiled, looking down at her as he dried himself.

She patted the spot next to her, inviting him to sit, and he immediately obliged. "We haven't had much time to talk since you came back. I'm sorry

I've kept you so busy."

"That's OK. I'll only be here a couple more weeks, and then I'll have to get back to school early for training."

"You've already completed a lot of the repairs, much more than I even hoped for. And you were right. Your father and brother did teach you well."

"Tomorrow, I'll take a look at your Volvo. If you plan on keeping it another year, it's going to need some maintenance done."

"I'd like to keep it running through the end of school, but it may not last that long, I'm afraid."

"I'll check everything out tomorrow and see what it needs."

"I kept watch of the newspaper and Cornell baseball. It looks like you had a good season."

He nodded and thought to himself that's encouraging. "It could have been better, but we did OK. I think we'll be better next year."

They sat in silence for a while, watching the boats on the lake, before Leah spoke again. "Can you tell me about your family? You know mine, but I know nothing of yours."

"Well, I don't really know where to start."

"Start at the beginning."

"There's not enough hours in a day to tell you everything about my family."

"Then just the highlights. I met Zak, so start with him."

"He's not family per se. But he has been like a brother to me. He was my first and best friend until his family moved away. We kept in touch, though, both committed to playing baseball at Cornell. That's when we reconnected."

"He seems like a nice guy. It's good to have a best friend who you can talk with and depend on."

"Yeah, he is a good guy. But I worry about him. He sat on the bench most of the season, and who knows what will happen next year."

"Why would he be benched? He had to be good to make the team, didn't he?"

"Sure. He has the skills, no doubt. But he doesn't have the size." Nate did not elaborate.

"And your family?"

"I've mentioned Todd to you before. Todd is three years older than me. Practically raised me until he turned nineteen and joined the Marines."

"What about your parents?"

Nate was reluctant to talk about them. Maybe someday. "Let's save that discussion for another time."

"OK. Any other brothers and sisters?"

"I have a sister, Gail. She is a year older than me."

"Are you two close?"

Nate chuckled. "No." Leah waited a moment for him to continue, but Nate remained elusive.

"So, just the three of you?" she continued.

Nate thought for a bit, deciding just how much he should say. "I had another brother, Billy. Billy was two years older than me." Nate took a deep breath before continuing. Talking about his brother had been very difficult for him in the beginning, and the years seemed to have lessened the pain, but he still had difficulty sometimes controlling his emotions. "He died when he was sixteen." Nate felt no need to elaborate now.

"I'm sorry, Nathan. That must have been hard for you and your family."

"We've had our share of tragedy," he admitted. "Over the years, I've determined that when tragedy strikes a family like that, things change. They can never be the same, and there are only two directions it can take. Pull together or fall apart. Unfortunately, mine did the latter."

"But it sounds like you and Todd remained steady. It sounds like he took the place of your parents, a lot like Molly and me."

"Some of those memories are still hard to talk about. Maybe we can talk more about them some other time. I am looking forward to Saturday, though, and whatever surprise you have in store for me."

"I am too." They bid each other goodnight and retired for the evening.

***

Nathan found Leah already outside on Saturday morning, loading a small trunk into the back of her Volvo wagon. "Good morning," she greeted him as she closed the tail lid.

"Good morning," he responded, taking a quick drink from his coffee cup. "What's in the trunk?"

"You'll see. I figured we could take my car this morning. We'll give it a test run and see how well you did on the repairs."

"There wasn't anything major to fix. I put new brake pads on and changed a couple of filters and the oil. Everything else looks fine."

"Thanks, Nathan. Are you ready now for our adventure?"

"I feel like a little kid again," he laughed. "Let's do it." Nate began walking toward the driver's door, but she nudged him away.

"Uh-uh. I'll drive," she insisted. He wasn't often a passenger ever since he got his license and preferred to drive, but he didn't insist as he climbed into the passenger seat.

"So, how far a drive is it?"

"About twenty minutes," she said, starting up the car and backing out of the drive.

As they drove, Nate decided it was his turn to ask questions of her, although he wasn't sure how receptive she would be to his questions. "So, tell me more about your family," he began.

"Not a lot to tell, really. There's just me, Grammy, and Molly."

He waited, but she didn't elaborate. "You mentioned a sister, Molly's mother. Any other siblings?"

"No, just the two of us."

"And your parents? Are they deceased?"

"My mother died a few years ago. That's when Grammy took me in."

"And your father?" She didn't respond immediately, and Nate sensed some reluctance on her part. "We don't have to talk about him if…"

"It's OK. I don't know much about him. He left when I was just a toddler. Not even sure where he is now."

"And you haven't seen nor heard from him since he left?"

She shook her head no as she turned onto a gravel road from the main route. They had been driving about twenty minutes into the countryside and were passing by fenced-in pastures. Up ahead, Nate could see a large farmhouse, a red barn, and some outbuildings. The pastures contained run-ins similar to the ones at the Elliott's farm, where he had learned to ride. They soon turned off the gravel road and onto a narrow dirt drive that led up to the house and barn.

"Here we are," she announced, parking the car. Nate observed several horses in the pasture feeding on grass. He was flooded with memories of days spent at the Elliott's, whether it be riding or baling hay. Then he was reminded of Todd and, of course, Billy and the accident. Leah was opening her door and climbing out when she noticed he wasn't moving. "Are you coming?"

Nate was aroused from his daydream and climbed out as well, following her up toward the barn in silence. He was taking in the surroundings when Leah got his attention once more. "Let me introduce you to the rest of my family," Leah said as they walked down the hallway past several stalls. She was first greeted by a chestnut mare who nudged the gate and stuck her head out over the stall door. "This is Sheba," she petted the horse's soft nose gently.

"You own her?' Nate put his hand up slowly to the horse, gently rubbing her head between her ears.

"I do."

"She's beautiful. Friendly too. A quarter horse," he observed.

Leah was surprised by his comment. "You know horses?"

Nate nodded. " I've known a few."

"Have you ridden?"

"Uh-huh," he nodded.

"Nathan, you continue to amaze me. Is there anything that you haven't done?" Nathan just smiled, continuing to scratch between Sheba's ears.

"Well then, let me introduce you to Sheba's brother here in the next stall." She led him further down the hallway, and another horse, a gelding this time, greeted her through the stall door. "This is Toby," Nate observed that Toby was slightly taller and trimmer than Sheba.

"A brother to Sheba? He looks more like a Morgan," Nate observed.

Leah raised her eyebrows in response. "Now I'm really impressed."

"I grew up next door to a horse farm. I spent a lot of time there, learning to ride and working on the farm. They had Quarter horses, an Arabian, some Saddlebreds, and someone was boarding a Morgan there." Thoughts of Billy came back to him, but he pushed them aside for now. "How do you find time for all this stuff?" he asked.

"Unfortunately, I don't. I haven't been here for a couple of months. It's hard to justify even hanging onto them. As much as I love them, the board has gotten too expensive, and I won't be able to afford them much longer. But that's a problem for another day. How about we go for a trail ride?"

" I haven't ridden in a while, but I guess it's like riding a bike, right? Once you learn."

"Here's a lead line. Bring Toby out, and we can saddle him up." Nate slowly entered the stall and introduced himself to Toby, gently rubbing his face and scratching between his ears. Toby was calm and responsive to his touch, so he attached the lead line and brought him out into the hallway, secured and then brushed him. Leah had already brought Sheba out and was brushing her before putting on the pad and saddle. After saddling Sheba, she checked on Nate's progress. He had already found Toby's bit and put it in his mouth without resistance and was tightening the girth of the saddle.

"I can tell you've done this before. Do you have a preference on which one to ride?"

"Toby and I are buddies already. I think we'll do fine together. I wish though that you had told me we were coming here today."

"Why is that?"

Nate put his left foot in the stirrup and climbed up on Toby. "I would have worn my cowboy boots and hat." He then prodded Toby forward and walked from the barn.

Leah led them around the edge of the property at a walk at first, then trotted with Nate close behind. She then led them into the woods onto a trail that led for several miles in a circle around the outskirts of the property. "Try and keep up," Nate said as he nudged Toby into a gallop and passed Leah. They continued their rapid return to the barn, where they put their horses back in the stalls, removing their saddles and bits.

They were soon greeted by the owner, who introduced herself as Natalie Strange, a woman in her mid-forties, Nate guessed. She was dressed in jeans, a flannel shirt, and work boots and was clearly a worker bee as well as an owner.

"I got us here; now you can take us home," Leah said, handing Nate the car keys. She then went to the passenger side and climbed in.

Nate was watching the owner enter the barn, then spoke to Leah. "I forgot something. I'll be right back." Before Leah could speak, he trotted off to the barn and disappeared inside.

"Ms. Strange," he called out to her and found her in her office. "How much is board for the two horses?"

"Usually, it's $300 a month for each horse, but since there are two, it's $500 total."

"If you would, send me a bill when board is due and I'll set it up for regular payments each month. Here is my address" he quickly wrote it down.

She agreed and took the information from him before he returned to the car. Leah was waiting with an inquiring look which he shrugged off. "Had to pee," he said, starting the vehicle and heading out the drive toward town.

As they arrived back at the BnB, Nate decided it was time to take a chance with Leah. They hadn't had much time together, just the two of them, during his stay, and certainly not any intimate moments which he found himself yearning for. He touched her arm before she could exit the car. "Thank you for this nice surprise today. It was fun."

"You're welcome. It did turn out a lot better than I expected. I saw myself leading you around the riding ring with a lead line." she laughed.

Nate laughed with her, then sprung it on her. "Would you go out with me tonight?" There was a momentary silence, and he worried she might flat-out reject his proposition.

When she finally spoke, he had to contain his excitement. "OK. Where to?"

"My turn for a surprise." He then exited the car.

***

He met her in the foyer with a guitar case in hand. She smiled broadly, now aware of their destination. "Will you be showing me another of your talents?"

"I'll let you be the judge of my talent. I like your outfit, by the way," he said, noticing the tight jeans and sweater that accentuated her figure.

"That's my talent," she flirted.

"Hm..."

It was open mike night again at the pub, and Nate had reserved himself a time slot to sing. They sat near the stage, watching various performers while drinking margaritas and waiting for Nate's turn to take the stage. He found himself nervous with anticipation, not to be on stage, but to be singing a song he had selected specifically for her.

He positioned himself comfortably on the stool in front of the mike, and with guitar in hand, he spoke to the packed audience of the pub. He hadn't realized until that moment just how many people were there and how quiet it had become. "This song is for someone special," he said, looking in Leah's direction. "The name of the song is 'Winter' because that's when we first met. He then began strumming the guitar and singing one of his favorite tunes, occasionally looking down at Leah in the crowd. She sat still, listening and watching him, with her hands folded as if in prayer, in front of her chin.

The crowd applauded politely as Nate finished his song and left the stage, rejoining Leah at the table. "You have proven yourself once more," she commented, patting his arm. Nate examined her expression, hoping for some hint of how she felt. Would his overture be welcomed? He couldn't read her. They sat through several more performers and decided it was time to go. It was after midnight when they entered quietly through the front door of the house. During the walk home, she slipped her hand into his and continued holding it as they entered the foyer. Nate was acutely aware of this gesture and posturing. As she looked up at him, he embraced her, then leaned down and kissed her for the first time. She was receptive to this, and they lingered for a time in that position. Nate was unsure how far to pursue this first intimate contact between them until she broke free from him. She then took his hand and silently led him up the two flights of stairs to his room.

Few words passed between them during their moments of passion. After, he simply lay back, deep in thought, with her head resting on his chest. He pondered whether this was all just a momentary reaction to the sentiments of the evening or whether she truly had affection for him. He had waited with anticipation for this moment since first meeting her, and it exceeded all his expectations. He gazed down at her half-exposed body as she lay quietly in the candlelit room. He felt her soft breaths across his chest, and then she stirred slightly before moving her hand down his body. He soon found himself aroused once more, and she opened herself again to him.

***

After, he slept restlessly. He found himself standing outside the Elliott's horse barn, staring down the long alleyway. Behind him, he could see Todd in the field. He waved to him, but Todd didn't respond. He turned back toward the barn when he heard some commotion and then entered. He heard a faint sobbing sound which became louder as he hurried down what seemed to be an endless hall, passing by stalls as he went. The sound became louder and louder and turned into a wailing sound. He stopped and looked inside the stall where his mother was seated on the floor, holding Billy's limp, blood-splattered body, across her lap. She was rocking him back and forth, holding him and pleading for him to "wake up...wake up...." but to no avail.

Nate thrashed about the bed and was perspiring as he called out Billy's name. He then heard Leah's voice and was aroused from his dream. "Wake up, Nathan...wake up," Leah pleaded. He was fully awake now, realizing it was but a dream...a bad dream. She touched his cheek and spoke softly to him. "You were dreaming. It was about your brother?"

"Hm...." was all that he could muster in response.

RUNNING SHOES

***

Nate awoke later to discover that she had left his bed. It was nearly nine now, and he had slept soundly the rest of the night. While he would have liked to have her there now as he awoke, he understood her reluctance to do so with Molly and Grammy in the house. He only hoped that this was not just a one-time dalliance.

He thought now of the dream during the night. He surmised it was a result of yesterday's adventure and returning to something that Billy loved that ultimately ended his life. And, of course, his mother, who spent her moments and days since in anguish, having lost her favorite son. And Todd, whom he could see clearly, but had lost touch with.

He went from the bed and showered, then dressed and descended the stairs, making his way to the dining room where Grammy and Leah were speaking in a soft voice.

"Good morning, Nathan," Grammy spoke first. "Would you like some coffee?" He scanned Grammy's face, then Leah's, for any sign that they had been discussing him or what had transpired in the night.

"Yes, coffee would be great."

"Did you sleep well?" Leah asked, sensing his need for reassurance that nothing had been said.

"I did, thanks. In fact, I just woke up. Riding yesterday made me more tired than I realized."

Grammy excused herself, leaving them alone to talk. "You know we can't say anything about this," Leah warned.

"You think Grammy would be upset?"

Leah chuckled. "No, Grammy is quite liberated. But Molly would be devastated!"

"Well, I guess it's good I'm leaving for Cornell today. It would be difficult hiding my affection for you from Molly."

"I don't like keeping secrets, but in this case, I think it's best for the time being."

Nate nodded but stopped and gave her a quick kiss on the lips before heading up to his room to pack.

***

When Nate arrived that afternoon at the dorm suite, there was a message from Zak to meet him at the gym. Nate changed, put on his running shoes and jogged to the gym where he found Zak lifting free weights in the weight room. He observed him from a distance before approaching. Zak was dressed in a muscle shirt. He had said he was going to focus on bulking up over the summer, but was it possible to bulk up that quickly?

"Hey Zak" he greeted, taking the lifting bench next to him. "How was your summer?"

"Nate, good to see you." He extended his fist for a fist bump. "As you can see..." Zak continued as he lay back down for another set, " I've been working out some."

"Pretty good results," Nate responded. He decided it best not to ask questions; just let him disclose whatever he chose.

"Yeah, I hired a trainer at the gym. Really put me through the mill every day. Sometimes twice. That and lots of protein. Gained over 20 pounds in just two months."

"It shows."

"What about you? How is life in Geneva?"

"Good. Kept busy doing a lot of maintenance and repairs on the house, the cafe, and Leah's car."

"And Leah? How is she?"

"Busy too between the cafe, Molly, and helping Grammy with the BnB."

"Hm...doesn't sound like there was much free time for the two of you."

"We had a few evenings and Saturdays free."

"Uh-huh." Zak's tone had changed, and was becoming more insistent on sharing details.

"We enjoyed each others' company. Nothing serious. We didn't want to upset Molly. She has a terrible crush on me. So we kept it on the DL."

"So you're telling me that you and Leah didn't...you know...do it?"

Nate remained silent. He had never disrespected any of his female partners by divulging intimate details of their relationships. And it was not like Zak to ask such personal questions. They had always respected each other's boundaries. They were discreet, not like many of the guys they knew who sought out one-night stands and kept scorecards. "So I met this really hot babe at the gym down there. She was really into some kinky stuff," Zak continued since Nate had remained silent about Leah.

"Sounds like you benefited from those workouts in more ways than one."

Zak sat up on the bench now and wiped the sweat from his brow. His mood had suddenly changed. "You know, you really got it easy, Nate." Zak looked sternly at Nate with what he detected as animosity.

"How's that, Zak?"

"Look at you. I have to work hard for this. With you, it just comes naturally. Just like with women. Whenever we go out, who do they flock to? But I'm tired of being your wingman."

The direction of their conversation was upsetting Nate. This was clearly not the Zak he knew, and things had changed in just the two months he was in Texas.

Nate hung his head, not wanting to provoke Zak, but at the same time, not giving into his self-pity. "I've worked for this my whole life," Nate finally spoke. "And I never asked you to be my wingman." Nate thought it best to end the conversation before it became adversarial. "I think I'm going to head on back to the apartment. I have some unpacking to do."

"Yeah, whatever," Zak called after him as Nate walked away. Once outside, Nate began to sprint with no particular destination in mind. He just needed to clear his head of what had just occurred between him and Zak. He knew it must be frustrating for Zak; he did have to work harder. He wasn't wrong about that. But it seemed he needed to place blame somewhere, and it just happened to be on him. He felt sorry for Zak, and he would do his best to be supportive of him, whatever he was going through. He wasn't going to let this affect their lifelong friendship.

When he entered the suite, Jake and Tom were watching a football game in the living room. "How was your summer?" Jake greeted.

"Great, how about yours?"

"It was good. Jeannie and I got engaged."

"Congratulations" Nate extended his hand for a congratulatory handshake.

"Tom here is going to be my best man," Jake continued. "And I was wondering, if you're not too busy right after graduation if you would be a groomsman?"

"I'd be honored, Jake. Thanks for asking me. Say, have you seen Zak since he got back?"

"He was here earlier; he said he was going to the gym."

"Yeah, I saw him there. What'd you think?"

Jake looked at Tom and nodded. It appeared to Nate that maybe they had already discussed something about Zak and were agreeing to talk to Nate freely about it. "That's a lot of bulk to put on in just two months' time." This time it was Tom doing the talking. Jake nodded in agreement.

Nate was hesitant to even say it but finally relented. "You think he's using steroids?"

"Well, unless he's having a late growth spurt, which is highly unlikely at 21." Tom scoffed.

"What do we do?" Nate was worried about his best friend and would do anything for him.

"Nate," Jake began, "There isn't anything we can do. Chances are, he is going to get caught. Coach isn't stupid, and he won't risk it with the NCAA."

"There has got to be something we can do."

"If you involve yourself in this, Nate, you risk your own chances of getting into the minors," Tom warned.

"What about if we confront him, like an intervention?" Nate suggested.

Jake was the realistic and rational one. He was not optimistic. "I think you're just going to piss him off. You've probably already noticed a change in him. He's aggressive and moody. He'll just deny everything. He has to want to fix this himself. Right now, he's on too much of a high to see anything wrong with it. He's seen what these drugs can do for him, and he likes what he sees."

"Then all I can do is try to talk to him myself," Nate concluded. "We've been best friends for years. Maybe he'll listen to me."

"That's your decision, Nate. But don't be surprised if it only drives you further apart...maybe even end your friendship. I've seen guys go through this before. It doesn't usually end well."

Nate was determined to get through to Zak that what he was doing was dangerous. The opportunity to talk to him came sooner than he expected. Nate was in the bathroom, brushing his teeth, when Zak entered to take a shower. Nate watched him in the mirror as Zak removed his shirt with his back to him. "Hey," Nate said casually, while noticing the crop of acne across Zak's shoulders.

"Hey," Zak responded. He then saw his back in the mirror and Nate watching him. He turned toward Nate to hide his back.

Nate seized the opportunity. "What's happening back there? You going through puberty again?" He forced a smile, attempting to keep the conversation light.

"Don't pretend you don't know." While Zak was on a high earlier, his mood had changed now. Not as upbeat or confident.

"You don't need me to tell you the risks then? I mean, you've thought about what they do to you physically, the good and the bad."

"It's a risk I'm willing to take. I'd be lucky to make the starting team this spring, let alone have a chance of getting into the draft without some help."

"And the health risks?"

Zak laughed. "Look at me, Nate!" He flexed arm muscles, pumped his chest, and punched his hardened abdomen. "I'm starting to look like you!" Nate didn't respond. He wasn't sure what to say now. "Look, buddy, lighten up. Like I said before, you've had it easy. All this comes naturally to you. I have to work harder to get there. I'm almost there now. Once I reach my goal and make the starting team, I'll quit the steroids. I'll just maintain then."

"Zak, I don't think it's something you can just quit. There are side effects. And what about the coach? You think he's not going to suspect anything?"

"What's to suspect? I got the steroids legally. They were prescribed by a physician."

"What? Did you get a physician to prescribe you steroids? Why would a legit doctor..." Nate stopped and stared at his friend.

"All I know is that he's a licensed physician, and he prescribed meds to 'adjust my hormone levels.' That's all I need to know, and I don't ask questions. Now if you'll excuse me, I'm going to jump in the shower."

CHAPTER 22
REVELATIONS

Nate returned to Geneva for the Christmas holidays to spend it with Leah, Molly, and Grammy. He needed the respite from school, baseball, and, more specifically, Zak. Their last conversation had not gone well, and Nate found he was distancing himself from him. But it was not purposeful. Zak was pushing him away with his change in behavior, and Nate would not condone his steroid usage, no matter Zak's justification. He looked forward to seeing Leah again and forgetting, at least temporarily, his conflict with Zak.

Nate was greeted in the BnB foyer by Molly, who was excited about his return. "I got your room all ready for you," she announced proudly, wrestling the suitcase from his grip.

"Hugs first," Nate responded and reached out to her. She wrapped her arms around his waste without hesitating, and he reciprocated her embrace.

"Leah is in the kitchen with Grammy. I'll take your suitcase upstairs for you." She took it with two hands and moved awkwardly up the first flight of stairs.

"You don't have to do that," Nate laughed, calling after her, but she was soon out of sight down the hallway. Nate removed his coat and hung it on the coat rack, then walked to the kitchen. Leah and Grammy were busy packaging cookies in tins for distribution to the church. "Good afternoon, ladies," Nate announced himself.

Leah wiped her hands on her apron and turned to him, smiling. "Hey, stranger." Nate hesitated to embrace her, unsure if Grammy knew of the depth of his relationship with Leah. Leah surprised him by initiating their embrace but did not offer an opportunity for him to kiss her when she quickly separated from him and returned to Grammy's side.

Grammy spoke next. "It's good to see you, Nathan. How have you been?" she asked cordially.

"I'm great. And you?"

"We're busy as usual but good."

"Well, I can see how busy you are, so I'll get myself settled upstairs and see you all for dinner." Nate dismissed himself and made his way up to his room. It wasn't quite the reunion with Leah he had hoped for, but it would have to do until he could spend some alone time with her.

After dinner, the four of them sat in the living room, engaged in idle conversation until it was time for Molly to retire. "Will you take me to get the tree like last year?" Molly asked Nate before leaving the room.

"Absolutely," Nate said. "Another tree, just like last year's."

Grammy bid Nate and Leah goodnight before dismissing herself for the night as well, leaving them alone finally. Nate re-positioned himself next to Leah on the couch. "I've missed you."

"I missed you too.'

He leaned in and kissed her, and she then rested her head on his shoulder. "How is the situation with Zak?" she finally asked. Nate had messaged Leah shortly after his confrontation with him, sharing what had transpired.

"I'm worried about him. He is oblivious to the side effects. Thinks he can just quit anytime with no consequences."

"Why is he doing steroids?"

"He's worried he won't be a starter in the spring unless he bulks up and becomes a power hitter. He's got the skills. He's just never had the size. And if he stands any chance of getting drafted by a minor league team, well, he has to be a starter at Cornell."

"What about you? Are you worried about a starting position?"

Nate looked at her, puzzled by the question. "Of course not."

She nodded. "That tells me a lot about Zak, then."

"What do you mean?"

"It's simple, really. You are confident you'll make it. You've probably always had that confidence. As Zak said, it comes easy for you, and he has to work for it. He may have the skills, but he doesn't have your confidence and thinks the only way he can achieve his goals is by doing what he's doing."

"But why the attitude? Why's he being such an ass toward me? What did I ever do to deserve that?"

"You didn't have to do anything. This is a result of the effects of the drugs. You know all this, Nate. I shouldn't have to tell you the effects steroids can have on you."

"I guess I thought our friendship ran deeper than this, and I was looking for an easy solution, but obviously, there isn't one." He thought for a minute before continuing. "He says he'll quit once he makes the starting team. But I'm not optimistic. He can't just quit."

"What are you going to do, Nate, if he doesn't quit?"

"All I can do is be supportive, try to be patient, and still be his friend. Maybe someday this will all pass." They sat for a while in silence. "Will you come upstairs with me?" Nate suddenly asked, hopeful she would stay with him the night.

"I'd like to, Nathan, but I can't. Molly is too impressionable, and she is very aware. She started asking me questions about sex. And about you."

"Not in the same sentence, I hope!"

"No. But she is curious about sex. And she obviously likes you. Not in a sexual way, but if she suspects you and I are in a sexual relationship, it wouldn't be good. She is too young to understand what it all means."

"How about if we, just you and me, take a trip? Right after Christmas. We could go to my lake house. It's about five hours, so we could stay a couple of nights."

"Won't your family be there?"

"No, not likely. And it will give me an opportunity to explain some things about my family. Probably overdue."

"I don't know, Nathan. Grammy's getting too old to run this place and be responsible for Molly too. It's just not a good idea right now." She saw the disappointment on his face but tried to reassure him. "I'm sorry, Nathan. We just have to be patient." He nodded and understood but was disappointed non-the-less. "On another note, Nathan, I tried to pay the board at the stable a few weeks ago. She wouldn't take my check. Said it had been taken care of. You wouldn't know anything about that, would you?"

Nate smiled. "Possibly."

"Oh, Nate. I can't let you do that."

"Consider it an early Christmas present. I enjoyed that day more than you know. It brought back some happy memories of home. There aren't a lot of those, you know. And it's the memories that stay with us. Not the days. I want to make sure there are more opportunities like that. Besides, I worked hard for my scholarship, and all my college savings are just sitting there unused. So I decided to spend some of that money on something and someone special to me."

"I guess if you put it that way. Thank you, Nathan. It's very generous of you. It's just that...I don't know how to say this..."

"Then don't say it. You don't owe me anything. And there are no strings attached. Whatever becomes of us isn't tied to this gift. This is a gift for me too. So let's say we take a ride to the stables tomorrow and see how Toby and Sheba are doing."

***

His time there so far had not been as he had hoped, until the moment she entered his room in the middle of the night. He had been sleeping lightly but awoke immediately and watched her shadowy figure make its way carefully across the floor to the bedside. He could see her clearly now in the moonlight that shone through the window as she let her nightgown fall to the floor, revealing herself to him. She pulled the covers back slightly, just enough to climb into the bed and lay down with her back to him. He immediately wrapped his arm over her and pulled himself close to her, making full contact with her body. They didn't speak but communicated nonetheless with their touch, being intimate in the ways that lovers do. It was not frantic like their first encounter. It was gentle and slow, both taking time to experience every sense, physical and emotional, and both being attentive to the pleasure of the other, measured by their breathing and bodily response to their touches.

When they had finally exhausted themselves, they lay back; she was by his side with her head resting on his chest. He with his arm wrapped around her, holding her securely to him. He spoke to her in a whisper. His words surprised both of them. "Thank you...for loving me." It was puzzling to her, but to him, it was clear. He hadn't felt love for a long time. She probably wouldn't understand that without some kind of explanation. So he began to talk, and she listened attentively.

He began with Zak and their friendship that started at such a young age and how devastated he was when Zak moved away. He recalled then, vividly, how he had reacted and how his mother tried to comfort him with his head in her lap as he cried. And that was the last time she had reached out to him and showed him a mother's love. Next, he described the beginning of the end for their family. His mother's accident killed a five-year-old boy. Then Billy's sudden death and how he had always been her favorite, which in itself wasn't such a bad thing, but when she lost Billy, she somehow lost the ability to express love for any of them. From there, it was a downward spiral. She went from a vivacious, loving mother and wife to a drug-dependent recluse with no semblance of a life.

"The last time I saw her was the day I left for Cornell. She wouldn't leave her room to say goodbye or to, wish me luck, or tell me she was proud of me or that she loved me. So I went to her room. I told her I was leaving now. She didn't respond. She wouldn't even look at me. She just lay there in her shell, like I didn't even exist."

"I'm so sorry, Nathan."

"My father gave up on her. I get it. He couldn't fix her. What I don't understand, though is how he could give up on us too. Sure, he made sure his children had everything they needed, except for the most important thing."

He didn't have to explain; Leah understood. "What a child needs and doesn't get, he searches for his whole life," she suggested.

"I guess I'm scarred for life then," he sighed.

"It takes a lot of strength to get through the things you've had to deal with. And I haven't seen you dwell on those difficult times. You have an amazing strength of character and, I think, an ability to love in spite of what was lost to you."

"Maybe. But I think the real test of my character still awaits me."

"Why is that?"

"I have some big decisions ahead of me when I get back to school. And I have no idea what direction I should take."

"You don't have to make any big decisions tonight," she said playfully, kissing and pulling him closer to her.

***

Nate took Molly with him the next day to pick out their Christmas tree at the farm. "We're going to do this every year" Molly declared. She was determined and left no room for argument. Molly picked the perfect tree, and Nate carried it to his car to load on the rooftop. As he lifted it onto the roof and tied it down, he swore to himself that he would buy himself a pickup truck someday. It would be more practical than his Civic.

When they arrived back at the BnB, Nate set up the tree, and Molly directed him, getting the tree as straight as possible. Leah was busy at the cafe, so they would wait until after dinner, when she was there, to decorate.

"Do you like Leah?" Molly suddenly asked Nate as he made some adjustments to the tree stand.

"Sure," Nate shrugged, smiling to himself.

"I see the way you look at her," Molly commented.

"What do you mean?" Nate was getting a little nervous about the direction of the conversation.

"I think you really, really like her."

"Maybe. Would that be a bad thing?"

"No," was her short reply.

Nate stopped for a moment and looked up at her. "What about you?" he started. "What about us? Wouldn't you be jealous if I did like her?"

Molly laughed.

"What's so funny?" Nate was a bit perplexed and then surprised by her response.

"You're silly. There is no us. You're too old for me," she giggled.

"Well, I don't know whether to be hurt or angry. I'm not that old, you know." He tried to be serious but was relieved by her response. So he continued. "I guess I do kind of like her."

"I know she likes you…a lot!"

"Oh? How do you know that?"

"Because she looks at you the same way you look at her. You two aren't fooling anyone, you know."

"OK. I admit it. I do like her. A lot."

Grammy was heard calling Molly from the kitchen. "I have to go help Grammy now. Good talk Nathan." She left him alone with his thoughts. What really struck him was her last words, the closing phrase of his conversations with Todd. He hadn't heard back from Todd and was worried about him, so he decided to send him a message.

"Hey, Todd. Just sending this note to wish you a Merry Christmas. I hope you are doing OK. I am well. Spending the holidays at Seneca Lake with some friends." He stopped to think for a moment. Should he elaborate on Leah? Probably not. It would require a much more lengthy message. "Wherever you are, be safe. And Merry Christmas. I miss our talks. Nate."

He then pushed send and waited, hoping that Todd would get the message and respond immediately. His phone then buzzed with the message, "The number you have texted is no longer in service." It was Christmas a year ago that he had tried to reach Todd, and that message had gone unanswered. Now he was worried.

Nate remained preoccupied through dinner and was noticeably quiet as they decorated the tree. "Another beautiful tree" Leah commented, handing him a cup of warm spiced cider.

"Thanks," Nate responded shortly.

"Are you okay? You've been quiet all evening." Nate simply nodded.

"Tomorrow is Christmas Eve. We can go out to the stables in the morning, then be back in plenty of time for church. I think Molly would like to go with us to see Toby and Sheba."

Nate nodded his approval, then conveyed his thoughts. "I sent a text message to Todd today to wish him a Merry Christmas. It came back to me as not deliverable."

"If he's still in the middle east somewhere, it's possible he just lost or broke his phone and hasn't been able to replace it, don't you think?"

Nate nodded. "I suppose so."

There were no guests staying at the BnB, so Grammy and Molly retired after finishing the tree, leaving Nate and Leah alone in the living room. "Molly and I had an interesting conversation today."

"Tell me more."

"She called me 'old,'" Nate chuckled.

"Oh? What prompted that?"

"Well, she started out by asking me if I liked you. And I asked her if that would be a bad thing, and she said absolutely not. So I asked her about her and me. That's when she told me that I was too old for her."

"So, did you tell her that you liked me?"

"I admitted that I have some feelings for you, yes. Then she said that she knows that you really like me."

"I've never said anything like that around her. I can't imagine where she got that impression."

"Evidently, she has seen the way you look at me. How do you look at me?"

Leah chose to treat the question as rhetorical. "If you're thinking that we don't have to keep our late-night rendezvous a secret…"

"I understand you believe she is too young to be exposed to that, but we could be a little more open about our relationship. She obviously knows more about us than you think. So which would be worse: her catching us sneaking around or her being aware of us together, in a loving relationship?"

"It's clear you have thought this through," she observed.

Nate thought for a moment, then stood and took her hand. "I thought about you all day. I kept thinking about last night. I love being with you. And I want to wake up in the morning with you still at my side."

"You know that's not possible. As liberal-minded as Grammy is, even she wouldn't approve of that, as long as Molly is in the house."

"OK. For now, I will just have to mollify myself with your infrequent late-night visits."

Leah stood and led him from the living room. "You are overdue for a tour of my room. Understand, though, that you will have to leave my bed before Molly wakes up in the morning."

"I can do that," Nate obliged and followed her down the hallway, past the kitchen, toward the back of the house, and into her bedroom. This was all new territory for him.

***

The three of them spent the next morning and early afternoon at the stable, grooming the horses. It had begun to snow again, so they decided not to ride. In the evening, they ate dinner, then attended the Christmas Eve service together with Grammy. Christmas day was spent playing games, eating, and watching holiday movies, all the things that Nate had enjoyed as a child growing up in Connecticut. He felt that he was truly at home with this new family, surrounded by love.

Following Christmas, Nate took Molly skiing again, Leah kept busy at the cafe, and Nate and Leah enjoyed each other's company long into the night. Another New Year's came and went before Nate had to return to Cornell, promising to return once more for the summer.

CHAPTER 23
THE GARDEN

Spring practice started shortly after returning to Cornell. The regular season wouldn't start for several months, and the snow cover would remain until the spring thaw, so practices were held in the field house, focusing primarily on strength training and drills. While Nate kept in touch with Leah, his focus remained on Cornell and the challenges of keeping up his studies while on the road with the team.

His relationship with Zak regained some of the camaraderie of their youth in spite of his continued use of steroids. Zak anticipated that he would be selected as the starting catcher for the team, and once this was accomplished, he promised Nate he would discontinue their use. Nate was careful not to contradict or criticize his friend, knowing how volatile he was, and just hoped for the best.

It was early April when starting positions were posted, and Nate, Zak, Jake, and Tom were all selected as starters. Nate breathed a sigh of relief for his friend Zak, who convinced Nate that he knew it would happen and that now was the time to celebrate. The four of them met at their favorite hangout, joined by other team members, and drank beer with an occasional shot in celebration. At some point in the evening, Nate observed Zak as he engaged a pretty lady, about their age, at the bar. Zak later came by Nate's table with the girl on his arm and advised Nate they were leaving, could he borrow Nate's car, and he would see him tomorrow.

As the evening wore on, Nate was approached several times by more coeds who were clearly tipsy, some wanting to engage him in some extracurricular activities and inviting him back to "their place". Nate politely declined but introduced them to other members of the team who were interested and appreciative of Nate as their "wingman." Jake later found Nate at the table and had Jeannie on his arm. "We're headed back to the suite. You need a lift?"

"Yeah, I think I've about drunk my limit," and Nate followed them out the door to Jake's car. Nate was awoken around nine the next morning by a phone call. Caller ID identified the caller as the coach's office. "Hello."

"Nate, this is Coach Myer. Could you come by my office?" the voice on the line said.

Nate didn't have time to think except to ask what time the coach wanted to see him.

"I need to talk to you as soon as possible, Nate."

"OK, coach. I'll be there in 15." Nate disconnected the call, his thoughts racing. His first thought was of Zak. Coach knew that he and Zak were friends, and if he was suspicious of Zak's recent physical transformation, he might have questions about it. He was in a difficult position. Defend Zak, deny he knew anything, or give full disclosure. Whatever the reason, it had to be important for the coach to be calling him at nine on a Saturday morning since they had the weekend off. He dressed quickly and was out the door, arriving shortly at the gym office. As he entered, he saw a familiar face sitting in a chair opposite the coach seated behind his desk.

Both men stood, and the familiar face extended his hand to Nate. It was Pastor Rick, now wearing a collar of an ordained pastor. Had something happened to Dani? His mind raced.

"Nate, I believe you know Pastor Middleton. I'll leave you two to talk, and I'll be just outside." The coach then excused himself.

"Nate," Pastor Rick began. "Please sit," he pointed to another chair by the desk.

"I'll stand. What brings you here?" Nate was in no mood for small talk and wanted to know the purpose of this unusual visit as soon as possible.

"I'm sorry to have to bring you this news. It's about your mother..." Nate was silent and waited for it, so Rick continued. "Your mother passed away last night. I'm sorry, Nate."

Nate closed his eyes, breathing deeply. This shouldn't be a surprise to him. It was a long time coming. But it made it all so real now. Her long-suffering death had finally arrived.

Rick continued to talk after a few moments of silence. "Your father needed someone to tell you, and I offered. He'd like me to bring you home for a few days."

"Can you excuse me for a minute?" Nate finally asked.

"Of course, Nate. I'll be right outside when you're ready." Pastor Rick left Nate alone in the office.

Nate slowly sat down in the chair as tears welled up in his eyes. He had always hoped for a miracle that somehow, someday, she would return to her normal self. That he could have that relationship with her again, which was lost so long ago. But in his heart, he knew it was unlikely to happen, and now it was all real...too real. Nate finally stood from the chair and was met by the coach and pastor outside the office.

The coach spoke first. "I'm sorry for your loss Nate. Take whatever time you need. Your spot will be here when you're ready to come back."

"I'll just be gone a few days and ready to play when I get back," he responded firmly.

"I'll take you by your apartment to pick up some things," Pastor Rick offered.

Nate nodded and led Rick out of the gym and onto the sidewalk leading to the suite.

Inside the suite, all was quiet. It had been a late night for the guys, and they were all still sleeping. Nate found it easier that way, not having to explain anything to them while he was on a roller coaster ride with his emotions. He went to his room, grabbed a suitcase, and threw some clothes into it before joining Pastor Rick, waiting for him downstairs.

There remained an awkward silence between them during the four-hour drive to Plainville. There was no sense in asking about his mother. He knew when she died and how she had died. So he searched for something else to talk about. "So, you're a full-bloodied pastor now?"

Rick smiled. "Yes, I guess I am. I finished divinity school last year. I'm not ordained yet, but I will be this summer if all goes well."

"Congratulations." They were quiet again until Nate decided to ask about Dani. He was making the assumption now that his suspicions from long ago were true. "How is she?"

Rick glanced his way briefly before responding. "Dani? She's doing OK. I'm sure she'll be at the funeral. She'll be glad to see you." They were quiet the remainder of the drive until Rick drove up the long drive to the house. There were a dozen cars parked along the drive. Rick drove past them and let Nate out by the front door.

"Thanks for driving all that way to get me."

"I'm glad I could help Nate. I'll stop by later this evening once all the arrangements have been made."

Nate took his bag from the trunk and walked in through the front door. He heard voices coming from the living room and kitchen areas but decided to go to his room and change before engaging the crowd. He found his bedroom undisturbed from when he had left nearly two years before. In the closet, he found a pair of pressed pants and a long-sleeved white shirt. His suit was still wrapped in plastic from the last time it was dry-cleaned. He would save it for the viewing at the funeral home and the church service.

He slowly changed and made his way down the back stairs into the kitchen. Bella was standing with a group of people around the kitchen island

and spotted him as he entered. "Nate," she called and moved to him. He hugged her for a moment and then let her go before speaking.

"Bella" was all he said.

"Your dad is in the living room with Gail. Can I get you something to drink?"

"Have any hot tea? I need to wake up before facing the mob."

"Sure." She put a tea bag in a cup and added hot water.

"Thank you, Bella." He was going to ask Bella if she was there when his mother died but thought better of it. Besides, what good would it do? He took the tea and walked into the living room. "Dad," he said softly to his father as he approached.

"Nate," Mark responded, extending his hand to his son.

Nate did not offer it in return. Only one thought came to his mind. The bitterness he had toward his father. "You gave up on her. You gave up on all of us," Nate whispered as he turned his back to him. Mark called after him as he walked away, but Nate wasn't ready to engage him fully at that moment. As he passed through the living room on the way to the stairway, several people stopped him to offer their condolences. He finally made it back up to his room.

He was both angry and sad. Angry at both his parents. Neither of them was willing to face their problems head-on. Both were willing to give up on their family. Sad that now there was no redemption for either of them. When Billy died, the family died. All he had left now was Todd, and he wasn't even sure about him. This contributed to the animosity he felt, now toward his whole family. He changed into some jogging shorts and a sweatshirt, then his running shoes. He thought about Leah. She was the only "family" he had now, and he hadn't even thought about calling her until now, maybe after his run. He made his way down the stairs and past the congregants in the living room, then out the door.

A voice called after him as he stepped down from the porch. Looking back, he saw Gail sitting alone in a rocker. "Escaping again, I see."

Why does she have to be this way, he thought to himself before responding. "Were you with her when she died?" His words came out without thinking. It was in the back of his mind, just waiting to be asked. He wanted to know the details, he admitted to himself, even though until then, he didn't believe it was important. Gail didn't respond. She simply stared at him, expressionless.

Nate turned and began running out the long drive past the baseball field, now overgrown with tall grass. His thoughts were racing as fast as his feet moved. The day Zak left and how his mother had comforted him, letting him lay his head in her lap. The gentle voice and soothing strokes of her hands through his hair, a moment that would forever be in his heart but never repeated. Then he was at the shortstop position the first time she came home from the hospital. He was distracted and missed an easy ground ball. And after, how she had changed, so distant and unfeeling.

Soon he was running past the horse farm. The pastures were empty, the barn door wide open. A large "for sale" sign sat at the side of the road near the end of the drive. It struck him that not only were the horses gone, but so were all the farm equipment, the rocking chairs on the front porch, and all evidence of life at the farm. How appropriate it all was. What once was no longer existed.

He turned and continued his run up the long drive in the direction of the barn and stopped at the entrance. He thought to himself that this could be his last chance to see where it happened. But why was that important? It had changed everything, but now it could change nothing. He walked slowly down the long, empty aisle.

He remembered the precise location where Billy breathed his last. He stood outside the stall, then opened the stall gate, letting himself inside. He looked for signs...signs of life, signs of death, anything that would serve as a memorial to what had transpired here those years before. But everything was gone now. First Billy, now his mother. He thought of his father. How much suffering can one man endure? But they had all endured these hardships, and their father should have helped them all through it, instead of just giving up on them.

He thought about Gail, but only for a fleeting moment. She was a survivor. Albeit testy, with a martyr complex, believing she had to stay behind, or else no one would continue to exist. And Todd. Without him, there was no one in the family that he could turn to, to talk about his anger and anxiety. Leah wouldn't understand. She had no real sense of their family dynamics or, in this case, dysfunction. And she had enough of her own challenges and responsibilities with Molly and Grammy.

He walked out of the stall, closing the stall door behind him. Turning, he took one last glance inside. This is how he would remember it. Just an empty place, like a part of him, now felt, with the loss of both his brother and mother.

He began running again now, slower than before. He found himself running up the short drive of what used to be Zak's house, then walking up the steps to the back deck and looking out upon the yard. At the edge of a freshly planted flower garden a short distance away, stood an older woman. She had her back to him and he couldn't see her face. He stood, immobilized, thinking maybe he should quietly leave. After all, Zak no longer lived here and he was trespassing.

He turned to walk quietly away, back down the steps, when he heard the woman's voice calling out. "Hello" she called after him.

Nate was about to leave, but looked back over his shoulder as she approached and was soon standing near his position on the deck.

"I'm sorry" Nate began as he faced her. In spite of her advanced years, he was immediately captivated by her beautiful smile and bright eyes. "I'm sorry to trespass. My best friend used to live here and I was just passing by."

"Oh, you're fine." She sauntered to his side and they both looked out over the yard to the garden below. "Isn't it beautiful? This is one of my favorite spots, especially in the springtime."

Nate nodded. "Zak's mother used to spend a lot of time out here."

"It's a gift you know. The ability to create something so beautiful that when finished, calms the soul. Imagine how God felt after he planted that first garden."

"I suppose so. But then, it didn't end well, did it?"

She patted his arm and spoke softly to him. "Through no fault of His" she chuckled. She sat down on one of two chairs and offered the second to Nate. "I saw you running earlier. Are you in a hurry to get somewhere? If not, take a break and sit a spell."

Her voice was strangely calming to Nate. Normally, he would be compelled to just excuse himself and not engage in a conversation with a stranger. But something about her kept him from leaving. He found himself sitting next to her, calm and relaxed in a time of grief and despair.

"I was running away from it all and I'm in no hurry to get back." He surprised himself by speaking his thoughts so freely to this stranger.

She was not fazed by his forthcoming. "I think that's fairly common for someone your age" she began. " When we are younger, we tend to run from things we don't understand or want to face. The uncertainty of it all. Eventually, we all have to stop running from and start running toward those things. If you don't, eventually they will catch up with you, like it or not. But if we face them and run toward them, the momentum we gain can help us power through them."

He was reminded of the sports analogies that he loved. "What happens then? What about the future? I need to know what I before I can run toward it" Nate responded.

"And you're not there yet, are you Nathan? You are a runner, but you don't always know where you're going to end up, do you?"

Her familiarity caught him off guard. How did she know anything about him? How did she even know his name?

She patted his arm again and continued her gaze into the gardens below. "Not to worry. You'll get there. But you will have to deal with the past and all this pain and suffering first."

"Sometimes I feel like I've been abandoned. So many people have just come and gone from my life" he started. "People I loved and depended on. My friend Zak, then my mother when I needed her most, then my brother Billy. He's gone and the only connection I have left is the pain. And Todd....the one who helped me get through it all. I lost one brother years ago. I can't face the thought of losing another." Nate found tears welling up in his eyes. He hadn't cried yet for his mother or for the combined losses of everyone he loved. But to allow his emotions to overtake him in the presence of a stranger...yet she didn't feel like a stranger to him. There was something about her.

"Your losses don't have to define you Nathan. You're stronger than you know. And all these thoughts going through your head...they're just a momentary distraction from what's in your heart. Someday, you will know exactly what to do. It's already in here." She gently reached over to him and placed her hand over his heart. He had never felt such peace, even at this tumultuous time in his life. "And you needn't worry about Todd" she continued. "He'll be there when you need him. And you'll be there for him too, when he needs you. Just try to be patient. You'll know when it's time. Everything will work out."

Nate sat in silence, trying to grasp all that she had said with words that continued to comfort and calm him. She was right about Todd, up to a point. He had been there when he needed him. But where was he now? And why would Todd ever need him? He was the big brother and he had always looked out for him.

Finally she stood and urged him to stand too. "It's time Nathan. Your family is waiting for you." Nathan nodded, at a loss for words, but sensed she was fully aware of his every thought. There was no need for him to speak again. With a faint smile, he acknowledged her kind words of wisdom, and he walked solemnly down the steps on his trek toward home. He turned one last time to reassure himself that she was real. He saw her clearly still. She had returned to the garden, standing over it, admiring the beauty of it's creation.

***

He had been gone for nearly two hours, and the crowd had dwindled to a few stragglers and the return of Pastor Rick. Nate found them all seated in the living room, discussing the funeral home visitation for two evenings, followed by the funeral service and burial in three days. He sat and listened quietly as minor details were discussed. Gail was seated in the large arm-back chair next to him. "You were gone a long time," she commented. "Dad was asking where you were."

"What did you tell him?"

"The usual. Running away."

Nate nodded. "Have you met the new neighbor?" he then asked.

"What new neighbor?" she quipped.

"Zak's old house. The lady there."

Gail mocked him. "You're losing it, Nate. No one has lived there for years."

CHAPTER 24
JUST ANOTHER MEMORY

They sat in silence as the remainder of the visitors left for the evening, leaving Mark, Gail, and Nate alone. Bella joined them, carrying a tray with a pot of tea and cups, setting it down on the coffee table.

"The attorney wants to meet with us about the will," Mark stated.

Nate responded. "I'm heading back to school right after the funeral. I don't need to be there."

Gail couldn't help but offer her opinion. "Baseball is more important than family? We just lost our mother, for god sake."

Nate ignored her without comment.

"I don't see any reason not to do it Wednesday morning before the service," Mark said.

"That's a little insensitive, isn't it, Dad?" Gail interjected, this time questioning her father's sensibility.

"Not at all," he responded. "Your mother's gone now. And I'd like you all to be there."

"What about Todd?" Nate asked. Were they avoiding the issue of Todd's absence because no one knew of his whereabouts, he wondered.

"Todd isn't able to come right now." Mark's response was measured.

"Do you know where he is?" Nate continued his questioning.

"He is safe" was all Mark would say.

He must be back in the States then, Nate surmised. "Why isn't he here then? Did you tell him about our mother?" Nate was becoming agitated now and having difficulty keeping calm.

He looked around the room, and all eyes were on him. Bella had remained silent throughout the exchange but chose to speak now in an attempt to become the peacekeeper that their mother had once been.

"Nate, we are all concerned about Todd. We do know he is back in the US. What we don't know yet is why he is unable to come. The military can be very evasive about these things, but they have assured your father that they will make sure Todd is in touch with his family as soon as he is able."

"Thank you, Bella," Mark concluded. "I don't know what Todd has been told. All I could do was try to have a message relayed to him about your mother. They assured me he would be told. This has been a long day for us all. I suggest we all get some rest. We're going to need it for the next few days." Mark excused himself and left the room.

Nate stood to leave and walked toward Bella. "Thank you, Bella." He then returned to his bedroom, debating in his mind if he should call Leah or wait until he had more time to deal with everything that was happening. He slowly dialed her number, believing she would be hurt and possibly angry that he hadn't contacted her.

Leah answered in her usual pleasant voice. "Nathan." It was unusual for him to be calling her on this day and time, which aroused her suspicions immediately. "Is everything OK?"

"It is...now that I hear your voice."

"Where are you? Are you at school?"

"No, I'm in Connecticut. My mother passed away last night, and I drove up this morning."

"Oh, I'm sorry, Nathan. I wish I could be there."

"I know. But it's not necessary. This has been a long time coming, and it will all be over soon. I just like hearing your voice."

"So, how are you doing?" Then she let him talk while she listened.

"I'm OK. Nothing much has changed. She's been missing from my life for so long now it's hard for me to feel like anything is different. I took my usual run just to clear my head and give me some time to think." He decided not to tell her about the encounter at Zak's; maybe someday. "Anyway, it got me thinking about all these opportunities that God has put right in front of me, and I just manage to screw it up somehow. I could have gone to any school I wanted or joined the military like Todd did, or just stayed home and tried to help my family. Maybe I screwed up. Maybe I should have stayed here and helped my mother. Maybe she'd be alive today if I had."

"You know I'm happy to just listen. But if you want to know my opinion on that..."

"I'm always happy to hear your opinion, as long as it's an affirmation that I have made the right decision."

Leah hesitated for a moment, then responded. "I can't affirm that, Nathan. It's not that I believe you made the wrong choice. It's that you won't know if you made the right decision for what may be years to come. Who knows what will happen over the next few years...what you'll be doing....where you'll be...We don't always get instant results or gratification from our choices. The rewards and consequences may not be known for a while. But I can say this. I don't see that you have made any blatant errors in your thinking or your plans. And you're pretty much on target where you want to be in five years, aren't you?"

Nate thought for a minute. "That's the problem. I'm not sure anymore where I want to be in five years. I thought I knew. But now I'm just not sure. And what does that mean for us, Leah?"

"You still have time to make those decisions," she reassured him. "And your current thinking may just be the result of what you're going through right now. Once you get passed this, maybe things will become more clear for you."

"Well, one of the first things you found out about me is that I'm not a patient person. I can't just sit around and wait."

"If it's any consolation at all, your patience has been tested by the circumstances surrounding your mother. I don't pretend to understand what you have been through all these years with her, but from what I have observed and seen, you have an amazing inner strength and ability to get by...to get through these things and remain true to yourself."

"Gail says I'm always running away. Avoiding it all."

"What do you think?"

"I have always felt the need to run. But I never thought about it from that perspective...running away from things. Maybe she is right."

"I don't think it's that simple, Nathan. We all have ways of dealing with stress. The good thing about your method, it doesn't hurt or endanger anyone. You are the only one it affects. That's a good thing, don't you think?"

"I much prefer your perspective over hers," Nate chuckled. "So, I still wonder about us. What will happen to us." It was no longer a question in his mind but more of an observation.

"I guess it will be another test of your patience and endurance. You know I am not free to do anything other than what I'm doing now. And I won't have that freedom for a least a couple of years. That will allow us both to think about what we want; something to look forward to, I think."

"I guess so. So, I will see you again in a couple of months."

"I'm looking forward to it."

"I love you, and I miss you."

"I love you too, Nathan. Take care of yourself, and I'll see you soon."

"Bye."

***

Nate unwrapped the suit from the plastic. It smelled faintly of some dry cleaning solution; not an unpleasant scent but enough to add to the uneasy sensation he had in his gut. The plan was for them to drive to the attorney's office together before the viewing at the funeral home. Mark, Gail, and Bella were waiting for him in the car in the drive. Unusual, Nate thought, that Bella would be going, but he wouldn't question it.

Mark drove the SUV with Nate in the passenger seat. Gail and Bella sat in the back. As they exited the car, Nate announced that he would not be going with them to meet with the attorney. "I'll meet you at the funeral home." He turned, and they watched him walk away.

He wished he could run, but he was dressed in a suit and wingtips, so he just walked vigorously down the sidewalk. He determined that the funeral home was only several streets away, and it would afford him the opportunity to calm his nerves and prepare for what was to come.

The funeral home was quiet when he entered. The small sign by the entrance into the chapel simply said, "Jean MacArthur Woods 7 to 9 PM". It was nearing 6:30 now, so he entered the chapel, passing rows of empty chairs toward the front where the open coffin rested. His mother lay before him now, finally at peace after years of suffering a pain she had no desire to quash. A pain she believed she deserved for all her failings.

And it brought back the memory of that day when she was taken so quickly from him and the loss he felt from that day on. For, in fact, she had been his best friend until that day. She was the one he would go to, for love and affection, for comfort, for understanding. All these things are lost in one single moment.

He observed her face. The years of medication had taken its toll. He remembered her as beautiful, and the mortician had done his best to restore what had been lost. Her smile, while diminished, was faint and almost mocking in appearance, for she had escaped to a better place. Her hair had not grayed; it maintained the vibrant auburn color of her heritage. She had brushed it frequently, never having to curl its natural waves, and that's how she would take it to her grave.

"I'm sorry Mom…" he began as he stood tall above her…" that I couldn't help you. I know it wasn't your fault. I just wish you could have accepted that too. I know in your heart that you still loved us but you couldn't overcome the thoughts in your head that you were somehow responsible for everything bad that happened and that you didn't deserve our love. But we loved you in spite of that. If you could only have accepted our love, then things would have been different. Well, I guess this is the last time we'll get to talk. I just wanted to say I love you and miss you." He bent down and kissed her on the forehead, then turned and took a seat in the front row.

His thoughts were interrupted by voices as they entered the chapel. Mark entered with Gail, and they walked directly to the front and stood before the casket. Others came and went before the casket, then took seats while a brief service took place. It was mostly a blur for Nate, and people were soon disbanding. When he arose from his seat and turned, he spotted Dani standing with Pastor Rick near the back entrance. Upon catching his attention, Dani walked by herself in his direction. She was as beautiful as he remembered. Her natural auburn hair had all grown back and was flowing down to her shoulders. She smiled demurely as she reached him and hugged him. "I'm so sorry, Nate."

"Thank you for coming. You didn't need to." He found himself speaking formally and not with the past familiarity.

"I know. I just wanted to show my support, as you did for me when I needed it. So, how are you doing? Is there anything I can do?"

"No, everything has been taken care of. Actually, I don't know anything except what they tell me. Dad and Gail have handled pretty much everything."

"How is school? And baseball? You're still playing, I assume."

Nate nodded. "Doing well enough at both to keep my scholarship intact. What about you? You going to school now?"

"Just locally. To the community college for now."

"No Quinnipiac? I thought after the year off, you were heading there."

"That was my plan, but things changed."

"What changed?"

"I don't think this is a good time to talk about that. How long will you be in town?"

"Just until after the funeral. I have to get back to baseball, you know. They won't win without me."

"I see you're as arrogant...I mean proud...as ever."

"It's all about confidence and believing in yourself. So what else are you doing? Besides going to Community College?"

"I'm actually working part-time at the church."

"At the church?" Nate was surprised. He then saw Rick from across the room. "With him?"

Dani looked at Nate with apprehension.

Nate nodded. "I guess it was inevitable," he concluded.

"I'm sorry, Nate. I didn't want you to find out this way. That's why I was hoping we'd have a chance to talk under different circumstances."

"There's no need to be sorry, really. I do have one question for you, though. Was there anything going on between you and him when we were together?"

"No, Nate. I was honest with you then, and I'm being honest with you now. Nothing ever happened between us until after you left. When I was with you, it was only you. And you helped me get through some rough times."

"And so did he."

"Yes, he did. But it wasn't like with you. You were my first love. Something that I will always cherish and remember right here." She touched her heart.

It was true for him as well, but expressing that now just didn't seem right. This was something else he felt he had lost. Along with all the other losses and now a couple of years separated from Dani, it was final. He had lost her too. There was an awkward silence between them when Dani finally spoke. "I guess I better go. I'll see you then at the church. Maybe we can talk more after."

Nate nodded and watched her walk back to Rick's side, thinking there was really nothing more to say.

***

Nate arrived at the church thirty minutes before the service. Bella rode with him, and he kept her by his side as the family met with the pastor before the service. They would wait to enter the sanctuary until everyone else was seated. Aunt Susan, Uncle Matt, and cousins Melissa and Jacob had arrived from Florida and would walk in behind Nate, Gail, Mark, and Bella. As they processed in, Nate recognized some familiar faces; others were strangers, probable friends of his mother or father. He spotted Dani and her parents, Mr. and Mrs. Lucas, Sarah and Jim Elliott, then Zak's father, Ben.

He was taken completely by surprise and moved by the next row of young men, all dressed in Cornell baseball jerseys.. Zak was seated nearest the aisle and caught his eye, giving him a nod as he passed by. They took their seats, and the service moved forward. Several guests took the opportunity to move to the podium to speak and share some of their fondest memories of his mother.

Nate took his turn and stepped forward. Behind the podium, he looked at the crowd before him. The sanctuary was crowded with people who had all come to pay their respects to this wounded and long-suffering woman. But their reverence for her was clearly for what she had been, not what she had become. And that's what he would focus on at this moment.

"Cesare Pavese, an Italian poet from the mid-1900, once said, 'We don't remember days, only moments.' This is one of those moments. I want to thank all of you for being here at this moment in time to honor the life of my mother, Jean MacArthur Woods. You have already heard from some folks here about how she was selfless in her service to others. Along with that service, she had four children to raise. And how she managed to do both, well, that just tells you how amazing she was. Back to my very first memory of her up until about age ten, she was not only my mother but my friend. I relied on her for everything. And she always came through. Most of you know that while growing up, I was a runner. I loved to run, and I did it every day. My mother would take me shopping for sneakers, and I had to explain to her, over and over, that I needed running shoes, the expensive kind, not sneakers. I think she knew the entire time that running shoes were just a fancy name for expensive sneakers. And after each pair of new running shoes, she would threaten me that if I didn't take good care of them, it would be the last pair of running shoes she would buy me. But it was like a game between us. It really didn't matter if I took good care of them. I would just outgrow them and need a new pair the next year anyway."

There were some chuckles in the audience as he continued. "My mother was the peacekeeper. We would sit around the table, each of us kids with our own ideas and torture tactics for each other, discuss the most absurd subjects, purposely contradicting each other, working up to a frenzy, when my mother would calmly and quietly negotiate a peace treaty, while never taking sides. Those are the moments I choose to remember, and nothing that has transpired since will ever take away the love I have for her. I'd like to finish with a poem I came across. The author is unknown. I don't know why because if I had written it, I would certainly take credit for it. I think it says everything I believe and feel at this moment in time. This is for you, Mom."

RUNNING SHOES

"Life is but a stopping place,

A pause in what's to be,

A resting place along the road,

to sweet eternity.

We all have different journeys,

Different paths along the way,

We all were meant to learn some things,

but never meant to stay…

Our destination is a place,

Far greater than we know.

For some, the journey's quicker,

For some, the journey's slow.

And when the journey finally ends,

We'll claim a great reward,

And find everlasting peace,

Together with the lord."

***

Nate was greeted on the sidewalk by his teammates outside the church. Each gave their condolences as they walked down the line. "You missed your calling; you should have been a poet," Zak commented.

"I can't believe you guys are here."

"We're brothers, right? Besides, I figured you wouldn't want to be staying here for long, and you might need a ride back to school. And the team needs you."

"Well, listen, guys, you don't know how much this means to me, you all being here. I think we should all head to the lake house, do some celebrating, then head back to school in the morning."

Jake and Tom were standing nearby and agreed. "That sounds like a plan, guys. Let's do it," Jake announced.

As they were about to leave, Dani passed by them on the walk. She clearly wanted to speak to Nate, but he turned away as she approached. One of the teammates took notice and asked Nate about her. "Wow, who is that?"

Nate glanced her way once more, then replied: "Just another memory."

CHAPTER 25
TRUST

Jake was the captain of the team and, when they traveled together, took charge, so it was no surprise when he divided the guys up for the ride to the lake house. "Zak, you know the way to the lake house, so you take the guys in the team van. Nate, Tom, and I will follow you in my car."

Nate decided to skip the reception at the house afterward; he had already seen and talked to most of the family and friends who would be there, and he just wanted it to be over. He had spoken to Bella briefly before leaving the funeral and asked her to let anyone who asked know that he was leaving for Cornell with his teammates. As far as his father, they hadn't spoken since he left them outside the attorney's office, and there was nothing left to say.

"Sit in the front," Jake instructed Nate as they climbed into his car. Tom climbed into the back seat without argument, so Nate did as Jake requested. They drove in silence for a while, following the team van, with some country music playing. Finally, Jake reached over and turned the radio off. "I know the timing is not ideal, but I wanted to take a few minutes to talk to you without the other guys around," Jake began.

Nate looked his way curiously. "It's not a problem. What's up?"

"Coach talked to me just before we left to come here. This is just between the three of us for now. The NCAA has started an investigation into alleged steroid abuse. That, in itself, is not unusual. It happens every few years, and then it just kind of all goes away quietly. But if this is any kind of serious investigation, Zak has put himself and the whole team at risk. Have you talked to him yet about his steroid use?"

Nate thought for a moment. He had discussed with Zak the consequences of using steroids but not the effect it could have on the team. "We talked briefly. He got defensive rather quickly. Talked mainly about how it was the only way he was going to make a starter on the team and be eligible for a spot in the minors. Other than that, all he said was that he got the steroids legally, by prescription."

"Yeah, we've heard that one before. Fake docs giving fake prescriptions," Tom scoffed from the back seat.

"I don't think that defense will get him far if he tests positive for steroid use," Jake continued.

"So what do we do?" Nate asked.

" If it were just Zak that would suffer the consequences, I'd say we do nothing. But it's the team at risk and anyone like me and Tom who are graduating this year and looking for a place in the minors. If the team is disqualified because of this, we may all lose our chances."

"You're telling me all this for a reason," Nate concluded out loud.

Tom spoke up after giving Nate time to think. "You may be the only one who can help us, to help the team."

"Look, Nate. I understand this may all come down to you making a decision based on what you think is right for yourself versus what is right for your friend and your teammates. I wouldn't want to be in your shoes right now and have to make that choice. Chances are, Zak will be targeted and tested. He may ask you to somehow take the test for him. So I just wanted to give you a heads up; give you time to think of the choices you may have to make and the ramifications."

Nate leaned back into the headrest of the seat and closed his eyes, his thoughts racing. Zak was his best friend. How far should he go to protect that friendship? And what would he do if he were in Zak's shoes? Would he ask his best friend to cheat on a drug test for him? And the stakes were high; it would be in his power to end Zak's college eligibility and even his career. And it troubled him that Zak might put him in this position.

And what about the team? If Zak was singled out and the only consequential loss, he could live with himself. But they were going into the season next week, and once they had played, then found steroid use on the team, the entire team could face disqualification. And that would fall on Nate's shoulders, if only because he could have stepped in to prevent it from happening.

They arrived at the lake house before Nate was derailed from his thoughts. He remained solemn throughout the evening while his teammates imbibed, attributing and accepting his non-participation as a consequence of the day's solemn events. The guys found various places to sleep, some in beds and others on the floor of the lake house. Nate retreated to Billy's room, the only one designated as off-limits to the guys. There was a knock on the door as Nate sat on the bed, observing the still undisturbed contents of the room, reminders of those days long ago.

"OK to come in?" Zak asked, cracking the door open just wide enough to see Nate seated on the bed.

"Sure, Zak. Come on in."

He looked around the room as he entered. "Nothing changed here. How long do you think it will stay this way?"

"No rush or reason to change it." Nate was reticent.

"You OK? You've been pretty quiet all night. Still thinking about the funeral?"

"I'm fine. Just a lot to take in these last few days. I meant to tell you 'thanks' for bringing all the guys. It meant a lot. You guys are family, something I'm missing these days." This statement resounded in his head after speaking it.

"Didn't take much convincing to get the guys here. They jumped on the chance. You're the golden boy, you know. All the guys speak highly of you. They think like I do...that you'd do anything for them."

Nate forced a smile as he watched Zak walk around the room, inspecting pictures and items, all reminders of Billy.

"There used to be a picture here on the dresser. Of you, Todd and Billy. I remember it. You were about nine or ten, I think. Great picture. Where'd it go?"

Nate just shrugged. "Not sure." He was thinking now about what Zak had just said, that the guys believed "he would do anything for them." Was this coincidental, or was it part of a plan by all of them to get into his head and convince him to do them all a favor? To volunteer himself to take Zak's drug test so no one would be at risk? He trusted Jake; would Jake betray that trust and set him up like this? How desperate were these guys?

When he looked up from his thoughts, Zak was standing over him, watching him closely. "You really seem lost in thought," he commented. "What's going on?"

Nate removed his shoes, then proceeded to put on his running shoes, which were nearby. If there were ever a time he needed Todd's advice, it was now. "I need to clear my head."

Zak nodded. "OK, bud. You do what you have to do. We all need clear heads to get through the next few days." He then turned and walked toward the door to leave.

Nate called after him. "No matter what happens, Zak, you've always been a good friend, and I appreciate that." Zak continued out the door without looking back, closing it softly behind him.

***

Rumors of the pending investigation spread quickly among the team and became a reality the following week. The entire team was gathered in the field house as the coach announced that urine samples would be needed from all team members so as not to discriminate against any particular individuals. "You have nothing to worry about as long as you don't have anything in your system that tests positive," he concluded.

"What if someone tests positive? Does that disqualify just him or the whole team?" one of the players called out.

"That's up to the NCAA. We don't know yet how deep this goes. One thing in our favor is that we haven't played any league games yet, so if this is resolved before a league game, chances are we will not be disqualified as a team."

This did not help to relieve Nate of his anxiety. There were still no definitive answers to the questions on his mind. "Everyone needs to be here an hour before practice tomorrow," Coach announced. "Drink plenty of water beforehand. And no alcohol."

After the coach dismissed them, Zak was waiting for Nate by the exit. They began their walk back to the suite in silence before Zak finally spoke. "What you said the other night at the lake house," he began. "Did you really mean it?"

Here it comes, Nate thought to himself. "Which part?"

"About us. Our friendship."

"Of course, Zak. You've always been one of my best friends."

"Which is why this is difficult for me to ask this...because we have been best friends for so long."

Nate stopped walking for a minute, looking directly at Zak and waiting for him to continue with what he feared most.

"I'm quitting the team," Zak suddenly blurted.

Nate was stunned. "What? What do you mean quitting the team?" This was a turn of events that Nate had not anticipated.

"I've put the team at risk. It's not right. They shouldn't have to pay the price for something I've done."

So what was the question? Nate was thinking to himself. They continued walking. Nate wasn't sure if he was relieved or simply feeling pity for his friend. "I don't know what to say, Zak," Nate finally spoke.

"That's alright. Just listen for a minute. You know I considered asking you to somehow take the test for me...I don't know...maybe get them to let us take the test at the same time..different stalls, of course," he laughed. "I would have just handed you my cup under the stall and had you fill it up for me. Sounds crazy, doesn't it? But I know that would have put you in a bad position, and that wouldn't have been fair at all to you. The other night, you reminded me just how important our friendship is...to both of us. So I want to clear the air. I've always considered you my best friend. Even when we were separated by a thousand miles for those years."

"So what will you do? I mean, after school..."

"Everyone needs a backup plan. I have mine. I'm majoring in sports medicine, and I'll continue to work toward getting a spot on a team as a trainer. It's all good. I really don't think I could have made it to the minors anyway, even with the steroids. So overall, it's best to get off the drugs and pursue a more realistic goal."

"You amaze me, Zak. I have been a little anxious the past few days since I heard about the drug testing. I have to admit, I was afraid you were going to ask me to take the test for you. So what is it you wanted to ask me?"

"Would you have?" Zak had stopped and was looking directly at Nate, waiting now for a response.

"I don't know, Zak. If I had said no, it would have affected our friendship and could have had an impact on the whole team. If I had agreed to do it, I'd have to deal with my conscience for who knows how long. Neither one was preferable to the other. I'm sorry that I just couldn't immediately agree to it."

"I've always admired your integrity. Friendships only run so deep. At some point, you would have had to choose what was best for you. I can't fault you for that, and I'm sorry for any expectation you may have had that I was going to put you in that position. Fortunately for us both, you don't have to choose. I've made my decision, and it's best for everyone involved. I wish we could go celebrate about now," Zak added. "But we'll have to save it until after your test," he patted Nate on the back.

***

He drove directly to the BnB, parking his Honda near the curb and carrying his suitcase into the house. It was a clear warm June day, and with no one around to greet him, he decided it was a perfect time to take a leisurely jog around the town. As he ran, he thought this could be his last summer trip to Geneva. He would soon have to decide something more permanent. He was still set on baseball as a career choice, but there were too many variables. First, if he would be invited to try out, then if he could make the minor league team. Then he would have to wait to be called up to the majors if it ever happened. He had heard many tales of older minor league players who never got called up and were left poor and desolate, monetarily and career-wise. It was all a risk you had to be willing to take, and in spite of self-confidence in his ability to achieve those goals, his patience would be tested daily, and he was not a patient person.

If he was successful in at least the first steps toward achieving his goal, it would mean leaving Leah behind. She had committed herself to care for Molly until she was of legal age and able to care for herself. And there was Grammy Nettles, getting on in years. Who knew how long it would be before Leah had to care for her as well? Nate had to accept that he was not the priority in her life; he only came in third at best. Leah also had her work to consider. She would be finishing school next year and wanted to move on to teaching. She still owned and managed the cafe, and as Grammy was able to do less and less at the BnB, Leah would be forced to either take over its management, hire someone to do it, or close it altogether.

At some point in time, he would have to address these issues with Leah. But it would have to wait for now. He hadn't seen her in months, and he missed her. For now, he would focus on the here and now and spend time getting reacquainted with her.

He found himself in front of the cafe, peering in through the front window. He spotted her immediately, standing behind the counter, dressed in her pale blue uniform and white apron, pouring coffee. He inspected himself in the reflection of the window, dressed in running shorts and a tank top, then decided it best to just return to the house and shower before letting her know of his return. He turned to leave but then heard her voice as she came out the front door. "Running off without even saying hello?"

Nate was apologetic but happy to see her. "I'm sweaty and not really dressed appropriately for such a fine dining establishment."

"Good retort. I won't hug you, not for my sake, but for the sake of my customers."

"Just a kiss then?" he asked slyly.

"For now, that will do." He leaned down and kissed her.

"How are you?" he asked as he was reminded just how beautiful she was.

"OK. Busy as usual. How did things go at home?"

"About as expected. I'll tell you more later when we have some time."

"I look forward to it."

"A quick kiss then until I see you later?"

"I guess that would be OK." She turned her face up to him to meet his lips and not so quick a kiss.

***

"Molly will be disappointed that she missed you tonight." Grammy was sitting with Nate and Leah at the dinner table. "She's staying at a friend's house."

"She'll be home tomorrow afternoon, which will be soon enough,"

RUNNING SHOES

Grammy observed.

Nate spoke next. "It looks like there are enough projects to keep me busy here most of the summer," he said, looking at the wish list that Grammy had given him. "Before I get started, though, my friend Jake is getting married next week. I'd like to take Leah, but it means being gone the entire weekend." He hadn't asked Leah yet, and he had only mentioned it to her in a previous message. She was non-committal.

Grammy responded while Leah sat quietly. "We don't have any guests booked for next weekend. The summer crowds won't arrive for another couple of weeks, just before the fourth, so between Molly and me, we'll be fine."

Nate turned his attention to Leah. "And the cafe? Can they do without you for the weekend?"

Leah smiled. "I'll have to check with the manager."

***

They sat alone in the living room after Grammy retired for the evening, and Leah encouraged him to talk about the past semester and all that transpired. First, he talked about Pastor Rick giving him the news about his mother and driving him back to Connecticut, and then the welcome surprise of his teammates showing up at the funeral. "There was a point though that I wondered what their real motive was for being there."

"Why?" was her simple response.

"I told you my concerns about Zak. About how he was doing steroids, which put not only him, but the whole team at risk. Jake shared with me that there was going to be an investigation and drug tests. If Zak tested positive, he'd be out, and maybe the team too. Maybe I was being paranoid, but when I heard this, I wondered if Jake was hinting that I needed to somehow make sure Zak didn't test positive. Not for Zak's sake but for the team. They could be disqualified, and this would have an impact on Jake and Tom's plans to play in the minors."

"It doesn't sound like you're being paranoid to me," she commented. "I can only imagine the internal conflict you must have been going through."

"I was. But the hardest thing for me was believing that Zak would put me in the position of deciding his fate. Take the test for him, or just let it all play out with the likelihood that he would be kicked off the team and lose out on the minors. And if I didn't do what the team needed, I would be ostracized by them."

"Well, the season is over now, so what did you decide?"

"That's the thing. I didn't have to. Zak did the right thing. He told me he couldn't put me in that position. He resigned his spot on the team."

Leah smiled. "Sounds like he proved himself to be a good friend. And both of you are left with your integrity intact." Nate nodded in agreement. "I was sorry to hear about your mom, and I'm sorry I couldn't be there."

Nate nodded. "She was depressed; suffered from anxiety for years. All those years on drugs finally took its toll."

"It must have had a terrible impact on your family."

"Over the long term, yes. My father eventually gave up on her and then abandoned us. I understand now why Todd felt the need to leave home when he did. And Gail...she sought affection in other less than virtuous places."

"And you?"

Nate became more somber and didn't respond immediately. "I'm not sure," he finally admitted.

Leah nodded, expanding upon her observation. "I've seen that about you, Nate. It seems to me that you have been unsure about a lot of things."

"I can't disagree. Maybe it has to do with her. I had an uncertain future without her involvement."

"What about Billy?"

"Billy was her favorite. I understood that. None of her kids looked like her except Billy. And she shared more interest in what he was doing than the rest of us. It wasn't planned, I'm sure. It just happened. Her family had horses growing up, and they were a big part of Billy's life. And ultimately his death," he added.

"Tell me about Billy."

He had never elaborated about Billy. It was time. "He was different. He liked most of the same things that Todd and I liked. Sports. Fishing. Boating and swimming. Skiing. But he was into horses, like our mother. He learned to groom and ride when he was pretty young. But he wasn't content with just that. He wanted to ride the show horses. He wasn't ready, and he took unnecessary risks. He was overconfident, and one night, it got him killed."

"I noticed that first time we went to the stables how you were hesitant at first."

"It just brought back some memories. I was actually glad to get back in the saddle. I hadn't ridden since Billy's accident."

"How are things with your father? Did you get to talk to him at the funeral?"

Nate shook his head. "We had one conversation, which didn't go well. I lost my cool. I probably said some things I shouldn't have about how he abandoned our mother and then the whole family. I basically accused him of being a terrible father."

"And that's how you left it?" Nate noticed the concerned expression on her face.

"I don't expect we'll be talking again soon...if ever."

Nate suddenly moved on to another topic. "I saw my old girlfriend. She came to the funeral." It was a reckless attempt to defer from further discussion about his father, he realized after saying it. Then he added, "She came with her new boyfriend."

Leah smiled. "Good rebound Nathan. For a moment there, you opened yourself up to a lot of questions. Now it sounds like there's not much to tell."

"It bothered me some that she was there with him."

"Why? You still have feelings for her?"

Nate shook his head no. "Maybe bothered is not the right word. It just made me wonder. The entire time we were together, I knew she was friends with him. But I don't think she was being entirely honest with me. How she really felt about him then. It's more about me being deceived than her being dishonest. With everything that's happened to me, I'm beginning to think I have trust issues, what with Zak and the team, Dani, my father's cheating on my mother."

Leah raised her eyebrows at this new surprise disclosure.

"I guess I never told you about that," Nate continued. "I came upon them accidentally in a restaurant. He and his 'secretary'".

"You sure it was an affair?"

"When I mentioned it to Todd, he said it had been going on for years."

Nate stood from the couch and extended his hand to her as she rose. "It's getting late. I'd love it if you could join me tonight…"

Leah smiled but resisted. "I would, but I have to open the cafe tomorrow at 6. Besides, I'm looking forward to this weekend when we can really be alone at the lake house. So, you will just have to wait," she teased.

"I look forward to that. I guess it's good night then."

She raised her face to his as he leaned down to kiss her. "Good night Nathan." He watched as she walked quietly toward her room.

CHAPTER 26
TRUTH BE TOLD

"Welcome to my hideout," Nate said, opening the door to his bedroom and setting the suitcase down.

"So this is where it all started." Leah was walking around the room, inspecting the various sports posters on the walls. "No women in bikinis, no race cars, no heavy metal rockers."

"I was focused," Nate replied. "No time for sex, drugs, or rock n roll."

"I assume there's a bathroom upstairs here somewhere."

"Sure, just down the hall. Make a left, and the bathroom is on the right."

"I'll be right back." Leah left him alone for a few minutes before he heard voices coming from the hallway. He recognized Gail's voice, now engaged in conversation with Leah. Gail acknowledged him as he approached. His attention was drawn immediately to her attire. She was wearing maternity pants and a top.

"Hi, Nate," Gail smiled her usual mischievous smile. She knew her appearance would catch him off guard and enjoyed his discomfort. "Leah and I were just getting acquainted."

"I was telling Gail that we were here for a wedding," Leah added.

Nate had just seen Gail a couple of months ago, and she was not showing, so this was a complete surprise to him. "So when is the happy occasion?" he asked.

"October," Gail said shortly.

"Boy or girl?" Nate continued. Leah quietly listened to their banter.

"Depends. You want to be an aunt or an uncle?" She laughed.

Nate simply smiled at her attempt at humor. "Congratulations. Do you know who the father is?"

Gail was not offended in the least by his remark. "Now that's the Nate I expect to hear. You remember Dale Polinski?"

"Sure. He was on the baseball team. Couldn't keep it in his pants." Leah was standing beside Nate now and took his hand.

Gail ignored the characterization. "It's OK, Leah. We always talk like this," she reassured her. "Anyway, Dale and I went to the prom together way back. We always seemed to have a connection."

"Like two peas in a pod," Nate concurred.

"Exactly," Gail agreed. "And now we're back together."

"Well, sis, if all that is true, I am happy for you. I just hope you two are better parents than we had."

"Shouldn't we get ready for the dress rehearsal?" Leah interrupted.

Nate nodded. "Good luck with your baby," he said, leading Leah back toward the bedroom. "And with Polinski," he added as they disappeared into his room.

Once inside, Nate closed the door behind them.

"You didn't know she was pregnant?"

"Nope. I pity the child."

"Oh, Nathan. Maybe having a baby will change her. Make her a bit more..."

"Likable?" he interjected.

"Not exactly the word I was looking for. Anyway, you two seem to have this mutual love/hate relationship. On the surface, you're all mean and nasty to each other. But on the inside, I'm not so sure."

"Trust me. There is no love lost between us. And that guy she is with. We once had a bit of an altercation right outside there." He pointed to the bedroom door. "I actually got the better of him until another guy jumped me and held me down while Polinski beat the shit out of me."

Leah frowned. "I'm sorry to hear that. I thought there might be a chance for you and Gail and whoever the guy is, to reconcile and actually be a family."

"That's not going to happen. And it probably doesn't matter who the guy is. I'm surprised she even knows who it is, the way she used to sleep around."

"There's that old double standard again," she observed. "A guy sleeps around, and it's no big deal. He's just labeled a bad boy. But if a girl does it, she's automatically labeled a slut."

"What's your point?"

"It's an injustice that has been perpetuated throughout history. Kings could have a wife and multiple mistresses. Women had to be virgins until they married, or else they were ostracized. That's all I'm saying." They were quiet for a minute before she continued. "Tell me, were you a bad boy? You had all those girls chasing after you all through high school, and I imagine it hasn't been much different at Cornell."

Nate thought for a second. Admitting anything to her would require him to put down his defenses, and he was not comfortable with that, even with her. He would have to admit, yes, the girls chased after him, but no, he had very limited experience with women. There had only been Dani and her. Besides, he knew Leah was no virgin the first time they slept together. And more importantly, he preferred not knowing her sexual history, only to find out she may have been promiscuous in the past.

"I don't like where this conversation is going," he said adamantly. From the firmness of the conviction that she heard in his voice, Leah knew better than to pursue it any further. She wasn't sure if he was just uncomfortable with the subject or had something to hide.

"Someday, I hope we can be comfortable enough with each other to talk about these kinds of things."

They continued to change in silence. Nate found the suit that he had worn to his mother's funeral hanging in the closet and put it on. His mood changed considerably as he watched Leah change into a blue lace chiffon dress and matching heels, which contrasted nicely with his dark suit and powder blue shirt.

"You are stunning," he said admiringly from across the room.

"You're not so shabby either," she said as she strode across the room to face him, then straightened his tie. "If you want to kiss me, do it now so I can put on my lipstick and makeup."

He obliged her and was reluctant to let her slip from his arms.

***

The rehearsal and dinner went down without a hitch, and they soon found themselves on the road to the lake house. It was nearly midnight when they arrived, so they joined together in the shower before climbing into bed. He would wait until the morning to show her around and, if they had time, climb to the top of the mountain to show her the view.

He gently washed her back as they enjoyed the relaxing steam of the shower together. When she finally turned to face him, he lifted her up with ease as she wrapped her legs around him. They enjoyed each other for a time before retreating to the bed which awaited them and completed what they had begun.

In the morning, when he awoke, he found her nestled close to him, and he felt her soft, steady breaths on his back. He rolled over gently to face her and began to explore her soft skin and body with his hand as he kissed her forehead, ears, nose, and then lips. By now, she began to stir in response to his touch, which had progressed ever so slowly down, and without words, she reached out, finding him eager and ready to be joined with her.

***

"You are amazing," she sighed, lying now in his arms.

"How so?" he queried, not looking for compliments or reassurance but simply curious as to her emotion.

"I have never felt so loved by anyone" She smiled and brushed her hand across his stubble. "And you are sooo sexy," she added.

"I'm the lucky one," he countered.

"How so?" she copied.

"To be with the most beautiful woman in the world."

"Hm...my compliment was at least believable. I feel loved, and you are sexy. But it's doubtful that I am the most beautiful woman in the world."

"You are to me," he stated simply. "And that is what matters."

"Go make me some breakfast. I need to wash this smell off of me." She hopped from the bed, wrapping the sheet around her.

"I've seen you naked," he called after her as she walked toward the bathroom. She turned briefly and stuck her tongue out at him, then disappeared behind the closed door.

***

They began the hike up the mountain shortly after breakfast. Upon reaching the top, Nate took his usual stance on the big rock, looking down at the valley below. Leah stood beside him, admiring the view. "I can see why you like it up here." He put his arm around her waist as they breathed in the cool morning air. "What's that over there?" She was pointing at the big oak with the carvings in the bark.

"Come, I'll show you." He jumped down from the rock, leading her to the tree for a closer look. "This is Todd here," he pointed out. "And Billy. And me. Here are Todd and Allie. And this is..." he paused.

"You and Dani." She took his arm and continued. "Wonderful memories here, Nate."

"They're not all wonderful." He took a knife from his pocket and peeled Dani's initials away, then began carving Leah's initials below where Dani's had been. "Maybe someday, we'll come back here with a fond memory of this moment. Do you think that we will? Be together, I mean, in a few years from now?"

"For now, I'm stuck in the present. But you, Nathan, you have some options and a great future ahead of you."

It saddened him to see her stuck in the present. And she was right about his future. The time was rapidly approaching when he would have to make decisions that would not bode well for the two of them.

"We better get going back to Plainville. I have to meet with my dad before we go to the wedding."

***

They arrived back at Nate's home by mid-afternoon and had several hours to spare before the church ceremony. Nate and Leah found Bella in her customary spot in the kitchen, cheerful as usual and pleased to see them. "Your dad is in the living room. He has a friend with him," she cautioned.

"Do I know him?" Nate responded.

"Her," Bella corrected.

"His secretary, I presume."

Bella looked up from her baking sheet for a moment without responding.

"Are you ready for this?" Nate asked Leah.

"Are you?" she responded.

"Never. But let's get this over with." He took Leah's hand and led her into the living room.

Mark was seated in one of two high-backed chairs, and a woman a few years younger sat beside him. Nate had only seen her a few times before when as a young boy, he visited his father's downtown office. Mark immediately stood as they both entered.

"Nate, It's good to see you," he began, extending his hand for his son to shake. Nate cordially responded with his hand, then stepped back to stand beside Leah and awaited an introduction. "You remember my assistant Pam" he continued, nodding in the direction of his companion.

"Of course. It's nice to see you, Mrs. Dawber," Nate said politely. He knew she was married at some point in time and wasn't aware of her current marital status. He never knew her first name and was intent on keeping their relationship formal and not familiar. "This is Leah."

Mark was still standing and extended his hand to Leah with a pleasant smile. "I'm very pleased to meet you, Leah."

"It's nice to meet you too."

Mark returned to his chair and beckoned them to sit as well. They talked for a bit about Nate's school and baseball, then about his future plans. "I haven't decided yet" was all Nate provided. Then they moved on to Leah, and she offered some general information about school and planning to teach music. Pam listened attentively and followed up with additional questions when given the opportunity. "And your family?" she asked.

"My grandmother raised me. I still live with her and help her when she needs it. And I have a ten-year-old niece who I help care for."

"No other family?"

"No, just the three of us."

There was an awkward silence for a moment before Nate seized upon the opportunity to speak. He was reluctant to at first and preferred to do it in private, but his father had made that impossible now. "Dad, I wanted to meet with you today to apologize for my behavior the last time we spoke."

"It was a difficult time for all of us, Nate," Mark responded.

"It's been difficult for a long time," Nate added. Mark watched him closely as Nate continued. "Mom was sick for so long, then Todd left and you… I'm not sure where you were." He looked in Pam's direction, and she stared at him blankly.

"I was here when I could be Nate. I still had my work, and life doesn't just stop when things go wrong."

"Things go wrong?" Nate said, barely under his breath. Leah sensed the acrimony toward his father and looped her arm through his.

"Your mother was ill for a long time Nate. You know when and how it started. And you know we tried…I tried…to get her help. And it didn't do any good."

"What about us?" Nate countered.

"What do you mean?" Mark asked.

Could he be completely clueless? Nate thought as he prepared to respond. "Maybe you couldn't help her. Maybe you did do all you could for her. But you had four…three children," he corrected himself before continuing. "Three children who needed you."

"That's why I brought Bella in," he shrugged.

Nate scoffed. "Unbelievable," he whispered under his breath.

"Nathan," Leah whispered to him. "This is not going to solve anything." She urged him to stop before exacerbating the situation.

Nate took a deep breath, then continued. "So you thought hiring Bella to do all the cooking and cleaning was enough to replace my mother and you?"

"Nate, I lost your mother to this illness, then I lost Billy…"

"I know, Dad" Nate had lowered his voice now but remained emotional. "So let's compare. I lost a mother, I lost Billy, and then I lost you. Top that off with Todd leaving. What was left for me here? It's rather obvious, don't you think? There was nothing then, and there is nothing now."

"I'm here now, Nate."

Nate slowly stood, shaking his head. "That's great, Dad. But you know what? I don't need you anymore. I've learned to get by without you being here." He turned his attention toward Leah. "We better get going. We don't want to be late." He strode past her and out of the room.

Leah stood now, too, and excused herself. She entered the kitchen and found Bella busying herself but clearly upset too by what she had overheard. She looked to Leah and motioned toward the back door. "I don't know that he'll ever forgive his father," Bella lamented. "He went outside, through the back."

Leah found him sitting quietly now in a rocker on the back porch. She sat down next to him but remained quiet. "There used to be a hammock here. Zak and I used to climb in and then swing it as high as we could until we both fell out." They sat in silence before Nate continued. "It's times like these that I would just put on my running shoes and run until I dropped. As bad as that sounds, it helped to clear my head. Forget the pain… Do you think he really doesn't get it? What did he do to us?"

"I don't know Nate. I understand you felt abandoned by both your mother and father. That was a terrible period of your life. But I can see from his perspective it wasn't just a terrible time; it was the rest of his life he was losing. The woman he loved and planned to spend the rest of his life with was gone. A son whom he loved was gone. He could never get those things back. But you...maybe he saw you as being resilient...able to move forward when he couldn't. You still had...have your whole life ahead of you. What does he have?"

"A mistress" was his short reply. After a moment of silence, he continued. "You think that justifies his behavior? Leaving his children to fend for themselves? Look where it's gotten us. A sister about to be an unwed mother, a brother who leaves home and is missing, and me, left on my own to fend for myself."

"We don't think rationally when we are overcome with grief. We just react the only way we know how. It's like you and running. You react to your anxiety in that way. And it works for you. Your father's behavior may not have been rational, but it's all he knew to do."

Nate took a deep breath. "Things will never be right between us," he concluded. "So, I guess it's time we go our separate ways and leave this miserable thing we once called family behind us. You ready?" He stood from the chair and pulled her up beside him. "At least I have you now. And that's all I need."

***

CHAPTER 27
SEASONS CHANGE

Nate and Leah spent one more night at the lake house together before returning to Geneva. His projects were numerous, and he had six weeks to complete them, which is where he spent most of his time. Little was discussed between him and Leah about their visit to Connecticut.

Nate organized his time well, completing repairs around the BnB and the cafe during the week while still allowing time for him and Leah to spend time together on the lake, hiking the trails at the glen, and visiting some of the local wineries around the Finger Lakes region. He found fulfillment and a new sense of worth in the completion of various projects. And his time with Leah allowed him to set aside much of the turmoil that had ruled his life up until that time.

He and Leah spent every evening together, and she would visit him frequently in the middle of the night, only to leave him again before dawn in an effort to keep that part of their relationship private and discreet, for Molly's sake.

On several weekends, they drove to the stable, and when Leah wasn't available, he took Molly, who was rapidly improving her equestrian skills. He continued teaching Molly how to play the guitar, and in the evenings, Molly, Leah, and Nate would sit on the dock, playing their guitars while other visitors sang along with them. Molly preferred country ballads, easy to learn, play and sing along with, which was amenable to Nate and Leah.

As guests continued to arrive throughout the summer at the BnB, Nate took an interest in their wants and needs, eagerly providing assistance whenever he could. He found he enjoyed spending time with the many guests who came and went, sometimes inviting them to join him and Molly on the docks to be entertained with their musical talents. His favorite place was sitting on the dock, which was one of the few memories from his childhood that he held tightly to.

As the end of summer approached, he became more solemn as he thought of what was to come. His final year at Cornell was his last chance to fulfill his childhood dream of playing the game he loved and the choices he would have to make that would impact not only his life but the lives of those he had come to love. These would be the most critical decisions of his life, and he still had no definitive plan.

***

Nate had gone for a late evening swim when he found Leah waiting for him at the end of the pier. She tossed him a towel as he ascended the ladder, then sat to dangle her feet into the warm summer water of Seneca Lake. This would be his last evening with her before returning to Cornell as a senior for the fall term. "This has become one of my favorite places now," he observed as he sat down beside her.

"It does have a certain appeal," she agreed thoughtfully.

"You've spent your whole life here. Have you ever wanted to go somewhere else?"

"I'd like to travel someday, but this is my home, and I've never even thought about leaving here."

"But would you, if you could?"

She knew he was referring to her obligation to care for her grandmother and Molly as long as necessary. "It's not a possibility right now, so I don't think about it. What good would it do?"

Nate thought about it before speaking. "Sometimes I wish I didn't have a choice...that I didn't have to make a decision. It would be easier to have my future written in stone than to have to choose."

"I think I know you well enough now to understand where your heart is. You've always wanted to pursue your first love, baseball. I can't be the reason you don't pursue your dream, Nathan. So whatever you ultimately decide, you need to leave me out of that equation. Do what's right for yourself. You don't need to worry about me or Grammy or Molly. We'll be fine."

"I don't want to leave you or what we have."

Leah slowly stood and looked out over the lake. "What we have, Nathan, will always be in my heart. But we are both young and have some amazing things to look forward to. Your life will change soon. Mine will take a while, but that's OK. I like where I am right now, and I can be patient enough to wait for whatever changes may come."

She began to walk away when he called after her. "One more night," he said, just loud enough for her to hear. She turned, smiled, then continued back to the shore. "That's all we have," he whispered to himself.

***

Molly and Grammy watched from the porch as Nate loaded the last of his belongings into the Civic. He had already said goodbye to Leah as she left him in the middle of the night. Molly decided at the last moment to run to him and hug him tightly before he climbed into the car. "Will we get a big tree at Christmas again?" she asked tearfully.

"We will, I promise. Do you remember that scarf you made me the first Christmas I was here? I've worn it out. Any chance you can make me a new one?"

"You bet I will," she smiled. He kissed the top of her head, then nudged her to return to the porch with Grammy. Then he watched and waved to them as he drove away.

***

The fall semester came and went quickly for Nate. He continued living in the suite with Zak and two new suitemates, both seniors on the baseball team with Nate. Zak had assumed a new role since leaving the team. He had made amends with the coach and team, stopped his steroid use, and, since his major was in PT and sports medicine, assumed a position as an assistant trainer for the team. This allowed him to travel with them and maintain close relationships with the team and with Nate.

Nate was happy for Zak, who was now back to his usual self, the person that Nate had always loved as a friend and brother. They spent many evenings talking about their past and hopes for the future. They even had visions of Nate playing baseball and Zak being a trainer on the same team.

Nate found himself worrying less and less about the decisions he would soon be forced to make. And in light of his last conversation with Leah, she had made it clear that whatever he decided to do, it had to be for himself and not based on their relationship. While that was difficult at first to accept, he grew to understand what it would ultimately mean. She might not be a part of his plan, and she would not affect his decision, whatever it ended up being.

He missed Leah, and in spite of the newfound tranquility he found in being ready to accept whatever was to come, the time to see her again seemed to pass too slowly. When Christmas finally arrived, he sought her out first, finding her in the usual place serving coffee at the counter of the cafe. He sat at the counter, unnoticed at first by her.

"Excuse me, miss," he called out while her back was turned to him.

"I'd like some coffee, please." She recognized his voice without turning and playfully admonished him for his impatience.

"Alright, alright. Keep your shirt on," she responded without turning. When she finally did face him, she smiled and touched his hand. "Or maybe not."

They both laughed at the suggestion as she poured him a cup of coffee. "What brings you to our beautiful city on the lake?"

"Just passing through," he responded with a smile. "Any suggestions on a place to stay for a few nights?"

"Try Grammy's BnB. The penthouse suite might still be available."

"I will do that. Maybe our paths will cross again during my visit."

"Maybe," she winked, then moved on to serve some other customers.

***

The Christmas and New Year's holidays were the happiest that Nate had experienced since his early childhood before all the troubles began. He set those thoughts aside and enjoyed the moments experienced through his family of here and now, Leah, Molly, and Grammy Nettles. The church Christmas pageant this year was directed by Leah and consisted of youth and adults. Nate was asked last minute to play and sing their favorite tune, the Little Drummer Boy, which was inserted into the program. As he played that Christmas, he sang the lines, and all those around him provided the drumming chorus. It was emotional for him, as he was reminded of his childhood, surrounded by his brothers and sister on Christmas Eve, but the joy he felt overcame any uncontrolled emotional response he could have had from things past.

He and Molly had found the perfect tree. And as asked, he received the perfect gift from her. It was a new scarf, this one much brighter and longer than the first one she had made, and he wore it proudly wherever they went during their short time together.

He and Leah found time for themselves, sometimes during the day, sometimes in the middle of the night. They talked again of their future plans, and the only uncertainty remaining was theirs and if their paths might ever cross again. It was a profound sadness that they quickly dispelled, choosing to focus on their current happiness and the opportunities that lie before them.

On their last night, as they lay together in the quiet of his room, he stroked her hair and spoke softly to her. "Regardless of what opportunity I may be offered after school, I want to come to see you before I go. Would you be

OK with that?"

"I guess this won't be our last goodbye then," she stated. "I would like that."

"And by then, I'll have my plan in place. I'll have a fair notion of where I'm headed. Will you watch me play? I mean, if I make the majors."

"When you make the majors," she corrected.

"When I make the majors makes me sound a bit arrogant, don't you think?"

"A couple of years ago, I would have said yes and just dismissed you as some arrogant, self-centered college boy. Now I know better. You told me back then it was pride, not arrogance. You weren't wrong. And you have the right to be proud of all you've accomplished. And something else has been reaffirmed from my time with you. Money can't buy happiness. Regardless of your status in this life, rich or poor, we all face adversity, but we can rise above that. You have shown that."

"You give me more credit than I deserve."

"You may think that way now, but your story isn't over yet. You still have some things to prove before you believe you deserve any kind of credit. And when you do make the majors, I'll be your biggest fan."

***

His return to Cornell for the last semester was nostalgic. He longed for what was left behind while yearning for what was still to come. Zak remained steadfast in his friendship and encouragement for Nate to achieve what he had always longed for. As the season progressed, Nate was keenly aware of the scouts sent to watch and recruit for various farm teams across the country. In rare instances, players were recruited directly into the majors. But that required a commitment on their part that most weren't willing to make. The preferred route was to draft them into positions in the minors, allowing time for closer observation of the players and determination of what was needed for the team based on player performances and injuries. Nate was well aware of the process and contented himself with the possibility of getting his foothold with an offer from at least one farm team and, ideally, two, affording him an opportunity to determine for himself where he might end up.

Midway through the season, an opportunity was presented to him as he met with a recruiter from the Gwinnett Stripers, the AAA farm team for the Atlanta Braves. There were farm teams in Syracuse and Binghamton that he preferred, which would have kept him closer to what he now considered home, but they were not forthcoming. He met shortly after with a recruiter from the Buffalo Bisons, the AAA farm team for the Toronto Blue Jays. It wasn't ideal, and the Blue Jays weren't at the top of his list, but he would settle for them, even if only because of their proximity to Leah, provided nothing more appealing was offered him. The final offer received came from the Dodgers farm team located in Oklahoma City. It was by far the best offer available, playing for a highly-rated team with lots of opportunities to move up into the big leagues. The downside was the location and it meant leaving everything behind that he knew and loved.

The weeks before he had to sign weighed on him heavily. She had told him not to base his decision on her, but on what was best for him. And if he were going, to be honest with himself and her, the choice was obvious. He waited until the last day to commit to the team and would have to report to them in Oklahoma City the second week of July. For the remainder of the school year, he focused on baseball along with his studies which, when completed, would grant him a multi-state teaching certificate in health and physical education. This was Nate's fall-back plan which his friend and teammate Jake had pushed for when they began their years at Cornell.

His current thinking was, with all due respect to his friend Jake, he wouldn't need it, and it would soon become just an afterthought. He was about to make his dreams come true. As the season ended and matriculation from school was complete, he packed up his things for one last trip to Geneva before heading out to his new job. Zak was preparing to leave as well. He was successful in his search for an athletic training position for Baltimore's minor league team in Aberdeen, TX, not far from his father's home. Parting ways was not easy for either of them, but they agreed to stay in touch, and their travels with the teams would reconnect them on occasion.

RUNNING SHOES

***

As Nate drove toward Geneva, he mapped out a schedule, allowing him to spend some time with Leah before heading to Oklahoma. During the process, he determined that if he were ever going to reconnect with his brother Todd, it would have to be now. He would have to make the time between Leah and Oklahoma City. Leah would undoubtedly understand and, in fact, probably encourage Nate to seek him out.

As he continued to drive, he telephoned his home, hoping that someone there could help him find Todd. He was relieved when Bella answered his call.

"Bella, this is Nate."

"Nathan. It's wonderful to hear your voice. How are you?"

"I'm fine. Schools done. And I have an offer to play in the minors."

"Congratulations! I'm so happy for you. And proud! I know it's what you always wanted."

"Thank you, Bella. How are things there?" he inquired.

"Things are OK here. Hectic at times, with the baby and all, but it keeps me busy, and everyone seems happy."

Nate had forgotten about Gail's pregnancy and, with no regular communication from home, knew nothing about the outcome. "Boy or girl?" he asked Bella.

"She is beautiful, Nate. Her name is Hailey."

"And the father? He in the picture?"

"Doubtful. Gail has moved on. I don't know if he has even seen the baby. But enough about that. You must have called for a reason."

"Yes, I did. I have some time to kill before I head to the farm team, and I was hoping you might know where Todd is."

"I don't have an address, but I overheard your father talking with the family attorney a while back. They mentioned Venice, Florida. It's not a big city, so you might be able to track him down, just knowing that."

"Thanks, Bella. You've been very helpful."

"Should I tell your father you called?"

"No. In fact, I'd prefer you didn't. We're not on the same page about a lot of things. So it's best to just leave things alone."

"I understand. Maybe someday."

"Maybe. Goodbye, Bella."

"Goodbye, Nathan."

***

The summer crowds had already begun to flock in, a yearly ritual for many that resulted in consternation by the locals. Were it not for the small businesses that benefited from the influx, there might have been even more animosity between the natives and the visitors.

Nate loved the area for its seasonal beauty and recreational opportunities. That would never change, and the moments he spent here would always be a part of him, no matter where he ended up. There was a distinct difference between this lake and the one in Connecticut. This one served as a hub for tourists from both within and without the upstate NY region, whereby Candlestick Lake was, on a much smaller scale, an attraction for mostly in-state residents.

He found all the rooms at the BnB rented out already. This didn't include the penthouse suite, which was never used now for commercial purposes but was reserved for special visitors like him. Unfortunately, that's what he felt like now. This was no longer his home; he was just visiting for a short time. The hard reality that this may soon just be a memory hit him hard, and he sat

RUNNING SHOES

for a time, sitting in his car outside the BnB before entering.

As he carried his suitcase up the first flight of stairs and down the hallway, he passed by each closed door, all rooms occupied from within. He passed by Molly's door as well and listened briefly for any sign of life inside but was greeted only by silence. He continued up the second flight of stairs to his room on the third floor. Nothing was changed. It was all the same like he had never left. It made him think back to his own room in Connecticut, how it was always the same as he had left it. And Billy's room too. He was gone almost ten years now. But his room remained a shrine dedicated to a brother and son who left this world much too early and before his time. It all seemed like a dream now. And by leaving things unchanged, he would finally wake up from his dream and be reassured that nothing had changed and all was as it should be.

He would walk down the hall and past the room next door where Billy was lying on his bed, reading the latest equestrian magazine. Then he would move on to the next open door, and Todd would smile and wave to him to come in as he strummed his guitar. Then turning and walking back toward his room, Gail could be seen flipping through the latest teen magazine. And before returning to his own room, the sound of his father and mother speaking in hushed tones behind the closed door of their bedroom.

All of these things reminded him of how his family was...how they should be. But it wasn't real. And it never would be. These were the harsh realities of his lost childhood. He had dealt with these feelings again and again and was finally able to put most of them to rest. He knew where he was today and where he was going. Those decisions had been made. But there was still one missing piece. That of a brother whom he idolized and wanted to emulate. The brother who once called him his best friend and spent hours with him, sometimes late at night, just talking from their bunks, or fishing and swimming in the river, and tossing the football or playing baseball in the yard or basketball by the garage. All of the things that brothers do together, all in limbo but not forgotten.

Todd had escaped. His absence for the past seven years had turned into abandonment. He had left Nate behind to fend for himself, knowing full well of the family's disintegration and gradual descent into oblivion.

The more he thought about it, the more angst he felt. It had been building inside him now for some time, and now that school was over and a deadline for reporting to the field team was set, he was becoming anxious and bitter. He had been left on his own to sink or swim, even by his brother, and he wanted to know why. Todd was the only one in his family that mattered to him now.

***

Leah detected a restlessness within him. She had sought him out to come down for dinner and found him pacing about his room. This was the first time she had seen him in six months, and she expected his stay to be short but intimate. But instead, he seemed distant and distracted.

"Nathan," she called from the top step leading into his room, having observed him quietly for a minute.

He turned to her with a momentary look of confusion before his head cleared, and she came into vision. "Hey," he acknowledged and moved toward her. She took the last step up to face and embrace him, not questioning his frame of mind. At least not now; maybe later. She would avoid further intimate contact or verbal play until she understood more. "It's time for dinner." She broke free of him, and he followed her down the stairs in silence.

Molly was already seated, and Grammy was setting a meat platter on the table before seating herself. "Welcome home, Nathan," Grammy greeted him with a smile.

"Thank you," Nate responded. "It's good to be home again."

"You look tired," Molly commented, looking at him curiously. Leah remained silent as they passed the dishes around the table.

"I guess maybe I am a little tired," Nate confessed. "A lot to do the last couple of days. Finishing up with school, graduation, then packing and driving here."

"You'll have plenty of time to rest here," Grammy commented. "We're not giving you any projects this visit. Just take some time for yourself. From what Leah has said, you have a wonderful opportunity ahead of you. I will say we'll be sad to see you go again."

"You're not staying the summer?" Molly asked, clearly disappointed by this news.

"Not this time, kiddo, I'm afraid. In fact, I'll only be here for a couple of days. Then I will have to leave."

Leah was caught by surprise at this latest pronouncement. She had expected he would stay for several weeks, and they could spend some time together before he headed to Oklahoma. "I thought you didn't have to be in Oklahoma until after the 4th," Leah commented.

"That was my original plan, but I have some unsettled business I have to attend to before Oklahoma."

Leah determined that it must be important enough to cut his visit short, and she could accept that. It concerned her more about his current frame of mind. He should be more excited about the opportunity ahead but seemed to be focused on something ominous.

Nate changed the subject to avoid any further discussion about his stay. "How about we visit the stables tomorrow? All of us."

"You all can go," Grammy resisted. "I have a full house and guests to tend to."

"I'll take the day off, so Molly and I can go," Leah agreed. "As long as you think you are OK with us leaving you here to handle the guests," she said, turning her attention to Grammy.

"I'll be fine. All I have to do is make breakfast for the guests. Then they are on their own, and so am I."

***

"Walk with me," Leah said as she led Nate from the dining room and out the back door, then onto the dock. They walked the length of the pier to the gazebo. Nate had rebuilt most of it and replaced any rotted wood the previous summer. They sat on the bench and watched boats pass by in the late evening sunshine. "I love the smell of the lake, the fresh air." Nate was quiet, still deep in thought. "Are you going to tell me, or am I going to have to pry it out of you?"

"I'm sorry. I shouldn't have blindsided you like that."

"It's not like you, Nathan. Clearly, something is bothering you. I can understand the anticipation of not knowing exactly what's ahead of you or what to expect. But I don't see that affecting you this way. Can you tell me what this unresolved business is that you referred to?"

"You deserve an explanation, but I hesitate because I don't know if you'll understand."

"Try me."

"OK. I've tracked Todd down."

She waited for him to continue, but he didn't, so she did. "So you're going to go see him. That's a good thing. I can understand that."

"It's why I'm going to see him that you won't understand."

"I know you love and miss your brother. What more reason do you need?"

"I need to know. I need to know why he left as he did. Why he hasn't been in contact in over four years? Why he abandoned the family."

"Why he abandoned you," she concluded.

"Do you think I'm wrong to feel this way?"

"I think I know you pretty well, Nathan, and you will never be able to let this go without knowing. I also know that when you get something in your head, you don't let anything or anyone deter you. It really doesn't matter what

I think."

"Of course it does. You matter to me, Leah."

"As I said before, Nathan, your decisions now can't be because of me. Decisions like that now will result in regrets later. I won't be the reason for your regret."

"You know I've weighed my options from every which way. I wanted to somehow achieve my lifelong goal with you by my side. I was hoping and praying I would get drafted by the Syracuse farm team, so I could stay close to you. It could have bought us both some time to work things through. But as luck would have it, I couldn't be much further away than Oklahoma."

"So what will you say to Todd when you see him?"

Nate shook his head. "I don't know. Whenever we used to talk, he was always the older brother, and I was just a kid. We're both adults now, and I don't know what to expect. How he will react if...when I confront him. I really don't know how it's all going to play out. I've always been non-confrontational. I try to avoid conflict. I run from it."

"I didn't see you avoid or run from your father."

"That's true, but it didn't end well either."

"All I can say, Nathan, is you need to go. You need to resolve this with your brother. And from what you have told me, your relationship with him is nothing like with your father. You may be able to just sit down with him and come to terms without the conflict."

***

Nate, Leah, and Molly spent the next day at the stable. Leah rode Sheba, Nate rode Toby, and Molly rode one of Natalie's other quarter horses. In the evening, after dinner, they all gathered in the gazebo for Nate's last night with them. Nate and Molly both played their guitars, and all joined in on some familiar country tunes. Guests of the BnB joined them as well, so Molly insisted they make it a going-away party for Nate. The celebration continued to almost midnight when the guests, Grammy and Molly, all retreated for the night, leaving Nate and Leah alone once more on the pier.

"Will you let me know when you get to Todd's and how your reunion goes?" Leah asked.

"Sure. Just allow me a few days to get there and settle things with him."

"Come," she stood and took his hand. No more words were spoken as she led him into the house and up the two flights of stairs to his room, where they would spend their last night together.

CHAPTER 28
LOST AND FOUND

He arose from their bed as soon as the morning light came through the window. He had a long drive ahead and wanted to get an early start. They had only a few hours of sleep between them, having spent much of the night joined together in intimacy. As he slowly dressed, he watched her as she lay sleeping, a sheet drawn up tightly to her chin, hiding what he had searched for during the night. When he was finally dressed and ready to go, he knelt over her and kissed her gently on the lips. She stirred and sighed, then continued into what must have been a deep, rejuvenating sleep.

He wouldn't wake her, for it would only be to say goodbye. This was one of those moments: difficult but never forgotten. It was hard to say those words. They seemed too permanent. But in reality, he believed their time together was over, and he needed to say it, so he whispered to himself as he looked at her one last time. "Goodbye, Leah." He then made his way quietly down the two flights of stairs, out the front door, and to his car.

***

It would take him roughly twenty hours to get there. He could have flown, but there was too much uncertainty on this trip. He didn't know exactly where Todd was, only that he lived somewhere in Venice. It was a small enough town that, with any luck, the locals would know him. He didn't know how long he would be there. In all likelihood, it would just be overnight once he had his say with him. And if he was just there the night, he would have several weeks to kill before he had to be in Oklahoma, so maybe he would need the car for a road trip across the south.

His thoughts went from Leah, whom he had just left behind, to Todd and where he was now going. His focus soon became only Todd. He wanted to know why Todd quit communicating with him. Had he written him off like he did the rest of the family? What kind of brother would do that? He thought their bond was stronger than that. He had made numerous attempts to reach him, up until the messages started coming back as "undeliverable." What was that all about? If he had lost his phone or it was damaged, he could have gotten a new one sometime during those years of no contact. He couldn't comprehend how his older brother, whom he loved so deeply, could treat him this way. The more he thought about it, the more bitter he became. And when he would finally have the chance to confront Todd, he would let him know how hurt and angry he was for the betrayal of everything they had.

***

He was so angry; he stopped only to refuel. He was certain he couldn't sleep, and normally, when he was anxious, he would simply run until his body outraced his mind. His adrenaline kept him alert and moving so that he could complete this journey as quickly as possible.

He entered the southern gulf Florida town of Venice around eight in the evening. As his car refilled with gas, he went inside the QuickStop and asked a woman behind the counter if she knew a man named Todd Woods, to which she responded, no.

"You don't have a phone book here, do you?" he then asked.

The woman formed a puzzled look on her face before responding. "Do they even print those anymore?" she quipped.

Nate turned away in frustration without speaking and returned to his car. He continued his drive down Route 19 until he came upon a small diner. He hadn't eaten all day, so he parked and went inside. A waitress with an excessive amount of makeup and curly red hair approached the table. Clowns wear less makeup, he thought to himself. He now focused on the rigorous bubble gum chewing and the resulting bubble that popped before she spoke.

"What'll you have, sweetie?" she asked with a smile that revealed a missing front tooth.

The cliché almost made him laugh, except that she certainly wouldn't have appreciated it and could do nasty things to his food. "A burger and fries will do. And a Coke."

"Sure toots, coming right up." She sauntered off and returned to the table with his coke.

"Say, you wouldn't know if Todd Woods lives around here, would you?"

"Who's asking?" she said, setting the Coke down on the table.

"Well, I'm his brother, and I lost directions to his house."

"I donno no Todd Woods." She then walked back toward the kitchen and yelled to the cook. "Hey Geoffrey, you know a guy named Todd Woods?"

Nate listened as a response resounded from the kitchen. "Never heard of him."

She returned to Nate's table with his plate in hand. "Here you go, sugar. Geoffrey says he never heard of the guy. And Geoffrey knows pretty much everybody in this town. You sure you're in the right state?" She then laughed, and Nate chuckled, just to keep the conversation light.

"Yes, I'm sure. Thanks for asking around, though."

"You got it, hon." Their interaction ended there and left Nate pondering, had he stayed longer, what other name she could possibly attach to him. He left the diner shortly after and continued further south, wondering how he would ever locate Todd. He was becoming even more frustrated by his own failure to figure this out ahead of time instead of driving around blindly in the dark. He came upon what appeared to be a biker bar, slowed down, but thought better of stopping and engaging with a group of bikers, considering his short curly hair and two days of stubble against their long hair and beards.

A little further down the road, he found a much larger bar with a packed parking lot. The front door was propped open, and smoke poured through it, accompanied by loud country music. It was nearly ten o'clock now. He would stop just for a beer and maybe ask around about Todd, then find a place to stay the night. His search would have to wait until morning.

He entered the place, which was packed; probably a violation of the local fire codes, but that was not his concern. His feet stuck to the floor as he walked past tables filled with people and pitchers of beer. A live band was set up in the corner, beginning another loud country tune. Nate finally found a lone empty stool at the bar and watched a muted Marlins baseball game on the TV overhead as he waited for the bartender to come his way.

A girl who looked barely old enough to drink, let alone serve beer, set a coaster in front of him. "Hi. What can I get for you?"

"Guinness," he answered, admiring her short shorts as she turned away to get his drink.

"I don't think I've seen you here before," she commented, setting a full mug in front of him. "You live around here?"

"Nope."

"Well, welcome to Venice. A great place for fishing but not much else." She stood there for a moment looking at Nate, waiting for him to respond, but he didn't feel like talking much, so he just smiled and gulped his beer. He sat there in silence and watched the game for a time, then downed a couple more guinesses before the girl tried once again to engage him in conversation.

"This one's on the house." She set a shot of tequila in front of him. He was already beginning to feel the three or four drafts...he had actually lost count already but figured it would be impolite to refuse a free shot.

"Thanks," Nate said, holding it up to her as if to make a toast, then downed the shot.

"Another Guinness?"

"Sure, why not" he responded. He drank a lot during his time at Cornell but rarely drank more than he could handle. He felt like he was nearly there and debated on quitting for the night. As he thought about it, another shot magically appeared in front of him.

"Hi, I'm Mandy." A girl had suddenly taken the stool next to him and was now talking to him.

"Hey," Nate responded, giving her the once-over. Pretty. Long black hair. Too much makeup and lipstick. Probably a bit older than him. He took the shot and downed it.

"Better slow down, cowboy," she commented, taking a cigarette from her purse and sipping on some green-colored drink in a martini glass.

"Appletini?" Nate asked, beginning to slur his words now. She nodded and smiled. "Bartender, another drink here for the lady," he requested. "Mandy, you said, right?" Nate asked, now noticeably drunk.

"That's right."

"What time is it, Mandy?"

"A little past twelve. You want another beer?"

"Sure. Why not. Bartender, another beer over here, pleeease…"

She came over and stood in front of him. "I think you've had enough for tonight."

"Awe, come on," Nate pleaded disingenuously. "Just one more."

"Sorry, I'm cutting you off," she replied.

"I want a fuckin beer," Nate shouted, and the crowd around him drew silent. The girl began to turn away to serve another patron when Nate reached across the bar.

"Hey," she shouted at him and pulled away. "Time for you to leave."

"OK...OK...I'm going," he slurred. As he got up from the stool, his head spun, and he blacked out, falling to the floor.

***

It was one AM when the phone rang, waking Allie out of a deep sleep. Who could be calling at this hour? She wondered. It couldn't be good. "Hello?" she answered sleepily.

"Is this the Woods' house?" a man's voice on the other end of the line asked.

"Yes, who is this?"

"Look, you don't know me, but I know Todd. We met at the VA a while back."

"OK."

"Is Todd there?"

"No, he's not."

"Well, does Todd have a brother named Nathan?"

"Yes, why?"

"Well, I'm over here at the West Corral Pub. This young fellow had a bit too much to drink. He passed out, so we checked his I.D. to see if he was local. He's got a Connecticut license. License says his name is Nathan Woods."

"Oh my gosh. You said he's passed out?"

"Yeah, but nothing that a good night's sleep won't cure. He'll have a helluva hangover, though. Listen, a couple of the vets here say they know Todd real well. They understand the situation and what Todd's been going through. We're happy to help out if we can. What would you like us to do with this young fella?"

Allie thought quickly. "Any chance you can get him here? That would really help us out. I'm sorry to put that on you."

"It's not a problem. If this fella is anything like his brother, he's a good man. Probably just working through some issues like all of us."

"What did you say your name was?" she asked.

"Frank. Frank Willows."

"Thank you again, Frank. I'll be waiting for you when you get here." Allie then gave him the address before hanging up.

***

Nate heard whispers around him, but his head hurt too much to even think about opening his eyes. He rubbed his temples, trying to relieve the pulsating pain that was in perfect rhythm with his heartbeat.

"I think he's waking up," came a voice, a little louder now than before. He squinted in the direction of the voice, and it took him a minute to focus his eyes enough to make out two small figures standing at the foot of the bed. Who these little people were or whose bed he was in, he had no idea. He had a vague recollection of the previous night, watching the Marlins on TV and having a couple of beers. Then someone put a shot in front of him, and everything else was a blur.

"What time is it?" Nate asked without further consideration for who they were or where he was. Not that the time really mattered, either.

"It's almost noon," the bigger of the boys responded. Nate rubbed his eyes and was finally able to open them wider to get a better look around him. He was in a bed, still fully dressed except for shoes, in a nondescript bedroom, clearly meant for guests. Two boys continued to stand at the foot of the bed, one a head taller than the other, just staring at him. "Mom says we gotta go in a few minutes. She wants you to come with us."

"Who are you, and why are you torturing me?" Nate groaned.

The older of the boys laughed while the other just stared. "I'm Josh, and this is Jacob," he said.

Nate began to realize where he must be and that the two boys in front of him looked like him, but even more like his brother and likely father, Todd. They both had short blond curly hair, which was a dominant feature of the Woods brothers.

"You're Uncle Nate," Josh spoke again.

"I guess I probably am," Nate responded, still trying to get his bearings. "So where are we going?"

"To see Daddy." These were the first words out of the younger boy's mouth.

"And where is Daddy? It's Saturday. He doesn't work on Saturday, does he?" Nate actually had no idea what job, if any, Todd would have, so in retrospect, the question was stupid.

"Daddy's in the hospital," Jacob responded.

"Oh." Nate was caught off guard by the response, just adding to his confusion. "Well, I guess I need to get moving then. Tell your mom I'll be ready in a few minutes."

"She wants you to shower and change first. She said you smell bad. I think you smell like puke." This was Josh talking again, and Jacob laughed.

"You said puke," Jacob laughed again.

"Here are some clothes to put on" he laid them on the foot of the bed "and put the dirty ones in the clothes hamper. That's where mom always makes us put them." The boys then turned to leave. "Hurry up, or we'll be late," were Josh's last instructions before closing the door behind them.

"Bossy little kid," Nate mumbled and pulled the sheet up to his chin, then just lay there for several minutes. "Shit," he mumbled and forced himself to sit at the edge of the bed. His head was still throbbing; maybe a hot shower would help. He got up from the bed and noticed now the stains on his shirt. He did smell like puke, and it nauseated him, so he quickly removed it. He peaked out the door, looked down the hallway, and made his way to the bathroom at the end of the hall.

Inside he quickly removed the rest of his clothes and stepped into the hot shower, inhaling deeply the steam which began to clear his head. He tried to remember what had happened the previous evening or even how he got to where he was, but nothing came to him. Whoever brought him there had clearly done him a favor. They could have just left him on his own, allowing him to drive his car into a tree, or simply abandoned him in the parking lot.

He finally stepped out of the shower, examining himself in the mirror. No new bruises or scars, which was good. He hadn't shaved now in four days, which was fairly typical of how he had been living since going to Cornell, but his eyes were red and swollen, clear evidence of last night's undertaking. He found a washcloth, soaked it with cool water, and placed it over his eyes while he sat on the closed lid of the toilet. The throbbing in his head had receded some and was now just a dull ache, so he dispensed with the washcloth and got dressed.

It was easy enough to find his way around the house. It was a typical one-story ranch common to the area. When he entered the kitchen, the same two boys were seated at a round oak table, eating PBJs and drinking glasses of milk. The woman at the sink eyed him curiously, and his head was clear enough to vaguely recognize her as someone he had last seen when he was thirteen. Todd had told him that Allie was the love of his life and he was true to his word.

"How are you feeling?" she asked him.

"Better than a few minutes ago. Thanks for the clothes."

"You and Todd are about the same size. You've grown a bit since I saw you last. You look amazingly like him. But he has a few years on you. Safe to say, you will age well, provided you don't make a habit of last night's activities," she smiled. She then set down a dish towel and walked over to Nate, put her arm around him, and hugged him tightly. "Nate, we are so happy to see you."

Nate reciprocated the hug. "I could have done a better job of it. I mean, showing up unannounced, and God knows how I even got here."

She laughed. "We can talk about that later. For now, do you have any interest in eating something? I can make you some eggs or maybe just a sandwich."

"I don't want you to put yourself out for me. Just tell me where the bread is, and I can fix myself a sandwich."

"OK, bread is in the bread box there," she pointed, "and you'll find some cold cuts in the refrigerator."

"Those PBJs look pretty good," Nate responded, eyeing the boys.

"Here you go, then." She handed him the jars of peanut butter and strawberry jam. "I'm going to finish getting ready to go. We're going to see Todd. You are welcome to join us now, or if you prefer, you can go later this evening when you're feeling better."

"Todd's in the hospital? Is he OK?"

She nodded. "He will be. He's recovering."

"From what?"

She was evasive and didn't answer.

"I'm sorry. I don't mean to push. This is all so…new…not at all what I was prepared for."

She then turned her attention to the boys. "Boys, go wash your sticky hands and put on your running shoes."

It brought a smile to Nate's face to hear those words.

"I never knew the difference until Todd explained it to me. And he said he learned it from you."

Nate chuckled. "There is a lot going on here right now that I just didn't expect."

"So, what exactly were you prepared for?"

Nate sat down with the sandwich and turned his eyes away from her. "I hesitate to tell you. I'm not proud of what I was prepared to do."

"I'm sure you and Todd have a lot to talk about. But I do need you to go easy at first. This has been a long road to recovery for him."

"What happened to him?"

"His last tour was three years ago. He was injured. Took some fragments from an IED. He was OK at first, but some were lodged near his spine. They moved, and he was paralyzed. So he had surgery. Started physical therapy and regained his ability to walk. Then it happened all over again. So he had a second surgery. That time was worse than the first. But he was strong and eventually able to continue with PT. Then about three days ago…well…it was a lot more risky this time. They had to make sure they removed all of the fragments this time."

"And did they?"

"They have assured us, yes."

"What about recovery?"

"That's what we're going to find out today. It will help to have you here. It will lift his spirits considerably. You know he's tough physically. Mentally, it's taken a toll on him. That's why he missed your mother's funeral. He couldn't travel. And somewhere along the way, he lost his phone when he was over there, and with everything going on, he never got it replaced."

"Does he know I'm here?"

She shook her head. "You arrived rather unexpectedly, and I haven't spoken with him since yesterday." The boys reentered the kitchen, ready to go. "I still have to make myself presentable."

"You go get ready. I'll get them settled in the car," Nate offered.

CHAPTER 29
REUNITED

It was mid-afternoon before they entered the hospital. Nate waited patiently outside the room while Allie took the boys in first to see Todd. Nate listened as the boys excitedly greeted their father. He then heard the familiar sound of Todd's voice, one he hadn't heard in years. But it was just as he remembered it. They talked for a while in muffled voices, interspersed with laughter before Allie finally hinted to Todd that they had brought someone else along who was anxious to see him.

Nate recognized his cue and walked through the doorway. They simply stared at each other for what seemed like minutes before either spoke. "Am I dreaming? Is that a grownup version of my little brother?" Todd smiled.

"And you're just as handsome as ever. I've been told we look a lot alike, and I have a lot to look forward to if that's true." They both laughed.

"Wow, I can't believe it's really you. I'd jump out of bed right now and give you a hug if I could."

Nate moved to the bedside. "No worries, brother. There will be plenty of time for that later."

"Why don't I let you guys talk for a while" Allie began. "We're going to run some errands and come back in a couple of hours."

"Thanks, hon," Todd agreed. She then kissed him before ushering the boys out the door.

"Two boys. Wow. There's no mistaking who they take after," Nate observed.

"They do look like Woods boys, don't they?" Nate took a chair near the bed as Todd continued. "So, when did you get into town?"

"Sometime last night. Late I think."

"How'd you find us?"

"Just lucky, I guess."

"OK," Todd laughed. "What gives? You look like hell. When was the last time you shaved? And finding us was luck?"

"We've always been honest with each other, right?" Nate asked.

Todd nodded. "Always."

"I had no idea where in this town you lived. I asked around. Nobody I asked ever heard of you. So I gave up. Went into this friendly bar, just for a couple of beers, you know. Who knew the folks here would be so friendly? Last I remember, someone gave me a shot. Tequila, I think. Next thing I know, I'm waking up in a strange bed with two boys, who look amazingly like their father, standing at the foot of the bed, telling me to get up."

Todd laughed. "Yeah, they do that to me sometimes too. Think of it as a welcoming party. So what prompted you to come? I mean, you're done with school. Don't you have someplace to be? A job lined up someplace? You can't live off our mother's insurance forever, you know."

"There's no rush. I have a little time."

"You came here without any idea of what you were getting into. It's not too late, you know…to just say hello, nice to see you, and goodbye. I wouldn't blame you."

"That was my plan."

"I figured I would have some explaining to do once I got past all this. You deserve an explanation."

Nate shook his head. "No, you don't have to explain anything. Allie told me some. And I get the picture. It was pretty selfish of me to expect you to check up on me regularly with what you've been going through. I just wish I could have been here for you. To help you get through it somehow."

Todd paused, and they just looked at each other for a few minutes. It was not an uncomfortable silence; they just needed time to take it all in. They were reunited after all this time. Todd finally broke the silence. "Well, you're here now, Nate. And you can help me. I want to get out of this bed and back on my feet as soon as possible. Allie's been good about it, but with the boys and her job, it's been a lot for her. If she can turn her attention back to the boys and stop worrying about me, that would help us out a lot."

"I'm here as long as you need me." It really wasn't true, Nate thought to himself, but it seemed right to say it, and they could talk more about that later. "Maybe we can even get back to running together."

"Spoken like the Nate I know. I still can't believe you're here. God, I missed you, Nate."

"Don't get all sentimental on me now. We do have a lot of catching up to do, though."

"You already know most of what's happened to me since leaving home," Todd began.

"There are some missing parts I'd like to hear about. "

Todd simply smiled. "And reminisce...on the good times."

They talked first about Todd's deployment and how he survived his third one in Afghanistan while his closest friend was killed by an IED. "It was my third deployment to Afghanistan that got the better of me. We were ambushed and had to abandon our Humvee and hoof it on foot. The guy next to me stepped on an IED. I was injured. He was killed. Something like that happens; you see why guys come back here suffering from PTSD. I am luckier than most. I got through it relatively unscathed."

"Yeah, right. Unscathed. How can you say that after three surgeries?"

"I still have all my limbs. I was able to come back, and I will eventually be restored to who I was. With your help."

"What about the boys?"

"Allie became pregnant with Josh before my first deployment. Then with Jacob before my second deployment. I have no regrets for anything I've done, except I was not here for their births. But Allie has been great. She understood I was doing what I was meant to do. And her mother still lives up in Sarasota and comes down to help her with the boys."

It was Nate's turn now for a quick update. "I'm not sure where to start. I guess I felt kind of lost for a while after you left. But I was already starting high school, so I adjusted. I found my mojo and met Dani. She was reluctant at first, but I used that Woods brothers' charm, and she caved."

"I was happy for you and relieved that you had found someone to take your mind off the family."

"She was a welcome distraction in the beginning, but when she got sick, it brought on a whole new level of concern. I just felt like it was something else I was losing...lost as it turned out." Nate continued to talk about his time with Dani and her illness and the breakup when he went off to Cornell when they were interrupted by Todd's surgeon, who had stopped by to check on him. He did a quick examination before speaking. "Things look good, Todd. Tomorrow, I want you up and out of that bed. Use a walker, and do some laps up and down the hall as many as you can until you're tired. Do that for a couple of days; then, we'll get rid of the walker. If all goes according to plan, you can start PT again."

"When can I get out of here?" Todd asked.

"We can get you into a rehab facility in a couple of days to start physical therapy. Going home before that would be risky."

"Can I do the PT at home?" Todd implored, not wanting to delay his return home any longer than necessary.

"You're going to need someone there to help you out if and when you need. Being alone would be risky, and your wife works, doesn't she?"

"That won't be a problem," Nate spoke up after listening quietly. "I'm Nate, Todd's brother. I plan on staying with Todd and his family for a while. I can handle Todd, no problem. And I'll make sure he does everything he needs to do to recover as quickly as possible."

The surgeon nodded. "We'll transfer you to the rehab center tomorrow. I'd like to keep you there for at least a couple of days. If things progress well and you have the right equipment at home, I'm OK with releasing you to continue the therapy there, provided you have your brother to help you out."

"Thanks, Doc. Any chance I can get out of this bed today and take a short walk? This bedpan is getting old."

The surgeon smiled as he made some notes on Todd's chart. "I'll have the nurse come in. She can disconnect the IV and assist you to the bathroom."

***

"Alright, Mr. Woods, swing your legs around to this side of the bed," the nurse instructed. "Sit there for a moment; make sure you're not light-headed."

"I'm fine."

Nate moved to his side. "I'll help him," he offered and assisted Todd as he rose to his feet. Todd rested his arm around Nate's shoulder, steadying him. "Ready?"

"Ready," Todd responded as he and Nate took slow steps toward the bathroom while the nurse observed. Nate reached for the door and pushed it open. "I got it from here," Todd insisted, and Nate waited outside the door..

When Todd opened the door to come out of the bathroom, Allie and the boys returned.

"Wow, look at you guys. Couldn't wait to get out of that bed, I see."

"Damn straight. Now that I got my buddy here to help, I'm going to take advantage of it."

Allie took Todd's other arm as she and Nate guided him back to the bed. "I take it you've decided to stay with us for a while," she said to Nate. Before he could respond, Allie reassured him. "We're lucky you showed up when you did."

"Doc says I'll need to stay in rehab for a couple of days, then continue PT at home as long as Nate is there."

***

Nate visited Todd in the rehab center daily, observing and participating when possible in his physical rehabilitation, learning the routines so that they could continue them at home. During those visits, they continued to reconnect, reminiscing about their years together as well as catching up on the years lost.

Todd was walking and steadying himself on the treadmill as Nate stood close by. "I didn't tell you what brought me here originally, did I, Todd." It was a statement, not a question, and Nate thought it needed to be said, so his brother would understand that his anxiety was the motivating factor, and for years, he blamed Todd.

"I blamed you...not at first. Not as long as we were at least able to communicate with each other. But once that stopped, I got really pissed at you. I felt like you abandoned me twice, in fact, first when you left, then when you stopped responding to my messages. Up until I was 16, you were the only constant in my life. The only one I could depend on." Todd listened closely and remained quiet as Nate poured out his heart to him.

"It's only now that I realize how selfish my motivations were. It was all about me. I never considered that something like this had happened to you."

"I never told you why I left. And you had no idea why I quit responding to your messages. I'm sorry I wasn't there and able to help you through those feelings." Todd was apologetic.

"I understand now why you quit responding. But why did you leave? Why the Marines? You could have gone to Cornell."

"Before I graduated, I planned to go to Cornell. Then I thought maybe I should stay home another year. Defer college. Maybe staying home one more year might help our family get through this crisis. It didn't take long to figure out my staying home wasn't going to help fix what had been going on for years. I knew I was going to have to leave eventually for my own welfare. I knew of Dad's affair, and I couldn't stand to see him do that to our mother. Gail had Bella to help her through it all. And you were 15 and going into high school. My biggest concern was you, but I believed you would be OK on your own. I was able to keep in touch...at least for a while. I also needed to prove to myself that I could make it on my own. So I decided the Marines was my best option."

"You helped me get through so much...adversity...tragedy."

"I inherited that job. I was your big brother. But it became a lot more than that. No mother around, then no father. We lost our brother. No one should have to go through that alone with no help from our parents."

"You helped me get through it," Nate said thoughtfully. "I feel like I've lost a lot of things during my lifetime. When Zak left, it felt permanent. Then our mother slowly drifted away after the accident and Billy's death, then our father. After you left, I had Dani for a time, but then I lost her."

"I was fortunate to have Allie. She helped me get through so much during those teenage years. She supported everything that I chose and encouraged me to follow what was in my heart. I knew from the start; she was the one I wanted to spend the rest of my life with."

"You make love look easy."

"It hasn't always been easy, Nate. We've had our struggles, our share of problems. I learned from her, though, that I couldn't fix every broken thing. And that when two people love each other, they can face those challenges together." Todd finished his therapy, and Nate handed him his crutches. "I worry about you, Nate," Todd said as they walked back to his room. "That you haven't found someone to share your life with yet."

"There is someone..was someone," Nate corrected himself. "But I had to make a choice. She told me not to base any decisions I make on her. But if you love someone, how can you not make it about her? Then I thought, well, if she can give me up that easily, maybe she didn't feel the same way about me as I felt about her."

"Or maybe she thought any decisions you made because of her; you might resent her for later. When I joined the Marines, I knew it wasn't Allie's first choice for me. She didn't relish worrying about me every time I was deployed. But she told me the same thing your girl told you. My choice had to be based on what I wanted for myself. And she would be supportive of whatever decision I made, just as long as I didn't do it because of her. It wasn't easy choosing between the two; the woman I loved and what I believed I was being called to do. But she made that choice possible. This girl you have feelings for, there is always the possibility that she does feel the same about you, but she doesn't want that to get in the way of you pursuing your dreams. Is baseball still on the table?"

Nate filled him in on the Triple A team he had been drafted for and the timeline. "The Dodgers weren't what I had hoped for, but I know I'm lucky to at least have been drafted. And Oklahoma City. I'm supposed to report there right after the 4th."

"Thanks to you, I'll be out of this place in a couple of days. That will still give me two weeks of home PT before you have to leave. It should be enough time for me to regain enough strength to do PT on my own without your supervision."

***

Nate spent the next few days preparing Todd's house for his arrival. He moved the exercise equipment into the lanai by the pool. Between the treadmill, weight machine, and pool, they could meet all the requirements of Todd's continued therapy under Nate's watchful eye and assistance when needed.

He kept busy, only to take a quick break to text Leah as he had promised. He let her know that he had found Todd and that all was going well. And that he expected to stay there for a couple of weeks before leaving for Oklahoma. That was the extent of his message, and she responded with just a short acknowledgment that she was happy for him and then wished him well on his new venture into minor-league baseball.

Nate also got acquainted with Todd's boys, Josh and Jacob. Both boys played in soccer leagues and spent time with Nate kicking the ball around the backyard. Nate took it upon himself to mow the lawn, trim the hedges and do some maintenance around the house. He took particular interest in Todd's jeep, which sat at the edge of the drive, covered by a tarp. He uncovered it and asked Allie about its condition.

"When did Todd last drive it?"

"It's been a couple of years now. After he was injured, we just covered it and left it."

"Do you mind if I try to get her up and running again?"

"Be my guest," she handed him the keys.

Nate tried turning it over, but the battery was dead. He popped the hood, and over time, the terminals had corroded, but the battery itself looked to be in good condition. In between visits to Todd, he worked on the jeep, hoping to get it running before his return home.

He cleaned the terminals, charged the battery, changed the oil and plugs, then started the Jeep. Todd had kept the registration and insurance up to date, hoping someday to get it back on the road, so when Nate got it running, he test-drove it around the block. "Let's go fishing." Nate gathered the boys. He had found a place where they could drive on the beach with the jeep and would spend the afternoon fishing there. Allie would go pick up Todd to bring him home, and the boys would be surprised when they returned from fishing to be reunited with their dad.

Allie and Todd arrived home around six. They sat in the car for a few minutes, Allie stalling, waiting for Nate to arrive with the boys, while Todd just looked out at the yard. "Our boy has been busy," Todd observed. "The yard looks better than I ever left it," he laughed. "Shrubs too. Hey, where is my jeep?" he suddenly noticed.

Allie laughed as the jeep pulled into the driveway behind them. Todd climbed out of the car as the boys came running to him, shouting, "Daddy!" Nate observed while quietly sitting in the jeep, thinking to himself that he still wanted to be just like his big brother someday, with a family to love and that loved him. Todd hobbled on his crutches over to Nate, still sitting in the jeep after hugging the boys.

"You've done well," Todd smiled.

"I had a good teacher," Nate responded.

"She is running, OK?"

"Like a top. She is in great shape too."

"I won't be driving her soon, and I've been thinking of getting something more practical. It's all yours if you want it."

"I'd take it in a heartbeat, but since I'm staying through the 4th, I'll have to fly."

CHAPTER 30
LIFE CHANGES

Nate took on his new role with a discipline not unlike his days at Cornell while training for the team. His schedule for Todd included morning stretches followed by light weights for his arms, shoulders, and back. The morning routine also included thirty minutes on the treadmill at a walking pace until Todd had regained some of his coordination and strength. Afternoons were similar, but instead of weights, Todd swam laps in the pool.

Nate also followed a strict regimen for himself, including heavy weights for his upper body and leg lifts for his lower body and abdomen. These were to maintain peak physical condition for his upcoming arrival at the training camp in Oklahoma. Each of his workouts ended with a five-mile runaround and through the neighborhood, including runs on the beach.

They were two weeks into the training, and Nate only had another week before he would have to leave for camp. While he saw definite progress in Todd's condition, he was worried that it wasn't enough soon enough and urged him to work harder. Todd's reaction was one of frustration and impatience based on his own inability, not on Nate's pressing to meet the goals he had set for him.

On Friday, Allie drove the boys up to Sarasota to spend the day with her parents. Nate and Todd finished up their morning routines and relaxed by the pool. "When's the last time you talked to Dad?" Nate inquired.

"He called the day Mom passed."

"He called you? He lied to us then. I shouldn't be surprised. He said he didn't know where you were but assured us the military would track you down and inform you about Mom."

"That's not totally inaccurate. He didn't know exactly where I was or that I was in the hospital. And he didn't reach me directly. My CO found me, told me what was going on, and then I called Dad back."

"So he conveniently left out the part about actually talking to you," Nate stated emphatically.

Todd became apologetic. "Nate, I asked him not to say anything about me, where I was, what was going on down here. You had enough on your plate with school, baseball, and then mom. I was afraid if you knew, you might drop everything and come here. And if you didn't, you would at least wish you could, and that would just add to your burdens. I didn't want that for you. I was hoping you would understand, eventually."

Nate just nodded, so Todd continued. "I'm going to go take a shower now. Why don't you just think about things, maybe go out for your run? Then we can go grab some lunch somewhere." Nate watched as Todd rose from his seat and clutched his crutches. He observed again that while Todd had improved, he still had a long road to recovery, which created doubt in his own mind about what role he might be able to play going forward. There just wasn't enough time before he would have to leave.

Nate took Todd's advice and donned his shorts and running shoes. It was sunny and already in the mid 80's by mid-morning. He began his run at a steady pace and maintained it throughout the run, going first down the street a couple of miles before coming to the beach access. Then he ran along the shoreline in the packed sand, taking notice of the fishermen along the way. Before long, he was on the return route. He felt good physically and happy about his own conditioning and fitness level. When he reached the house, he took a long swig of water, then did some stretching so as not to cramp.

Nate continued inside and went straight to the kitchen to find Todd. The kitchen was empty. Nate could see out into the lanai and pool area, but Todd was nowhere in sight. "Todd," Nate called, next searching the living room and then on toward the master bedroom. In the distance, he thought he heard the shower running and thought to himself that Todd must have gotten sidetracked and was only now taking his shower. "Todd," he called again as he entered the bedroom. The bathroom door was closed, so he moved in closer to it. "Everything OK in there?"

Todd still did not respond, so Nate tried the door. It was unlocked, so he entered slowly, thinking that maybe Todd hadn't heard him. "Todd, you OK?" It was then that he spotted Todd sprawled out on the floor of the tiled shower. He lay there, just looking up at Nate, without speaking. The water had turned cold and was still beating down on him. "Damn," Nate cursed as he turned off the water.

"I can't move," Todd said weakly, shivering. Nate grabbed a towel and wrapped it around him.

"Let me help you up."

"No," Todd responded quickly. "Better not. I slipped. I don't want to take any chances."

"I'll call an ambulance." Nate took his cell phone from his shorts pocket. "I need an ambulance," he told the 911 operator. As they waited, Nate climbed into the shower and sat down next to Todd. "I'm here, Todd. I'm not going anywhere." The proclamation was more to himself than to his brother.

***

Nate followed the ambulance to the hospital. He alerted the EMTs to Todd's previous spinal injury and subsequent surgeries, so they stabilized him before moving him. Once they arrived at the hospital, Todd was taken in for xrays, and Nate took the opportunity to call Allie. "Hey. Todd's OK, but he fell. We're at the hospital to have him checked out. He's in xray right now. I'll fill you in when you get here."

Everything had happened so fast; now Nate finally had time to think about what had happened. He should have been there. Instead, he had decided to go for a run, and as a result, Todd had laid there for...how long? He didn't even know. But it was obvious it was long enough for the water to run cold. It was his fault. He was pushing too hard because he was in a rush for Todd to heal. It was selfish on his part, wanting everything to be more on his own timeline, so he could report to baseball camp on time. Now what? How severe was the injury? It could be catastrophic or maybe just a minor setback. In any case, he couldn't leave now. He had to be there for his brother. Make sure he watched him more closely. And not push so hard this time.

Allie found Nate in the waiting room. "Todd's doctor has to take a look at the xrays. Then he'll be out to talk to us. I'm sorry, Allie." Nate had teared up, and Allie hugged him.

"This is not your fault," she reassured him.

"I should have been there."

"Nate, stop. Your brother is strong. We've made it this far. And this is probably just a minor setback. Let's just wait for the doctor."

A nurse joined them and led them to Todd's room. He was awake and alert when they entered. Allie walked over and kissed him as Nate stood at the foot of the bed.

"I guess an afternoon workout is out of the question," Todd joked, but obviously in pain.

Nate forced a smile. Todd's doctor then joined them and examined him, checking for sensations in his feet and legs. Then he looked at Todd's back, poking and prodding along the way. Todd responded to the pain, flinching on occasion, which was a good thing, as the doctor explained. "No loss of sensation anywhere. That's good. And nothing new in the xrays. It looks like you just bruised yourself. How'd this happen?"

"I was getting into the shower, and my leg just kind of slipped out from under me. I was afraid to move, didn't want to risk further injury to my spine, so I just stayed there until help arrived."

Nate was about to speak but was cut short by the doctor. "It was wise not to move until we were sure. You were lucky this time. But for the next few weeks, you need to have someone there with you. Don't take any more chances. Understood?"

"Sure, Doc," Todd responded.

"I want you to stay off your feet for a couple of days. I'm releasing you, but I want you back in the chair, ice your back, and take ibuprofen until the back pain and swelling subside. You can restart your rehab routine in about a week. Any questions?

Todd shook his head, no, and Allie thanked the doctor before he left them alone. "Boys, boys, boys," Allie began. "I leave you alone for a few hours, and the trouble begins. While we wait, I need to update my parents and the boys. I'll be back in a few minutes."

After she left the room, Todd and Nate just looked at each other blankly. "What are you thinking, Nate?" Todd asked.

"I'm sorry. I never should have gone for that run. I should have been there."

"You couldn't have prevented my fall."

"No, but you were left there for how long? The water was running cold. You were shivering."

Todd smiled. "That was nothing. Do you know what kind of training you go through in the Marines? You think a few minutes of cold water is going to hurt me?"

"Well, next time, I won't let you fall. I won't let that happen again."

"Nate, let's be realistic. I don't want to risk this again either, but you're going to be gone in a week. We are going to have to figure out something else."

"I'm not going," Nate suddenly declared. "Not until I know you'll be OK."

"Stop" Todd raised his hand. "Stop right there. You have to be in Oklahoma next week. Baseball has been your dream your whole life. And I'm not letting you give up that dream because of this minor setback."

Nate found himself saying something totally unexpected, even to himself. "But it's not. Not anymore. I thought it was what I wanted for the longest time. But not now. My brain tells me to just get up and go. But, my heart is not in it. Not anymore."

They were silent for several minutes, considering what Nate had just revealed. "You still have some time to think about it."

"Thinking only gets you in trouble. It's a distraction. You told me that, remember?"

"So then tell me, Nate. What is in your heart? Where is it leading you?"

"I don't know. All I do know is that I'm not going to Oklahoma. It's a sign, I think, telling me if I really want to pursue baseball, I have to go someplace far away that has absolutely nothing else to offer. So until I know for sure what I want to do someday, I'd like to just stay here. Be there for you, just like you were for me way back when. It's the least I can do."

"You can't do this just for me."

"I'm not. Being here now gives me purpose. I feel needed. It's been a while since I felt anyone needed me."

"It would feel really weird right now if I told you, 'I need you,'" Todd chuckled.

"Afraid to let down your guard?" Nate laughed.

Allie re-entered the hospital room, overhearing the last of their conversation. "So what are you boys so happy about?" she queried.

Nate spoke up. "I've decided to stick around awhile, provided you'll let me. And I promise I will watch over our boy here," pointing to Todd, "and provide much better care than I have up to this point."

Allie looked at Todd, who was still smiling. "Well, if you can get him smiling like this and keep him smiling, then absolutely, stay. As long as you like."

***

Nate's flight to Oklahoma City was scheduled for the 5th. He canceled the reservation, giving up the opportunity to report to the farm team on time and his chances of playing. Todd resumed the daily therapy sessions under Nate's supervision. "I can see how seniors find no dignity in this kind of treatment," Todd commented as he prepared to step into the shower with Nate's assistance. "I'd much prefer to have Allie in here with me."

"She is too little to catch you falling, and you would probably crush her. Besides, knowing you, it could only lead to risky sex, and you falling on your ass again."

"Speaking of which, what about you?" Todd asked as he continued to wash himself. "You know, Allie could set you up. She knows a few single female teachers in the school."

"I'm not there yet."

"Want to talk about it? I know you spent the last few Christmases and summers in Geneva. What's in Geneva?"

"Leah." Nate had never mentioned her to Todd by name before but simply alluded to someone else of importance in his life. "Her name is Leah."

"So, is it serious?"

"Was." Nate's response was short, without elaboration.

"What happened?"

"Life happened. She has her life, and I have mine. We were on different paths."

Todd stopped asking questions and stepped out of the shower with Nate again assisting him. "If you ever want to talk more about her, I have lots of time to listen," he offered.

"I know. You've always been a good listener and offered me sound advice."

"By the way," Todd began. "We're having a barbecue here. I'd like you to meet some of the guys. I think a couple of them were responsible for bringing you here that night."

"Not a night to be proud of," Nate laughed. "Embarrassing, really, but I guess I do owe them a debt of thanks."

"And so do I," Todd added.

"You can help me on the grill and keep the keg flowing. I think Allie has invited some of her coworkers..single ladies."

"Like I said, I'm not ready."

"Nate, do me a favor. This is a time in your life to just have fun. I want you to have fun and be happy. If you are going to be here, I'm going to have to insist that you at least meet some new people, make friends, and let whatever happens happen. Suppose you are lucky enough to hook up; well, good for you. It's not like you're making a lifelong commitment."

"Lucky? I will have you know, big brother, that I don't get lucky. I have mastered the art."

"I'm sure you have," Todd laughed. Nate continued to fill Todd in on the details of his adventures at the lake house, including his naked swim to the middle of the lake and failed rendezvous later that evening. They were quiet for a few minutes before Todd spoke again. "I guess there was some good that came out of me leaving when I did. It forced you to grow up quickly and assume responsibility for your behavior."

"It helped to know you were watching out for me, even from afar. Now it's my turn to watch out for you."

"I think from now on; we'll be watching out for each other little brother."

Nate simply nodded. "Good talk."

"Yeah, good talk," Todd agreed.

***

"You OK?" Todd was standing at the grill, his crutches supporting him as he flipped the burgers. Nate had brought him a draft, and they stood together looking out over the gathering.

"Yeah, I guess so. Just getting used to the idea. It's actually a relief. At least I don't have to go to Oklahoma now."

"There's a lot of pretty ladies out there," Todd commented. Nate just smiled. "You should mingle."

Nate considered for a minute. "I promised Allie I'd stay close by, just in case you need me."

"Come on, Nate. I'm feeling good. We've made a lot of progress, almost back to where we were before I fell."

They were interrupted by two guys that Todd obviously knew. The first extended his hand to Todd in a vigorous handshake. "Todd, good to see you up and about again."

"Frank, glad you could make it. I think you and Nate have met."

Frank extended his hand to Nate and grinned. "Yeah, we've met, but I doubt he remembers."

"I heard you were the one who rescued me and helped me find my long-lost brother. Thank you."

"I think you were the lost one," Todd interjected. "Frank, we both appreciate it. Steve..." Todd reached out to the other man standing nearby. "Thanks for coming. Nate, Steve, and I served together. Several tours."

Steve returned the greeting. "It's good to see you back on your feet, brother." Steve then introduced the girl on his arm. "This is my wife, Stephanie. She and Allie teach at the same school. In fact, Allie introduced us. Best day of my life," he proclaimed.

Introductions to new faces continued throughout the afternoon for Nate. He was later approached by an older woman who introduced herself as Janet. "I've heard a lot about you, Nate," she began. "Allie says you're going to be staying here for a while."

"As long as they need me." Nate was curious about this lady, who was obviously older and stood out in the crowd. Her hair was ashe blonde but graying at the temples. She reminded him of someone..the lady in the garden.

She interrupted him from his thoughts. "What happens when he doesn't need you anymore?"

Nate shrugged. "I don't know. I've made a lot of decisions lately that kind of changed my long-term plans. I haven't really had time to think about what's next."

"Baseball," she nodded. "Todd has spoken about you often. About Cornell and your baseball scholarship. The farm team and your chance to someday play in the majors. And I just heard you gave that all up. Why?"

Nate looked at her and began to speak, but she touched his arm. "You don't have to answer that. We don't always end up where we planned. Circumstances change; people change. What you did says a lot about you and what's most important. It all goes without saying." They stood in silence for a moment. It was not an awkward silence, and Nate was relaxed and reassured by her words. Her next question surprised him. "Do you have any interest in teaching?"

Nate shrugged. "I haven't thought much about it. Not since Cornell when my advisor told me I needed a backup plan. I didn't think I needed one at the time, but I took his advice. I majored in health and phys ed."

"There's an opening at the high school in August you'd be perfect for if you're interested," Nate observed her for a moment, and the calming effect she had on him made him think again of the lady in the garden. "Whatever you decide, it will all work out." She touched his arm once more before walking away to join another group nearby.

"Who is that lady?" Nate asked Todd, returning to his side and handing him another draft.

"She's the high school principal."

"No kidding. I feel like I've met her before."

Todd chuckled. "She has that effect on people."

"I think she just offered me a job."

Todd nodded.

"You knew?"

"You're going to be here for a while, and I will become less and less dependent on you. Once I've recovered, it doesn't mean you have to leave. You'll always be welcome here. But that doesn't mean you can sit on your ass all day by my pool, working on your tan. We thought maybe you'd like to try teaching for a while. See if you like it. And the high school baseball team needs a good coach. I think they only won three games all season last year. It has to be your decision, though, Nate. There is absolutely no pressure either way."

"Still looking out for your little brother."

"Brothers forever," Todd responded, draping his arm around Nate's neck.

CHAPTER 31
The Backup Plan

"Are you sure it will be OK?" It was mid-August, and Nate sat by the pool with Todd and Allie, sipping iced tea.

"I've made good progress with your help Nate. It's been six weeks since I fell, we're well past the risky part of my rehab, and I'm fine on my own."

"No showers while we're not here" Allie patted Todd's arm.

"I promise I will wait to shower until you can join me there," he winked.

"They've also asked me to coach the JV football team," Nate continued. "With teaching two health classes and four PE classes, plus coaching, it's going to significantly cut into our therapy time."

"It'll be fine, Nate," Todd reassured him.

"We're happy that you've decided to do this," Allie added.

***

Nate's schedule kept him busy, but he still managed to make time to work out with Todd, usually in the evenings before dinner. He enjoyed teaching more than he expected, especially the juniors and seniors in the high school, who found him easy to relate to and interact with. Coaching the JV football team brought back fond memories of his high school football days and even happy times spent with Dani. The highlight of his day was totally unexpected, however, when as the Health teacher, he was assigned a sex ed class. It wasn't teaching the class itself, but that the boys and girls were separated, and a female teacher near his age was assigned to the girls. Together, they had to collaborate on lesson plans and quite often ended up sharing stories about the kids in their classes and the questions they asked.

Her name was Jenna. She was a short, petite brunette with pretty green eyes and a bubbly personality. He found her attractive, and their personalities complemented each other, both finding humor within the strict curriculum.

"It's amazing to me some of the misinformation these guys have," Nate commented during one of their afternoon meetings in the teacher's lounge. "They all pretend to know everything there is to know about sex, and that misinformation just keeps getting repeated over and over until, for them, it becomes fact."

"The girls are the same way. It's scary, really. But weren't we like that too, back when we were teenagers?"

"I suppose so. But I learned early on." Nate stopped, embarrassed by the admission.

She smiled and looked at him curiously. "Do tell."

Nate shrugged. "Well, most of these boys are like 17, and they don't have a clue."

"And you did?"

"I knew enough. What about you? When did you learn about sex?"

"I led a pretty sheltered life until college. Then I learned a lot, quickly."

"Would you go out with me sometime?" Nate suddenly asked her.

"Interesting segue," she commented. "Right from talking about our sex lives to asking me out."

"This is awkward. I'm sorry. We work together. It's probably inappropriate. I shouldn't have even asked."

Jenna reached across the table and touched his hand. Nate recovered from his embarrassment and looked up at her. It was odd talking to her. He wasn't usually uncomfortable in this type of situation, but this was different. They had never really talked other than about the curriculum and students in the sex ed class. For all he knew, they had nothing else in common, and it probably was a mistake for him to pursue anything outside their current relationship. But it was too late to back out now, as she responded. "When?"

Her response caught him by surprise. He had almost hoped for rejection.

"What? Oh, um...how about this weekend? Saturday? "

"I can't, Saturday." Nate was almost relieved. "I could do Friday, though," she countered.

"Sure. Friday works. Here is my number. Text me your address, and I'll pick you up around eight." She seems nice enough, he thought. Maybe he would learn more about her over dinner Friday, and they would have more in common than just the class they shared.

***

This would be the first time since Leah that he had dated, and he just couldn't get excited about the prospect of dating someone new. Maybe he should just cancel it; explain that he had just broken off a three-year relationship and didn't think he was ready to date again. She would understand, but it would be more awkward than having to work with her every day. So he sought out Todd's advice..

"You've always had a habit of overthinking things," Todd noted as he and Nate finished their routines under the lanai. "Grab me a beer, will you?" Todd took a seat by the pool, and Nate soon came back with two beers in hand. "I think you should just give it a chance. It's just one date. Either it will go a lot better than you anticipate, or it will be sheer agony. Who knows, maybe you'll be pleasantly surprised. Nothing ventured, nothing gained, right?"

***

Nate picked her up promptly at eight for a late evening dinner at a local seafood restaurant. The conversation drifted from the most recent classroom discussions to topics of a more personal nature.

"So you're from Connecticut, and then you went to Cornell. Impressive. Ivy League. But why Cornell? There are a lot of Ivy League schools in the Northeast. Isn't Yale closer to your home?"

"That's the point, right? Get away from home, I mean."

"I guess that may be true for some people. What about girlfriends?"

"I've had a few along the way. How about you?"

"I've had a few...girlfriends," she laughed. It forced a smile from Nate. "Oh, so you can smile. There seems to be a lot going on in that head of yours."

"Sorry," Nate apologized.

"I just broke up with my fiancee," she suddenly confessed. "Found out he was cheating on me. Three years together, then poof! All done. Takes some getting used to. Spending, or should I say wasting, all that time with someone, then finding out they're a two-timing ass."

"That's a shame."

"What about you, Nate?"

"No, I'm not a two-timing ass if that's your question. I never cheated on anyone."

"That wasn't my question, but it's nice to know. Tell me about your lost love."

"Hm...I'm not really ready to talk about her."

"Too soon?"

Nate nodded. "You know, I have to confess. I almost regretted asking you out. Not because I don't find you attractive; I do. I just didn't know how good a company I would be."

She reached across the table to touch his hand; she had done that once before to reassure him, he thought. "I understand that. This is all new to me, too, Nate. I had second thoughts after I accepted your invitation for tonight. But then I thought, why the hell should I put my life on hold? You're a nice guy, and we deserve a nice night out. So we're both on the rebound. So what? What we do now isn't anyone's business. I have no expectations that this is going to blossom into some new romance overnight. I just want to have some fun. And it might possibly help us forget what we've lost."

They continued talking through the evening, and Nate began to feel more comfortable in this new girl's presence. They listened for a time to some live music, then decided it was late and time to leave. Nate drove her home and walked her up to her apartment door. He expected just a quick kiss goodnight, but she took his hand and held onto it. "Would you like to come in for a nightcap?"

Nate hesitated before responding.

"I don't make a habit of inviting men into my apartment after the first date. But I've had fun tonight, and I'm not ready for it to be over."

"OK," Nate agreed, and they entered her apartment. "You live here alone?" Nate asked, observing the bright sea-foam painted walls of the living room.

"No, I have a roommate. She's staying at her boyfriend's tonight. There is a bottle of wine in the fridge if you want to pour us some." She disappeared through a door that Nate speculated must lead to one of the bedrooms.

He went to the kitchen, found some wine glasses, and poured two glasses of pinot. He returned to the living room, set the glasses on the table, and moved to some bookshelves, one shelf filled with vinyl. He flipped through them and found a REM album, one that had been a part of Todd's collection years ago. She returned to the living room as he put the album on. "Didn't think you'd mind."

"Of course not." She picked up her drink and took a sip. Nate followed her lead and took a drink from his glass. They sat on the couch for a while, talking and refilling their glasses as needed. She then stood and searched for some different music, finding the perfect album and song, "Fallen" by Gert Taberner. It was a slow melodious tune, and she beckoned Nate to get up and slow dance with her. Nate was feeling the effects of their dinner and after-dinner drinks, which, combined with the new bottle of wine, now fully consumed, had him light-headed. As they danced, he sensed that she, too, was feeling the effects, but they continued to dance in slow steps to the music.

At some point, he found her looking up at him, and he bent down to kiss her. They lingered for a bit before she took his hand and led him to the bedroom, where they would complete their time together.

The effects of the alcohol made him sleep soundly through the night, and he was awakened late morning by the sound of voices coming from the living room. The bed was empty except for him, and she had managed to arise without disturbing him. He heard laughter and the sound of two female voices. He sat up and searched for his clothes, which lay on the floor beside the bed. He put them on and escaped into the bathroom. He noticed his five o'clock shadow had an extra day's growth as he splashed cool water on his face and ran his wet hands through his curly hair. "Could be worse," he commented to himself as he patted his face dry.

Jenna was back in the bedroom when he came out of the bathroom.

"Good morning," she greeted. "Sleep well?"

"I did, thanks. How about you?"

"I slept great! And last night was fun, wasn't it?"

"It was fun. I'm glad we took a chance."

"Me too."

Nate wasn't sure what his next move should be with her standing across the room. He didn't want to cheapen their time together, but at the same time, it was just a one-time thing, right? After all, they were both on the rebound.

"This isn't going to be weird, is it?" she then asked. "I mean, we had fun; maybe we can do it again sometime, but there's no commitment by either of us. And we can still work together, right?"

"Kind of like 'friends with benefits,'" Nate reflected.

"Exactly! Now as one last contribution to our fun date, let's go get some breakfast."

Nate agreed and reassured himself. *I'm OK with this.*

***

It was nearly lunchtime when Nate returned home. Todd and the boys were waiting for him, fishing poles in hand. This would be their first attempt at fishing since Todd began his recovery, and Nate had agreed to take them all. Todd eyed him curiously as Nate found them all by the pool.

"Have a good night?" Todd asked with a smile. It was obvious to Todd that Nate must have spent the night as he had returned in the same clothes which he left the previous day. But it was OK with Todd. He was glad to see Nate in a good mood.

Nate nodded and smiled.

"Good. You're a little overdressed for fishing, so go change. The boys have been waiting patiently here."

Nate quickly changed and met Todd and the boys already sitting in the jeep. They spent the afternoon fishing on the pier and brought home several whiting, which Nate cleaned when they returned.

"Do you think you'll be seeing her again?"

"Not much choice in that. I work with her every day."

"Oh. I didn't realize that's who you went on a date with. Will it be awkward?"

Nate stopped and thought, then shook his head. "No, I don't think so. She was actually pretty cool about it. We're kind of on the same page right now. She recently broke up with her boyfriend, and I'm not with Leah now. This is a rebound thing for both of us, that's all."

"Well, I'm glad you're back in the saddle. With all the time you've had to spend with just me, you deserve to go out and have some fun. I'm happy for you."

"Thanks, Todd. For the push, I mean. You were right. I just needed to take a chance."

***

The holidays came and went with Nate occasionally thinking of Leah and how she might be spending this holiday without him, the first time in three years. He continued to work with Jenna daily and see her occasionally on weekends as they continued their casual 'friends with benefits time together.

Springtime meant baseball, and Nate was in his full element once again, albeit in a different role, as coach of what had been a losing baseball team. Under his guidance, the team succeeded in improving their record to over five hundred, which met with the approval of the administration and an excited team and supporters. Todd continued his recovery and was soon rid of the crutches, able to walk on his own around the block. Nate walked with him and set new goals. They would be running together in a few months' time.

By summer, Todd had improved to the point of doing heavier weights and jogging alongside Nate. They limited their runs to a mile around the neighborhood, with Nate often continuing on for an extra two miles by himself. The boys enrolled in a neighborhood summer soccer league, and

Todd coached. It was the off-season for Nate, so he assisted, and they led the boys to an undefeated season. "We are good together," Todd toasted Nate as they drank a beer beside the pool.

Nate turned down an offer to be assistant coach of the varsity football team in favor of staying with the JV squad. His team had done reasonably well the first year, and now going into the second year, he was confident they had gained the skills needed for a winning season. His intuition paid off, losing only one game.

***

During the Christmas holidays, Todd, Allie, and Nate were invited to Steve's for a holiday celebration. Nate took Jenna as his plus one. Allie knew Jenna, but not well, as they worked in different schools. Allie took the opportunity to speak with Jenna at the party once she was alone.

"So, Nate seems to be enjoying himself. You two have become good friends, I see."

Jenna agreed. "Yes, he's a really nice guy. He's fun."

"To be honest, when he first came here, I didn't know if this would work out. One thing I do know, he's been a real blessing for us. Especially Todd."

"Todd looks to be doing really well." They watched Todd as he engaged his friends around the room.

"He is. How is school going for you? Nate tells us stories about some of his classes. Especially his sex education class. You both must have some stories to tell."

"Yes, it's been an adventure, that's for sure." They were quiet for a moment before Jenna spoke again. "I'm falling for him," she suddenly blurted.

Allie acknowledged the revelation with a nod. "I get that. Those Woods boys are hard to resist. That's why I married one."

"I really like Nate. I never planned on that happening. I was just getting over a breakup. And we agreed, Nate and I, that this would just be a rebound thing. But I don't think I can continue this as a rebound thing. Has he said anything to you? About me?"

Allie shook her head no. "He talks to Todd a lot. But Todd hasn't said much about it to me. I sense that Nate is getting a bit restless. I know he likes being near his brother, but I'm afraid that it won't be enough to keep him here. He's still searching for where he is meant to be."

"So, any advice for me? What should I do?"

"I don't know Jenna. All I can say is I wouldn't plan my life around him. He may stay here forever, or he may suddenly decide to up and leave. If you want to stay close to him, unless and until he lets on otherwise, I think you have to accept things for what they are. Your feelings for him have obviously changed. But I don't know if his feelings for you have."

"I just don't know how much longer I can do that. Hold back my feelings for him. The more I'm around him, the harder it gets."

Their conversation abruptly ended as Nate joined them with coats in hand. "It's getting late. Ready to go?"

Jenna nodded. "I'll see you later at home," he said to Allie as he and Jenna turned to leave.

"Thank you," Jenna called to Allie as they walked away.

Nate had seen them talking from across the room, apparently engaged in a very serious discussion. "What was that all about?"

She brushed it aside. "Just chit-chat."

***

They were silent throughout the drive back to Jenna's, and when they arrived, she quietly opened the door and got out. "Is it OK if I come in?" Nate called to her.

She leaned in through the open car door and spoke softly. Nate sensed she was holding back but wouldn't push her to say what was on her mind. "I'm really tired, Nate. And my roommate is here. I'll see you back at school after Christmas break." She closed the door behind her, and he watched her move slowly up the sidewalk. Something was amiss, but he had no clue what.

He found Allie and Todd seated at the island in the kitchen. Their conversation lagged when he entered. "My ears are burning," Nate commented as he went to the refrigerator to retrieve a bottle of water.

"Not everything's about you," Todd responded.

Nate stood across from them both and waited. "But this time, it was, wasn't it?"

"I'm surprised to see you home so early." Todd was now awaiting Nate's response.

Nate turned his attention to Allie. "You and Jenna appeared to be having a serious talk, huddled together on the other side of the room." Allie continued to look at Nate. He suspected they were sympathetic eyes. "So I'll talk if no one else will. She was strangely quiet when I dropped her off. Somber. I'm not sure what I did, but it appears I won't be seeing much of her outside of school."

"What did she say?" Todd asked.

"Nothing. Not a damned thing." Nate turned away and left for his room.

***

Nate returned to the classroom after the holidays in a melancholy mood. He hadn't heard from or tried to speak to Jenna since the night of the party. He admitted to himself that he missed her friendship. She was someone he could talk to and have fun with. That's all that he had expected or really wanted from her. For some reason, though, she no longer wanted that from him, and he didn't understand why.

He didn't purposely avoid her or seek her out. She had made the decision to make their contactless frequent and possibly limited to only school. He waited for her in the teacher's lounge to discuss the upcoming sex ed lesson plan at their regularly appointed time, but Jenna didn't show. This was clearly avoidance on her part which both frustrated and annoyed him. While he liked some games that women played, this was not one of them. So he wasn't going to play, and he would ignore any attempts by her to engage him in it.

He saw little of her the following months except in passing in the hallway. She was cordial and polite, and he reciprocated. As the baseball season approached, his melancholy deepened. He tried to remain focused on the task at hand, readying his team for their first game and plans for a second winning season.

Todd once again became his refuge. They took long runs together in the evenings, and Nate poured out his heart to him while Todd just listened. "Your mood has changed," Todd observed.

"I feel different. It's like a mix of things that are changing too fast and, at the same time, things that need to change but aren't. There's something missing in my life. Something is staring me straight in the face, and I just can't see it."

"Is it Jenna?"

Nate shook his head no. "It's not her. She was nice, but she was just a distraction. I think part of it is you, Todd. I got here at the right time when you needed me. It's been almost two years now. I don't think you need me here anymore."

"I love having you here, and you know that. But you're right; I've recovered fully now, and you don't have to be here any longer to help me through it. It's been great. You don't know how good this has been. For me. For you. For Allie and the kids. You mean so much to us all, Nate. But we aren't what you need. At least not anymore. And I think you believe you need to be needed. Wherever that may be."

"What about coaching? I love it, and I don't want to let the boys down."

"You think that's enough to satisfy your need? These boys come and go.

Every year it's a new group. What you've done with these teams has been amazing. They have a new attitude and have regained their sense of pride. But they will survive, with or without you. And if you really do love coaching, you can do that practically anywhere."

"I've had a lot of time to think, Todd. And I know now that you were right."

"Right, about what?"

"You said it a couple of times to me. The first time was camping on the river; you, me, and Zak. And the second time was at the lake house right after Billy died. You said to me, 'Our thoughts are just a distraction from what is in our hearts.' You were right. I know that now."

"So tell me, Nate. What's in your heart that is taking you from us?"

***

Nate was honored at the end of the season Sports Banquet for his baseball team and its first undefeated season. As he accepted the trophy, he stood before the mike to address the crowd. "It's an honor and a privilege to accept this on the team's behalf. These are an amazing group of boys, and you should all be as proud of them as I am." The crowd applauded as groups of students chanted his name. Once it had quieted again, he continued. "I came here just two years ago, straight out of college, and it's been incredible. You all welcomed me, and you gave me an opportunity to work with these boys, to teach them and coach them in the game I have lived for my whole life, baseball. I'll be forever thankful for that, and no matter where I go from here, I'll always have these fond memories to take with me." The room became very quiet as he finished. "All that said, I'm sorry to have to tell you all, but I will be leaving Venice at the end of this term. Thank you all, and God bless you." He held up the trophy to a stunned yet appreciative audience, who continued their applause after he had left the stage.

***

Nate was busy packing the last of his belongings when Todd checked on his progress. "It's amazing how much junk one can accumulate in just two years."

Todd agreed. "One more thing to take with you." He placed a set of keys in Nate's hand.

"What's this?"

"The Jeep. I want you to take it. It's yours."

"No, I can't take your jeep. You love that thing."

"And so do you. Every time you take me out for a drive, I can tell. So it's yours now. Something to remember me by. Besides, I got my eye on a new Tundra. Something to remember our mother by."

"I don't know what to say."

"Consider us even now. Payment for what you helped me get through. Have you decided where you're headed?"

Nate nodded. "I have a good idea where I need to be."

"Text me when you get there?"

"I will."

"I'm really gonna miss you, little brother." He pulled him in close and hugged him tightly.

"Let's not lose touch, OK?"

Todd nodded. "Never again. I'll be watching out for you. Looking over your shoulder."

"Promise?"

"Promise."

"Good talk."

"Yeah, good talk."

CHAPTER 32
LET ME TELL YOU ABOUT BILLY

He had driven all night, stopping only for fuel and to relieve himself. His thoughts had turned the hours into moments in time, and he was now caught up to the present. It had been over two years since he last saw her. His departure had been a painful one. They had stayed in touch for awhile, but it had digressed to the point of only a courtesy. There were no expectations from either of them for anything more. His decision had been made, and she had made it clear. She would not be the one to deter him from pursuing his lifelong dream. As it turned out, she wasn't the reason. It was all about timing and where he was needed. And it had been a healing process for both he and Todd.

The moment had finally arrived. He had become restless these past few months. In spite of his brother and family, the friends he had made, and the satisfaction he had found in coaching and teaching, he felt more empty every day. Maybe it was seeing Todd and his family together that affected him most. Todd had said he "had no regrets" for everything that happened to him. The reason was obvious. He had found happiness and was living life to the fullest. Todd had identified a restlessness in Nate and urged him to move on. "I think you're ready, Nate. Pursue what's in your heart."

And so it was. She was still in his heart. Even though he had tried to put her out of his mind, he would often wake up in the middle of the night thinking of her, yearning to be with her once again. His mind wandered as he entered the town. What if? What if she didn't feel the same way? What if she had moved on? Found someone new? What if he was too late?

He drove down the main street and slowed the jeep as he approached the cafe where they had first met. The Nettles Cafe sign still hung, albeit precariously, above the door. He debated whether to stop. If she was there, he would be impatient to discover how she felt. He would want to sweep her into his arms, seeking immediate reassurance that she still felt about him as he felt for her. But he thought better of it, at least for now. There were too many variables. Too many "what ifs" to make such a bold move.

He continued down the main street two blocks and turned to the right. He pulled the jeep to the curb in front of the BnB. The silver Volvo sat at the side of the drive. It appeared to not have been moved for some time, now covered by a thick coating of dried leaves and pollen. He made his way up the walk to the front porch and found the front door locked. This was unusual, it being summer when they should be fully occupied. It raised concerns that maybe Grammy was no longer able to keep up the BnB and accommodate guests. She was getting on in years, and with Leah teaching full time, it might have just been too much for the both of them.

He searched for the front door key. Surely they wouldn't mind if he just let himself in. He was like family to them. But then he thought better of it. It was an unfair expectation. He had been gone over two years. Some things had changed for sure, and he didn't know what their reaction would be to his sudden return.

He decided to walk the short distance back to the cafe. He would take a chance that Leah was there. After all, it was summer, and school was out. It was late afternoon, and the lunch crowd had dwindled to several small groups scattered about the cafe. The server behind the counter was not Leah and not a familiar face. He took a seat on a stool at the counter, and the server approached him.

"Hi. Can I get you something to drink? Coffee or iced tea, maybe?" She was younger than Leah, probably in her late teens or early twenties, he observed.

"Iced tea would be great."

"Here you go." She placed it in front of him, then handed him a menu. "We close at four, but you still have a few minutes if you want something to eat."

Nate recalled that they used to stay open and serve dinner until seven. Another change.

"Just tea, thanks." He tried to engage her in casual conversation. "When I was last here, you served dinner up until seven."

The girl nodded. "They quit serving dinner last year. We just do breakfast and lunch now. I think the owner just had too much going on. She wanted to keep the place open but couldn't manage the evening hours."

Nate nodded. "Does Leah still manage the cafe?"

"Oh, so you know Leah? Yes, she still manages it. Doesn't spend much time here, though. Only when we're short-staffed."

"I guess teaching keeps her pretty busy," Nate concluded.

The girl looked at him curiously. "Oh, she hasn't been teaching; she's been too busy..." She then stopped in mid-sentence. "What did you say your name was?"

"Nate. Nathan." That's how she knew him back then.

She then changed the subject. "You look tired." Nate hadn't really thought about it. He had been up for thirty hours straight now. He needed a shower and a change of clothes. And he hadn't shaved in several days.

"I had a long drive. Hey, do you know if the Nettles BnB is open? I used to stay there when I was in town."

The server just shrugged. "Not sure what's going on over there these days."

Nate finished his iced tea and stood to leave. He noticed the server had gone into the kitchen, and he could see her talking on a phone in a hushed tone. The phone she used was an extension, and she had avoided using the phone by the counter where he sat. "Probably talking to her boyfriend," he concluded, smiling to himself.

***

"Hi, it's me. No, things here are fine. There are only a few folks left, so I'll lock up at four. I thought you should know there is a guy here asking about you. He says his name is Nathan. You're welcome." She then hung up the phone.

***

Nate walked back to the BnB, took a suitcase from the jeep, and walked up the steps of the porch. He needed a shower. He hoped they would understand. The front door was locked, so he searched for a key and found one under the flower pot by the door. Everything inside looked the same. No changes, no updates to speak of. He listened for sounds coming from the kitchen or from the rooms upstairs. Nothing. So he headed up the stairs to the third floor. The room was unchanged except that the bed was unmade. There was a faint odor, more of a musty smell from being closed up and probably unused for quite some time.

He quickly removed his clothes and jumped into the shower. He stood there, just letting the hot water run over him for minutes, his mind now running wild. Maybe it was the caffeine or the adrenaline rush, or a combination of both. He was anxious. If he ran, maybe it would clear his mind of any expectations. But he was in the shower already. It could have waited until after his run, but it was too late now and silly to concern himself with. He would run and then shower again if needed.

He soon found himself jogging up and down the streets he had come to know from the previous times spent in Geneva. He began at a jog, then increased his speed. His thoughts kept pace as he thought back to growing up in Plainville, the lake house, his mother, Billy, and Todd. All those things brought him to this moment in time when his fate would finally be determined. He thought again of Leah, reaffirming his belief that this was where he was meant to be. It felt good. He was re-invigorated, and his mood changed from nervous anticipation to one of relief. He would soon know his chances with Leah and if she still felt for him what he felt for her. If she had moved on, he would do what was necessary to rekindle their relationship, to get back what they once had. It was decided.

***

Nathan was back. It was, at first, a shock. When reality set in, she thought about what it meant and the ramifications of his return. It was possible that he was on the road with the baseball team and that this was just a stop along the way. That would make sense, but there were things she hadn't told him, things that she couldn't and wouldn't say. If he was only going to be there a couple of nights, she could work it out. If he stayed longer, it could be a problem.

She and Grammy returned to the BnB right after she had gotten the call. "He has a right to know," Grammy said as they unpacked the groceries in the kitchen.

"I know. But I need to understand what he's thinking first; why he is here. Once I know his plans, then I'll decide how to handle it."

***

The door was unlocked now as Nate returned from his run. A Honda minivan now sat in the driveway next to the Volvo. He chuckled to himself. A minivan? He set the thought aside now, excited at the prospect of finally seeing her again. He entered the front foyer and overheard voices coming from the kitchen. Maybe he should shower again. His tank top was drenched in sweat. But it was too late. She entered the hallway and stopped in her tracks, feigning surprise at his arrival.

"Nathan," she smiled.

His heart raced. She looked as beautiful...maybe more beautiful than he remembered. He wanted to sweep her off her feet, but he resisted. A broad smile would have to do for now. "Hey. How are you?"

She walked toward him. "This is a nice surprise."

"I wanted it to be. A nice surprise."

"So what brings you back to Geneva? A road trip with the team?"

"It's a long story," he responded.

"Tell you what. Why don't you go take a shower, and I'll meet you under the gazebo in a few minutes. You can fill me in there."

Nate's thoughts began racing again. This could be going better. She didn't seem overly excited to see him after such a long absence.

***

She was waiting for him under the gazebo, dressed in a yellow sundress with a pattern of small sunflowers. He watched her as he approached, her shoulder-length blonde hair blowing in the breeze. He sat down beside her as they looked out over the lake. "I've always loved this spot," she sighed.

"There is an abundance of beauty here." She chuckled as she eyed him curiously.

"You found Todd?" she asked. Nate nodded. "A good visit then?"

"It started out rough. My fault, not his. I was angry when I sought him out. I needed to know why he abandoned us. Me, I mean. But you know all that already."

She nodded. "So what happened?"

"I made too many assumptions. I was wrong about everything. But as it turned out, I arrived at the right time. He needed me, and I was finally in a position to be able to help him, the way he helped me when I needed him."

"I'm glad you were able to work things out and be there for him. So then what? Tell me about baseball."

Nate took a deep breath. It was time for full disclosure.

"I was supposed to report to the field team in Oklahoma right after July 4th. I never made it there. I didn't go."

"Oh, Nathan. Your dream. What happened?"

"I was helping Todd in his recovery, but we...he had a setback. It was my fault. I might have been able to prevent it from happening. So I decided not to go. He still needed me. And the more I helped him, the less I had the desire to leave or pursue the minors. So I just stayed."

"You stayed there for two years?"

"Once Todd was well on the road to recovery, I wasn't sure of my purpose anymore. I mean, we still worked on his PT, but eventually, he could do it on his own. When he didn't need me anymore, I decided to just keep busy until I knew for sure what I wanted. So I got a teaching job at the high school and coached the baseball and football teams."

"I can't believe you gave up your dream. Were you happy, Nathan? Are you happy? Teaching and coaching?"

"I was for a time." He paused before continuing. "But it wasn't enough." He focused his eyes now on her. "It took me some time to figure it out. It was never going to be enough. At the end of the day, there was always an emptiness..." He stopped again, waiting for her to speak. But she didn't speak. She was too busy repeating those last words in her own head. An emptiness.

"I thought I knew what I wanted when I left here," he continued. "It's amazing how things just worked out the way they did. It didn't take me long to figure out that I wasn't looking forward to going to Oklahoma. In fact, playing baseball in the minors just lost its appeal. It would have been a huge mistake for me to have followed through on that. Fortunately, the timing of Todd's surgery and recovery made my decision not to go so much easier. Todd was more important to me than something I had dreamed about my whole life."

"I'm happy for you, Nathan. But you haven't told me why you're here. You said you stayed with Todd until you knew what you wanted."

He stood now and moved directly in front of her. Taking both her hands, he raised her to her feet and looked into her eyes. "You. You are what's been missing. I came back because of you."

He saw the tears fill her eyes and run down her cheeks. She was unable to speak. "I've loved you from the start." he continued. "I thought about you every day I was away. Only you can fill that empty part of me. When I'm with you, I feel whole again. I love you, Leah."

Without speaking, she wrapped her arms around his neck, and they stayed that way for some time. "I tried to stop loving you," she suddenly confessed. "You were gone, and I didn't want to feel that pain anymore. I never wanted you to leave; you know that. But you needed to find on your own what you wanted, regardless of how I felt. That was one of the most difficult days of my life...the day you left."

"I'm sorry I put you through that. I never wanted to hurt you. And I'll never hurt you again like that. That is if you'll still have me."

She brushed the last of the tears from her cheeks and smiled. "I need to show you something. Come with me." She took his hand and led him up the wooden pier toward the house, then up the driveway to the sidewalk.

They walked several blocks. "Where are you taking me?"

"You'll see." They walked another block before coming to a park and playground. In the distance, Nate could see and hear kids of all ages playing in the park. They entered through the gate and closed it behind them. Leah searched the grounds. For what, Nate didn't know, until he spotted Molly in the distance. She was standing behind a child's swing, gently pushing a toddler.

"Is that Molly?" Nate asked as they approached her. "I forget it's been two years already. She's old enough to babysit now, I see."

"Thankfully. She has been a tremendous help to me these past months." Nate's thoughts about her words were interrupted by Molly's voice.

"Nathan," Molly waved to him. She didn't run to him this time. She was older and much more mature now. Happy to see him but a little more reserved in her greeting.

Nate smiled and waved to her before his attention was drawn to the child in the swing. He was not good at guessing toddlers' ages, but he saw the little boy with curly blonde locks of hair. "And who is this little guy?" he asked as he moved closer to the swing. He was waiting for a response and looked from Molly to Leah. Neither of them spoke. "Cute little guy. Hey buddy." Nate had knelt down now on his knees in front of the child. "I'm Nathan." He reached out and touched his small hand. The little boy looked up at Nate with his blue eyes and a big smile. "What's your name, little man?"

"His name is Billy," Leah finally responded. Nate was stunned when he heard the name and looked questioningly up at her as she smiled broadly.

Nate turned back to the boy and took his tiny hand in his. "Billy, that's a great name. I had a brother, Billy, a long time ago. Let me tell you about Billy…"

ABOUT THE AUTHOR

Clifford James is a native Upstate New Yorker, a graduate of the University of Bridgeport CT, and resident of North Carolina for over thirty years, splitting his time between Raleigh and the coastal community of Bogue, NC. He has three children and seven grandchildren. This is his first work of fiction with more to follow.

Made in the USA
Columbia, SC
14 August 2023